Before We Were Yours

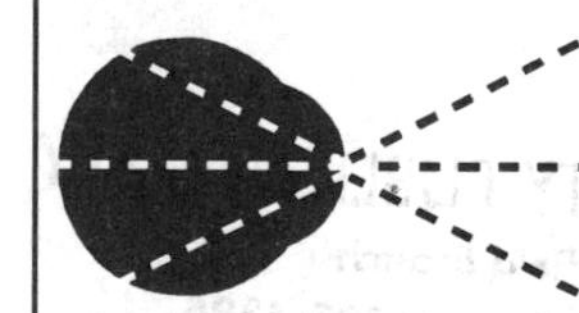

This Large Print Book carries the Seal of Approval of N.A.V.H.

Before We Were Yours

Lisa Wingate

LARGE PRINT PRESS
A part of Gale, a Cengage Company

Large Print Press, a part of Gale, Cengage Learning.

The text of this Large Print edition is unabridged.
Other aspects of the book may vary from the original edition.
Set in 16 pt. Plantin.

LIBRARY OF CONGRESS CIP DATA ON FILE.
CATALOGUING IN PUBLICATION FOR THIS BOOK
IS AVAILABLE FROM THE LIBRARY OF CONGRESS.

ISBN-13: 978-1-4328-7758-3 (paperback alk. paper)

Published in 2019 by arrangement with Ballantine Books, an imprint of Random House, a division of Penguin Random House LLC

Printed in the United States of America
1 2 3 4 5 6 7 23 22 21 20 19

For the hundreds who vanished
and for the thousands who didn't.
May your stories
not be forgotten.

For those who help today's orphans
find forever homes.
May you always know the value
of your work
and your love.

"Did you know that in this land of the free and home of the brave there is a great baby market? And the securities which change hands . . . are not mere engraved slips of paper promising certain financial dividends, but live, kicking, flesh-and-blood babies."

— FROM THE ARTICLE "THE BABY MARKET,"
The Saturday Evening Post,
FEBRUARY 1, 1930

"They are, [Georgia Tann] said repeatedly, blank slates. They are born untainted, and if you adopt them at an early age and surround them with beauty and culture, they will become anything you wish them to be."

— BARBARA BISANTZ RAYMOND,
The Baby Thief

tion swell the room, stretching it like a helium balloon. Any more joy and we'll all float away.

Someone touches my hand and wrist, fingers encircling me so unexpectedly that I jerk away, then stop myself so as not to cause a scene. The grip is cold and bony and trembling but surprisingly strong. I turn to see the woman from the garden. She straightens her humped back and gazes up at me through eyes the color of the hydrangeas back home at Drayden Hill — a soft, clear blue with a lighter mist around the edges. Her pleated lips tremble.

Before I can gather my wits, a nurse comes to collect her, taking a firm hold. "May," she says, casting an apologetic look my way. "Come along. You're not supposed to bother our guests."

Rather than releasing my wrist, the old woman clings to it. She seems desperate, as if she needs something, but I can't imagine what it is.

She searches my face, stretches upward.

"Fern?" she whispers.

CHAPTER 2

May Crandall

Aiken, South Carolina, Present Day

On occasion, it is as if the latches in my mind have gone rusty and worn. The doors fall open and closed at will. A peek inside here. An empty space there. A dark place I'm afraid to peer into.

I never know what I will find.

There's no predicting when a barrier will swing wide, or why.

Triggers. That's what the psychologists call them on TV shows. Triggers . . . as if the strike ignites gunpowder and sends a projectile spinning down a rifle barrel. It's an appropriate metaphor.

Her face triggers something.

A door opens far into the past. I stumble through it unwittingly at first, wondering what might be locked inside this room. As soon as I call her Fern, I know it's not Fern I'm thinking of. I've gone even further back.

It's Queenie I see.

Queenie, our strong mama, who marked all of us with her lovely golden curls. All but poor Camellia.

My mind skitters featherlight across treetops and along valley floors. I travel all the way to a low-slung Mississippi riverbank to the last time I saw Queenie. The warm, soft air of that Memphis summer night swirls over me, but the night is an impostor.

It is not soft. It does not forgive.

From this night, there will be no returning.

Twelve years old, still thin and knobby as a front porch post, I dangle my legs under the rail of our shantyboat, watching for a gator's eyes to catch the amber flicker of lantern light. Gators shouldn't stray this far upwater on the Mississippi, but there's been gossip about sightings around here lately. This makes looking for them a game of sorts. Shantyboat kids take their entertainment where they can find it.

Right now, we need a distraction worse than usual.

Beside me, Fern climbs the rail and searches the woods for fireflies. At nearly four years old, she's learning to count them. She points a stubby finger and leans out, mindless of gators. "I seen one, Rill! I seen

’im!” she cries.

I grab her dress to pull her back. “You go fallin’ off, I ain’t jumping in after ya this time.”

Truth told, it probably wouldn’t hurt her if she tumped over. It’d teach her a lesson. The boat’s tied up in a nice little backwater across the river from Mud Island. The water is only hip deep on me off the *Arcadia*’s stern. Fern might could touch the bottom on her tiptoes, but all five of us swim like pollywogs anyhow, even little Gabion, who can’t talk a full sentence yet. When you’re born on the river, you take to it as natural as drawing breath. You know its sounds and its ways and its critters. For river rats like us, the water’s a homeplace. A safe place.

But something’s in the air just now . . . something that’s not right. A spat of goose-flesh runs up my arms and needles my cheeks. There’s always been a knowing in me. I’d never tell a living soul of it, but it’s there just the same. A chill settles through me in the airless summer night. Overhead, the sky is thick, and the clouds are ripe as melons fair to bursting. There’s a storm coming, but what I feel is something more than that.

Inside the shanty, Queenie’s soft groans come faster now, mindless of the midwife woman's molasses-thick voice: "Now, Miz Foss, you gots to stop pushin', and you gots to stop now. This 'ere child come out wrong sided, he ain't gon' be long fo' this world, and you ain't neither. That's it now. You jus' quieten down. Be easy."

Queenie gives a low, wrenching sound that's like a boot sucking out of thick bayou mud. She's birthed the five of us with hardly more than a heavy breath, but it's taking so much longer this time. I rub the sweaty chill off my arms and feel like something's out there in the woods. Something evil. It looks our way. Why is it here? Did it come for Queenie?

I want to scamper down the gangplank and run along the shore and yell, "You git on now! You git away! You can't have my mama!"

I'd do it. I'm not afraid there might be gators. But instead, I sit still as a killdeer bird on a nest. I listen to the midwife's words. She's loud enough, I might as well be in the shanty.

"Oh, lands! Oh, mercy. She got more'n one inside. She do!"

My daddy mutters something I can't hear. His boot steps cross the floor, hesitate, cross again.

The midwife says, "Mista Foss, ain't

nothin' I can do 'bout this. You don't git this woman to a doctor quick, them babies ain't gon' set eyes on this world, and this be their mama's dyin' day too."

Briny doesn't answer right off. He pounds both fists hard against the wall so that Queenie's picture frames rattle. Something slips loose, and there's the clink of metal against wood, and I know what it is by where it falls and how it sounds. In my mind, I see the tin cross with the sad-looking man on top, and I want to run inside and grab it and kneel by the bed and whisper mysterious Polish words, the way Queenie does on stormy nights when Briny is away from the shantyboat, and the rainwater flows over the roof, and waves pound the hull.

But I don't know the strange, sharp language Queenie learned from the family she left behind when she ran off to the river with Briny. The few Polish words I have would be a mouthful of nonsense if I strung them together. Even so, if I could grab Queenie's cross in my hand just now, I'd say them to the tin man Queenie kisses when the storms come.

I'd try pretty near anything to help get the birthing over with and see Queenie smile again.

On the other side of the door, Briny's boot scrapes the planks, and I hear the cross clatter over the floor. Briny looks out the cloudy window that came from the farmhouse he tore down to build the boat before I was ever born. With Briny's mama on her deathbed and the crops droughted out for another year, the banker was gonna get the house anyway. Briny figured the river was the place to be. He was right too. Time the Depression hit, him and Queenie were living just fine on the water. *Even the Depression can't starve the river,* he says every time he tells the story. *The river's got her own magic. She takes care of her people. Always will.*

But tonight, that magic's gone bad.

"Mista! You hear me talkin' at you?" The midwife turns mean now. "I ain't havin' they blood on my hands. You git yo' woman to the hospital. You do it now."

Behind the glass, Briny's face pulls tight. His eyes squeeze shut. He hammers a fist to his forehead, lets it fall against the wall. "The storm . . ."

"I don' care if the devil hisself is dancin' by, Mista Foss. Ain't nothin' I can do fo' this gal. Nothin'. I ain't gon' have it on my hands, no, suh."

"She's never . . . had trouble . . . not with the others. She . . ."

Queenie screams high and loud, the sound whirling off into the night like a wildcat's call.

" 'Less'n you fo'got to tell me somethin', she ain't never had two babies at once befo' neither."

I shift to my feet, and take Fern around, and put her on the shanty porch with Gabion, who's two, and Lark, who's six. Camellia looks my way from where she's staring in the front window. Closing the gate across the gangplank, I trap them all on the porch and tell Camellia not to let the little kids climb over. Camellia answers with a frown. At ten years old, she's got Briny's muley streak along with his dark hair and eyes. She doesn't like being told what to do. She's stubborn as a cypress stump and twice as thick sometimes. If the little ones go to fussing, we'll be in a bigger fix than we already are.

"It's gonna be all right," I promise, and pat their soft, golden heads like they're puppies. "Queenie's just havin' a hard time is all. She don't need nobody botherin' her. Y'all stay put now. Old rougarou, he's rootin' round tonight, I heard him breathin' minute ago. Ain't safe to be out." Now that I'm twelve, I don't believe in the rougarou and the buggerman and Mad Captain Jack of the river pirates. Not much anyhow. I doubt if Camellia ever did swallow Briny's wild tales.

She reaches for the door latch.

"Don't," I hiss. "I'll go."

We were told to keep out, which Briny never says unless he means it. But right now, Briny sounds like he's got no idea what to do, and I'm worried about Queenie and my new baby brother or sister. We've been, all of us, waiting to see which one it'd be. It wasn't supposed to come yet, though. This is early — even earlier than Gabion, who was such a little thing, he came sliding into the world before Briny could get the boat to shore and find a woman to help with the birthing.

This new baby don't seem much inclined to make things so easy. Maybe it'll look like Camellia when it comes out and be just as stubborn.

Babies, I remind myself. It sinks in that there's more than one, like puppies, and this ain't normal. Three lives lay half-hidden by the bed curtain Queenie sewed from pretty Golden Heart flour sacks. Three bodies try to pull themselves apart from each other, but they can't.

I open the door, and the midwife is on top of me before I can decide whether to go in or not. Her hand locks onto my arm. It feels like her fingers go around twice. I look down and see the circle of dark skin against pale. She could snap me in two if she'd a mind to. Why can't she save my baby brother or sister? Why can't she pull it from my mama's body and into this world?

Queenie's hand grips the curtain, and she screams and tugs, arching up off the bed. A half-dozen wire hooks rip loose. I see my mama's face, her long, corn-silk blond hair matted to her skin, her blue eyes, those beautiful, soft blue eyes that have marked all of us but Camellia, bugging out. The skin on her cheek stretches so tight, it's crossed with lacy veins like a dragonfly's wings.

"Daddy?" My whisper comes on the end of Queenie's scream, but still it seems to upset the air in the room. I don't ever call Briny Daddy or Queenie Mama unless something's real wrong. They were so young when they had me, I don't think they even thought to teach me the words *Mama* and *Daddy.* It's always been like we were friends the same age. But every once in a while, I need them to be a daddy or a mama. The last time was weeks ago when we saw the man hung in the tree, dead, his body bloated up.

Will Queenie look like that if she dies?

Will she go first and then the babies? Or will it be the other way around?

My stomach squeezes so tight I don't even feel that big hand around my arm anymore. Maybe I'm even glad it's there, holding me on my feet, keeping me anchored to the spot. I'm afraid to go any closer to Queenie.

"You tell him!" The midwife shakes me like a ragdoll, and it hurts. Her teeth glare white in the lantern light.

Thunder rumbles not far off, and a gust of wind hits the starboard wall, and the midwife stumbles forward, taking me with her. Queenie's eyes meet mine. She looks at me the way a little child would, like she thinks I can help her and she's begging me to do it.

I swallow hard and try to find my voice. "D-Daddy?" I stutter out again and he still stares straight ahead. He's froze up like a rabbit when it senses danger nearby.

Through the window, I see Camellia with her face mashed to the glass. The little kids have climbed up on the bench to look in. Lark's got big tears rolling down her fat cheeks. She hates to see any living creature hurting. She throws all the baitfish back in the river if she can get away with it. Whenever Briny shoots possums, or ducks, or squirrels, or deer, she carries on like her best pal's been killed dead right there in front of her.

She's looking at me to save Queenie. They all are.

There's a spit of lightning someplace off in the distance. It pushes back the yellow coal-oil glow, then goes dark. I try to count the seconds before I hear the thunder, so I'll know how far off the storm is, but I'm too rattled.

If Briny doesn't get Queenie to the doctor soon, it'll be too late. Like always, we're camped on the wild shore. Memphis is all the way on the other side of the wide, dark Mississippi River.

I cough a lump out of my throat and stiffen up my neck so the lump won't come back. "Briny, you gotta take her across-water."

Slowly, he swivels my way. His face is still glassy, but he looks like he's been waiting for this — for somebody besides the midwife to tell him what to do.

"Briny, you gotta carry her off in the skiff now, before that storm comes in." It'd take too long to move the shantyboat, I know. Briny would realize that too if he could think straight.

"You tell him!" the midwife eggs me on. She starts toward Briny, shoving me ahead of her. "You don' get that woman offa this boat, this child's mama be dead befo' mornin'."

Chapter 3

Avery Stafford

Aiken, South Carolina, Present Day

"Avery! We need you down here!"

Nothing takes you from thirty years old to thirteen faster than your mother's voice rebounding up the stairs like a tennis ball after a forehand slice. "Coming! I'll be right there."

Elliot chuckles on the other end of the phone. The sound is both familiar and comforting. It calls up a memory trail that stretches all the way back to childhood. Between Elliot's mother and mine giving us the hawkeye, we never had a prayer of stepping out of line, much less getting away with the sorts of miscreant deeds *other* teenagers were guilty of. We were more or less doomed to be good. Together. "Sounds like you're *on,* sweetheart."

"The family Christmas picture." Leaning toward the mirror, I brush blond corkscrews away from my face only to have them fall again. My quick walk down to the stable after returning from the nursing home event has brought out the Grandma Judy curls. I knew it would, but a broodmare foaled last night, and a new baby is more than I can resist. Now I'm paying the price. No hair straightener known to man is a match for the water-laden breeze off the Edisto River.

"Christmas pictures in July?" Elliot coughs, and I'm reminded of how much I miss him. This business of living so far apart is hard, and we're just two months into it.

"She's worried about the chemo. They told her that Daddy wouldn't lose his hair with this kind, but she's afraid he will." There's really no doctor on the planet who can comfort my mother about Daddy's colon cancer diagnosis. Mama has always been in charge of the world, and she's determined not to abdicate now. If she says Daddy's hair will thin, it probably will.

"Sounds like your mother." Elliot laughs again. He should know. His mother, Bitsy, and mine are cut from two corners of the same cloth.

"She's just scared to death of losing Daddy." I choke a little on the last word. These past few months have rubbed us raw from the inside out, left each of us silently bleeding beneath our skins.

"Of course she is." Elliot pauses for what seems like an eternity. I hear computer keys clicking. I remind myself that he has a fledgling brokerage firm to run and its success means everything to him. He doesn't need his fiancée calling in the middle of a workday for no particular reason. "It's good that you're there, Aves."

"I hope it's helping. Sometimes I think I'm adding to the stress rather than reducing it."

"You need to be there. You need the year in South Carolina to reestablish your residency . . . just in case." Elliot reminds me of the same thing every time we have this conversation — every time I'm fighting the urge to catch a flight to Maryland and return to my old digs at the United States Attorney's Office, where there was no need to worry about cancer treatments, early Christmas pictures, constituents, and people like that desperate-looking woman who grabbed my arm at the nursing home.

"Hey, Aves, hang on a minute. Sorry. Things are crazy here this morning." Elliot puts me on hold to answer another call, and my thoughts drift back to this morning. I see the woman — *May* — standing in the garden, wearing her white sweater. Then she's beside me, her face barely at the level of my shoulder, her bone-thin hands clenched over my wrist, the walking cane dangling from her arm. The look in her eyes is haunting, even in retrospect. There's such a sense of recognition there. She's certain she knows who I am.

Fern?

I'm sorry?

Fernie, it's me. Tears frame her eyes. *Oh, dear, I've missed you so. They told me you were gone. I knew you'd never break our promise.*

For a second, I want to be Fern, just to make her happy — to give her a respite from standing by herself gazing into the wisteria. She seemed so very lonely out there. Lost.

I'm saved from having to tell her that I'm not the person she's looking for. The attendant intervenes, red-faced and clearly rattled. *I apologize,* she whispers just to me. *Mrs. Crandall is new here.* She wraps an arm firmly around Mrs. Crandall's shoulder and drags her hand from my wrist. The old woman is surprisingly strong. She surrenders inch by inch, and the nurse says quietly, *Come on, May. I'll take you back to your room.*

I watch her go, feeling as if I should do something to help, but I don't know what.

Elliot comes back on the line, and my mind snaps to the present again. "Anyway, stiff upper lip. You can handle it. I've seen you take on the big-city defense attorneys. Aiken can't be too much of a problem."

"I know," I sigh. "I'm sorry for bothering you. I just . . . needed to hear your voice, I guess." A blush rushes up my neck. I'm not usually so dependent. Maybe it's a by-product of Daddy's health crisis and Grandma Judy's issues, but a painful sense of mortality clings to me. It's thick and persistent like fog off the river. I can only feel my way through it, blind to whatever might be lurking.

I've lived a charmed life. Maybe I never understood that until now.

"Don't be so hard on yourself." Elliot's voice turns tender. "It's a lot to deal with. Give it some time. You can't solve anything by worrying ahead of yourself."

"You're right. I know you're right."

"Can I have that in writing?"

Elliot's joke pulls a laugh from me. "Never." I grab my purse from the bureau, looking for something to tie back my hair. A dump-out on the bed scores two silver bobby pins. Those will do. I'll pull back the front and do a wavy look for the picture. Grandma Judy will love it when she sees the photo. It's *her* hair I'm working with, after all, and she always wore it curly.

"That's the way, Aves."

Elliot greets someone who's just entered his office, and we say a quick goodbye as I do my hair and give the mirror a final glance, straightening the green sheath dress I've pulled on for the photo. I hope my mother's stylist doesn't do a label check. The dress is a store brand from the mall. The hair actually looks decent, though. Even the stylist will approve . . . if she's here . . . and she probably is. She and Leslie are in agreement that I need *a bit of work,* as they put it.

There's a knock at the door, just a little one. "Don't come in. I've got an octopus locked in the closet!" I warn.

My ten-year-old niece, Courtney, pokes her curly blond head in the door. She's a throwback to Grandma Judy too. "Last time you said there was a grizzly bear in there," she complains, rolling her eyes to let me know that, while this little joke may have been cute when she was nine, it's lame now that she has officially reached the double digits.

"A *shape-shifting* mutant grizzly bear, thank you very much," I say, taking a poke at the videogame she's way too obsessed with. With a set of surprise triplets occupying the household, Courtney is left to her own devices much of the time. She doesn't seem to mind the new freedom, but I worry about her.

She puts a hand on her hip and gives me attitude. "If you don't get downstairs, you're gonna need that grizzly bear, because Honeybee's gonna sic the dogs on you." Honeybee is my father's pet name for my mother.

"Ohhhh, now I'm scared." The Scottish terriers here at Drayden Hill are so pampered, they'd probably expect an intruder to come equipped with designer goodies from the dog bakery.

I ruffle Courtney's hair and slip past her. "Allison!" I yell down the stairs, and start running. "Your daughter is holding up the family picture!"

Courtney squeals, and we race to the lower landing. She wins because she's an agile little thing and I'm wearing heels. I don't need the extra height, but mother will not be happy if I show up for the Christmas photo in flats.

In the formal receiving room, the staff and the photographer are on a mission. Christmas photo mania ensues. By the time we're done with the shoot, my eldest sister's teenagers are exasperated, and I'm ready for a nap. Instead, I grab a toddler and start a tickle war on the sofa. The others quickly join in.

"Avery, for heaven's sake!" my mother protests. "You're making a wreck of yourself, and you're supposed to leave with your father in twenty minutes."

Leslie cocks an eye my way, showing her iguana-like ability to focus in two directions at once. She wags a finger at the green dress. "That's too formal for the town hall forum, and this morning's outfit isn't formal enough. Wear the blue pantsuit with the cording around the bottom. Very senatorial but not overstated. You know the one I mean?"

"Yes." I'd rather wrestle with the triplets or talk to Missy's kids about their plans to be junior counselors at summer camp, but nobody's offering me those options.

I kiss my nieces and nephews goodbye and hurry upstairs to change. In short order, I'm sharing another limo ride with my father.

He pulls out his cellphone and scrolls to the recorded brief for this afternoon's events. Between Leslie, numerous aides and interns, the staff here and in D.C., and the newspapers, the man is always well informed. He needs to be. In the current political climate, there's a very real danger of a change in the senatorial balance should his bout with cancer force him to step down. Daddy would go to his deathbed before he'd let that happen. The length of time he ignored his symptoms and remained in D.C. for the congressional session is proof, as is the fact that I have been called home for grooming and reestablishment of residency, as Elliot put it, *just in case.*

In South Carolina, the Stafford name has always trumped political dividing lines, but the publicity about the nursing home scandal has everyone sweating like tourists on a Charleston summer afternoon. There's a new story breaking every week — residents who've died after bedsores were left untreated, care facilities with unlicensed staff, places that were far from complying with the federal regulations requiring at least 1.3 hours of care per day for each patient yet were still allowed to bill Medicare and Medicaid. Devastated families who believed that their loved ones were in competent hands. It's heartbreaking and horrible, and the slim connection to my father has provided his political enemies with endless emotionally charged ammunition. They want everyone to believe that if the pockets were deep enough, my father would use his influence to help a friend profit from human suffering and escape prosecution for it.

Anyone who knows my father knows better. He isn't in a position to insist that supporters and campaign contributors offer up their balance sheets, and even if he were, the truth would be hidden beneath layer upon layer of corporate entities that look fine at a glance.

"Better brush up," Dad says, and hits play on the voice memo. He holds the phone between us and leans my way, and suddenly I'm seven years old again. I get the gushy, warm feeling I always had when Mom walked me through the hallowed halls of the Capitol, stopped outside my father's door, and allowed me to go in alone. Very quietly, with great gravity, I'd march to the secretary's desk and announce that I had an appointment with the senator.

"Oh, well, let me confirm that," Mrs. Dennison would say each time, lifting an eyebrow and restraining a smile as she picked up the intercom. "Senator, I have a . . . Miss Stafford here to see you. Shall I send her in?"

After I'd successfully been admitted, my father would greet me with a handshake, frown, and say, "Good morning, Miss

Stafford. Wonderful of you to come. Are you prepared to go out and greet the public today?"

"Yes, sir, I am!"

His eyes always twinkled with pride as I twirled to display that I had dressed for the occasion. One of the best things a father can do for his daughter is let her know that she has met his expectations. My father did that for me, and no amount of effort on my part can fully repay the debt. I'd do anything for him, and for my mother.

Now we sit shoulder to shoulder, listening to the details of the day's remaining activities, the topics that should be covered and the issues that must be avoided. We're given carefully spun answers to questions about care facility abuse and foiled lawsuits and shell corporations that magically go bankrupt before damages can be paid out. What does my father intend to do about this? Has he been leaning on people, shielding political contributors and old friends from the long arm of justice? Will he now use his office to help the thousands of older adults who struggle to find quality care? What about those still living in their own homes, dealing with damage from the recent historic flooding, forced to choose between taking care of repairs, eating, paying the electric bill, and refilling medications? What does my father think should be done to help them?

The questions go on and on. Each comes with at least one well-scripted response. Many have several options we can use depending on the context, plus possible rebuttals. This afternoon's town hall forum will be a carefully regulated press op, but there's always the remote possibility of a mole sneaking to the microphone. Things could get heated.

We're even told how to respond should someone manage to dig up the issue of Grandma Judy. Why are we paying for a facility that costs over seven times the per-day amount that low-income seniors are allotted by Medicaid?

Why? Because Grandma Judy's doctor recommended Magnolia Manor as our best option given my grandmother's familiarity with the place. One of her childhood friends lived on the estate before it was converted, and so it's like going home for her. We want her to have whatever will comfort her, but we're also concerned for her safety. We, like many families, find ourselves confronted with a complex and difficult issue for which there is no simple answer.

Complex and difficult issue . . . no simple

answer . . .

I commit those lines to memory verbatim in case I'm asked. I'll be better off not trying to ad-lib when such deeply personal issues are involved.

"Good op at the nursing home this morning, Wells," Leslie comments when she slips into the car during a coffee stop a few blocks from the venue. "We're on our way to nipping this thing in the bud." She's even more intense than usual. "Let Cal Fortner and his team try to make mileage off this business about senior care. They're only putting out the rope we'll hang them with."

"They're putting out plenty of rope." Dad's joke falls flat. There's a well-thought-out attack plan in the opposition's camp, a systematic strategy of painting my father as an out-of-touch elitist, a Washington insider whose decades in D.C. have left him blind to the needs of the people in his home state.

"More for us to work with," Leslie answers confidently. "Listen, slight change of plans. We'll be coming into the building from the back. There's a protest under way across the street from the entrance."

She shifts focus to me then. "Avery, we'll bring you onstage for this one. We're doing the forum with the senator seated across from the host, for a casual feel. You will be beside your father on the sofa, to his right, the concerned daughter having moved home to look after his health and manage the family's business concerns. You're the one who's single and not busy raising children; you have a wedding to plan here in Aiken, et cetera, et cetera. You know the drill. Nothing too political, but don't be afraid to show your knowledge of the issues and the legal ramifications. We're looking for a relaxed, unscripted tone, so the opportunity may arise to filter a question of a more personal nature your way. Only *local* news outlets will be present, which makes this a perfect chance for you to gain a little face time without too much pressure."

"Of course." I've spent the last five years with juries scrutinizing my every move and defense lawyers breathing down my neck. Participants in a carefully monitored town hall meeting do not scare me.

Or so I tell myself. For some reason, my pulse is racing, and my throat feels rough and dry.

"Game face, kiddo." Daddy sends me what we sometimes call "the million-dollar wink." It oozes confidence like warm honey, thick and irresistible.

If only I had half of my father's charisma.

Leslie moves on with the briefing for the

event. She's still talking when we arrive at the hall. Unlike the nursing home appearance earlier, there's security this time, including local DPS officers. I can hear the commotion out front, and a squad car sits at the end of the alleyway.

Leslie looks like she's ready to punch someone's lights out as we're hustled from the limo. A nervous sweat beads under my conservative navy suit.

"Honor thy father and mother!" a protester shouts above the din.

I want to hang a right turn, march to the curb, and tell these people off. How dare they!

"No concentration camps for seniors!" That one follows us through the door.

"What are these people, *nuts*?" I mutter, and Leslie gives me a warning look, then shrugs covertly toward the police officers. I'm being told to keep my opinions to myself in public, unless they're preapproved. But now I'm fighting mad . . . which may be a good thing. My pulse slows resolutely, and I feel my game face settling into place.

The minute the door closes, things calm down. We're met by Andrew Moore, the program coordinator for the hosts of today's forum — a seniors' rights PAC. Andrew seems surprisingly young to be in such a position. He can't be past his mid-twenties. The neatly pressed gray suit combined with slightly askew necktie and haphazardly bunched shirt collar make him seem like a boy whose clothes were laid out for him in the morning but who had to get into them himself. He tells us that he was raised by his grandparents, who made huge sacrifices to provide for him. This is his way of giving back. When someone mentions that I was a federal prosecutor, he eyes me and quips that the PAC could use a good attorney on staff.

"I'll keep that in mind," I joke.

We make a bit more small talk while we wait. He seems likeable, honest, energetic, and committed. My confidence that this will be a fair discussion of the issues ratchets upward.

Other introductions quickly take place. We meet the local reporter who will act as our moderator. We slide microphones under our jackets, clip them to our lapels, and hook the transmitter boxes over our waistbands.

We wait in the wings while the host takes the stage, thanks the organizers, then reminds everyone of the format for today's forum before finally introducing us. The crowd applauds, and we ascend the stage, waving cheerfully at the audience. Everyone is well behaved, though looking out at the group, I see quite a few faces that seem concerned, skeptical, and somewhat unfriendly. Others eye the senator with what could only be classified as hero worship.

My father does a reasonable job of responding to the simple questions and deflecting a few inquiries that can't be answered in a sound-bite. There are no easy solutions to the problem of funding retirement years that last much longer than in previous generations or the issue of fractured families and the cultural shift toward relying on professional care rather than tending to senior relatives at home.

Despite the well-thought-out replies, I can tell that he's a little off the mark today. He's a bit slow when a young man asks, "Sir, I'd like to hear your response to Cal Fortner's accusation that the goal of corporate-owned senior care chains is to warehouse the elderly in the cheapest way possible so as to increase profits, and that your repeated acceptance of campaign contributions from L. R. Lawton and his investment partners indicates your support of this profits-over-people model. Do you acknowledge that in these facilities seniors were tended to by minimum-wage workers with little or no training, if they were seen to at all? Your opponent calls for federal legislation to hold anyone who profits from a care facility or its holding companies personally accountable for the care provided there, as well as any damages awarded in lawsuits. Fortner is also calling for taxes on wealthy individuals such as yourself to fund an increase in benefits for our poorest senior citizens. In view of recent events, would you support this in the Senate, and why or why not?"

I can almost hear Leslie gnashing her teeth behind the curtain. Those questions weren't anywhere in the script, and no doubt they're not on the index card the guy is holding.

My father hesitates, appearing to be momentarily bewildered. *Come on,* I think. Sweat drips down my back. My muscles tense, and I clutch the armrest of my chair to keep from fidgeting.

The silence is agonizing. Minutes seem to pass, but I know it's not that long.

My father finally launches into a lengthy explanation of the existing federal regulations on nursing homes and the taxes and federal trust funds that pay for Medicaid. He seems competent and unruffled. Once again in charge. He makes it evident that he is not in a position to single-handedly alter Medicaid funding, the tax code, and the current state of senior care but that these issues will have his foremost attention in the next Senate session.

The forum then returns to a more acceptable script.

A question eventually comes my way, and the host looks at me indulgently. I give the prescribed response about whether or not I am being groomed for my father's Senate seat. I don't say yes, and I don't say, *Never in a million years.* Instead, I end with "In any case, it's premature to even think about it . . . unless I want to run against the man himself. And who would be crazy enough to do that?"

The audience chuckles, and I follow up with the signature wink I inherited from my dad. He's so pleased, he looks ten feet tall as he responds to a few more simple questions and the discussion wraps up.

I'm ready for pats on the back from Leslie as we exit the stage. Instead, she catches me with a worried look and leans close as we walk out the door. "The nursing home called. Apparently you lost a bracelet there?"

"What? A bracelet?" Suddenly, I remember putting one on this morning. There's no movement on my wrist, and yes, the bracelet is gone.

"One of the residents was found with it. The director looked at her cellphone photos from the event and determined that it was yours."

The woman in the nursing home . . . the one who grabbed my hand . . .

Now I remember the tiny gold legs of three little dragonflies raking down my wrist as May Crandall was pulled away. She must have ended up with my jewelry. "Ohhhh, I know what happened."

"The director apologized profusely. The patient is new and struggling to adjust. She was found two weeks ago in a house along the river with her dead sister's body and a dozen cats."

"Oh, how horrible." My mind takes flight, and I see the dismal, gruesome scene, even though I don't want to. "I'm sure it was an accident — the thing about the bracelet, I mean. She grabbed my hand while we were listening to Daddy. The nurse sort of had to peel her off."

"That shouldn't have happened."

"It's okay, Leslie. It's fine."

"I'll send someone to pick it up."

I remember May Crandall's blue eyes, the way she regarded me with such desperation.

I imagine her coming away with my bracelet, examining it alone in her room, draping it over her wrist, and admiring it with delight.

If it weren't an heirloom, I'd just let her keep it. "You know what? I think I'll go back and get it myself. The bracelet was my grandmother's." The day's agenda calls for my father and me to part ways from here. He'll be spending a little time at his office before having supper with one of his constituents while my mother hosts a DAR meeting at Drayden Hill. "Is there someone who can drive me? Or can I take one of the cars?"

Leslie's eyes flare. I'm afraid we're about to lock horns, so I add a more compelling excuse. "I should run by and have tea with Grandma Judy while I've got a little time anyway. She'll enjoy seeing the bracelet." The town hall forum has left me feeling guilty that I haven't visited my grandmother in almost a week.

Leslie's jaw twitches as she acquiesces, making it clear that she finds my silly whim disturbingly unprofessional.

I can't help it. I'm still thinking about May Crandall and remembering the plethora of newspaper stories about nursing home abuse. Perhaps I just want to make sure that May didn't come to me because she's in some sort of trouble.

Perhaps my curiosity has been piqued by her sad, macabre story. *She was found two weeks ago in a house along the river with her dead sister's body. . . .*

Was her sister's name Fern?

Chapter 4

Rill Foss

Memphis, Tennessee, 1939

Queenie is as pale as skimmed milk, her body tight and hard as Briny lays her on the edge of the shanty porch and goes after the skiff, which is tied up to a drift pile downwater. Queenie cries and screams, out of her head, her cheek pushed to the smooth, wet wood.

Lark backs herself into the night shadows by the shanty wall, but the little ones, Fern and Gabion, sidle closer on hands and knees. They've never seen a grown person act this way.

Gabion leans down to see, like he's not sure this thing in Queenie's pink flowered dress is even her. Queenie is light, and laughter, and all the old songs she sings with us as we travel along from one river town to another. This woman with the bared teeth and the cuss words and the moans and sobs *can't* be her, but it is.

"Wiw, Wiw!" Gabion says, because, at just two, he can't say my name, Rill. He grabs my skirt hem, tugging it as I kneel down to hold Queenie's head. "Keenie owww?"

"Hush up!" Camellia slaps at the little kids' hands as Fern stretches to stroke Queenie's long, gold curls. It's the hair that first caught Briny's eye and made him set his sights on her. *Don't your mama look like a princess in a storybook?* he asks me sometimes. *Queen of Kingdom Arcadia, that's your mama. That makes you a princess sure enough, don't it?*

But my mama's not beautiful now, not with her face sweat streaked and her mouth twisted in pain. The babies are busting her open. Her stomach clenches and bulges under the dress. She grabs hold of me and hangs on, and inside the cabin, the midwife wipes her hands, gathering her birthing tools in a grass basket.

"You gotta help her!" I scream. "She's dyin'."

"Ain't havin' nothin' else to do wit' this bidness," the woman says, her heavy body rocking the boat and making the lantern sway and sputter. "No mo'. Fool, river trash."

She's mad as a camptown dog because

Briny wouldn't pay her cash money. Briny says she promised to deliver a baby, which she didn't, and she oughta be glad he's letting her take the two fat catfish he pulled off the trotlines earlier in the day plus some coal oil for her carry lamp. She'd get back at us if she could, but she's still blacker than tar, and we're white, and she knows what could happen if she gives us trouble.

The catfish was supposed to be our dinner, which leaves us with nothing but one little cake of cornpone between the five of us. That spins through my mind with a half-dozen other things.

Should I gather up clothes for Queenie? The hairbrush? Her shoes?

Has Briny got enough money to pay a real doctor? What'll happen if he don't?

What if the law nabs him? Once before, when we were hustling pool halls in river towns, he got snagged. Briny's a good hustler. There's nobody can beat him at a game of eight ball, and he can play a pool hall piano good enough that people will pay him to do it, but this Depression has made cash hard to come by. Mostly now he hustles pool and plays for things he can trade off to get what we need.

Is there money hid somewhere? Should I ask Briny when he comes back? Remind him he might need it?

How'll he make the trip across-river in the dark with the storm already lifting whitecaps on the water?

The midwife turns sideways to get out the door, her basket slapping her behind. Something red hangs out the top, and I know what it is, even in the dim light — Queenie's pretty velvet hat with the feathers on top, the one Briny won in a pool game in a dirty little place called Boggyfield.

"You put that back!" I say. "That's my mama's!"

The woman's dark eyes fold up in her face, and she wags her chin at me. "Done been here all day long, and I ain't gonna be takin' no two fish. I gots me enough fish. I take this hat." She looks around to see where Briny's at, and then she starts for the gangplank at the side of the porch.

I want to stop her, but I can't. On my lap, Queenie screams, thrashing around. Her head lands on the deck with a hollow thud, like a watermelon. I grab her with both hands.

Camellia hurries ahead of the woman and stretches herself across the gate, her thin arms stretched from rail to rail. "You ain't takin' my mama's hat nowheres."

The woman moves another step, but if she

knew Camellia, she wouldn't. My sister might be only ten, but she didn't just get Briny's thick black hair; she got his temper to go with it. When Briny gets mad, he's *blind-fool mad,* Old Zede calls it. *Blind-fool mad is the kind that'll get you killed on the river.* Zede's warned my daddy of that more than once when our boats have been tied near each other, and a lot of times they are. Zede's been Briny's friend since Briny first took to the river. He taught Briny the way of things.

"You li'l saucy thang. Sass mouth." A big dark hand clamps over Camellia's arm, and the woman yanks her up, and Camellia clings on to the rail so hard, I think her shoulder bone's bound to snap from the socket.

Two seconds don't pass before Camellia whips around and sinks in her teeth. The woman howls and stumbles back, rocking the boat.

Queenie screams.

Thunder rumbles far off.

Lightning flashes, and the night turns to day, then puts on its black veil again.

Where's Briny? Why's he taking so long?

A bad thought hits me. What if the skiff broke loose and Briny can't find it? What if he's gone to borrow one off somebody in the shantyboat camp? Just for once, I wish Briny wasn't so stuck on keeping to himself. He never ties up in the river camps, and folks who know our boat know not to come calling unless they're invited. Briny says there's good folks on the river and folks you can't trust, and it's best to figure out who's who from a distance.

Queenie kicks and knocks Gabion over, and he bangs his arm and howls high and long. Lark bolts inside the cabin to hide now that the midwife is clear of it. Queenie's dying right here in my arms. She's gotta be.

At the head of the gangplank, Camellia ain't budging. The sneer on her face dog-dares the woman to try her again. Camellia would just as soon fight something as look at it. She'll catch snakes barehanded and scrap with the boys in the river towns and not think twice about it.

"You leave my mama's hat!" she yells over Gabion's squalling. "And you don't need no fish neither. Just git off our boat 'fore we go on and find the po-lice and tell them some colored woman done trieda kill our mama and steal us blind. They'll hang you up a tree, they will." She lets her head go slack and lolls her tongue, and my stomach turns heavy. Just two weeks ago Wednesday, we saw the man hung in the tree downriver.

Big colored fella in overalls. There wasn't a house round for miles, and he'd been there long enough the buzzards had got after him.

Only Camellia would use something like that to try to get her way. It makes me sick just thinking about it.

Maybe that's why Queenie's in a bad way now, a voice whispers in my head. *Maybe it's all because Briny didn't stop and cut that man down and find his people so's they could bury him proper. Maybe it's him lookin' on from the woods now.*

Queenie begged Briny to go up to the shore and take care of the body, but Briny wouldn't. *We got the kids to think about, Queen,* he said. *No tellin' who did that to him or who's watchin'. We best get on down the river.*

The midwife snatches Queenie's red hat from her basket, throws it down, and walks over it, her weight rocking the deck as she wobbles down the gangplank, then grabs the lantern she left onshore. The last thing she does is take the stringer with the two catfish. Then she wanders off, cussing us all the way.

"And the devil can come get you too!" Camellia echoes back at her, hanging over the porch rail. "That's what you get for thievin'!" She stops short of repeating the woman's naughty words. Camellia's eaten enough soap to clean up the inside of a whale in her ten years. She's practically been raised on it. It's a wonder bubbles don't pour out her ears. "Someone's comin'. Hush up, Gabion." Grabbing Gabby and slapping a hand over his mouth, she listens into the night. I hear the sound of a motor too.

"Go look if it's Briny," I tell Fern, and she hops up to do it, but Camellia shoves Gabby at her instead.

"Keep him quiet." Camellia crosses the porch and leans over the waterside rail, and for the first time, I hear relief in her voice. "Looks like he's got Zede."

Comfort wraps me like a quilt. If anyone can make things all right, it's Old Zede. I didn't even know he was here around Mud Island, but Briny probably did. They always keep track of each other on the river one way or another. Last I'd heard, Zede was inland, seeing after a sister who had to move to a sanatorium because she had the consumption.

"Zede's here," I whisper to Queenie, leaning close. She seems to hear, maybe settles a little. Zede will know what to do. He'll calm Briny's wildness, push the clouds from my daddy's eyes, and get him to think.

"Zede's here, Queenie. It's gonna be fine. It's gonna be fine. . . ." I repeat it over and over until they're pitching the line to Camellia and climbing the gangplank.

Briny crosses the porch in two steps, falls to his knees beside Queenie, and scoops her up, bending his head low over hers. I feel her weight leave me, her warmth vanishing from my skin. The night dew closes in, and all of a sudden, I'm cold. I stand up and turn the lantern higher and wrap my arms tight around myself.

Zede squats down close, looks Queenie in the eyes, unwraps the sheet a little, and there's blood everywhere. He lays a hand on her belly, where a watery red stain rises up her dress. "Miz Foss?" His voice is steady and clear. "Miz Foss? You hearin' me now?"

She lets out what might be a *yes,* but the sound dies behind clenched teeth, and she buries her face in Briny's chest.

Zede's mouth turns grim inside his thick gray beard. His red-lined eyes hang loose in their sockets. His breath sucks in through wide, hairy nostrils, then pours out between tight lips. The smell of whiskey and tobacco hangs heavy, but it's a comfort. It's the one thing about this night that's like always.

He locks eyes with Briny and shakes his head a little. "Queenie girl, we're gonna git you offa the boat, ya hear me? Gotta carry you on down to the hospital in the *Jenny*. Be a rough trip, across-water. You be a brassy gal fer me now, ya hear?"

He helps Briny lift her from the floor, and her screams tear the night like the women shredding funeral veils down in New Orleans. She goes limp in Briny's arms before they can even get her in the boat.

"Hold her now," Zede tells Briny, and then he looks at me and points the crooked finger that was broke in the Spanish War. "You take the young'uns in the shantyhouse, and you git 'em all to bed, sis. Stay inside. I'll hist on back 'ere, 'fore mornin' if'n the storm holds off, but if'n it don't, the *Lizzy Mae*'s tied up downwater just a bit. Yer skiff's there. Got a boy on the *Lizzy* with me. He's a rough looker just now — tried hoboin' the train, and the railroad bulls got after 'im. He won't hurt you none, though. Told 'im to row on up here come mornin' if'n he didn't hear elsewise from me."

He cranks the Waterwitch motor, and it rumbles to life, and I stare at the sludge churning in the lantern's glow. I don't want to see Queenie's eyes closed and her mouth hanging slack that way.

Camellia casts off the line, and it lands

neatly in the jon boat's bow.

Zede points a finger Camellia's way. "You mind yer sister, li'l spitter. You don't do nothin' without askin' Rill first. You savvy?"

Camellia's nose scrunches up so tight the freckles on her cheeks run together.

"You savvy?" Zede asks again. He knows which one of us is most likely to wander off and roust up trouble.

"Mellia!" Briny's clouds clear a minute.

"Yessir," she agrees, but she ain't happy about it.

Briny turns to me then, but it's like he's begging me, not telling me. "You watch over the babies, Rill. Keep care of everybody, till we get back — Queenie and me."

"We'll be good. I promise. I'll look after everybody. We won't go nowhere."

Zede turns the tiller handle and cranks up the throttle, and the Waterwitch carries my mama away into the dark. All five of us hurry to the rail and stand there side by side, watching until the blackness swallows the *Jenny* whole. We listen while the hull slaps over whitecaps, rising and falling, the kicker roaring and quieting and roaring again. Its voice gets a little farther away each time. Off in the distance, the tugs blow their foghorns. A boatswain's whistle sounds. A dog yaps.

The night turns quiet.

Fern wraps around my leg like a monkey, and Gabby wanders inside the cabin with Lark because she's his favorite. Finally, there's nothing more to do but go in the shanty and figure out how we're gonna eat. All we've got is the one cornpone cake and some pears Briny traded for over in Wilson, Arkansas, where we stayed three months and went to school until it let out for summer. By then, Briny had the itchy feet again. He was ready to take to the water.

Any normal time, he'd never bring us to shore nearby a big city like Memphis, but Queenie'd been complaining of cramps since day before yesterday. Even though it was sooner than she figured it should be, after five babies, she knew we'd better tie up the boat and stay put.

Inside the *Arcadia* now, everyone's whiny, and worried, and hot, and cranky. Camellia complains because I've shut the door instead of just the screen, and it's sticky hot, even with the windows open.

"Hush up," I hiss, and get the dinner ready, and we sit in a circle on the floor, all five of us, because it doesn't seem right to be at the table with two spots empty at the end.

"I 'ungee." Gabion's lip pooches out after

his food is gone. He eats faster than a stray cat.

I tear off a scrap of my cornpone slice and twirl it close to his mouth. "You gobbled yours up too quick." He opens up like a bird every time I get near, and finally I pop the bite in.

"Mmmmm," he says, and rubs his tummy.

Fern plays the game with him, and so does Lark. By the time it's all over, Gabby's gotten most of the food. Except Camellia's, because she eats all of hers.

"I'll run the trotlines in the mornin'," she says, like that makes up for her selfish streak.

"Zede told us to stay put," I say.

"When Zede gets back. Or the boy comes. Then I'll do it."

She can't run the trotline by herself, and she knows it. "The skiff ain't even here. Briny rowed it down to Zede's boat."

"It will be tomorrow."

"Tomorrow, Briny'll be back. And Queenie with the babies."

We look at each other then — just Camellia and me. I feel Lark and Fern watching us, but it's only us two that understand enough to share the worry. Camellia looks toward the door, and so do I. We both know that nobody's gonna walk through it tonight. We've never stayed alone in the dark before.

There's always been Queenie, even when Briny was gone hunting, or hustling pool halls, or gigging frogs.

Gabion topples over onto Queenie's braided rug, his eyes closed, long sandy-brown lashes touching his cheeks. I still need to get a diaper on him for overnight, but I'll do it after he's out cold, just like Queenie does. Now that Gabby's using the potty during the day, he gets mad if we come at him with a diaper.

Outside, thunder booms and lightning flashes, and the sky starts to spit out mist. *Did Zede and Briny make it across-water with our mama?* I wonder. *Is she someplace where the doctors can fix her, the way they did Camellia when her appendix went bad?*

"Batten down the windows that're toward the river. No sense rain comin' in," I tell Camellia, and she doesn't even argue. For the first time ever, she's lost. She's not sure what's best. The problem is, I'm not either.

Gabion's mouth falls open, and he starts to snore. That's *one* of the little kids, at least, who won't be raising a fuss tonight. Lark and Fern are another matter. Lark's big blue eyes fill up, and she whispers, "I wa-a-ant Queenie. I'm skeered."

I want Queenie too, but I can't tell them that. "Hush up, now. You're six years old.

You're not a baby. Close the windows before the wind starts blowin', and get your nighty on. We'll change the big bed and sleep there, all of us. Just like when Briny's gone."

My body's boneless and weary, but my mind is running crazy. It can't think a clear thought; it's just spinning up nonsense words, like the Waterwitch turning the shallows, stirring leaves and twigs and bait grubs and muck.

It keeps on so that I don't hear all the whining and complaining and sniggling and sniffing and Camellia egging it on by calling Fern a ninny and Lark a baby and another dirty word she ain't even supposed to say.

Last thing, once they're all in the big bed and I turn the lanterns down, I take the tin man's cross off the floor and hang him back on the wall where he belongs. Briny hasn't got any use for him, but Queenie does, and tonight he's the only one here to watch over us.

Getting on my knees before I climb into bed, I whisper every word of Polish I know.

Chapter 5

Avery

"I'll only be a little while," I tell Ian, Leslie's intern, as he parks under the nursing home portico.

He stops halfway out the driver's side door. "Oh . . . okay. I'll just sit here and take care of some email, I guess." He seems disappointed that no escort is needed. I feel his curious gaze following me as I exit the car and make my way through the lobby.

The director is waiting in her office. Grandma Judy's bracelet lies on her desk. The dragonflies' gemstone eyes glitter as I slip the lost treasure back onto my wrist.

We chat a bit about the day's event before the director apologizes for my trouble. "We've had quite a time with Mrs. Crandall," she admits. "Poor thing. For the most part, she doesn't speak to anyone. She just . . . wanders the halls and the grounds until lockup at night. Then she stays in her room, unless the volunteers are here to play the piano. She does seem to love music, but even at the sing-alongs, we can't persuade her to engage with the other residents. Grief and a change of location can often be more than the mind and body can handle."

Immediately, I imagine someone saying the same thing about Grandma Judy. My heart aches for this poor woman, May. "I hope she isn't upset. I'm sure she didn't take the bracelet on purpose. I would've let her keep it, except it's been in the family for so long."

"Oh, goodness, no. It's best that she gives it back. One of the things our residents sometimes have difficulty accepting is that many of their belongings haven't come here with them. They tend to see things around the facility and think someone has made off with their possessions. We return heisted goods quite often. Mrs. Crandall is still adjusting to leaving her house. She's confused and unsettled right now, but it's natural."

"I know that's a hard transition." My grandmother's estate on Lagniappe Street is still closed up with everything inside it. We haven't been ready to decide what should happen to a lifetime of mementos and countless family heirlooms. Eventually, the house will pass down to the next generation, as it always has. Hopefully, one of my sisters will move in, and most of the antiques can stay. "Does Mrs. Crandall have family who come to visit?" I purposely don't mention the story about the dead sister. I already feel guilty talking about this woman as if she's some sort of . . . case study. She's a *person,* like Grandma Judy.

The director shakes her head, frowning. "No one locally. Her son passed away years ago. She has grandchildren, but it's a remarried and blended family, and none of them live nearby, so it's complicated. They're doing their best, and to be honest, Mrs. Crandall hasn't been making it any easier. She was taken to a facility closer to her home to begin with, and she tried to run away. The family moved her here thinking that a bit of distance might help. She has attempted to leave us three times in two weeks. Some amount of disorientation and difficulty isn't unusual for new residents. Hopefully, she'll improve once she has adjusted a bit. I'd hate to see her transferred to the Alzheimer's Unit, but . . ." She clamps her lips over the sentence, apparently realizing that she's not supposed to be telling me all of this.

"I'm so sorry." I can't help feeling as if I've made a bad situation worse. "Could I see her . . . just to tell her thank you for returning my bracelet?"

"She didn't return it . . . exactly. The nurse found her with it."

"I'd at least like to tell her I appreciate having it back." Mostly, I'm just concerned that the director seems so . . . clinical about all of this. What if I've stirred up trouble for May? "The bracelet was one of my grandmother's favorites." I look down at the ornately fashioned golden dragonflies with their garnet eyes and multicolored spines.

"We don't restrict our residents' visitors here, but it might be better if you didn't. Mrs. Crandall most likely wouldn't speak with you anyway. We'll let her know the bracelet was returned and everything is fine."

We end the conversation with a bit of pleasant chatter about the birthday party earlier, and then we part at her office door. On the way back to the entrance, I pass a hallway sign with names and room numbers neatly arranged in metal slots.

MAY CRANDALL, 107. I turn the corner.

Room 107 lies at the end of the hall. The door is open. The bed in the front half of the room is empty. The curtain in the middle has been drawn. I step in, whisper, "Hello? Mrs. Crandall?" The air smells stale, and the lights are off, but I hear the raspy sound of someone breathing. "Mrs. Crandall?" Another step, and I can see feet protruding from the blankets on the other bed. The feet are shrunken and curled. As if they haven't borne weight in a long time. That must not be her.

I study the area that is undoubtedly Mrs. Crandall's. It's small and bland and somewhat depressing. While Grandma Judy's new mini-apartment is outfitted with a sofa, a chair, and a game table, and adorned with as many favorite photos as we could fit, this room looks as if its occupant has no intention of staying. Only one personal item sits on the bedside table — a photo frame with a faded, dusty velvet stand on the back.

I know I shouldn't be nosy, but I can still see May looking up at me with her robin's-egg-blue eyes, seeming to *need* something. Desperately. What if she's tried to run away from this place because someone is mistreating her? As a federal prosecutor, you can't help being aware of horrible elder-abuse cases. When federal crimes such as telemarketing fraud, identity theft, and the pilfering of Social Security checks are involved, the cases fall under our jurisdiction. There are too many instances where young people are just waiting to get their hands on the older folks' money. Mrs. Crandall may have perfectly wonderful grandkids, but it's hard to imagine why they would leave her alone here in this condition instead of moving her to someplace where one of them could monitor her care.

I just want to be sure, I tell myself. There is, inbred in me, the Stafford sense of duty. It makes me feel responsible for the well-being of strangers, especially those who are helpless and marginalized. Charities are my mother's full-time, unofficial second job.

The ornate frame is turned toward the wall, unfortunately. It was molded from the sort of pearlescent ivory celluloid that would have matched ladies' powder jars and brushes, combs, and buttonhooks back in the thirties and forties. Even leaning over, I can't see the photo.

Finally, I just do it. I turn the frame. Sepia-toned and bleached white around the edges, the image is a snapshot of a young couple on the shore of a lake or pond. The man wears a battered fedora and holds a fishing pole. His face is difficult to make out — dark eyes, dark hair. He's handsome, and the way he stands with one foot propped on a fallen log, his slim shoulders cocked back, speaks of confidence — defiance almost. It's as if he's challenging the photographer to capture him.

The woman is pregnant. The wind catches her floral dress, outlining a stomach that seems too large to be carried on her long, thin legs. Her thick blond hair hangs in long spirals almost to her waist. The front of it is pulled up in a bedraggled bow, like a little girl's. That's the first thing that strikes me about her — she looks like a teenager dressed up for a role in a school play. *The Grapes of Wrath* maybe.

The second thing that strikes me is that she reminds me of my grandmother. I blink, lean closer, think of the photos we carefully hung in Grandma Judy's room not long ago. There's one in particular — an image from her high-school graduation trip. She's sitting on a pier at Coney Island, smiling for the camera.

I'm probably just imagining the resemblance. Judging by the clothing, this photo is too old to be of Grandma Judy. My always-fashionable grandmother would never have been dressed that way, but right now all I can think as I peer through the glass is *That could be her.* I also see the resemblance to my niece Courtney and, of course, to me.

I whip out my cellphone and try to get its camera to focus in the dim light.

The camera's crosshairs weave in and out. I snap a photo. It's blurry. I shift toward the bed, try again. For some reason, turning on the lamp feels like stepping over the line, and if I use the camera flash, it'll just glare off the glass. But I want a photo. Maybe my father can tell me if he recognizes these people . . . or maybe, once I get home and look again, I'll realize I'm overthinking the resemblance. The picture is old, and it's not that clear.

"It's rude to invade someone's space without being invited."

I jerk upright before the camera snaps again. And the phone slips loose. It tumbles end over end, and I'm like a cartoon character moving in slow motion, grasping at air.

May Crandall makes her way through the door while I retrieve my phone from under the bed. "I'm so sorry. I just . . ." There is no good explanation for this. None.

"What are you up to exactly?" When I turn, she draws away, surprised. Her chin turtles into her neck, then slowly pokes out again. "You came back." Her visual sweep takes in the picture frame, telling me that she knows it's been moved. "Are you one of *them*?"

"Them?"

"These people." A hand flits through the

air, indicating the nursing home staff. She cranes closer. "They've got me in prison here."

I think of the story Leslie told me — the house, the dead sister's body. Maybe there's more than just grief and disorientation involved here. I really know nothing about this woman.

"I see you have my bracelet." She points at my wrist.

The director's words come to mind. *For the most part, she doesn't speak to anyone. She just . . . wanders the halls and the grounds. . . .*

But she's talking to *me.*

I catch myself pulling the dragonfly bracelet close, holding a hand over it, pinning it against my chest. "I'm sorry. The bracelet was mine. It must have slipped off when you held my wrist earlier . . . today . . . at the birthday party?"

She blinks at me as if she hasn't a clue what I'm talking about. Maybe she's forgotten the party already?

"Did you have one like it?" I ask.

"A party? No, of course not." Her resentment boils just below the surface, potent and acidic.

Maybe the nursing home director has underestimated this woman's problems? I've heard that dementia and Alzheimer's can manifest in paranoia and agitation; I've just never experienced that behavior. Grandma Judy is confused and sometimes frustrated with herself, but she's as sweet and kind-hearted as ever. "Actually, I meant, did you have a bracelet like this?"

"Why, yes, I did . . . until they gave it to you."

"No. I was wearing it when I came here this morning. It was a gift from my grandmother. It was one of her favorites. Otherwise, I would've . . ." I stop before saying, *Otherwise, I would've let you keep it.* It seems like it would be disrespectful, as if I'd be treating her like a child.

She stares long at me. Suddenly, she seems completely lucid, acute even. "Perhaps I could meet your grandmother, and we can iron this out. Does she live nearby?"

There's an abrupt change in the atmosphere of the room. I feel it, and it has nothing to do with the vent kicking on overhead. She wants something from me. "I'm afraid that isn't possible. I wish it were, but it's not." In truth, I would never expose my sweet grandmother to this strange, bitter woman. The more she talks, the easier it is to imagine her holing up with her sister's body.

"Is she gone then?" Suddenly, she seems crestfallen, vulnerable.

"No. But she's had to move out of her house and into a care facility."

"Recently?"

"About a month ago."

"Oh . . . oh, what a shame. Is she happy there, at least?" A beseeching, desperate look follows the words, and I'm hit with a penetrating sadness for May. What has her life been like? Where are the friends, the neighbors, the co-workers . . . the people who should be coming to see her now, out of duty if nothing else? Grandma Judy has at least one visitor per day, sometimes two or three.

"I think she is. To tell you the truth, she was lonely in her home. Now that she's at the facility, she has people to talk to, and there are games days and parties she can attend. They do craft projects, and there's a library with plenty of books." No doubt, they offer some of those options here. Maybe I can gain a little mileage with May Crandall — encourage her to give her new life an honest try and stop battling the staff. The shift in our conversation is leading me to suspect that she's not as addled as she's been pretending to be.

She smoothly ignores my implication and

changes the subject. "I believe I knew her. Your grandmother. We shared bridge club, I think." She points the knuckle of a bent, craggy finger in my direction. "You favor her quite a bit."

"People say so. Yes. I have her hair. My sisters don't, but I do."

"And her eyes." Things turn intimate. She looks through me to the very marrow of my bones.

What is happening here?

"I — I'll ask her about you when I see her. But she may not remember. She has good days and bad days."

"Don't we all, though?" May's lips twitch upward, and I catch myself chuckling nervously.

Shifting, I hit the bedside lamp with my elbow, then catch it, knocking the frame this time. I grab it before it can fall, hold it, and try to resist taking a closer look.

"They're always bumping that. The girls here."

"I could put it over on the dresser."

"I want it close to me."

"Oh . . . okay." I wish I could sneak a new phone photo. At this angle, there's no glare, and the face looks even more like my grandmother's. Could it be her . . . maybe dressed up for a play? She *was* president of the drama club in prep school. "I was wondering about this, actually, when you came in." Now that we're on friendlier terms, it seems permissible to ask. "The woman in the picture reminds me of my grandmother, a little."

My phone buzzes, still on silent from the town hall forum. I'm reminded that I've left Ian waiting in the car all this time. The message is from my mother, though. She wants me to call her.

"Same hair," May Crandall agrees blandly. "But that's not so uncommon."

"No, I suppose not." She doesn't offer any more information. Reluctantly, I put the frame back on the nightstand.

May watches my phone as it buzzes a second time, my mother's text message demanding acknowledgment. I know better than to leave it unanswered.

"It was lovely meeting you." I attempt to excuse myself.

"Do you have to go?"

"I'm afraid I do. But I'll ask my grandmother if she recognizes your name."

She moistens her lips, emits a small cluck as they part. "You'll come back, and I'll share the story of the photo then." Pivoting with surprising agility and without using her cane, she starts toward the door, adding, "Perhaps."

She's gone before I can answer.

I grab a better shot of the picture, then hurry off.

In the lobby, Ian is scrolling through emails on his cellphone. Apparently, he gave up on waiting in the car.

"Sorry that took so long," I say.

"Oh, hey, no problem at all. It gave me the chance to sort my inbox."

The nursing home director walks by and frowns, probably wondering why I'm still here. If I weren't a Stafford, she'd undoubtedly stop and ask questions. As it is, she pointedly looks away and moves on. Even after two months back in South Carolina, it's still strange, getting the rock-star treatment just because of my family name. In Maryland, I often knew people for months before they even realized my father was a senator. It was nice having the chance to prove myself *as* myself.

Ian and I proceed to the car, and we're quickly bogged down in road construction traffic, so I use the time to call my mother. There will be no getting answers from her at home, with the DAR meeting being hosted there. After it's over, she'll be busy making sure every china plate and punch glass is back in its rightful place. That's

Honeybee. She's an organizational whiz.

She also never forgets a name.

"Do we know a May Crandall?" I ask after she has requested that I "happen by" the DAR gathering so as to make an appearance, shake hands, and score a few points with all the right wives. *Get the women, and you've got the vote,* my father always says. *Only foolish men underestimate their power.*

"I don't think so," my mother muses. "Crandall . . . Crandall . . ."

"May Crandall. She's around Grandma Judy's age. Maybe they played bridge together?"

"Oh, goodness, no. The women Grandma Judy played bridge with are *friends.*" By *friends,* she means long-term acquaintances of the family with ties that are generations old for the most part. People of our social circle. "Lois Heartstein, Dot Greeley, Mini Clarkson . . . they're all people you already know."

"Okay." Perhaps May Crandall really is just an addled old woman with a headful of jumbled memories that bear only a partial resemblance to reality. That doesn't explain the photo on the nightstand, though.

"Why?"

"No real reason. I met her today at the nursing home."

"Well, how sweet. That was kind of you to chat with her. Those people get so very lonely. She probably just knows *of* us, Avery. Many people do."

I cringe and hope Ian can't hear my mother's end of the conversation. It's embarrassing.

The question of the photograph still nibbles at the corner of my brain. "Who's going by to see Grandma Judy tonight?"

"I was planning to. After the DAR meeting, if it's not too late." Mom sighs. "Your father won't be able to." Unfailingly, Honeybee holds down the family responsibilities when Dad's job prevents him from doing so.

"Why don't you stay home and rest after the meeting?" I suggest. "I'll go."

"But you're coming by the meeting first?" Mom presses. "Bitsy is back from her trip to Lake Tahoe. She's dying to see you."

Suddenly, I have the horrible, desperate feeling a wild animal must experience when the door swings shut on a cage. No wonder my mother wants me to come by her DAR get-together. Bitsy is back in town. Given the party attendees, I can count on a multipronged interrogation about whether Elliot and I have set a wedding date, selected china and silver patterns, talked about a venue and season — indoor, outdoor, winter, spring.

We're not in any rush. We're both really busy right now. We're just waiting to see what feels right isn't what Bitsy wants to hear. Once she and the DAR ladies have me cornered, they won't let me go until they've used every tool in their arsenal to get the answers they're after.

I have a sinking feeling I might not be making it by Magnolia Manor this evening to ask Grandma Judy about the photo after all.

Chapter 6

Rill

In my dream, we're free on the river. The Model T engine Briny fixed to the back of the boat drives us upwater easy, like we haven't got any weight at all. Queenie sits up top of the cabin like she's riding an elephant. Her head's tossed back, her hair flowing out from under her feathery red hat. She's singing a song she learned from an old Irishman in one of the shanty camps.

"Ain't she pretty as a queen?" Briny asks.

The sun is warm, and the song sparrows sing, and the fat bass jump out of the water. A flock of white pelicans flies over in a big old arrow shape pointing north, which means the whole summer's still ahead of us. There's not a paddle-wheeler, or a flatboat, or a tug, or a barge in sight anywhere. The river is ours.

Only ours.

"And what's that make you?" Briny asks

me in my dream.

"Princess Rill of Kingdom Arcadia!" I yell out.

Briny sets a honeysuckle flower crown on my head and pronounces it so, just like the kings in the storybooks.

In the morning when I wake, there's a sweet taste still in my mouth. It lasts until I open my eyes and think about why we're all five in Queenie and Briny's bed, flopped across the mattress like a fisherman's catch, sweaty and slick.

Queenie's not here. It barely gets through my head before I know what's pulled me from my dream.

Somebody's knocking on the door.

My heart jumps up, and I jump with it, tugging one of Queenie's shawls over my nightgown while I cross the shanty floor. It's Zede on the other side of the door, and even through the window glass, I can see that his white-whiskered face is long and sad. My gut turns into a slipknot.

Outside, the storm's gone. It'll be a nice day. The morning air's turned warm and steamy, but I open the door and step outside and feel cold right through the old cotton nighty Queenie sewed a ruffle to because I'd gotten so tall. Queenie said a girl my age hadn't oughta have her legs showing so much.

I pull the shawl tighter over my chest, not because of Zede or because I've got any woman parts to hide — Queenie says that'll happen when it's time, and it just ain't time yet — but because there's a boy in Zede's jon boat. He's a skinny thing, but tall. He's got dark skin like a Cajun or an Indian. Not quite a man yet, I'd say, but older than me. Maybe fifteen or so. Zede's always got somebody under his wing. He's the grand-pappy of the whole river.

The kid hides his face under a raggy newsboy cap, looking at the bottom of the boat, not at me. Zede skips the introducing.

I know what that means, but I wish I didn't.

Zede's hand feels heavy on my shoulder. It's meant for a comfort, but I want to run away from it, scat off somewhere down the bank, my feet flying so fast they barely leave tracks in the washed-up sand.

Tears shove up my throat and I swallow hard. Fern's face presses against the window behind me. Figures she'd wake up and follow along. She never lets me get far.

"Queenie's babies didn't make it." Zede's not one to chase round the bush with his words.

Something dies inside me — a little brother or sister I was planning to hold like a new china doll. "Not either one?"

"The doc said no. Couldn't save neither of 'em. Said it wouldn't of made no matter if'n Briny'd got yer mama to the hospital sooner. The babies just wasn't meant for this world, that's all."

I shake my head hard, trying to wick those words out of my ears like water after a swim. That can't be true. Not in Kingdom Arcadia. The river is our magic. Briny always promised it'd take care of us. "What'd Briny say?"

"He's pretty broke up. I left him there with yer mama. They had some hospital papers to sign and whatnot. They hadn't told her 'bout the babies yet. Reckon Briny will when she's woke up good. She'll be all right, doc said."

But I know Queenie. She won't be all right. Nothing makes her happier than a brand-new, sweet baby to cuddle.

Zede tells me he figures he'd better go back to the hospital. Briny wasn't in a good way this morning. "I was gonna see if'n there wasn't a woman down in the river camp who'd come look after y'all young'uns, but the pickin' was sparse. Been some trouble with the police, and most all the shanty folk done took to the river. I brung Silas to watch out over ya till I can git yer daddy back home." He motions to the boy in the boat, who looks up, surprised. He didn't know that Zede meant to leave him, I guess.

"We can look after ourselves all right." Mostly, I just want Queenie and Briny to come home and get us on down the river. I want that so bad, I hurt for it deep underneath the knot in my belly.

"We ain't got nothin' to feed him." Camellia is in the door now, offering up her two cents.

"Well, good mornin' to you, Miss Rosy Ray a' Sunshine." Zede calls Camellia that all the time on account of she's the exact opposite of that very thing.

"I was gonna go gig us some frogs." She announces it like she's been made captain of the *Arcadia.*

"No, you ain't," I tell her. "We're not supposed to leave the boat. None of us."

Zede points a finger at my sister. "You kids stay put." He narrows an eye back toward the river. "Don't know what's spooked the folks out of Mud Island camp. It's good y'all are over in this li'l backwater by yerselves, anyhow. Just keep quiet. Don't be callin' any attention or nothin'."

Something new weighs on my chest. Something heavy. Worry scratches a setting spot inside me and takes up nesting. I don't want Zede to leave.

Fern sidles over to hang on my leg. I pick her up and snuggle her wild curls under my chin. She's a comfort.

Gabion comes out, and I pick him up too, and their weight pins my feet to the floor. Queenie's shawl binds tight around my shoulders and squeezes into my skin.

Zede puts me in charge again, and he brings the boy, Silas, onto the *Arcadia.* Unfolded, Silas is taller than I thought. He's skinny as a rail, but he'd be handsome if it weren't for the busted lip and the shiner. If he was hoboing trains, like Zede said, he's lucky the railroad bulls didn't do worse to him.

He hikes himself up on the porch rail, like that's where he means to stay.

"You watch after them now," Zede tells him.

Silas nods, but it's clear enough he ain't happy about it. A Cooper's hawk flies by looking for prey, and he watches it pass, then keeps his face pointed toward Memphis.

Zede leaves food behind — a bag of cornmeal, a bundle of carrots, ten eggs, and some salt fish.

Silas watches as Zede climbs into his boat and disappears.

"You hungry?" I ask him.

He turns my way, and it's then I remember I'm in my nighty. I feel the sticky air touching my skin where the neck pulls low from the babies on my hips.

Silas looks away, like he noticed. "Reckon." His eyes are dark as midnight on water. They reflect everything he looks at — a heron bird fishing nearby, branches drooping from a half-broke tree, the morning sky with its foam-white clouds . . . me. "You cook?" The way he says it makes it sound like he's already decided I can't.

I lift my chin, square up my shoulders. Queenie's shawl cuts in deeper. I don't think I like Silas much. "Yeah. I can cook."

"Pppfff!" Camellia spits.

"You hush up." I set down the little kids and push them toward her. "And watch after them. Where's Lark?"

"Still in bed."

"Look after her too." Lark can slip off quick and quiet as a whisper. One time, she laid up in a little clearing by a creek and fell flat asleep, and it was a whole day and half the night before we found her. Scared Queenie clean outa her mind.

"Reckon I better make sure you don't burn the place down," Silas grumbles.

I decide it right then: I don't like this boy at all.

But when we go through the door, he looks my way, and his split lip turns upward on one side, and I think maybe he ain't so bad.

We light a fire in the stove and cook the best we can. Between Silas and me, neither of us knows much. The stove is Queenie's territory, and I've never cared a thing about it. I'd rather be outside watching the river and its animals and listening to Briny spin stories about knights, and castles, and Indians out west, and far-off places. Briny's seen the whole world, near's I can figure.

Silas has seen a bit himself. While we cook and sit down to eat, he tells tales about riding the rails, and thumbing his way across five states, and scratching up food in hobo camps, and living off the land like a wild Indian.

"Why ain't you got a mama?" Camellia asks as she finishes the last of a hoecake that's just a little bit burnt on the edges.

Lark nods, because she wants to know too, but she's too shy to ask.

Silas waves a fancy silver fork that Briny dug up in the sand by the wreck of an old riverboat. "Had a mama. Liked her all right, till I was nine. Then I left and ain't seen her since."

"How come?" I look hard at Silas to see if he's teasing. As much as I miss Queenie already, I can't imagine being away from your mama on purpose.

"She married a fella that liked drinkin' whiskey and handin' out whippin's. I took me a year of that, and I figured I was better off makin' my own way." The sparkle leaves his eyes for a minute, and there's nothing left but dark. But quick as it's there, he shrugs and smiles, and the little dents come back in his cheeks. "I struck off with a harvest crew that was movin' through. Went clear up to Canada, pickin' apples and combinin' wheat. After that was over, worked my way back south again."

"When you was just ten?" Camellia smacks her lips to let him know she's not believing a word of it. "You done all that? I just bet."

Smooth as a cat, he turns in his chair, lifts up the tail of his faded-out shirt, and shows us the scars across his back. All five of us jerk away from the table. Even Camellia hasn't got a smart-mouthed answer now.

"Be glad if you got a nice mama and daddy." Silas looks hard at her. "Don't ever get it in your head to leave them behind, if they're good to you. Some sure enough ain't."

We all go quiet for a minute, and tears build in Lark's eyes. Silas sops up the last of his egg and drinks a swig of water. He looks at us over the rim of the tin cup and frowns like he can't figure what we're so long faced about. "Say, li'l bit" — he reaches out and tweaks Lark's nose, and her lashes flutter like butterfly wings — "did I ever tell you about the night I met Banjo Bill and his dancin' dog Henry?"

Just like that, he's off on another story and then another. Time goes by in a wink while we finish the last of the food and then clean up the mess.

"Your cookin' ain't half bad." Silas licks his lips after we're done washing dishes in the pail on the porch. By then, Fern's got her dress on wrong side out, because she's changed herself out of her nighty, and Gabion's running around half-naked, looking for somebody to clean him up after he sneaked to the outhouse off the back of the shanty all by himself. It's a good thing he didn't fall right through into the river. There's no bottom on a shantyboat outhouse, just the water.

I tell Camellia to take him on the porch

and dunk his rear in the river and then dry him off. It'll be easiest.

Camellia's nostrils flare. The only thing that scares her in the whole wide world is poop. Which is exactly the reason I'm making her go clean Gabby. She deserves it. She hasn't helped with a thing all morning.

"Mellia! Mellia!" our baby brother cheers as his fat little legs wobble him toward the door, bare bottomed. "I metsy!"

My sister sneers at me, then whips open the screen and drags Gabion out, pulling him up by one arm, so that he stands on his tippy-toes.

"I'll do it," Lark whispers, hoping to end the fight.

"You let Camellia see after it. You're not big enough."

Silas and I look at each other, and he smiles a little. "Ain't you ever gonna get dressed?"

I look down and realize I never did change and never even thought about it, I was so caught up in Silas's stories. "Guess I better," I say, and laugh at myself and get my dress down from the hook, then stand there holding it. "You gotta go outside, though. And no peeking."

There's been a funny little thought in my head while Silas and me been cooking and taking care of the babies. I've been play-pretending like I was the mama and Silas was the daddy and this was our house. It's helped me not think about Queenie and Briny still being gone.

But there's no way I'd get undressed in front of him, or anybody. I've come up big enough this past year that I dress behind the curtain in the shanty, like Queenie does. I wouldn't stand still for somebody seeing me in the altogether any more than I'd let somebody whip me across my back and leave scars.

"Heck," Silas says, and rolls his eyes, "why'd I be lookin'? You ain't nothin' but a kid."

My skin goes hot from head to toe, and my cheeks boil.

Outside the screen door, Camellia laughs.

I blush harder. If I could, I'd knock her and Silas both off into the water right now. "And take the little kids out with you," I snap. "A woman needs privacy."

"How would you know anythin' about that? You ain't no woman. You ain't nothin' but a li'l curly-headed Kewpie doll," Silas teases, but I don't think it's funny, especially when Camellia can hear. On the porch, she's lined up with Fern and Lark, enjoying the show.

Every muscle in my body goes stiff. I don't get mad easy, but when I do, it's like a fire inside me. "Well, you ain't nothin' but a . . . a stick! A stick boy. The wind don't even have to slow down to blow around you. That's how skinny you are." I square up on him, hateful as I can, and poke my fists into my hips.

"Least I don't got hair that'd do to mop a floor with." He grabs his hat off the hook and stomps out the door. From someplace near the gangplank, he yells, "You oughta join the circus. That's what you oughta do. You could be a clown!"

I get a look at myself in the mirror on the wall, and there's blond curls flying everywhere, and my face is red as a woodpecker's head. Before I can even catch hold of how I look, I'm running to the door to holler out, "Well, you can just keep walkin', Silas . . . Silas . . . whatever your last name is, if you got one. We don't need you anyhow, and . . ."

Onshore, he drops down to a squat all of a sudden and bats a hand at me. I can't make out his face under the hat, but it's clear enough there's trouble. He's seen something in the woods.

The heat in my skin changes direction and sucks inward.

"Yeah, you can just keep walkin'!" Camellia shouts, jumping into the wrangle. "Git off our boat, stick boy!"

Silas glances over, shoves his palm at us again. The brush closes around him as he scoots in.

"You ain't hidin'! I see you there!"

"Hush, Camellia!" I whip open the screen door and yank Fern and Lark inside.

Camellia gives me a crosswise frown. She's bent over the rail, dangling Gabion by his arms. His bottom swirls in the water while he kicks and giggles. Camellia pretends to drop him, then catches his arms again, and he lets out a squeal before I can get to them.

"Come on inside." Leaning out, I reach for my brother's arm, but Camellia swats me away and lets Gabby dangle by one hand.

"He's havin' fun. And it's hot inside." Her thick, dark hair falls forward, the tips reaching to the water, touching it like a spill of ink. "You wanna go swimmin'?" she asks Gabby. For a minute, I think she's gonna climb into the water with him.

Onshore, Silas pokes out of the brush and puts a finger to his lips, trying to throw quiet our way.

"Somethin's wrong." I catch Gabion's

hand and swing him up like a wishbone, bringing my sister with him.

"Owww!" She's mad when her elbow hits the rail.

"Get inside!" Down shore, the leaves shiver apart, and I see black — a man's hat maybe. "Somebody's out there."

Camellia snorts. "You just want that boy to come back." She can't see Silas, but he's probably not ten feet from where a branch snaps and a raven takes off, cawing out complaints.

"There. See?"

Camellia catches sight of the black. It's somebody coming, for sure, but instead of going in the door, Camellia slips around toward the other side of the boat. "I'll sneak off the back and check who it is."

"No," I hiss, but the truth is I'm not sure what to do. I want to toss off the lines, and push the *Arcadia* out of the sand, and take to the river. The water's still and calm this morning, so it'd be easy for us to put her out, except I wouldn't dare try it. With nobody but Camellia and me and maybe Silas to keep the *Arcadia* from hitting a bar or getting plowed through by a barge or a paddle-wheeler, there's no telling what could happen to us on the river.

"Let's get inside," I say. "Maybe he'll

think the boat's empty and move on about his business." But who'd have business down this little backwater where there's nothing around?

"Maybe it's just somebody out squirrel-in'," Camellia says hopefully. "Maybe he'd give us one for dinner if we're nice." She knows how to be sweet when she wants to, when somebody's got sugar candy to hand out or fry cakes to share around a campfire.

"Zede told us to keep quiet. And Briny'd tan us good if he found out." Briny's never tanned any one of us, but he threatens it sometimes. The idea worries Camellia enough that she hurries across the porch with me, and we go inside.

We bar the doors and climb up in the big bed and pull the curtain and wait and listen. I think I can hear the man walking onshore. Then I think he must've left. Maybe he was just a hunter or a hobo —

"Hallooo, the boat!"

"S-s-shhhh." My voice trembles. Wide, worried eyes turn my way. You grow up on the river, you know to be mindful of strangers. The river's a place men take to sometimes when they're running from the bad things they done someplace else.

Camellia leans close. "That ain't Zede."

Her whisper ruffles the fine hairs on my neck.

The hull rocks a little. Someone's trying the plank.

Lark scoots close, and Fern crawls into my lap, her cheek pushing against my heart.

The *Arcadia* sways toward shore, tipped by the man's full weight. He's big. Whoever he is, Silas isn't any match for him.

I push a finger to my lips. The five of us freeze the way fawns do when the doe leaves them behind so she can go feed.

The man is on the porch now.

"Halloo, the boat!" he says again.

Go away. . . . There's nobody here.

He tries the door, the handle turning slowly. " 'Loo, in the boat?" The door hits the bar and can't go farther.

A shadow hovers in the square of window light on the shanty floor. A man's head, the outline of a hat. There's a stick or a bat in his hand. He taps it against the glass.

A policeman? I'm afraid it is. The police come after shantyboat folk when they feel like it. They raid the camps, rough up the river rats, take what they want, send us on our way. That's one reason we always tie up by ourselves unless Briny's got some particular need for other people.

"I help you, Officer?" Silas's voice stops

the stranger as he crosses to the other window to look in. Their shadows stretch along the floor together, one a head longer than the other.

"You live here, son?"

"Nope. I'z just out huntin'. My daddy's over yander a ways."

"Some children live here?" The voice isn't hateful, but it means business. What if Silas gets himself arrested for lying?

"Don't reckon I know. I just now seen the place."

"That so, is it? Think you might be handing me a fib there, little river rat? I heard you talking to somebody on this boat."

"No, sir." Silas sounds sure as sunrise. "I seen these people go off in a skiff . . . oh . . . couple hours ago maybe. Must've been somebody down in the river camp you'z hearin' just now. Sound goes a long ways on the river."

The man takes a quick step toward Silas. "Don't tell me about the river, sonny boy. This is *my* river, and I been hunting these kids half the mornin' on it. You get them to come out, so I can take them into town to their mama and daddy." When Silas doesn't answer, the officer bends close, their shadows connecting at the face. "Sonny boy, I'd sure hate to see you land yourself in trouble with the law. How'd you get that shiner on your eye anyhow? You been into somethin' you shouldn't be? You got folks lookin' after you, or you a stray?"

"My Uncle Zede. He looks after me."

"I thought you said you came out here hunting with your daddy."

"Him too."

"You lie to a policeman, you'll find yourself in jail, river rat."

"I ain't lyin'."

I hear other voices nearby now. Men yelling in the woods and a dog barking.

"Tell the kids to come on out. Their mama and daddy sent us after them."

"What's their daddy's name, then?"

Camellia and me look at each other. Her eyes are big as walnuts. She shakes her head. She's thinking the same thing I am: *Briny wouldn't send the police here, and if he did send them, they would've known right where to find the boat.*

What does this man want with us?

We stare out the gap in the curtain as the big shadow lifts the little one up by the shirt collar. Silas coughs and gags. "Don't you sass-mouth *me,* boy. I didn't come for you, but you gimme any more trouble, we'll just take you with us. You'll see where scrawny little guttersnipes like you wind up in this city."

I'm out of the bed before Camellia can latch on and try to stop me. "No! Rill, no!" She grabs at my nighty, but it slips through her fingers.

When I open the door, the first thing I see is Silas's feet dangling six inches off the deck. His face is purple. He tries a punch, and the officer just laughs. "You want at me, boy? How about we put you under that water a minute or two and cool you off."

"Stop! Don't!" I can hear other men coming. There's some onshore, and off the starboard there's a motorboat rumbling up. I don't know what we've done wrong — other than being river gypsies — but we're caught for sure. It won't help for Silas to get himself killed or hauled off with us.

The officer drops Silas all at once so that he lands against the shanty wall, hitting his head hard. "Go on, Silas," I say, but my voice shakes so bad the words are barely anything. "You go home now. You ain't even supposed to be here. We *want* to go see Mama and Daddy." I figure it'll go better if we cooperate. By myself, I might be able to jump off the porch and get away to the woods before the men could catch me, but with my little sisters and Gabion, there's no way it'd work. One thing I know about Briny is he'd want us to stick together, no matter what.

I straighten my back, look at the police officer, and try to be as grown up as I can.

He smiles. "That's a good girl now."

"Is my daddy okay?"

"Sure he is."

"And my mama?"

"Real fine. She asked for you to come visit."

I don't even have to see in his eyes to know that's a lie. It ain't possible that Queenie's real fine right now. Wherever she is, she's heartbroke about the babies.

I swallow hard and feel it go all the way down, sharp like a piece of ice chipped fresh off the block. "I'll get the other kids."

The officer steps up, grabs my arm like he means to stop me. "Ain't you a pretty little river rat?" His tongue slides across his teeth, and for the first time, he's close enough that I can see his face under the shiny hat brim. His eyes are gray, and they're mean, but they're not cold like I thought they'd be. They're interested, except I don't know why. His look moves from my face down my neck toward the shoulder that's hanging out of the nightgown right now. "Somebody oughta feed you up a little."

Behind him, Silas wobbles to his feet, blinks, and staggers. He settles a hand on the axe that's standing by the woodpile.

No, I try to say without saying it. Doesn't he hear the men down shore and the motorboat coming closer?

From inside the shanty, there's a soft, high squeak, just loud enough that I catch it. The outhouse door. Camellia's trying to sneak away through the back.

Do something. "M-my little brother just got off the pot. I need to clean him up before we go, or there'll be poop everywhere. Unless y-you wanna do it." It's the only thing I can think of. Men don't like messy babies. Briny won't touch one at all except to dunk it in the river if Queenie or Camellia or me aren't there to do it.

The officer curls his lip, lets me go, and turns to listen over his shoulder. Silas jerks his hand away from the axe, stands with fists gripped at the ends of his skinny arms.

"Better hurry along." The policeman's lips spread into a smile, but there's no kindness in it. "Your mama's waitin'."

"You go on now, Silas. Just git." I stop in the doorway, stare at him, thinking, *Go. Run!*

The officer looks from me to Silas. He reaches toward his belt, toward the gun, the club, the black metal wristlets. What's he planning to do?

"Go on, git!" I yell, and give Silas a shove. "Briny and Zede wouldn't want you here!"

Our eyes lock. He shakes his head a little. I nod mine. He closes his lashes real slow, then opens them again and turns and runs down the gangplank.

"There's one in the water!" another policeman yells from the riverbank. The men in the motorboat holler, and the kicker throttles up.

Camellia! I spin around and rush inside, the officer's heavy footsteps coming after me. He shoves me, and I land against the cookstove, and he thunders to the back, where the stern door is hanging open. Fern, Lark, and Gabion are clustered along the rail. The man throws them back inside, hard, and they land in a pile screaming and crying.

"Mellia! Mellia!" Gabion wails, and points toward the outhouse, where our sister has shinnied down the privy hole into the river. She's slogging her way toward shore now, her wet nightgown clinging to her long, sunbrowned legs. A police officer runs after her, and the men in the motorboat follow along in the water.

She climbs a drift pile, as quick and nimble as a doe.

Gabion lets out a high-pitched scream.

The policeman on the back porch yanks his pistol from its holster.

"No!" I try to lunge forward, but Fern's got my legs. We land on the floor, toppling Lark with us. She lets out a sharp cry, and the last thing I see before the woodbox blocks my view is the man onshore leaping over a branch, stretching out a hand, and catching Camellia by her long, dark hair.

When I come up again, she's fighting like crazy, kicking and screaming and growling. Her arms and legs flail as the policeman holds her away from his body.

The guys in the motorboat throw their heads back and laugh like drunks at a pool-hall fight.

It takes three of them to get my sister in the boat and two to hold her down once she's there. When they pull up to the *Arcadia,* they've got Camellia pinned on the floor. They're muddy and mad because she smells like the bottom of an outhouse, and she's gotten it on everybody.

The officer on the *Arcadia* stands himself in the doorway, crossing his arms and leaning like he's comfortable there. "You get your clothes changed real nice now . . . out here where I can see. We're not gonna have anybody else running off."

I'm not about to get dressed in front of him, so I take care of Gabion, Lark, and Fern first. Finally, I just put my dress on over my nighty, even though it's way too hot for that.

The policeman laughs. "All right, if that's the way you want it. Now you come on real sweet and quiet, and we'll take you to see your mama and daddy."

I do what he says and follow him from the shanty, pulling the door closed behind us. I can't swallow, or breathe, or think.

"Good thing the other four weren't so tough," one of the policemen says. He has Camellia stuffed to the floor of the motorboat with her arms pinned up behind her. "This one's a wildcat."

"Smells more like a wild hog," the other officer in the boat jokes. He helps us settle in, lifting Gabion and then Fern and then Lark in and telling them to sit on the floor. Camellia gives me a wicked look when I do the same.

She thinks this is my fault, that I should've fought back and stopped it somehow.

Maybe I should've.

"She'll like these, all right," one of the men hollers as the motor kicks up and pushes us away from the *Arcadia.* He puts his big hand on Lark's head, and she ducks away, crawling up against me. Fern does the same. Only Gabion doesn't know enough to be scared.

"She likes the blonds, don't she?" The officer who came on the *Arcadia* laughs. "Not sure what she'll do with li'l stinky there." He wags his chin at Camellia, and she hocks up a wad of spit and sends it at him. He lifts a hand like he'll swat her, but then he just laughs and wipes the mess on his trousers.

"To the Dawson Warehouse lot again?" the man running the motor asks.

"Last I heard."

I don't know how long we're on the water. We travel across the river, then toward the channel where the Wolf pours into the Mississippi. When we round the tip of Mud Island, Memphis comes into full view. The big buildings stretch toward the sky like monsters waiting to swallow us whole. I think about jumping out into the water. I think about making a run for it. I think about fighting. I watch boats pass by — tugs, and paddle-wheelers, and fishing boats, and barges. Even a shantyboat. I think about yelling and waving my arms and calling for help.

But who would help us?

These men are the police.

Are they taking us to jail?

A hand settles on my shoulder, like someone's been reading my thoughts. It stays there until we finally dock. Up the hill, I can see more buildings.

"You be real good now, and keep your brother and sisters out of trouble," the officer from the *Arcadia* whispers against my ear. Then he tells the other men to hold the wildcat back a minute, till *she's* seen the four of us.

We march up the boardwalk in a line, me carrying Gabion on my hip. The clang-clang-swish of machines and the smell of hot tar catch me, and I lose the scents of the river. We cross a street, and I hear a woman singing, a man yelling, a hammer striking metal. The loose fluff from cotton bales floats in the air like snow.

In a scrappy bush at the edge of a parking lot, a cardinal sings his sharp song. *Weep, weep, weep.*

There's a car nearby. A big car. A man in a uniform gets out and walks around to the back door and opens it so a woman can heave her way out of the seat. She stands looking at us, squinting against the sun. She's not a young woman or an old woman but someplace in between. She's thick and heavy, her body settling in rolls inside her flowered dress. Her hair is short. Some of it's gray, and some of it's brown.

Her face makes me think of a heron bird. That's the way she watches while the policemen line us up. Her gray eyes move quick and jerky, tracking everything that's going on. "There should be five," she says.

"The other's coming, Miss Tann," one officer says. "She was a shade more trouble. Tried to get away in the river."

Her tongue clicks against her teeth, *tsk, tsk, tsk*. "You wouldn't do that, would you?" She fingers Fern's chin and leans down until they're almost nose to nose. "You wouldn't be a bad girl, would you?"

Fern's blue eyes go wide, and she shakes her head.

"What a lovely little bunch of foundlings," the woman — *Miss Tann* — says. "Five precious blonds with curls. How perfect." She claps her hands and folds them under her chin. Her eyes crinkle at the corners, and her mouth presses tight, so that she's smiling but her lips are gone.

"Only four." The officer nods toward Camellia, who's coming up from the river with a policeman holding her by the scruff of the neck. I don't know what they've told her, but she's not fighting anymore.

Miss Tann frowns. "Well . . . *that* one

didn't get the looks in the family, did she? She's rather common. I suppose we'll find a taker for her, though. We almost always do." She pulls back, putting a hand over her nose. "Good heavens. What is that smell?"

Miss Tann isn't happy when she sees up close what a mess my sister is. She tells the officers to put Camellia on the floorboard of the car and the rest of us on the seat. There are two other kids on the floorboard already — a blond-headed girl about Lark's age and a boy who's a little bigger than Gabion. Both of them look at me with big, scared brown eyes. They don't say a word or move an inch.

Miss Tann tries to take Gabion out of my arms before I climb in. She frowns when I hold on. "Behave yourself," she says, and I let go.

Once we're all in the car, she holds Gabion in her lap, standing him up so he can see out the windows. He bounces and points and babbles, excited. He's never been in a car before.

"My, my, look at those curls." She slides her fingers along my baby brother's head, pulling his corn-silk hair upward, so it has peaks on the top like the baby dolls at the county fair.

Gabion points out the window, cheering.

"Ohsee! Ohsee!" He's spotted a little girl having her picture made on a black-and-white pinto pony in front of a big house.

"We just need to wash the stench of the river from you, don't we? Then you'll be a fine little boy." Miss Tann's nose crinkles up.

I wonder what she means by that. Who's going to clean us up and why?

Maybe the hospital won't let us in this way, I tell myself. *Maybe we have to wash up first . . . to see Queenie?*

"His name's Gabion," I say, so she'll know what to call him. "Gabby for short."

Her head turns quick, the way a cat's does when it's seen a mouse in the pantry. She looks at me like she forgot I was in the car. "Restrain yourself from answering questions unless you're asked."

Her arm snakes out, fleshy and pale, and surrounds Lark, pulling her away.

I look down at the two scared kids huddled together on the floor and then at Camellia. My sister's eyes tell me that she's figured out what I already know, even though I don't want to.

We're not headed to the hospital to see our mama and daddy.

CHAPTER 7

Avery

The retirement home lies bathed in soft morning sunlight. Even with the newly added parking lot on what was once a sprawling front lawn, Magnolia Manor speaks of a bygone era — of the elegance of afternoon teas, and glittering cotillions, and formal dinners at the long mahogany table that still stands in the dining room. It's easy to picture Scarlett O'Hara fanning herself beneath the moss-draped live oaks that shade the white-columned veranda.

I remember this place's former life, if only a tad. My mother brought me to a baby shower here when I was nine or ten. Driving over, she shared the story of attending an important cocktail reception here for a cousin who was running for the South Carolina governorship. A college girl at the time, my mother had anything but politics on her mind. She wasn't at Magnolia Manor for thirty minutes before she noticed my father across the room. She made it her business to find out who he was. When she learned that he was a Stafford, she set her cap.

The rest is history. A marriage of political dynasties. My mother's grandfather had been a North Carolina representative before his retirement, and her father was in office at the time of the wedding.

The story makes me smile as I climb the manor's marble steps and punch the code into the incongruously modern keypad beside the front door. Important people live here still. Not just anyone is allowed to enter. Sadly, not just anyone is allowed to exit either. Behind the manor, the expansive grounds have been carefully fenced in decorative iron too tall to climb over. The gates are locked. The lake and reflecting pool can be looked at but not reached . . . or fallen into.

Many of the residents must be protected from themselves. That's the sad truth of it. As they decline, they move from one wing to the next, slowly progressing to higher levels of delicately provided care. There's no denying that Magnolia Manor is more upscale than the nursing home May Crandall lives in, but both places face the same underlying challenge — how to provide dignity, care, and comfort as life turns difficult corners.

I wind my way to the Memory Care Unit — here, no one would even think of crassly calling it the Alzheimer's Unit. I let myself through another locked door and into a salon, where the television plays a rerun of *Gunsmoke* turned up loud.

A woman by the window stares at me blankly as I pass. Beyond the glass, the climbing roses are dewy and fresh, pink and filled with life.

The roses outside Grandma Judy's window are a cheery yellow. She's sitting in the wingback chair admiring them when I walk in. I stop one step inside the door and steel myself before drawing her attention from the plants.

I prepare for her to look at me the same way the woman in the lounge did just now — without a hint of recognition.

I hope she won't. There's never any telling.

"Hi, Grandma Judy!" The words are bright, and loud, and cheerful. Even so, they take a minute to garner a reaction.

She turns slowly, leafs through the scattered pages in her mind, then in her usual sweet way says, "Hello, darling. How are you this afternoon?"

It's morning, of course. As I'd predicted, the DAR meeting ran late last night, and try as I might, I couldn't get away from the wedding interrogation. I was like a hapless grasshopper dropped into a henhouse. My head is now full of suggestions, dates I shouldn't plan on because someone important will be out of town, and offers to loan china, silver, crystal, and linens.

"Wonderful, thank you," I tell Grandma Judy, and cross the room to hug her, hoping the moment of closeness will draw a memory from her.

For an instant, it seems to. She looks deep into my eyes, then finally sighs and says, "You are so very pretty. What lovely hair you have." Touching it, she smiles.

Sadness expands in my chest. I came here hoping for answers about May Crandall and the old photograph on her nightstand. That doesn't look very likely now.

"There was a little girl, who had a little curl, right in the middle of her forehead." My grandmother smiles up at me. Cool fingers with paper-thin skin stroke my cheek.

"And when she was good, she was very, very good," I add. Grandma Judy always greeted me with this poem when I visited her house on Lagniappe Street as a child.

"And when she was bad, she was horrid," she finishes, and grins and winks, and we laugh together. It's just like old times.

I sit in the chair across the little round table. "I always loved it when you teased me with that rhyme." In Honeybee's home, little girls were expected to be anything but horrid, but Grandma Judy had always been known for having a spunky streak that bordered on impropriety. She'd spoken out on issues like civil rights and education for women long before it was acceptable for a female to have an opinion.

She asks if I've seen Welly-boy, her pet name for my father, Wells.

I fill her in on yesterday's press op and the town hall forum, then the long, long, long DAR meeting at Drayden Hill. I skip over the wedding chatter, of course.

Grandma Judy nods with approval as I talk, narrowing an eye and offering shrewd comments about the town hall meeting. "Wells mustn't let those people run riot over him. They'd love to catch a Stafford meddling in the dirt, but they won't."

"Of course not. He handled it beautifully, just like he always does." I don't mention how tired he looked or his seeming mental lapse under questioning.

"That's my boy. He's a very good boy. I don't know how he could've given rise to a girl who can be horrid."

"Pppfff! Grandma!" I slap a hand over hers and squeeze. She's actually cracking jokes and drawing connections between us. It *is* a good day. "I think it skipped a generation."

I'm expecting a quick-witted retort. Instead, she says blandly, "Oh, many things do." She sinks back in her chair, her hand pulling away from mine. I sense the moment fading.

"Grandma Judy, I wanted to ask you something."

"Oh?"

"I met a woman yesterday. She said she knew you. May Crandall. Does that sound familiar?" The names of old friends and acquaintances she can often recall with ease. It's as if her memory book has fallen open, a persistent wind tearing out the most recent pages first. The older the memories are, the more likely they are to remain intact.

"May Crandall . . ." As she repeats the name, I can tell immediately that she recognizes it. I'm already reaching for my phone to show her the photo when she says, "No . . . it doesn't ring any bells." I glance up from my purse, and she's looking at me very directly, thin white lashes narrowed over seawater eyes that suddenly seem strangely intense. I'm afraid we're about to have one of those moments where she stops in the middle of a conversation and without warning starts the visit over with something like *I didn't know you were coming by today. How have you been?* Instead, she says, "Is there a reason you would ask?"

"I met her yesterday . . . at the nursing home."

"Yes, you said. But many people know *of* the Staffords, dear. We must always be careful. People look for scandal."

"Scandal?" The word jolts me.

"Of course."

The phone suddenly feels cold between my fingers. "I didn't know we had any skeletons in the closet."

"Gracious. Of course we do *not.*"

I scroll to the photo, look into the face of the young woman who reminds me even more of my grandmother now that I'm right across the table from her. "She had this picture. Do you know the person in it?" Maybe these are woodpile relatives? People my grandmother doesn't want to acknowledge as part of the family tree? Every clan must have a few of those. Perhaps there was a cousin who ran off with the wrong sort of man and got pregnant?

I turn the screen toward her, watch for her reaction.

"Queen . . ." she murmurs, reaching out to pull the phone closer. "Oh . . ." Moisture wells up in her eyes. It beads and spills over, sketching trails down her cheeks.

"Grandma Judy?"

She's a million miles away.

Not miles, *years.* Years away. She's remembering something. She knows who that is in the photo. *Queen.* What does that mean?

"Grandma Judy?"

"Queenie." Her fingertip trails across the image. Then she turns my way with an intensity that bolts me to my chair. "We mustn't let people find out. . . ." she says, her voice lowered. She glances toward the door, leans close, then adds in a whisper, "They can never know about *Arcadia.*"

It's a moment before I can answer. My mind swirls. *Have I ever heard her mention that word before?* "What? Grandma Judy . . . what's Arcadia?"

"Sssst!" The sound is so sharp she spits a fine spray across the table. "If they ever found out . . ."

"They? They *who*?"

The doorknob rattles, and she sits back in her chair, folds her hands neatly one over the other. An eye flash silently instructs me to do the same.

I pretend to relax, but my head is cluttered with possibilities — everything from a Watergate-style cover-up involving my grandfather to some secret society of political wives acting as Cold War spies. What has my grandmother been involved in?

A friendly attendant enters with coffee and cookies. At Magnolia Manor, residents not only have meals, they also have snacks and drinks in between.

My grandmother jerks a secretive backhand toward my phone, her head turning to the server. "What do you want?"

The attendant isn't flustered by the uncharacteristically gruff greeting. "Morning coffee, Mrs. Stafford."

"Yes, of course." Grandma Judy again covertly indicates that I should put the phone away. "We'll enjoy a cup, certainly."

I glance at the time. It's later than I thought. I'm supposed to join my father for a luncheon and ribbon cutting in Columbia. *A golden opportunity to be seen rubbing elbows in the home state,* as Leslie put it. Press will be there, as will the governor. With the recent rumbles about Washington insiders and career politicians, these local events matter. I *get* it, but what I really want to do is stay with Grandma Judy long enough to see if I can gain some clarity on this May Crandall issue and find out what Arcadia has to do with it.

Maybe she's talking about a place? Arcadia, California? Arcadia, Florida?

"I really have to go, Grandma. I'm scheduled to accompany Daddy to a ribbon cutting."

"Heavens, then I shouldn't be holding you up."

The attendant moves in and pours two cups of coffee anyway. "Just in case," she says.

"You could take it to go," my grandmother jokes. The coffee is in a china cup.

"I probably don't need any more this morning. I'll be bouncing off the walls. I just stopped by to ask you about May —"

"Tsst!" A hiss and a raised finger stop me from finishing the name. I'm given the snake eye, as if I've just cursed in church.

The attendant wisely gathers her cart and leaves the room.

Grandma Judy whispers, "Be careful, Rill."

"W-what?" The intensity is once again startling. What's going on in that mind of hers? *Rill.* Is that a name?

"Ears" — Grandma Judy points to hers — "are everywhere."

Just as quickly, her mood changes. She sighs, tips up the tiny china pitcher, and pours a dab into her coffee. "Cream?"

"I can't stay."

"Oh, I'm so sorry. I wish you had time for a visit. It was lovely of you to pop in."

At this point, we've been chatting for at least thirty minutes. She's already forgotten. Arcadia, whatever it is, has disappeared into the mist.

She gives me a smile as blank as a freshly washed blackboard. It's completely genuine. She's not sure who I am, but she's trying to be polite. "Come again when you don't have to rush off."

"I will." I kiss her on the cheek and walk out of the room with no answers and even more questions.

There's no way I can let this thing drop now. I need to find out what I'm dealing with here. I'll have to unearth some other source of information, and I know where I intend to start digging.

Chapter 8

Rill

The shadow of the big white house slides over the car, swallowing it whole. Tall, thick magnolia trees line the curb, making a leafy green wall that reminds me of Sleeping Beauty's castle. It hides us from the street, where kids play in yards and moms push prams along the sidewalks. There's a baby carriage on the front porch of this house. It's old, and a wheel is missing, so it leans. It'd likely dump the baby out if you put one in it.

A little boy squats in one of the magnolia trees like a monkey. He's about Lark's size — maybe five or six. He watches us drive in but doesn't smile, or wave, or move. When the car stops, he disappears into the leaves.

A second later, I see him crawl from the tree and squeeze under a tall iron fence that circles the backyard of this house and the place beside it. The little building next door looks like it might've been a school or a church once. Some kids are playing on the teeter-totters and swings there, but the doors and windows are boarded shut, and there's hardly any paint on the wood. Brambles grow over the front porch, which makes me think of Sleeping Beauty again.

Camellia stretches upward from the floorboard to see. "This the hospital?" She gives Miss Tann a look to let her know she don't believe it for a minute. My sister has rested up on the drive, and she's ready for another fight.

Miss Tann turns her way and shifts Gabion, who's gone plumb asleep on her lap. His little arm flops down, chubby fingers gripping and ungripping. His lips move like he's blowing kisses in a dream. "You can't go to the hospital looking like that, now, can you? Stinking of the river and infested with vermin? Mrs. Murphy will take care of you, and *if* you are very, very good, then we will see about the hospital."

A hope spark tries to catch fire in me, but I can't find it much tinder. It snuffs out when Miss Tann looks my way.

Fern crawls up my chest, her knees poking into my belly. "I want Briny," she whisper-whines.

"Hop to. Time to go inside. You'll be just

fine here," Miss Tann tells us. "*If* you're good. Am I understood?"

"Yes'm," I try to answer for all of us, but Camellia's not giving up so easy.

"Where's Briny?" She ain't happy about this whole thing and she's working up to a blind-mad fit over it. I can feel it like a storm blowing in.

"Hush, Camellia!" I snap. "Do what she says."

Miss Tann smiles a little. "Very good. You see? All of this can be quite simple. Mrs. Murphy will take care of you."

She waits for the driver to come around and open the car door. Then she climbs out first, taking my little brother and pulling Lark by the hand. Lark looks at me with wide eyes, but like always, she won't fight. She's quiet as a kitten in the hay.

"You next." The woman wants me, and I scoot across, my knees knocking into the brown-eyed boy and girl on the floorboard. Fern wraps her arms around my neck so tight I almost can't get a breath.

"You two, now."

The kids who were in the car before us clamber out onto the driveway.

"Now *you.*" Miss Tann's voice lowers when she looks at Camellia. She turns Gabion and Lark over to me and stands right at the car door, her legs braced apart, her body blocking the way out. She's not a small woman. She towers over me and she looks strong.

"Come on along, Camellia." I'm begging her to be good, and she knows what I'm asking. So far, she hasn't moved an inch. She's got her hand around behind her back, and I'm afraid she's planning to try the other door. What use would there be in that? We don't know where we are or how to get back to the river or find the hospital. Our only hope is that, if we're good like Miss Tann says, we really will get to see Briny and Queenie.

Or that Silas will tell them what happened and our folks will come find us.

Camellia's shoulder jerks a little, and I hear the handle click. The door sticks, and Camellia's nose flares. She turns around to push, and Miss Tann sighs and leans inside.

When she lumbers back out, she's dragging Camellia by her clothes. "That is enough of *that*! You will straighten up and behave yourself."

"Camellia, stop!" I yell.

"Mellia, no, no!" Fern's voice is like an echo.

Gabion throws back his head and screams, the sound bouncing off the house and floating into the trees.

Miss Tann twists her grip so she's got a good hold on Camellia. "Do we understand one another?" Her round cheeks are red and sweaty. Her gray eyes bug out behind her glasses.

When Camellia squeezes her lips tight, I think Miss Tann might swat that look right off her face, but she doesn't. Instead, she whispers something close to Camellia's ear, then stands over her. "We'll be just fine now, won't we?"

Camellia's mouth still looks like she's sucked a lemon.

The moment teeters like a bottle on the edge of the *Arcadia*'s deck, waiting to topple down and be swept off in the river.

"*Won't* we?" Miss Tann repeats.

Camellia's dark eyes burn, but she nods.

"Very well then."

Miss Tann puts us in a line, and Camellia marches up the steps with the rest of us. From behind the iron fence, boys and girls of all sizes watch. Not a single one smiles.

Inside, the big house smells. The curtains are pulled everywhere, and it's shadowy. There's a wide staircase in the front hall. Two boys sit on the top step. One of them reminds me of Silas but bigger, except his hair is red as fox fur. These boys don't look a thing like the kids in the yard or the boy in the tree. They can't all be brothers and sisters.

Who are they? How many are there? Do they live here? Are they all here to clean up so they can see their mamas and daddies at the hospital?

What *is* this place?

We're taken into a room where a woman waits behind a desk. She's small compared to Miss Tann, her arms so thin the bones and veins show. Her nose pokes from her glasses, hooked like an owl's beak. It wrinkles when she looks at us. Then she smiles and stands and greets Miss Tann. "How are you today, Georgia?"

"Very well, thank you, Mrs. Murphy. It has been quite a productive morning, I daresay."

"I can see that it has."

Stroking her fingers along the desk, Mrs. Murphy draws trails in the dust as she moves toward us. One side of her lip comes up and an eyetooth flashes. "Good gracious. Where did you unearth these little waifs?"

The kids cluster close to me, even the ones I don't know. I hang on to Fern on one hip and Gabion on the other. My arms are starting to go numb, but I'm not letting go.

"Aren't they a pitiful lot?" Miss Tann says.

"I do believe we've removed them just in time. Have you space for all of them? It would be the simplest thing. I expect to move some of them quite quickly."

"Look at that hair. . . ." Mrs. Murphy comes closer, and Miss Tann follows. Miss Tann's bulky body shuffles side to side as she walks. For the first time, I notice that she's got a bum leg.

"Yes, quite something, isn't it? Four curly blonds all from the same family and . . . that one." She snorts and turns an eye on Camellia.

"Oh, surely *she* isn't one of this batch." Mrs. Murphy looks at me. "Is this your sister?"

"Y-yes'm," I say.

"And her name is?"

"C-Camellia."

"Quite a fancy name for such a common little thing. And all those silly freckles. Looks as though the stork dropped you into the wrong nest."

"She isn't one to cooperate," Miss Tann warns. "We've had trouble with her already. A little black sheep, in more ways than one."

Mrs. Murphy's eyes narrow. "Oh my. Well, I *do* expect good behavior in this house. Those who *fail* to meet my expectations will *not* be allowed to keep company above stairs with the rest of the children." She runs her tongue along her teeth.

My skin turns cold. Fern and Gabion wrap their arms tighter around my neck. It's clear enough what Mrs. Murphy means. If Camellia makes her mad, they'll take her away and put her . . . someplace else.

Camellia nods, but I can tell she don't mean it a bit.

"These other two with the dirt-blond hair were . . . found along the way." Miss Tann gathers the boy and girl who rode on the floor with Camellia. Both have long, straight straw-brown hair and big brown eyes. The way the little boy is hanging on to the girl, I'm sure she's his big sister. "More river rats, of course, although the camp down there was nearly empty. They must have gotten word somehow."

"Such darling faces."

"Yes, truly. These with the curls are almost angelic. They'll be in great demand, I predict."

Mrs. Murphy pulls away. "But good gracious! They stink of the river. I can't have that in my house, certainly. They'll have to stay outside until bath time."

"Don't let them out until you're certain they *fully* understand the rules here." Miss Tann drops a hand on Camellia's shoulder, and Camellia's head twitches so that I can tell the woman's fingers are digging in hard. "This one is a runner. She tried to bolt from the car, of all things. Those cows along the river bottom do know how to produce them, but not how to teach them to behave. This batch will need some work."

"Of course. Don't they all?" Mrs. Murphy nods. She focuses on me again. "And your name is?"

"Rill. Rill Foss." I try not to say anything more, but it spills out. I can't make sense of what they're talking about, and my heart is pounding. My knees tremble under the weight of my baby brother and sister, but that's not the only reason. I'm scared to death. Miss Tann plans to leave us here? For how long? "When can we go see our mama and daddy? They're at the hospital. Mama had a baby, and —"

"Hush," Mrs. Murphy says. "First things first. You will take the children into the hallway and sit them on the floor along the stairwell wall, smallest to largest. Wait there, and I'll expect *no* noise and *no* shenanigans. Understood?"

"But . . ."

Miss Tann lays a hand on my shoulder this time. Her fingers squeeze around the bone. "I do *not* expect to have trouble from *you.*

Surely you are smarter than your sister."

A pain shoots down my arm, and I feel Gabion slipping. "Y-yes'm. Yes, ma'am."

She lets go of me. I hike Gabby up again. I want to rub my shoulder, but I don't.

"And . . . *Rill.* What sort of *name* is that?"

"It's from the river. My daddy gave it to me. He says it sounds pretty as a song."

"We'll call you something proper. A *real* name for a real girl. *May* will do. May Weathers."

"But I'm . . ."

"May." She shoos me out the door, the other kids dragging along with me. Camellia gets warned again not to do anything except sit quiet in the hallway.

The little ones whine and whimper like puppies as I try to skin them off and set them down. Up the stairs, the two boys are gone. Somewhere outside, kids play Red Rover. I know that game from the schools we've gone to. When it's the school year, Queenie and Briny usually try to tie up someplace near a river town so Camellia and me, and now Lark, can go. The rest of the time, we read books, and Briny teaches us arithmetic. He can make a cipher out of almost anything. Camellia's a whiz at numbers. Even Fern knows her alphabet already, and she's still too young for school. Next fall, Lark will start the first grade. . . .

Lark looks up at me now, with her big mouse eyes, and a sick feeling bubbles in me like a black-water eddy. It's got no place to go. It just spins round and round in circles.

"Are they takin' us to jail?" the little girl — the one whose name I don't even know — whispers.

"No. 'Course not," I say. "They don't put little kids in jail." *Do they?*

Camellia's eyes slant toward the front door. She's wondering whether she can light out of here and get away with it.

"Don't," I spit under my breath. Mrs. Murphy told us not to make noise. The better we are, the more chance they'll take us where we want to go, I figure. "We need to stay together. Briny's gonna come get us soon's he knows we're not on the *Arcadia.* Soon's Silas tells him what happened. We've gotta be all in one place when he shows up. You hear me?" I sound like Queenie when there's breaking ice on the water and she won't let us hang over the rail in case a floe might hit the boat and shake us off into the river. Times like that, she wants us to know she means it when she says no. She don't get that way too often.

Everybody nods but Camellia. Even the

other little girl and boy nod.

"Mellia?"

"Mmmm-hmm." She gives in and pulls her knees up and crosses her arms and sticks her face in the middle, letting her head bump hard enough to make sure we know she ain't happy about it.

I ask the other kids' names, and neither one will say a word. Big tears roll down the little boy's cheeks, and his sister hugs him close.

A bird flies into the front-door glass and hits with a thud, and all of us jump. I stretch to see if it got up and flew off okay. It's a pretty little redbird. Maybe he's the one we heard by the river, and he followed us here. Now he staggers around, his feathers glittery bright in the long, lazy afternoon sun. I wish I could scoop him up before a cat can get him — we saw at least three in the bushes on the way in — but I'm afraid to. Miss Tann will think I'm trying to run.

Lark gets up on her knees to see, her lip trembling.

"He'll be all right," I whisper. "Sit down. Be good."

She does like she's told.

The bird wobbles off toward the steps so that I have to crawl away from the wall a little to see him. *Fly,* I think. *Hurry up. Fly off before they get you.*

But he just stays there, his beak hanging open, his whole body panting.

Fly away. Go on home.

I keep watch. If a cat comes, maybe I can scare it off through the window.

Words drift from under the door across the hall. I stand up real careful, tiptoe closer.

I catch bits and pieces of what Miss Tann and Mrs. Murphy are saying, but none of it makes any sense. ". . . surrender papers right at the hospital on the five siblings. Simple and straightforward. The easiest way to sever ties. The most difficult thing was finding the exact location of their shantyboat, actually. It was moored by itself across from Mud Island, the police tell me. The little freckle-faced one tried to swim out through the loo. That's more than just the river you caught a whiff of."

Laughter twitters, but it's sharp like a raven's call.

"And the other two?"

"Found them picking flowers near a hive of shantyboat vermin. We'll have their papers issued soon enough. Certainly it won't be any trouble. They seem quite mild mannered too. Hmmm . . . Sherry and Stevie. Those should do for names. Best to begin retraining them to them immediately.

They are darling, aren't they? And young. They might not stay long. We've a viewing party planned next month. I'll expect them to be ready."

"Oh, they will be."

"May, Iris, Bonnie . . . Beth . . . and Robby for the other five, I think. *Weathers* should do for the last name. May Weathers, Iris Weathers, Bonnie Weathers . . . It has a ring to it." Laughter comes again. It rises high and loud so that it pushes me back from the door.

The last words I hear are Mrs. Murphy's. "I'll see to it. You can rest assured that they'll be properly prepared."

By the time they come out, I've scooted into my place and checked that everyone is lined real neat along the wall. Even Camellia picks up her head and sits Indian style, the way we do in school.

We wait, still as statues, while Mrs. Murphy walks Miss Tann to the door. Only our eyes turn to watch them talk on the porch.

The little redbird has hopped to the stairs, but he just sits there helpless. Neither one of them notices.

Fly away.

I think of Queenie's red hat. *Fly all the way to Queenie, and tell her where to find us.*

Fly.

Miss Tann limps a few steps, almost hitting the bird. My breath turns solid and Lark gasps. Then Miss Tann stops to say something else.

When she starts off again, the redbird finally flies away.

He'll let Briny know where we are.

Mrs. Murphy comes back inside, but she's not smiling. She goes into the room across the hall and closes the door.

We sit and wait. Camellia buries her face again.

Fern lays on my shoulder. The little girl — *Sherry,* Miss Tann called her — holds her baby brother's hand. "I'm hungwee," he whispers.

"I 'ungee," Gabion echoes, way too loud.

"Ssshhh." His hair feels soft under my hand as I rub his head. "We have to be quiet. Like hide-and-seek. Like a game."

He clamps his mouth and tries his best. Being only two, he's always left out of our "Let's pretend" games on the *Arcadia,* so he's happy to be part of it this time.

I wish this was a good game. I wish I knew the rules and what we get if we win.

Right now, all we can do is sit and wait for whatever happens next.

We sit, and sit, and sit.

It seems like forever before Mrs. Murphy

comes out. I'm hungry too, but I can tell by her face we'd best not ask.

She stands over us with her fists poked into her sides, her hip bones sticking out under her flowered black dress. "Seven more . . ." she says, frowning and looking up the stairs. A breath comes out and sinks like fog. It smells bad. "Well, there isn't any *choice* about it, what with your parents unable to care for you."

"Where's Briny? Where's Queenie?" Camellia blurts out.

"You will be *silent*!" Mrs. Murphy teeters on her feet as she moves down the line of us, and now I know what I smelled when she came out the door. Whiskey. I've been around enough pool halls to recognize it.

Mrs. Murphy stabs a finger toward Camellia. *"You* are the reason everyone must *sit* here rather than going outside to *play."* She stomps off down the hall, her steps drawing a crooked line.

We sit. The little ones finally sleep, and Gabion falls flat out on the floor. A few other kids pass by — older and younger, boys and girls. Most wear clothes that are too big or too small. Not a single one looks our way. They walk through like they don't notice we're there. Women in white dresses with white aprons move up and down the hall in a hurry. They don't see us either.

I wrap my fingers around my ankles and squeeze hard to make sure I'm still there. I almost think I've turned into the Invisible Man, like Mr. H. G. Wells wrote about. Briny loves that story. He's read it to us a lot and Camellia and me play it with the kids in the river camps. Nobody can see the Invisible Man.

I close my eyes and pretend a while.

Fern needs to potty, and before I can figure out what to do about it, she wets herself. A dark-haired woman in a white uniform walks by and spots the mess running across the floor. She grabs Fern up by the arm. "We will have none of that here. You'll use the bathroom properly." She pulls a sack towel from her apron and throws it over the mess. "Clean that up," she tells me. "Mrs. Murphy will have a fit."

She takes Fern with her, and I do what she says. When Fern comes back, her drawers and dress have been washed out, and she's wearing them wet. The lady tells the rest of us we can go to the bathroom too, but to hurry up about it and then sit down by the stairs again.

We haven't been back in our places long before someone blows a whistle outside. I hear kids clambering around. Lots of them.

They don't talk, but their footsteps echo beyond the door at the end of the hall. They're in there a while, and then there's a racket like they're hurrying up stairs, but not the stairs next to us.

Overhead, the boards creak and groan the way the gunwales and planking do on the *Arcadia.* It's a home sound, and I close my eyes to listen and pretend I can wish us back aboard our safe little boat.

My wish dries up pretty quick. A woman in a white dress stops by and says, "Come this way."

We climb to our feet to follow. Camellia goes first, and we keep the little kids between us, even Sherry and Stevie.

The lady takes us through the door at the end of the hall, and everything looks a lot different back there. It's plain and old. Strips of paper and cheesecloth hang off the wall. There's a kitchen to one side where two colored women are busy with a kettle on the stove. I hope we'll get to eat soon. My stomach feels like it's shrunk to the size of a peanut.

Even thinking *that* makes me hungry for peanuts.

A big staircase rises off to the other side of the kitchen. Most of the paint's rubbed off, like it's been walked on a lot. Half the bars are missing from the railing. A couple loose ones hang out like the leftover teeth in Old Zede's smile.

The woman in the white uniform takes us upstairs and stands us along a hallway wall. Other kids form lines nearby, and I hear water running in a tub someplace. "No talking," the woman says. "You will quietly wait here until it's your turn for the bath. You will take off your clothing now and fold it neatly in a pile at your feet. *All* of it."

Blood prickles in my skin, hot and sticky, and I look around and see that all the other kids, big and small, are already doing what we've just been told to do.

CHAPTER 9

Avery

"May Crandall. Are you sure that name isn't familiar?" I'm sitting in the limo with my mother and father, en route to the ribbon-cutting ceremony in Columbia. "She's the one who found my bracelet at the nursing home yesterday." I say *found* because it sounds better than *lifted it right from my wrist.* "The Greer design with the garnet dragonflies — the one Grandma Judy gave me. I think this woman recognized it."

"Your grandmother wore that bracelet frequently. Anyone who'd seen her in it certainly might remember it. It's quite unique." Mom searches her memory banks, her perfectly lined lips compressing. "No. I really don't recall that name. Perhaps she's one of the Asheville Crandalls? I dated a boy from that family when I was young — before your father, of course. Did you ask who her people are?" For Honeybee, as with all well-bred Southern women of her generation, this is a natural question upon meeting. *Wonderful to know you. Isn't this a lovely day? Now, tell me, who are your people?*

"I didn't think to ask."

"Honestly, Avery! What are we going to do with you?"

"Send me to the woodshed?"

My father chuckles, looking up from a briefcase filled with documents he's been reading. "Now, Honeybee, I *have* been keeping her busy. And nobody could file away all those details the way you do."

Mom swats at him playfully. "Oh, hush."

He catches her hand and kisses it, and I'm pinned in the middle. I feel thirteen years old.

"Eeewww. PDA, y'all." Since coming home I've readopted words like *y'all,* which I had expunged from my vocabulary up north. They're good words, I've now decided. Like the humble boiled peanut, they serve perfectly in many situations.

"Do you recall a May Crandall, Wells — a friend of your mother's?" Honeybee retracks our conversation.

"I don't think so." Dad reaches up to scratch his head, then remembers that he's been amply hair-sprayed. Outdoor occasions require extra preparation. Nothing worse than ending up in the newspaper looking like Alfalfa. Leslie made sure I pulled my hair back. Honeybee and I match, actually. It's French twist day.

"Arcadia," I blurt out, just to see if the word draws a reaction. "Was that one of Grandma Judy's clubs . . . or maybe a bridge circle . . . or did she know someone who lived in Arcadia?"

Neither my mother nor my father seems to have any unusual reaction to the word. "Arcadia, Florida?" Mom wants to know.

"I'm not sure. It came up in the conversation about her bridge groups." I don't tell her that the way Grandma Judy said it left me uneasy. "How could I find out more?"

"You're awfully concerned about this."

I almost pull out my phone to show her the photo. Almost. My hand stops halfway to my purse, and I smooth my skirt instead. The ember of a new worry is clearly visible in my mother's face. She doesn't need one more thing to stress about. If I show her the photo, she'll be certain a nefarious scheme is being perpetrated and May Crandall wants something from us. My mother is a professional worrier.

"I'm really not concerned, Mama. I was just curious. The woman seemed so lonely."

"That's sweet of you, but Grandma Judy

wouldn't be much company for her, even if they *did* know one another. I've just had to ask the Monday Girls not to visit Magnolia Manor anymore. Too many old friends stopping by just frustrates your grandmother. She's embarrassed that she can't place names and faces. It's harder when it's not family. She worries that people are talking about her."

"I know." Maybe I should let this go. But the question nags me. It whispers and pesters and teases. It will not leave me alone all afternoon. We chat; we schmooze; we clap when my father cuts the ribbon. We spend time in the VIP lounge at the local country club, rubbing elbows with the governor and talking with corporate higher-ups. I'm even able to offer some free legal advice on the battle over natural gas fracking and ongoing legislation that could throw the doors wide open to it in neighboring North Carolina. Economy versus environment — so often it comes down to those two heavyweights duking it out in the ring of public opinion and, of course, upcoming legislation.

Even as I'm discussing the cost-benefit questions, which I honestly do care about passionately, in the back of my mind, I'm thinking of the cellphone in my purse and

Grandma Judy's reaction to the photo.

I know she recognized the woman. *Queen . . . or Queenie.*

It's not a coincidence. It can't be.

Arcadia. Arcadia . . . what?

In the car on our way back to my father's Aiken office, I offer up a few innocent-sounding excuses to slip away from my parents for a while — errands and whatnot. The truth is that I'm going to see May Crandall again. If there *is* something going on here, I'm better off knowing about it. Then I can decide what needs to be done.

Daddy actually seems a little disappointed that we're parting ways. He has a strategy meeting with his staff before finally going home for supper. He was hoping I'd sit in.

"Oh, for heaven's sake, Wells. Avery *is* allowed a personal life," Mom interjects. "She has a handsome young fiancé to keep up with, remember?" Her slim shoulders rise, and she offers me a conspiratorial smile. "And a wedding to plan. They can't *plan* if they never talk." The end of the sentence rises, singsong with anticipation. She pats my knee and leans close. A meaningful look flashes my way. *Let's get this show on the road,* it says. She busies herself with her purse, lets a moment pass, and pretends to be casually switching topics. "The gardener brought in some new form of mulch the other day . . . for the azaleas . . . on a recommendation from Bitsy's landscaper. They put it out last fall, and their azaleas were twice as thick as ours. Next spring, the gardens at Drayden Hill will be the envy of . . . well . . . everyone. Around the end of March. It should be just . . . heavenly."

The phrase *perfect for a wedding* hangs unsaid in the air. When we announced our engagement, Elliot made Bitsy and Honeybee promise they wouldn't sweep in and hijack the decision-making process. It's killing them, really. They'd have this thing all sewn up if we'd just get out of the way, but we're determined to make plans in our own time, in the way we think is best. Right now, my father and Honeybee should be focusing one hundred percent on Dad's health, not worrying about wedding arrangements.

You can't tell Honeybee that, though.

I pretend not to get the drift. "I think Jason could grow roses in the desert." Jason has managed the gardens at Drayden Hill since long before I left for college. He'd be thrilled to have the chance to show them off. But Elliot will never go for a wedding idea that originated with the moms. Elliot loves his mother, but as an only child, he's exhausted by her constant focus on arranging his life.

One thing at a time, I tell myself. *Daddy, cancer, politics.* Those are the big three right now.

We pull up in front of the office. The driver opens the door for us, and I slip out, glad that I'm free.

One last thinly veiled hint follows me out the door: "Tell Elliot to thank his mother for the suggestion about the azaleas."

"I will," I promise, then hurry off to my car, where I do call Elliot. He doesn't pick up. Chances are he's in a meeting, even though it's after five. His financial clients are international, so demands come in around the clock.

I leave a quick message about the azaleas. He'll get a laugh out of that, and he often needs it at the end of a high-stress day.

A block down the road, I get a call from my middle sister, Allison.

"Hey, Allie. What's up?" I say.

Allison laughs, but she sounds frazzled. The triplets are fussing in the background. "Is there any way . . . *any* way at *all* you could pick Courtney up from dance class? The boys are sick, and we've been through three sets of clothes today already, and . . . yeah. We're naked again. All four of us. Court's probably standing outside the dance studio wondering where in the world I am."

I make a quick U-turn toward Miss Hannah's, where I was a ballet and pageant class failure back in the day. Fortunately, Court has real talent. At her spring recital, she was amazing. "Sure. Of course I'll do it. I'm not even very far away. I can be there to get her in ten."

Allison answers with a long sigh of relief. "Thank you. You're a lifesaver. Today, you're my favorite sister." It's been a running joke since childhood, the question of who was Allison's favorite. As the middle kid, she had her pick. Missy was older and more interesting, but I was younger and could be bossed around.

I laugh softly. "Well, that's totally worth an extra trip across town."

"And please don't tell Mama the boys are sick. She'll come over here, and I don't want to take any chances on Daddy being exposed to whatever this bug is. Drop Courtney off at Shellie's house. I'll text the address to you. I already called Shellie's mom. They're fine with Court spending the night."

"Okay, will do." Of the three of us, Allison is the most akin to Honeybee. She operates like a four-star general, but since the boys came along, she's been overpowered by an invading army. "I'm almost at the studio. I'll text you once I've rescued your daughter."

We hang up, and a few minutes later, I'm pulling up to Miss Hannah's. Courtney is standing out front. She brightens when she sees that she hasn't been abandoned.

"Hey, Aunt Aves!" she says as she slides into the car.

"Hey, yourself."

"Mom forget me again?" She rolls her eyes and lets her head sag to one side, a motion that makes her seem way more than ten years old.

"No . . . I was just lonesome for you. I thought we could hang out, go to the park, slide down the slide, play in the play fort, that kind of thing."

"Okay, *seriously,* Aunt Aves . . ."

It bothers me that she's so quick to reject the idea. She's too grownup for her own good. Wasn't it just yesterday that she was tugging my pants leg and begging me to climb trees with her at Drayden Hill? "All right, your mom did call me to pick you up, but only because the boys are sick. I'm supposed to take you to Shellie's house."

Her face lights up, and she straightens in the passenger seat. "Oh, awesome!" I give her the stink eye, and she adds, "Not about the boys being sick, I mean."

I offer an ice cream stop, our favorite activity once upon a time, but she tells me she's not hungry. She only has eyes for Shellie's house, so I turn on the GPS and strike out in that direction.

She whips out her cellphone to text Shellie, and my thoughts switch tracks. Arcadia and May Crandall overshadow the pangs of watching my niece rush headlong toward teenagerhood. What will May's response be when I ask her about that word, *Arcadia*?

It's looking less likely that I'll find out today. By the time I drop Courtney off, it'll be supper hour at the nursing home. The staff will be busy, and so will May.

I turn off the main road and wind through tree-clad streets lined with stately turn-of-the-century homes surrounded by perfectly manicured lawns and gardens. We've gone quite a few blocks before I realize why the trip to Shellie's house has such a familiar feel to it. Grandma Judy's home on Lagniappe is not far away.

"Hey, Court. Want to run by Grandma Judy's house with me before I drop you at Shellie's?" I don't like the idea of going alone, but it has just occurred to me that there might be some answers to be found among Grandma Judy's belongings.

Courtney lowers the phone, giving me a bemused look. "It's kinda creepy, Aunt Aves. Nobody's there, but all Grandma Judy's stuff is still around." Her bottom lip pouts outward. Big blue eyes regard me earnestly. It's hard for the kids to accept the rapid change in Grandma Judy. This is their first real brush with mortality. "I'll go with you if you *really* need me to."

"No, that's all right." I continue past the turn-off. There's no reason to involve Courtney. I'll run over to Lagniappe after I drop Court at her friend's.

She's clearly relieved. "Okay. Thanks for picking me up today, Aunt Aves."

"Anytime, kiddo."

A few minutes later, she's trotting up the driveway to Shellie's house, and I'm bound for Lagniappe Street and the past.

Blunt-force grief strikes me as I pull into the drive and step from the car. Everywhere I look, there's a memory. The roses I helped my grandmother tend, the willow tree where I played house with the little girl from down the street, the Cinderella's castle bay window upstairs, the yawning porch that served as a backdrop for prom photos, the water garden where the multicolored koi bobbed for cracker crumbs.

I can almost *feel* my grandmother on the Charleston-style piazza along the side of the house. Climbing the stairs, I half expect her to be there. It's painful to realize that she's not. I'll never again come to this place and be greeted by my grandmother.

In the backyard, the greenhouse is stale and dusty smelling. The moist, earthy scents are gone. The shelves and pots have been removed too. No doubt my mother gave them to someone who could use them.

The hidden key is right where it has always been. It catches a beam of late-afternoon light as I remove a loose brick along the foundation. From there, it's easy enough to slip inside and turn off the alarm. After that, I stand in the living room thinking, *What next?*

The floorboards crackle beneath me, and I jump, even though it's an old, familiar sound. Courtney was right. The house seems vacant and spooky, no longer the second home it has always been. From the age of thirteen on, I stayed here during the school year whenever my parents were in D.C., so I could attend classes in Aiken with my friends.

Now I feel like a sneak thief.

This is silly anyway. You don't even know

what you're looking for.

Photos, maybe? Is the woman on May Crandall's nightstand in any of the old albums? Grandma Judy has always been the family historian, the keeper of the Stafford lineage, the one who tirelessly pecks out labels on her old manual typewriter and attaches them to things. There isn't a stick of furniture, a painting, a piece of artwork, or a photo in this house that isn't carefully marked with its origins and previous owners. Her personal items — any that matter — are similarly stored. The dragonfly bracelet came to me in a well-worn box with a yellowed note taped to the bottom.

July 1966. A gift. Moonstones for first photographs sent back from the moon by American exploratory spacecraft Surveyor. Garnets for love. Dragonflies for water. Sapphires and onyx for remembrance. Custom by Greer Designs, Damon Greer, designer.

Beneath that, she'd added:

For Avery,
Because you are the one to dream new dreams and blaze new trails. May the dragonflies take you to places beyond

your imaginings.

— Grandma Judy

It's strange, I now realize, that she didn't say whom the gift was from. I wonder if I can find that information in her appointment books. Never a week passed that she didn't carefully document the details of her days, keeping track of everyone she saw, what she wore, what was served at meals. If she and May Crandall were friends or shared a bridge circle, May's name will probably be there.

Someday, you'll read these and know all my secrets, she told me once when I asked her why she was so meticulous about writing everything down.

The comment seems like permission now, but as I pass through the shadowy house, guilt niggles at me. It's not as though my grandmother has passed away. She's still here. What I'm doing amounts to snooping, yet I can't get past the feeling that she *wants* me to understand something, that this is important, somehow, for both of us.

In her little office off the library, her last appointment book still sits on the desk. The page is open to the day she disappeared for eight hours and ended up lost and confused at the former shopping mall. A Thursday.

The handwriting is barely legible. It trembles and runs downhill. It looks nothing like my grandmother's lovely, curving script. *Trent Turner, Edisto* is the only notation for that day.

Edisto? Is that what happened when she disappeared? Somehow, she thought she was going to the cottage on Edisto Island to . . . meet someone? Maybe she had a dream overnight and woke up believing it was real? Perhaps she was reliving some event from the past?

Who is Trent Turner?

I leaf through more pages.

There's no mention of May Crandall among Grandma Judy's social engagements over the past months. Yet, somehow, May gave me the impression they'd seen each other recently.

The farther back I go, the clearer the handwriting becomes. I feel myself sinking into the familiar routines around which I once shadowed my grandmother — events for the Federation Women's Club, the library board, the DAR, the Garden Club in the spring. It's painful to realize that seven months ago, before her rapid downward spiral, she was still functioning reasonably well, still keeping up her social calendar, though a friend or two had mentioned to my parents that *Judy has been having some lapses.*

I leaf through more pages, wondering, remembering, thinking about this watershed year. Life can turn on a dime. The appointment book reinforces my new awareness of this. We plan our days, but we don't control them.

My grandmother's January notes begin with a single line scrawled haphazardly in the margin just before New Year's Day. *Edisto* and *Trent Turner,* she'd written again. There's a phone number jotted underneath.

Maybe she was talking to someone about having work done on the cottage? That's hard to imagine. My dad's personal secretary has been handling Grandma Judy's affairs since my grandfather died seven years ago. If there were any arrangements to be made, she would have taken care of them.

There's one way to find out, I guess.

I grab my cell and dial the number.

The phone rings once, twice.

I start wondering what I'm going to say if someone answers. *Ummm . . . I'm not sure why I'm calling. I found your name in an old notebook at my grandmother's house, and . . .*

And . . . what?

A machine picks up. "Turner Real Estate. This is Trent. There's no one here to answer the phone right now, but if you'll leave a message . . ."

Real estate? I'm gobsmacked. Was Grandma Judy thinking about selling the Edisto place? That's hard to fathom. The cottage has been in her family since before she married my grandfather. She loves it.

My parents would've told me if we were letting go of the place. There must be another explanation, but since I have no way of knowing, I return to my browsing.

In the closet, I find the rest of her appointment books stored in a well-worn barrister bookcase, right where they've always been. They're neatly arranged in order from the year she married my grandfather to the present. Just for fun, I take out the oldest one. The milky leather cover is dry and crazed with brown cracks so that it looks like a piece of antique china. Inside, the handwriting is loopy and girlish. Notations about sorority parties, college exams, bridal showers, china patterns, and date nights with my grandfather fill the pages.

In one of the margins, she has practiced signing her soon-to-be married name, the flourishes on the letters testifying to the giddiness of first love.

Visited Harold's parents at Drayden Hill, one entry says. *Horseback riding. Took a few fences. Harold said not to tell his mother. She wants us in one piece for the wedding. I have found my prince. Not the slightest bit of doubt.*

Emotion gathers in my throat. It's bittersweet.

Not the slightest bit of doubt.

Did she really feel that way? Did she really just . . . *know* it was right when she met my grandfather? Should Elliot and I have experienced some sort of . . . lightning bolt moment, rather than the relaxed drift from childhood adventures to adult friendship to dating to engagement because, after six years of dating, it seems like it's time? Is there something wrong with us because we haven't tumbled in headfirst, because we're not in a rush?

My cellphone rings, and I grab it, wanting it to be him.

The voice on the other end is male and friendly, but it isn't Elliot's.

"Hello, this is Trent Turner. I had a call from this number. Sorry I missed you. What can I help you with?"

"Oh . . . oh . . ." Every possible icebreaker flies from my mind, and I blurt out, "I found your name in my grandmother's date book."

Papers shuffle in the background. "Did we have an appointment set up here on Edisto? To look at a cottage or something? Or is this about a rental?"

"I don't know what it's about. Actually, I was hoping you could tell me. My grandmother has been experiencing some health problems. I'm trying to make sense of the notes on her schedule."

"What day was the appointment for?"

"I'm not sure if she had one. I thought she might've called you about selling a property. The Myers cottage." It's not uncommon around here for properties to be known by the names of people who owned them decades ago. My grandmother's parents built the Edisto house as a place to escape the hot, sticky summers inland. "Stafford. Judy Stafford." I prepare myself for the change in tone that almost invariably comes with the name. Anywhere in the state, people either love us or hate us, but they usually know who we are.

"Staff . . . for . . . Stafford . . ." he mutters. Maybe he's not from around here? Come to think of it, his accent doesn't even hint of Charleston. It's not Lowcountry, but there is some sort of drawl there. Texas maybe? Having spent so much of my childhood mingling with kids from other places, I'm good with accents, both foreign and domestic.

There's a strange pause. His tone is more guarded afterward. "I've only been here about nine months, but I can promise you that no one's ever called here about selling or renting the Myers cottage. Sorry I can't be of more help." Suddenly, he's trying to shuffle me off the phone. *Why?* "If it was before the first of the year, my grandfather, Trent Senior, was probably the one she was talking to. But he passed away over six months ago."

"Oh. My condolences." I instantly feel a kinship that goes beyond his presence in a place I have always dearly loved. "Any idea *what* my grandmother was in touch with him about?"

There's another uncomfortable pause, as if he's carefully weighing his words. "Yes, actually. He had some papers for her. That's really all I can say."

The lawyer in me surfaces. I catch the scent of a reluctant witness who's harboring information. "What kind of papers?"

"I'm sorry. I promised my grandfather."

"Promised what?"

"If she'll come down here herself, I can give her the envelope he left for her."

Alarm bells ring in my head. What in the world is going on? "She isn't able to travel."

"Then I can't help you. I'm sorry."
Just like that, he hangs up.

Chapter 10

Rill

The room is quiet and wet-smelling. I open my eyes, shut them real tight, let them come open again slow. Sleep haze hangs over me so that I can't see too clear. It's like the river fog came crawling through the shanty windows overnight.

Nothing's where it's supposed to be. Instead of the *Arcadia*'s doors and windows, there're thick stacked-stone walls. The air smells like the closed compartments where we keep crates of stores and fuel. The stink of mold and wet dirt crawls up my nose and stays there.

I hear Lark whine in her sleep. There's the squeak of hinges instead of the soft rustle of the pull-down pallets where Lark and Fern sleep.

Blinking, I look up and make out one tiny, high-up window near the ceiling. Morning light pushes through, but it's dull and shadowy.

A bush scrapes over the glass. Its branches raise a soft squeal. A scrappy pink rose hangs down, half-broke.

Everything comes back in a rush. I remember going to bed on the musty-smelling cot, staring out the window at the rose as the day faded and my brother and sisters breathed longer and slower around me.

I remember the worker in the white dress bringing us down the basement stairs and walking us by the furnace and the coal piles to this tiny room.

You'll sleep here until we find out whether you're staying for good. No noise and no carrying on. You're to be quiet. You are not to leave your beds. She pointed us to five folding cots, the kind that soldiers use in their practice camps along the river sometimes.

Then she left and closed the door behind her.

We huddled quiet on our beds, even Camellia. Mostly I was just glad we were by ourselves again, just the five of us. No workers, no other kids watching with curious eyes, worried eyes, sad eyes, mean eyes, hollow eyes that're dead and hard.

All of what happened yesterday plays in my head like a picture show. I see the *Ar-*

cadia, the police, Silas, Miss Tann's car, the bath line upstairs. A sickness runs over me from head to toe. It swallows me like a backwash of stagnant water, hot from the summer sun, poisoned by everything that's fallen into it.

I feel dirty from the inside out. It's not got a thing to do with the cloudy bathwater that was brown with the sand and soap of all the kids who'd used it before me, including my sisters and Gabion.

Instead, I see the worker standing over me while I step into the tub, turning my shoulder to hide myself. "Wash." She points at the soap and the rag. "We ain't got time for dallyin'. You river rats ain't exactly known for bein' prude anyhow, are you?"

I don't know what she means or how to answer. Maybe I'm not supposed to.

"I said, wash up!" she hollers. "You think I got all day?" I know for sure she doesn't. I've already heard her yell the same thing to other kids. I've heard whining and whimpering and sputtering when heads got dunked to rinse them off. Luckily, none of us Foss kids mind going underwater. The babies and even Camellia made it through the bath line without much trouble. I want to do the same, but the woman seems like she's got it in for me, maybe on account of I'm the oldest.

I squat down over the water because it's dirty and cold.

She moves to get a better look at me and stares in a way that raises gooseflesh on my skin. "Guess you ain't too grown-ish to be in with the little girls after all. Won't be long, though, we'll have to move you someplace else."

I turn my shoulder even more and wash quick as I can.

This morning I still feel dirty from having somebody look me over like that. I hope we'll be gone from here before it's time for another bath.

I want the little pink rose outside to disappear. I want the window to change, the walls to turn to wood, the cement floor to shift, and melt, and go away. I want old planks worn down by our feet and the river rocking under our beds and the soft sound of Briny playing his harmonica outside on the porch.

I've come awake at least ten times overnight. In the wee hours, Fern squeezed herself in beside me, the sagging canvas pulling us together so tight it's a wonder she can breathe, much less sleep.

Each time I let myself go under, I'm back

on the *Arcadia* again. Each time I wake up, I'm here, in this place, and I try to make sense of it.

You'll sleep here until we find out whether you're staying for good. . . .

What's that mean . . . *for good*? Aren't they taking us to the hospital to see Briny and Queenie now that we've stayed the night here and got cleaned up? Are all of us going or just some? I can't leave the babies here. What if these people hurt them?

I have to protect my brothers and sisters, but I can't even protect myself.

Tears turn my mouth sticky. I've told myself I won't cry. It'd only scare the little kids. I promised them everything'll be all right, and so far, they believe it, even Camellia.

I close my eyes, curl around Fern, let the tears come and seep into her hair. Sobs heave through my stomach and push up my chest, and I swallow them like hiccups. Fern sleeps right through it. Maybe her dreams make her think it's just the river rocking her bunk.

Don't fall asleep, I tell myself. I have to put Fern back in her own cot before anybody comes. I can't get us in trouble. The lady told us not to leave our beds.

Just a minute or two more. Just a minute or

two, then I'll get up and make sure everybody's where they're supposed to be.

I drift and wake and drift and wake. My heart slams hard against my ribs when I hear somebody breathing nearby — not one of us, somebody bigger. A man. Maybe it's Briny.

No sooner does the thought come than the scents of old grease and green grass and coal dust and sweat sift into the room. It's not Briny. He smells of river water and sky. Morning fog in the summer and frost and woodsmoke in the winter.

My mind clears up, and I listen. Feet shuffle a couple steps in the door, then stop. That's not Briny's walk.

I pull the covers over Fern's head, hope she won't wake up and move just now. It's still pretty dim, that same faint light coming through the window. Maybe he won't notice Fern's not on her cot.

When I turn my head, I can barely see him from the edge of my eye. He's big, taller and fatter than Briny by a lot, but that's all I can make out. He's a shadow, standing there. He doesn't move or say anything. He just stands and looks.

My nose runs from all the crying, but I don't wipe it or sniffle. I don't want him to know I'm awake. Why is he here?

Camellia rolls over in her bed.

No, I think. *Ssshhhh.* Is she looking at him? Can he see whether her eyes are open?

He moves into the room. Moves, then stops, then moves, then stops. He bends over Lark's cot, touches her pillow. He stumbles a little and bumps the wood frame.

I watch through the narrow slits of my eyes. He comes to my cot next, looks down for a minute. The pillow rustles near my head. He touches it twice, real light.

Then he stops at the other cots and finally leaves and closes the door.

I let out the breath I've been holding and suck in another one and catch the smell of peppermint. When I throw off the covers and wake Fern, there're two little white candies on the pillow. They make me think of Briny right off. When Briny hustles money at a pool hall or works on a showboat that's docked up, he always comes back to the *Arcadia* with a roll of Beech-Nut Luster-Mints in his pocket. They're the best kind. Briny plays little riddle games with us, and if we get the answers right, we get a candy. *If there's two redbirds up a tree and one on the ground and three bluebirds in a bush and four on the ground and a big ol' crow on the fence and an owl in the barn stall, how many birds on the ground?*

The older you are, the tougher the questions get. The tougher the questions get, the better the Beech-Nut candies taste.

The peppermint smell makes me want to run to the door and look out and see if Briny's here. But these peppermints are another kind. They don't feel right in my fist when I scoop them up and carry Fern to her bed.

By the door, Camellia pops hers into her mouth and munches it.

I think about leaving the peppermints on the little kids' pillows, but instead, I decide it'd be better to pick them up. If the workers come, I'm afraid we might get in trouble for having them.

"Stealer!" Camellia talks for the first time since the bath line last night. She's sitting up in her bed, the shoulder of a too-big nighty sagging halfway down her arm. After the baths, one of the workers rooted through a pile and handed us these to wear. "He gave us *each* a candy. You can't have 'em all. That ain't fair."

"Ssshhh!" She's so loud, I half expect the door to swing open and we'll all be in a fix. "I'm saving them for everybody for later."

"You're stealin'."

"Am not." Sure enough, Camellia's back to herself today, but like usual in the morning, she's in a mood. She don't wake up easy, even with peppermints. Most times, I'd square off with her, but right now, I'm too tired for it. "I'm saving them till later, I said. I don't want us to get in trouble."

My sister's bony shoulders sag. "We *already* got trouble." Her black hair falls forward in mats, like a horse's tail. "What're we gonna *do,* Rill?"

"We're gonna be good so's the people will take us to Briny. You can't try to run away anymore, Camellia. You can't fight them, okay? If we make them mad, they won't take us."

She stares hard at me, her brown eyes squinted into slits so that she looks like the Chinamen who wash river town laundry in big, boiling kettles along the bank. "You think they'll take us, for sure? Today?"

"If we're good." I hope it's not a lie, but maybe it is.

"Why'd they bring us here?" The question chokes her. "Why didn't they just leave us be?"

My mind scrambles around, trying to figure it out. I need to explain it to myself as much as to Camellia. "I think it's a mistake. They must've figured Briny wasn't comin' back to look after us. But Briny'll tell them soon's he finds out that we're gone. He'll tell them this is all somebody's big mistake, and he'll take us home."

"Today, though?" Her chin quivers, and she pushes her bottom lip up hard, bolts it the way she does when she's about to pick a fight with a boy.

"I bet today. I bet today for sure."

She sniffs and wipes snot with her arm. "I ain't lettin' them women get me in that bathtub again, Rill. I ain't."

"What'd they do to you, Camellia?"

"Nothin'." Her chin pokes up. "They just ain't gettin' me in there again, that's all." She stretches a hand toward me, opens it. "If you ain't gonna give them candies to everybody, let me have 'em. I'm starved."

"We'll save the rest for later. . . . If we get to go outside where the kids were yesterday, I'll pull them out then."

"You said Briny was gonna come later."

"I don't know *when.* I just know he will."

She screws her lips to one side like she's not believing it for one minute, then turns herself toward the door. "Maybe that man can help us get away. The one who brung us the peppermints. He's our friend."

I've already thought about that. But who *was* the man? Why did he come in here? Does he *want* to be our friend? He's the first one who's been nice to us at Mrs.

Murphy's house.

"We'll wait for Briny," I say. "We've just gotta be good till then, that's —"

The door handle rattles. Camellia and I fall into our beds both at the same time and pretend we're sleeping. My heart pumps under the scratchy blanket. Who's out there? Is it our new friend or someone else? Did they hear us talking?

I don't have long to wonder. A brown-haired lady in a white dress comes in. I watch her through a thin place in the blanket. She's stout as a lumberjack and round in the middle. She isn't one of the women we saw yesterday.

At the door, she frowns, then looks toward our beds, then at the keys in her hand. "All of you, out of bet." She talks like the family from Norway whose boat was tied up down the way from ours for a month last summer. *Bed* sounds like *bet,* but I know what she means. She doesn't seem mad, really, just tired. "On your feet, and folt the blankets."

We scramble up, all except Gabion. I have to rustle him from his cot, and he stumbles around and lands on his rear while I take care of the blankets.

"Someone *else* was in this room duringk the night, yes?" She holds up a key pinched between her fingers.

Should we tell her about the man with the peppermints? Maybe he wasn't supposed to be in our room? Maybe we'll get in trouble if they find out we didn't tell.

"No'm. Not nobody. Just us," Camellia answers before I can.

"And *you* are the troublemakingk one, I am tolt." A hard look comes Camellia's way, and my sister shrinks a little.

"No'm."

"Nobody came in." I have to lie too. What else can I do now that Camellia told a fib? "Unless it happened while we were sleepin'."

The woman pulls the chain on the lightbulb overhead. It flickers, and we blink and squint. "This door shouldt have been lockedt. It was, yes?"

"We dunno," Camellia pipes up. "We was in our beds the whole night."

The woman looks at me, and I nod, then make myself busy with cleaning up the room. I want to get rid of the peppermints, but I'm too scared to, so I keep them stuck in my hand, which makes it hard to fold the blankets, but the lady doesn't notice. Mostly, she's just in a hurry to get us out of there.

When we leave the room, I see the big

man standing there in the basement, leaning on a broom handle next to the fat black boiler stove with slats that look like the mouth on a Halloween pumpkin. The man watches us go by. Camellia smiles over at him, and he smiles back. His teeth are old and ugly, and his thin brown hair hangs down around his face in sweaty strings, but still, the smile is nice to see.

Maybe we do have a friend here after all.

"Mr. Riggs, if you have *nothingk* else that must be done, see to the branch that has fallen in the yardt duringk the night," the woman says, "before the children are goingk out."

"Yes'm, Mrs. Pulnik." His lips curve up at the edges, and he moves the broom a little as Mrs. Pulnik starts up the stairs, but he doesn't sweep anything.

Camellia looks back over her shoulder, and he winks at her. The wink makes me think of Briny, so maybe I do like Mr. Riggs a little bit.

Upstairs, Mrs. Pulnik takes us to the laundry room and gives us some things off a pile. She calls them playclothes, but they're really not much more than rags. She tells us to get ourselves dressed and use the bathroom, and we do, and breakfast looks a lot like the supper they gave us last night after the bath — a little scoop of cornmeal mush. We're late getting to the table. The other kids have already gone to play. After we've scraped our bowls clean, we're told to get outside too and not to try leaving the backyard and the churchyard, or *else.*

"Andt you will not be goingk near to the fence." Mrs. Pulnik grabs Camellia's arm and Lark's before we can make it through the door. She leans over us with her round cheeks red and sweat shiny. "A boy tunneledt underneat yesterday. Mrs. Murphy has given him *the closet.* To be given *the closet* is very, very bat. In the closet, it is *dark.* Do you understandt?"

"Yes'm," I croak out, picking up Gabby and reaching for Lark to get her away. She's standing still as a stump, not a thing moving but the big old tears dripping down her cheeks. "I'll make sure they mind the rules till we can go see our mama and daddy."

Mrs. Pulnik's big lips push together and curl. "Goot," she says. "This is a wise choice for you. *All* of you."

"Yes'm."

We get out the door quick as we can. The sun feels like heaven, and the sky stretches out big between the poplars and maples, and the bare dirt at the bottom of the steps is cool and soft. Safe. I close my eyes and listen to the leaves talking and the birds singing their morning songs. I pick out their voices, one by one, Carolina wren, redbird, house finch. The same birds that were there yesterday morning when I woke up on our little shantyboat.

The little girls grab on to my dress, and Gabby hitches himself back against my arms, trying to get down, and Camellia complains that we're just standing there. I open my eyes, and she's looking at the tall black iron fence that circles the yard. Honeysuckle and prickly holly and azaleas grow thick over most of it, higher than our heads. There's only one gate that I can see, and it goes to the playground behind the run-down church house next door. That's got more of the same fence around it too.

Camellia's way too big to squeeze under, but she looks like she's searching for the best spot to try it.

"Let's go over on the swings at least," she whines. "We can watch the road from there . . . for when Briny comes to get us."

We move across the yard, Gabion in my arms and my sisters in a tight knot behind me, even Camellia, who usually picks a fight at every school we go to quicker than you can say *spit.* The kids eyeball us because we're new. We pretend we don't notice it.

We're usually good at this game — don't act too friendly; look out for each other; let them know that if they mess with one of you, they'd better be able to whip the bunch of you. But this time it's different. We don't know the rules in this place. There's no teacher around watching. There's not a grown-up in sight. Nobody but kids, all stopping their games of jump rope and Red Rover to stare at us.

I don't see the little girl who came with us from the river yesterday. Her baby brother — the one Miss Tann named Stevie — sits in the dirt with a tin truck that's missing all its paint and one wheel.

"Where's your sister?" I squat down beside him, Gabion's weight putting me off balance so that I have to brace a hand on the ground to keep from falling over.

Stevie's shoulders lift and fall, and his big brown eyes turn watery.

"You can come with us," I tell him.

Camellia grumbles, "He ain't our problem."

I tell her to hush.

Stevie rolls a pouty lip and nods and lifts both arms. There's a big bite mark on one of them, and I wonder who did it. I scoop him up and push myself back to my feet. He's older than Gabion, but he weighs about the same. He's a skinny little thing.

Two girls playing with dented tin dishes look our way. They've raked the old dead leaves and made a pretending spot in the shade of the well house, like Camellia and I do in the woods sometimes. "You wanna play?" one of them asks.

"Bugger off," Camellia snaps. "We ain't got time. We're goin' over to the churchyard to watch for our daddy."

"You hadn't oughta." The girls turn back to their game, and we move on along.

At the gate to the churchyard, a big boy pops out from behind the hollies. Now I see they've got a tunneled-out spot in the bushes. There's four or five of them back there with a deck of cards. One's carving a spear with his pocketknife. He gives me a squinty look and tests the sharp point with his finger.

The big redheaded boy stands in the gate, his arms crossed over his chest. "You come down here," he says, like he's in charge of me. "They can go over and play." It's clear enough what he means. He wants me to clamber up under the bushes with the four of them. Otherwise my brother and my sisters can't go in the churchyard.

My face turns hot. I feel the blood pouring in. *What's he got in mind?*

Camellia says what's just gone through my head. "We ain't goin' no place with you." She braces her feet apart and pokes her chin out about even with his chest. "You ain't the boss of us."

"I ain't talkin' to you, mudpuppy. You're hound-dog ugly. Anybody ever tell you that? I'm talkin' to your pretty sister here."

Camellia's eyes bug out. She's on her way to getting full-out mad. "Ain't ugly as you, carrothead. Your mama cry when you was born? Bet she did!"

I hand Gabby over to Fern. Little Stevie doesn't want to turn loose. His arms stay locked tight around my neck. If we're gonna have a fight, I don't need a baby hanging on me. The redheaded boy is probably more than Camellia and me can handle, and if his chums come out of there, we're in real trouble. There's still no workers anyplace in sight, and one of those ugly mugs has a knife.

The redhead's nostrils flare, and he uncrosses his arms. Here it comes. Camellia's put in a bid we can't pay this time. The boy stands at least a half foot taller than me, and I'm tall.

My mind runs like a squirrel on a spring day, jumping from branch to branch. *Think. Think of something.*

Always use your brains, Rill, Briny says in my mind, *and you'll find your way out of a scrape quicker'n anything.*

"I got peppermints," I blabber, and reach into the pocket of my borrowed dress. "You can have the whole bunch, but you gotta let us pass."

The boy pulls his chin back and squints at me. "Where'd you get peppermints?"

"I ain't a liar." I can barely choke out the four words because Stevie's hanging on to me so tight. "You gonna let us pass or not?"

"You gimme the peppermints." The other rowdies are already shinnying out of their hidey-hole so they can grab their share.

"Those are ours!" Camellia argues.

"Be quiet." I pull out the mints. They're a little dirty from being stuck to my hand this morning, but I don't reckon these boys care.

The redhead opens his fingers, and I dump the candy in. He lifts it up so close to his face, his eyes go crossed, and he looks even dumber than before. A slow, mean smile spreads his lips. He's got a chipped tooth in front. "You get these from ol' Riggs?"

I don't want to bring trouble on the man from the basement. He's the only one who's been nice to us so far. "Ain't your business."

"He's our *friend.*" Camellia can't keep her

mouth shut. Maybe she thinks it'll scare the boys if they know the big man likes us.

But the redheaded boy just grins. He leans close to my ear, near enough that I can smell his stinky breath and feel his heat on my skin. He whispers, "Don't let Riggs get you off by yourself. He ain't the kind of friend you want."

CHAPTER 11

Avery

Spanish moss drips from the trees, as delicately spun as the lace on a bridal veil. A blue heron launches itself from the salt marsh, disturbed by the passage of my car. It flies clumsily at first, as if it needs a moment to become at home in the air, to find its wings. It beats hard, then finally floats into the distance, in no hurry to be earthbound again.

I know the feeling. For two weeks, I've been trying to sneak away and make the drive to Edisto Island. Between the meetings and press ops that were already scheduled and an unexpected complication with Dad's health, it's been impossible.

I've spent the last six days in doctors' offices, holding my mother's hand as we tried to discern why, when the cancer and intestinal bleeding were supposed to have been cured by the surgery, Dad was once again anemic and so weak he could barely stay on his feet. After endless tests, we think the cause has been found. The solution was simple — a laparoscopic surgery to fuse broken blood vessels in his digestive system, a problem unrelated to the cancer. Outpatient. Quick and easy.

Except nothing is simple when you're trying to hide from the whole world, and Dad insists on not telling anyone he has experienced a minor setback in his health. Leslie is completely onboard with that. She's reporting that my father had a nasty case of food poisoning; he'll be back to his regularly scheduled activities in a few days.

My eldest sister, Missy, stepped in to handle appearances at a couple of charity events that couldn't be canceled. "You look exhausted, Aves," she said. "Why don't you get away for a little while, since Leslie has pretty much cleared the schedule anyway? Go see Elliot. Allison and I can keep an eye on things at Drayden Hill."

"Thanks . . . but . . . Well, you're sure?"

"*Go.* Talk wedding plans. Maybe you can convince him to knuckle under to the mom pressure."

I didn't tell her that, other than a few rushed conversations, Elliot and I haven't even discussed wedding ideas. We have too much else going on. "Elliot had to fly to Milan to meet with a client, but I think I'll go down to the old place on Edisto. Has anyone been there lately?"

"Scott and I took the kids for a few days . . . oh . . . I guess it was last spring. The housekeeping service keeps the place in such great shape. It should be all ready for you. Go have a little vacay."

I was packing a suitcase almost before she could tell me to say hello to the beach for her. On the way out of town, I paid a long-overdue visit to May Crandall's nursing home. An attendant there told me May had been hospitalized with a respiratory infection. The attendant didn't know how serious it was or when to expect May back.

Which means that the mysterious packet of papers on Edisto is my one possible lead, at least for now. Trent Turner won't take my phone calls. Period. My only option is to confront him in person. The envelope he's holding has begun to haunt my every waking moment. I'm getting a little obsessed, making up stories in which he plays different parts in each scene. Sometimes he's a blackmailer who has discovered a horrible truth about my family and sold the information to my father's opponents; that's why he won't answer my calls. Other times, he's the man in May Crandall's photograph. The pregnant woman he's holding close is my grandmother, and she had some sort of hidden life before she married my grandfather. A teenage love affair. A scandal that's been covered up for generations.

She gave the baby away, and it's been living somewhere all this time. Now our dispossessed heir wants a fair share of the family money, *or else.*

All my scenarios seem crazy, but they're not completely unfounded. I've learned things from reading between the lines in my grandmother's appointment books. My dragonfly bracelet has some sort of deeper history on Edisto. *A lovely gift for a lovely day on Edisto,* the entry read. *Just us.*

It's the *just us* part that niggles at me. Only a page before, she'd noted receiving a letter from my grandfather, who had taken the children fishing in the mountains for the week.

Just us . . .

Who? Who was buying gifts for her on Edisto in 1966?

My grandmother often came here alone over the years, but many times she wasn't alone after she arrived on the island. That much was obvious from her daybooks.

Could she have been having an affair?

My stomach roils as the Dawhoo Bridge rises ahead. That can't be the case. Despite the pressure of a life lived in public, my family has always been known for rock-solid marriages. My grandmother loved my grandfather deeply. Aside from that, Grandma Judy is one of the most upright people I know. She's a pillar of the community and a fixture at the Methodist church. She would never, *ever* keep a secret from the family.

Unless that secret is something that could hurt us.

And that's exactly what scares me.

It's also why I can't have an envelope floating around heaven knows where with my grandmother's name on it and some sort of clandestine information inside.

"Ready or not, here I come," I whisper into the salt air. "What was it that you wanted with my grandmother, Trent Turner?"

While sitting in cars and doctors' waiting rooms these past few weeks, I've tried researching Trent Turner, Sr., and Trent Turner, Jr., the grandfather and father of the Trent I talked to on the phone, who is Trent Turner III. I've looked for political connections, criminal records, or whatever might explain ties to my grandmother. I've used all my favorite prosecutor tricks. Unfortunately, there is nothing obvious. According to an obit from seven months ago in the Charleston paper, Trent Turner, Sr., was a lifelong resident of Charleston and Edisto Island and the owner of Turner Real Estate. Just an ordinary fellow. Plain and simple. His son, Trent Turner, Jr., is married and lives in Texas, where he owns a real estate agency.

Trent Turner III doesn't seem to be anyone out of the ordinary either. He played basketball at Clemson and was pretty good at it. He was in the commercial real estate business until recently, mostly in New York. A local press release from a few months ago indicates he left the city behind to take over his grandfather's business on Edisto.

Why, I can't help but wonder, *does a man who's been brokering high-rises suddenly move to an out-of-the-way place like Edisto and start dealing in beach cottages and vacation rentals?*

I'll find out soon enough. I've looked up his work address. One way or another, I plan to leave the Turner Real Estate office with my grandmother's envelope and all of its contents, whatever they may be.

Despite the nervousness that stirs inside me, Edisto begins to work its magic as I descend the island side of the bridge and continue along the highway, passing small, sea-weathered homes and a few businesses tucked among pines and live oaks. Overhead, the sky is a perfect shade of blue.

This place is still so much like I remember it. It has a peaceful, gracious, untraveled feel. There's a reason the locals have nicknamed the island Edi-*slow.* The ancient oaks bow low over the road, as if seeking to shield it from the outside world. Moss-laden trees paint deep shade over the small SUV I've spirited away from the barn at Drayden Hill for the trip. The back roads on Edisto can be a little rugged, and beyond that, showing up in a BMW didn't seem like a good idea considering that I'm wondering if the contents of the envelope have anything to do with blackmail.

The Turner Real Estate building is easy to find. It's quaint but not necessarily impressive — the sort of place that's happy to be just what it is, a seawater-blue vintage cottage on Jungle Road, just a couple blocks from water. Now that I'm here, it does look vaguely familiar, but as a kid, of course, I never had any reason to go inside.

As I park and cross the sand-sprinkled lot, I'm momentarily jealous of the man I've come here to find. I could work in a place like this. I could live here even. Just another day in paradise, every single morning. From not far away, laughter and beach sounds drift over. Colorful kites fly above the treetops, kept in the air by a steady sea breeze.

Two little girls run down the street, trailing long red ribbons on sticks. Three women pedal by on bicycles, laughing. Once again, I'm envious, and then I think, *Why don't I come here more often? Why don't I ever call my sisters or my mother and say, "Hey, let's just take off and go sit in the sun awhile. We could use some girl time, right?"*

Why haven't Elliot and I ever come here?

The answer tastes bitter, so I don't chew on it very long. Our schedules are always filled with other things. That's why.

Who chooses the schedules we keep? We do, I guess.

Although, so often it seems as if there isn't any choice. If we aren't constantly slapping new paint on all the ramparts, the wind and the weather will sneak in and erode the accomplishments of a dozen previous generations of the family. The good life demands a lot of maintenance.

Walking up the porch steps to Turner Real Estate, I grab a fortifying breath. The sign says COME ON IN. WE'RE OPEN. . . . So I do. A jingling bell announces my entry, but there's no one behind the counter.

The front room is a lobby area with colorful vinyl chairs lining its edges. A watercooler waits with paper cups. Racks display endless brochures. A popcorn machine reminds me that I've missed lunch. Beautiful photographs of the island line the walls. The base of the counter across the room is decorated with children's artwork and photos of happy families posing in front of their new beach homes. The display randomly mixes past and present. Some of the black-and-whites appear to be from all the way back in the fifties. I stand and I scan them, looking for my grandmother. There's no sign of her.

"Hello?" I venture, since nobody seems to be materializing from the rooms down the hall. "Hello?"

Maybe they've stepped out for a minute? The place is dead quiet.

My stomach growls, crying out for popcorn.

I'm about to raid the machine when the back door opens. I slap the popcorn bag down and turn around.

"Hey! I didn't know anyone was in here." I recognize Trent Turner III from the photo online, but that picture was taken from a distance, a full-body shot in front of the building. He was wearing a ball cap and had a beard. It didn't do him justice. Now he's clean-shaven. Dressed in khakis, well-worn loafers with no socks, and a nicely fitted polo shirt, he looks like he belongs under an umbrella table somewhere . . . or in an ad for casual living. He's sandy blond and blue-eyed, the hair just shaggy enough to backhandedly say, *I live on beach time.*

He moves up the hall, juggling a couple to-go bags and a drink. I catch myself ogling the haul. I think I smell shrimp and chips. My stomach offers another audible protest.

"Sorry, I . . . there was no one here." I thumb over my shoulder toward the door.

"Ran out for some lunch." Placing the food on the counter, he looks around for a napkin, then settles for swiping up stray cocktail sauce with a piece of printer paper. Our handshake is sticky but friendly. "Trent Turner," he says with casual ease. "What can I do for you?" His smile makes me *want* to like him. It's the kind of smile that assumes people *do* like him. He seems . . . honest, I guess.

"I called you a couple weeks ago." No sense starting right off with names.

"Rental or buy-and-sell?"

"What?"

"A place. Were we talking about a rental or a property listing?" He's searching his memory banks, clearly. But there's also more than casual interest coming my way. I feel a spark of . . . something.

I catch myself smiling back.

Guilt niggles at me instantly. Should an engaged woman — even a lonely one — be reacting this way? Maybe it's just because Elliot and I have barely talked in almost two weeks. He's been in Milan. The time difference is difficult. He's focused on the job. I'm focused on family issues.

"Neither one." I guess there's no sense postponing this any longer. The fact that this guy is good-looking and likeable doesn't change reality. "I called you about something I found at my grandmother's house." My fledgling friendship with Trent Turner is, no doubt, doomed to be short-lived. "I'm Avery Stafford. You said you had an envelope addressed to my grandmother, Judy Stafford? I'm here to pick it up."

His demeanor changes instantly. Muscular forearms cross over a ripped chest, and the counter quickly becomes a negotiation table. A hostile one.

He looks displeased. Very. "I'm sorry you wasted the trip. I told you, I can't give those documents to anyone but the people they're addressed to. Not even family members."

"I have her power of attorney." I'm already pulling it from my oversized purse. Being the lawyer in the family, and with my mother and father preoccupied by the health issue, I am the one designated on Grandma Judy's documents. I unfold them and turn the pages toward him as he's lifting his hand to protest. "She's in no shape to handle her own affairs. I'm authorized to —"

He rejects the offering without even looking at the papers. "It's not a legal matter."

"It is if it's *her* mail."

"It's not mail. It's more like . . . cleaning up some loose ends from my grandfather's files." His eyes duck away, take in the swaying palms outside the window, evading my probing.

"It's about the cottage here on Edisto then?" This *is* a real estate office, after all, but why maintain such secrecy over real estate documents?

"No."

His answer is disappointingly brief. Usually, when you throw a wrong assumption at a witness, the witness responds by inadvertently giving you at least a piece of the right one.

It's obvious that Trent Turner has been

through many a negotiation before. In fact, I sense that he's been through *this* very negotiation before. He did say *those documents* and *people,* as in *multiple.* Are other families being held hostage as well?

"I'm *not* leaving until I find out the truth."

"There's popcorn." His attempt at humor only serves to stoke the fire in my belly.

"This isn't a joke."

"I realize that." For the first time, he seems slightly sympathetic to my plight. His arms uncross. A hand runs roughly through his hair. Thick brown lashes close over his eyes. Stress lines form around the edges, hinting at a life that was once considerably more high-pressure than this one. "Look, I promised my grandfather . . . on his deathbed. And trust me — it's better this way."

I don't trust him. That's the point. "I'll go after them legally if I have to."

"My grandfather's files?" A sardonic laugh indicates that he doesn't take to threats very well. "Good luck with that. They were his property. They're my property now. You'll have to be satisfied with that."

"Not if this could damage my family."

The look on his face tells me I've struck close to the truth. I feel sick. My family *does* have a deep, dark secret. What is it?

Trent lets out a long sigh. "It's just . . .

This really is for the best. That's all I can tell you." The phone rings, and he answers it, seeming to hope the interruption will drive me away. The caller has a million questions about Edisto beach rentals and activities on the island. Trent takes the time to talk about everything from fishing for black drum to finding mastodon fossils and arrowheads on the beach. He gives the caller a lovely history lesson about wealthy families who resided on Edisto before the War Between the States. He talks about fiddler crabs and pluff mud and harvesting oysters.

He pops fried shrimp into his mouth, savors them while he listens. Turning his back to me, he leans against the counter.

I return to my original seat by the door, perch on the edge, and stare at his back while he offers an endless litany about Botany Bay. He seems to describe the four-thousand-acre preserve inch by inch. I tap my foot and drum my fingers. He pretends not to notice, but I catch him peeking at me from the corner of his eye.

I pull out my phone and thumb through email. If worse comes to worst, I'll scroll through Instagram or dawdle around with the wedding ideas my mom and Bitsy want me to look at on Pinterest.

Trent bends over a desktop computer,

looks up information, talks about rentals and dates.

The customer finally settles on a time and place for the ideal vacation. Trent confesses that he's not the one who handles logging the rental bookings. His secretary is home with a sick baby, but he'll email her, and she'll take care of the confirmations.

Finally, after what seems like at least thirty minutes of chatterboxing, he straightens to his full height and looks in my direction. A staredown ensues. This man is, quite possibly, as stubborn as I am. Unfortunately, he can probably hold out longer. He has food.

Hanging up the phone, he taps a knuckle to his lips, shakes his head, and sighs. "It won't matter how long you're here. It's not going to change anything." His frustration is starting to show. I'm getting somewhere. I've got him rattled now.

I proceed calmly to the popcorn machine and the watercooler and help myself.

Thusly equipped for the sit-in, I wander back to my seat.

He yanks an office chair into position behind the computer, sits down, and disappears behind a four-drawer file cabinet.

At the first taste of popcorn, my stomach lets out an indelicately loud roar.

The shrimp basket suddenly appears on the edge of the counter. Manly fingers shove it my way, but he doesn't say a word. The kindness makes me feel guilty, even more so as, with a resolute thump, he adds an unopened soda. I'm undoubtedly ruining his perfectly good day.

I help myself to a little handful and return to my spot. Guilt and fried shrimp go quite nicely together, it turns out.

Computer keys click. Another sigh comes from behind the file cabinet. More time passes. The desk chair squeals in protest, as if he's rocking back in it. "Don't you Staffords have *people* to do this kind of thing for you?"

"Sometimes. But not in this case."

"I'm sure you're used to getting what you want."

His insinuation burns. I've been fighting it all my life — the idea that my only qualifications are a cute blond head and the Stafford name. Now, with the speculation heating up about my political future, I'm incredibly sick of hearing it. The family name didn't get me through Columbia Law School with honors.

"I work for what I get, thank you."

"Ffff!"

"I don't ask for any special favors, and I

don't expect any."

"So I can call the police and have you removed from my waiting room, just like I would with anyone else who stakes out the place and won't leave when they're asked?"

Shrimp and popcorn merge to form a lump just below my breastbone. He wouldn't . . . would he? I can just imagine the newspaper coverage. Leslie would string me up singlehandedly. "Does that happen often?"

"Not unless someone's tipped back a few too many brewskies on the beach. And Edisto's not really that kind of place. We don't get much excitement here."

"Yes, I know. And I have a feeling that's one reason you won't want the police involved in this."

"One reason?"

"I doubt you're unaware that there are people who wouldn't have hesitated to threaten my family with information that could be damaging . . . if there were any such information. And that sort of behavior is illegal."

Trent is out of his chair in a heartbeat, and I'm out of mine. We face each other like generals across a war room table. "You're about a half inch from meeting the Edisto Beach police."

"What did your grandfather want with my grandmother?"

"It wasn't blackmail, if that's what you're getting at. My grandfather was an honest man."

"Why did he leave an envelope for her?"

"They had business in common."

"*What* business? Why didn't she tell anyone about it?"

"Maybe she thought that was for the best."

"Was she coming here to . . . meet someone? Did he find out about it?"

He draws back, his lip curling. "No!"

"Then *tell* me!" I'm in courtroom mode now, focused on one thing — getting to the truth. "Give me the envelope!"

He slams a hand on the counter, rattles everything there, then whips around the end. In a few strides, we're face-to-face. I stand as tall as I can, and still he towers over me. I refuse to be intimidated. We're settling this thing. Right here. Right now.

The bell on the door rings, and it barely registers at first. I'm focused on white-rimmed blue eyes and clenched teeth.

"Whew! It's a hot one outside. Got any popcorn today?" When I glance over my shoulder, a man in an official-looking uniform — a Park Service employee or perhaps a game warden — is standing in the doorway, looking back and forth between Trent Turner and me. "Oh . . . didn't know you had company."

"Come on in and take a load off, Ed." Trent beckons the incomer with friendly enthusiasm, which quickly wanes when he turns my way again and adds, "Avery here was just leaving."

CHAPTER 12

Rill

It's two weeks before I learn that the kids here are wards of the Tennessee Children's Home Society. I don't know what *wards* means when I first hear Mrs. Murphy say it on the telephone. I can't ask either, since I'm not supposed to be listening in. I've figured out that if I shinny up under the azalea bushes alongside of the house, I can get close enough to hear through the screens on her office windows.

"Certainly, all of the children are wards of the Tennessee Children's Home Society, Dortha. I do understand your daughter-in-law's predicament. When unhappy, many men turn to liquoring and . . . dalliances. It is so difficult for a wife. Adding a child to the home at long last might well brighten up the atmosphere and solve the entire problem. Fatherhood has a way of changing a man. I'm certain it won't be a problem, as you'll have no trouble paying the fees. Yes . . . yes . . . quickly, of course. A surprise for their anniversary. How sweet. If I could just *give* you one of these, Dortha, I certainly would. I have some darling little cherubs just now. But Miss Tann controls all of the decisions. I'm only paid to board the children and . . ."

I figure it out from the conversation quick enough — that new word. *Wards* means that these kids' parents didn't come back for them. The kids here say that if your parents don't come get you, Miss Tann gives you to somebody else, and they take you home. Sometimes those people keep you, and sometimes they don't. I'm scared to ask too many questions because we're not supposed to talk about it, but I've got a feeling that's why Stevie's big sister hasn't turned up again since the day we got here. Miss Tann gave her to somebody. Sherry was a ward.

We're lucky we're not. We belong to Briny, and he'll fetch us, soon as Queenie gets well. It's taking longer than I thought, and that's why I've started listening under Mrs. Murphy's window. I've been hoping to hear something about Briny. When I ask the workers, they just tell me to behave myself, or else we'll have to stay here longer. I can't think of anything much worse than that, so I do my best to see that all of us behave.

I'm taking a chance, coming up under the window like this, and I know it. We're not allowed to get anywhere near Mrs. Murphy's flower beds. If she knew I was listening to her phone calls and talks on the front porch when folks come by . . . I've got a few ideas about what might happen to me.

She comes to the screen, and through the azalea leaves I see cigarette smoke puff out. It hangs in the wet air like the genie floating over Aladdin's lamp, and my nose tickles with a sneeze. I slap my hand over my face, and the branches move. A hammer pounds against my ribs from the inside.

"Mrs. Pulnik!" she yells. "Mrs. Pulnik!"

My skin goes cold. *Don't run. Don't run,* I tell myself.

Fast steps come up the hallway inside.

"What is it, Mrs. Murphy?"

"Instruct Riggs to put out poison this evening under the azaleas. Those infernal rabbits have gotten into my flower beds again."

"I will be puttingk him to the task immediately."

"And have him tidy up the front yard and pull the weeds. Tell him to make use of the older boys in any way he sees fit. Miss Tann will be coming tomorrow. I'll have the place presentable, or else."

"Yes, Mrs. Murphy."

"What's become of the ones in the sickroom? The toddler boy with the deep violet eyes in particular. Miss Tann wants to see him. She has promised him for an order in New York."

"He is lethargic, I am afraidt to say. As well, he is thin. He takes little bit of corn mush. I do not belief he will travel well."

"Miss Tann will *not* be pleased. *I* am not pleased. You'd think that, having been raised in back alleys and ditches, the little guttersnipes would be hardier."

"That is true, yes. The girl in the sickroom is decliningk as well. For two days, she refuses to eat. The doctor shouldt be summonedt, yes?"

"No, of course not. Why in heaven's name would I have the doctor called over a bit of the runs? Children *always* have the runs. Give her some gingerroot. That should do it."

"As you wish."

"How is little Stevie coming along? He *is* roughly the size of the boy in the sickroom. Older, but that can be changed. What color are his eyes?"

"Brown. But he has become stubborn in

wettingk the bed as well. Andt he will not speak even a wordt. I do not belief a client wouldt be content with him."

"That will *not* do. Secure him to the bed and leave him in it for the day if he wets again. A blister or two will teach the lesson. In any case, brown eyes won't satisfy for this order. Blue, green, or violet. Those have specifically been requested. Not brown."

"Robby?"

My throat catches. Robby is the name they call my little brother. There's not another Robby in the house.

"I am afraid not. The five are being saved for a special viewing event."

I swallow the burning in my throat, push it all the way down to my stomach. *A special viewing event.* I think I know what that means. I've seen parents come here a few times. They wait on the porch, and the workers bring their kids to them, clean and dressed and with their hair all combed. The parents carry presents and give hugs and cry when they have to go. That must be what a viewing event is.

Briny's coming to see us soon.

But that worries me too. Last week, a man showed up to visit his little boy, and Mrs. Murphy told him the boy wasn't here. *He's been placed for adoption. I'm very sorry.* That was what she said.

He's gotta be here, the man argued. *Lonnie Kemp. He's mine. I didn't sign him over for adopting. The children's home is just boardin' him till I git back on my feet.*

Mrs. Murphy didn't seem worried, even when the man broke down and cried. *Nonetheless, he is gone. The family court deemed it best. He has been taken in by parents who can provide very well for him.*

But he's my *son.*

You mustn't be selfish, Mr. Kemp. What's done is done. Think of the child. He will be given what you could never provide for him.

He's my son. . . .

The man fell down on his knees and sobbed right there on the porch.

Mrs. Murphy just went back inside and shut the door. After a while, Mr. Riggs hauled the man up and walked him to the street and put him in his truck. He sat there all day watching toward the yard, looking for his boy.

I'm worried that Briny might come here and have the same problem. Only, Briny won't stand there and cry. He'll bust his way in, and something terrible will happen. Mr. Riggs is a big man. Miss Tann knows the police.

"Take the utmost care of the little one in

the sickroom," Mrs. Murphy says now. "Give him a nice hot bath and some ice cream. Maybe a gingersnap. Pep him up a bit. I'll ask Miss Tann if she might delay the order a day or two. I want him well enough to travel. Do you understand?"

"Yes, Mrs. Murphy." Mrs. Pulnik's words hiss through clenched teeth, which tells me I sure don't want to get caught here under the azalea bushes today. When she's in *that* mood, you better run fast and hide good, because she's looking for somebody to take it out on.

The last thing I hear is Mrs. Murphy crossing the room and yelling into the hall, "And don't forget about poisoning those rabbits!"

I grab up a broken branch and quietly start stirring the leaves over my knee prints, so Mr. Riggs won't be able to see that I've been here. I wouldn't want him to tell Mrs. Pulnik.

But that's not what scares me most. What scares me most is Mr. Riggs knowing someone's been going up under here at all. To make it to the azalea bushes, you've got to slip past the cellar doors. Riggs keeps them open, and if he can, he'll get kids in there with him one way or another. Nobody talks about what goes on down there, even the big boys. *If you talk about it,* they say, *Riggs'll get you and snap your neck and say you fell out of a tree or tripped on the porch steps. Then they'll cart your body off to the swamps and feed it to the gators, and nobody'll ever hear about you again.*

James, the big redheaded boy, has been here long enough, he's seen it happen. We give him peppermints, and he tells us what we need to know to get by here at Mrs. Murphy's place. We're not friends, but candies will buy you a lot around here. Every morning when we wake up, there's a little wad of peppermints shoved under the door of our room. At night, I hear Mr. Riggs come around. He tries the knob, but it's locked, and the workers always take the keys when they put us in bed. I'm glad. Sometimes, after Mr. Riggs comes by our room, I hear him walking up the stairs to the house. I don't know where he goes, but I'm glad we're down in the cellar. It's cold, and the army cots are scratchy and smelly, and we have to use a slop pot at night, but at least nobody can get at us when we're in there.

I hope Briny comes before enough beds empty out to move us upstairs.

Riggs is just headed in the cellar door when I get to the end of the azalea hedge. I almost don't see him quick enough to let the branches fall back and hide me.

He looks right at me before he walks down the steps, but he can't see me. I'm like the Invisible Man again. The Invisible Girl. That's who I am.

I wait until I'm sure he's gone, and then I creep out of my spot, quiet as a little bobcat. The thing about bobcats is, they can be two foot from you and you'll never know it. One big breath, and I run past the cellar door and around the fig tree. After you're past it, you're safe. Riggs knows the workers look out the kitchen windows a lot. He won't do things where anybody else can see.

Camellia's waiting for me on the hill behind the church house playground. Lark and Fern are riding a teeter-totter with Gabion in the middle. Stevie's sitting in the dirt beside Camellia. He climbs over into my lap soon as I sit down.

"Good," Camellia says. "Get him offa me. He stinks like pee."

"He can't help it." Stevie wraps his arms around my neck and lays against my chest. He's sticky, and he does smell bad. I rub a hand over his head, and he whimpers and pulls away. There's a goose egg under his hair. The helpers here like to thump kids on the head where it won't show.

"Yes he *can* help it. He could talk too, if

he wanted to. He's just gettin' hisself in trouble with the workers. I told him he better stop it or else." Camellia's a fine one to talk. If any of us does get *the closet* while we're here, it'll be her. I still don't know for sure what happens in *the closet,* but it must be bad. Just a couple days ago, Mrs. Murphy stood over the breakfast table and said, *When the food thief is caught, it'll be the closet, and not just for one day.*

Nothing's disappeared from the kitchen since.

"Stevie's just scared. He misses . . ." I stop without saying it. It'll only make him upset if I bring up his sister. Sometimes I forget that, even though he won't talk anymore, he can still understand everything we say.

"What'd you hear at the window?" Camellia hates it that I won't let anybody else go under the azaleas. She always looks me over and sniffs at me to see if I found any peppermints while I was there. She thinks the big boys are lying about Mr. Riggs. If I don't watch her, she'll try to sidle off over there while we're out to play. I can't turn my back on her for a minute, unless I'm leaving her with the babies to watch.

"She didn't say anything about Briny." I'm still trying to make sense of what I heard under Mrs. Murphy's window. I'm not sure how much of it I should tell Camellia.

"He ain't comin'. He's got hisself in jail or somethin', and he can't get out. Queenie's dead."

I scramble to my feet, taking Stevie with me. "No she ain't! Don't you say that, Mellia! Don't you *ever* say that!"

On the playground, the teeter-totters stop, and feet scrape the ground to hold swings still. Kids look our way. They're used to watching the big boys get in fights and roll around and kick and punch. It don't usually happen with girls.

"It's true!" Camellia's on her feet quick as a whip, her chin poking out, her long, skinny arms cocked on her hips. Wads of freckles seem to squint her eyes down to practically nothing, and her nose scrunches up. She looks like a spotted pig.

"It ain't!"

"Is so!"

Stevie whines and squirms to get away. I figure I'd better let him. He runs off to the teeter-totter, where Lark grabs him up in her arms.

Camellia rears back a fist. It won't be the first time we've gotten in a knockdown, spit-flying, hair-pulling match.

"Hey! Hey, you cut that out!" Before I even see it coming, James is out of the big boys' hidey-hole, and he's headed our way.

Camellia hesitates just long enough for him to get to her. His big hand snakes out and grabs her dress, and he slings her into the dirt, hard.

"Stay down," he growls, and points a finger.

She doesn't, of course. She pops to her feet madder than a swatted hornet. He shoves her down again.

"Hey!" I yell. "Stop it!" She's my sister, even if she was about to punch my lights out.

James looks my way and grins, the chipped tooth showing the pink tip of his tongue. "You want me to?"

Camellia takes a swing at him, and he grabs her arm, holding her far enough away that she can't kick him. She's like a daddy longlegs spider with one foot stuck in a door. He squeezes so hard her skin goes purple. Her eyes fill up and spill over, but she just keeps on fighting.

"Stop!" I yell. "Let her alone!"

"You want me to, then you be my girlfriend, pretty girl," he says. And, "Elsewise, she's fair game."

Camellia roars and squeals and goes wild.

"Let her be!" I take a swing, and James grabs my wrist, and now he's got us both.

My bones crush together. The babies run over from the playground, even Stevie, and start pounding James's legs. He swings Camellia around and uses her to knock down Fern and Gabion. Fern's nose spouts blood, and she screams, grabbing her face.

"All right! All right!" I say. What else can I do? I look around for grown-ups, and like always, there aren't any.

"All right, what, pretty girl?" James asks.

"All right, I'll be your girlfriend. But I ain't gonna kiss you."

That seems good enough for him. He dumps Camellia in the dirt and tells her she better stay there. He makes me follow him up the hill and drags me around an old outhouse that's nailed shut so nobody can get in it and get snakebit. For the second time that day, a hammer pounds inside me. "I ain't kissin' you," I tell him again.

"Shut up," he says.

Behind the outhouse, he pushes me to the dirt and plops down next to me, still squeezing my arm. My breath comes fast and hangs in my throat. I taste my stomach.

What's he plan to do to me? Growing up on a boat and with four babies born after I came along, I know a little bit about what men and women do together. I don't want somebody to do that to me. Ever. I don't like boys, and I never will. James's breath smells like rotten potatoes, and the only boy I've ever thought I might let kiss me was Silas, and that was only for a minute or two.

The chants of his gang wind their way around the building. "James's got a girlfriend. James's got a girlfriend. James and May sittin' in a tree, k-i-s-s-i-n-g . . ."

But James doesn't try to kiss me. He just sits there with red splotches working up his neck and over his cheeks. "You're pretty." His voice squeaks like a baby pig's. It's funny, but I don't laugh. I'm too scared.

"No I ain't."

"You're real pretty." He lets go of my wrist and tries to hold my hand. I pull it away and wrap my arms around my knees, holding myself in a tight ball.

"I don't like boys," I tell him.

"I'm gonna marry you someday."

"I don't wanna marry anybody. I'm gonna build a boat and go down the river. Take care of *myself.*"

"I might get on your boat too."

"No you ain't."

We sit there a while. The boys down the hill chant, "James's got a girlfriend. . . . K-i-s-s-i-n-g . . ."

He lolls his elbows over his knees, looking

at me. "That where you come from? The river?"

"Yep, it is."

We talk about boats. James is from a dirt farm in Shelby County. Miss Tann picked him and his brother up off the side of the road when they were walking to school one day. He was in the fourth grade then. He's been here ever since and not seen a day of school this whole time. His brother is long gone. Adopted.

James lifts his chin. "I don't want me some new parents," he says. "I figure I'll be too big pretty soon, and I'll get outa here. I'm gonna need me a wife. We can go live on the river, if you want."

"My daddy's comin' back to get us." I feel bad saying it. I feel sorry for James. He seems lonesome more than anything. Lonesome and sad. "He'll be here pretty soon."

James just shrugs. "I'll bring you some tea cakes tomorrow. But you gotta still be my girlfriend."

I don't answer. My mouth waters thinking about tea cakes. I guess now I know who's been sneaking around in the kitchen at night. "You hadn't oughta. You might get the closet."

"I ain't scared." He puts his hand over mine.

I let it stay there.

Maybe I don't mind it too much.

Pretty soon, I figure out it's not so bad being James's girlfriend after all. He ain't hard to talk to, and he only wants to hold my hand. Nobody bothers me the rest of the day. Nobody's mean to Camellia or Lark or the babies. James and I walk around the yard and hold hands, and he tells me more things I need to know about Mrs. Murphy's house. He promises me tea cakes again. He describes just how he'll sneak down and get them tonight.

I tell him I don't like tea cakes.

In the bath line, the big boys don't look at me. They know they better not.

But the next day, James isn't at breakfast. Mrs. Pulnik stands over the table, tapping a wood spoon in her big, meaty hand. She says they sent James off to a place where the boys have to earn their keep instead of getting it by the kindness of the Tennessee Children's Home Society.

"A boy who is oldt enough to pursue after the girls is oldt enough for *work* and too oldt to be wanted by a goot family. Mrs. Murphy will be havingk *none* of this behavior between boys and girls here. Each of you *knows* of our rules." She slaps the spoon hard against the table, her breath coming in heavy snorts that make her wide, flat nose flare out. We jerk upright like puppets with strings bolted to our heads. She leans toward the boys' side of the table. They duck and stare at their empty bowls. "Andt for the girls" — the spoon and the jiggly arm come our way now — "so much *shame* to you for causing trouble to the boys. Mind yourselfs, keep down your skirts, and behave as little women shouldt." The last word comes with a hard look at me. "Or I do not want to think of *what* may happen to *you.*"

Blood rushes hot up my neck and burns in my cheeks. I feel bad for getting James sent away. I shouldn't have been his girlfriend. I didn't know.

The workers don't bring Stevie down for breakfast either. He's not on the playground. The other kids tell me he has to stay in his bed because he wet it again last night. I see him in the upstairs window later with his nose pushed against the screen. I stand in the yard and whisper up at him. "Be good, all right? Just be good, that's all."

Later on that afternoon, the workers line us up on the porch, and I gather my sisters and my brother close because I'm scared. Even the other kids don't seem to know what's happening.

Mrs. Pulnik and the workers march us by

the rain barrel one by one. They swipe dirty faces and arms and knees with wet cloths and brush hair and have us wash our hands. Some kids are made to change their clothes right there on the porch. Some kids get fresh clothes or pinafores to put right on top of their playclothes.

Mrs. Murphy comes outside and stands on the top step and looks us over. A wire rug beater dangles off her arm. I've never seen the kitchen women use it to knock the dirt out of the rugs, but I've seen it used on kids a lot. The kids call it the *wire witch.*

"Something very special will be happening today," Mrs. Murphy says. "But it's *only* for good little boys and girls. Anyone who isn't on best behavior will *not* be allowed to participate. Do you understand?"

"Yes, ma'am." I say it right along with the rest of the kids.

"Very well." She smiles, but the smile makes me back up a step. "Today, the bookmobile will be coming. The kind ladies of the Aid Society will be giving of their time to help you select books. It is very important that we make a good showing. Each of you may have one book to read *if* you are good." She goes on and tells us to mind our manners, say *yes ma'am* and *no ma'am,* don't grab and touch all the books, and if the workers ask whether we're happy here, we're to tell them we're very grateful to Miss Tann for finding us and to Mrs. Murphy for taking us into her home.

I lose track of the rest. All I can think of is that we're going to have a chance at a book, and there's not much I like better than books, especially books I haven't read yet. With five of us, we can get *five* books.

But when the workers unlock the yard gate and the line starts out, Mrs. Murphy stops Camellia and me and the babies. "Not you," she says. "Since you haven't a place upstairs yet, you've no good spot to keep books, and we can't have the library's property being damaged."

"We'll treat them real careful. I promise," I blurt out. Normally, I'd never talk back to Mrs. Murphy, but I can't help it this time. "Please. Could we get one book at least? And I can read it to my sisters and my brother? Queenie used to . . ." I button my lips before I can get myself in more trouble. We're not allowed to talk about our mamas and daddies here.

Sighing, she hangs the rug beater on a nail in one of the porch posts. "Very well. But there is no need for the little ones to go. Just you. And be quick."

It takes me a second to decide whether to

leave the babies. Camellia grabs their arms and drags them toward her. *"Go."* She pops her eyes at me. "Get us somethin' good."

I give them one last look before scooting out the gate. It's all I can do not to run across the yard and bust through the magnolias. It smells like freedom out here. It smells good. I have to make myself stay in line and follow the rest of the kids around to the driveway, real orderly.

On the other side of the tree wall, there's a big black truck. Two more cars pull up. Miss Tann gets out of one, and a man with a camera gets out of the other. They shake hands, and the man takes a notepad and pen from his pocket.

The big black truck says SHELBY COUNTY LIBRARIES on the side, and once we get closer, I can see that there're shelves coming right out the back of it. And the shelves are full of books. The kids mill around them, and I have to put my hands behind my back and lace my fingers tight to keep from touching things while I wait my turn.

"As you can observe for yourself, we provide the children with many stimulating opportunities," Miss Tann says, and the man writes on his notepad like the words are going to get away if he doesn't catch them fast enough. "Some of our little ones have never enjoyed the luxury of books before coming to us. We provide wonderful books and toys in all of our homes."

I duck my head and fidget and wish the crowd would thin out. If Miss Tann has other places like this, I don't know what they're like, but there's not a single book around Mrs. Murphy's, and all the toys are broke. Nobody even cares enough to fix them. Miss Tann's been here enough. She's got to know that.

"Poor little waifs," she says to the man. "We take them in when they are unwanted and unloved. We provide them with all that their parents cannot or will not give them."

I bolt my eyes to the ground and make fists behind my back. *It's a lie,* I wish I could scream at the man. *My mama and daddy want us. They love us. So did the father who came to see his little boy, Lonnie, and ended up broke down on the porch crying like a baby when they said Lonnie'd been adopted.*

"How long does the average child remain with the society?" the man asks.

"Oh, we have no average children here." Miss Tann pushes out a high little laugh. "Only extraordinary ones. Some may remain longer than others, depending on the condition in which they come to us. Some are weak and small when they arrive and so wan they cannot even run and play. We plump them up with three nourishing meals per day. Children require good food to grow properly. Plenty of fruits and vegetables and red meats always put the glow back in their little cheeks."

Not at Mrs. Murphy's house. At Mrs. Murphy's house, it's cornmeal mush, one little bowl, morning and night. We're hungry all the time. Gabby's skin is pale as milk, and Lark and Fern's arms are so thin you can see the muscles and the bones.

"We monitor all of our boarding homes to be certain the children are properly fed and well treated." She acts like it's true for a fact.

The man nods and writes and says, "Mmmm-hmm," like he's swallowing it whole and it tastes real good.

Go look in the backyard, I want to tell him. *Go look in the kitchen. You'll see how it really is.* I want to say it so bad. But I know if I do, I won't get a book, but I *will* get the closet.

"The children are so very grateful. We pull them from the gutters and . . ."

Someone touches my arm, and I jump without meaning to. A lady in a blue dress looks down at me. Her smile is bright as sunshine.

"And what do *you* like to read about?" she asks. "What sort of books? You've been so patiently waiting all this time."

"Yes, ma'am."

She leads me toward the bookshelves, and my eyes about pop out of my head. I forget all about Miss Tann, and all I can think about are books. I've been to libraries in river towns before, but back then we had books of our own on the *Arcadia* too. Now we haven't got anything, and when you haven't got a single book, the idea of putting your hands on one is like Christmas and a birthday rolled up together.

"I . . . I like any kind," I stammer out. Just looking at the shelves and seeing all those colors and words makes me smile real big. I feel happy for the first time since we came here. "Maybe a long book would be good, since we just get one."

"Smart girl." The woman winks at me. "Are you a good reader?"

"Yes'm, real good. Back on . . ." I duck my head because I was about to say, *Back on the* Arcadia, *Queenie had us reading all the time.*

There's a worker standing not two foot from me, and Miss Tann isn't far off either. If she heard that, I'd be out of here quick as spit.

"All right then," the book lady says. "Let's see. . . ."

"I like adventures. Adventure stories."

"Hmmm . . . adventures about what?"

"Queens and princesses and wild Indians. All kinds of things." My mind fills with tales.

"Maybe a western, then?"

"Or the river. Have you got a story about that?" A book about the river would be like going home again. It'd keep us till Briny takes us back to the *Arcadia.*

The woman claps her hands together. "Oh! Oh, yes I do!" She lifts a finger into the air. "I have the perfect thing for you."

After a minute of looking, she hands me *Adventures of Huckleberry Finn* by Mr. Mark Twain, and I figure that one really was meant just for me. We've never had this book, but Briny has told us tales about Tom Sawyer and Huckleberry Finn and Injun Joe. Mark Twain is one of Briny's favorites. He used to read those books when he was little. You'd think him and Tom Sawyer were personal friends even.

The lady in the blue dress writes my new name, May Weathers, on the card. When she stamps the date in the book, I realize yesterday was Fern's birthday. She's four now. If we were on the *Arcadia,* Queenie would bake her a little cake and we'd all give her presents we made by hand or found along the riverbank. Here at Mrs. Murphy's, the library book will have to do. When I get back to the yard, I'll tell Fern it's her birthday surprise, but she only gets to keep it awhile. We'll make a mud cake and use flowers for frosting and add twig candles with little leaves balanced on top, so Fern can play like she's blowing them out.

The library lady gives me a hug before she sends me off, and it feels so good, I want to stay right there and hang on to her and smell the books, but I can't.

I hold *Huckleberry Finn* real tight against my chest and start across the yard. Now we can leave this place behind anytime we want. All we gotta do is join up with Huckleberry Finn. There's room on his raft for all five of us, I'll bet. Maybe we'll find the *Arcadia* out there somewhere.

Even though I have to head back to Mrs. Murphy's house, it feels like a whole new place.

Now it's got a river in it.

That very night before bed, we open Fern's birthday book and start on our adventures with Huck Finn. We've been traveling downwater with him for almost a week when Miss Tann's shiny black car rolls up the driveway one afternoon. It's a sunny day and hot as fry grease in the house, so her and Mrs. Murphy meet out on the porch to talk. I skitter around the fig tree and go up under the azaleas to listen.

"Oh yes, the advertisements have already run in all the papers!" Miss Tann is saying. "I've had such a brilliant vision, I must admit. *Fair-haired cherubs for a fair summer season. Yours for the asking!* Perfect, isn't it? All the little blonds."

"Like a gathering of wood nymphs. Little elves and fairies," Mrs. Murphy agrees.

"It is almost as compelling as the Christmas Baby Program. Customers have been calling already. Once they see the children, they'll be vying against one another."

"Without a doubt."

"You'll have all of the children ready on Saturday morning, then? I will expect them well dressed — dirndls and bows and all the niceties. Baths all around and scrub every one of them down to the nubbins. No grimy fingernails or dirt behind the ears. Be sure they know what is expected of them and what will happen to them if they humiliate me in public. Make an example of someone ahead of time, and be certain the other children see it. This party represents an important opportunity to grow our reputation for offering the finest. With the new advertisements, we'll have all of the best families in Tennessee and a dozen states beyond. They'll all be coming to see our children, and when they see them, they won't be able to help themselves. They'll *have* to have one."

"We'll make certain the children are properly prepared. Just let me look again at the list." They stop talking. Papers rattle. The wind shifts and blows the azalea branches, and I see Miss Tann's head. Her short gray-brown hair catches the breeze and stands up straight when she bends close to Mrs. Murphy.

I press against the wall and hold real still, afraid they'll hear me and look over the railing. The wind brings up the smell of something dead. I can't see it, but it probably ate the poison Mr. Riggs put out. Once the stink gets bad enough, he'll find the body and bury it someplace.

"Even *May*?" Mrs. Murphy asks, and my ears perk up. "*She's* hardly a cherub."

Miss Tann gives a sharp little laugh. "She'll be a help with the little ones, and she is quite a pretty thing to look at, as I recall."

"I suppose so." Mrs. Murphy doesn't sound happy. "She isn't a troublemaker, to be sure."

"I'll have cars come for them at one o'clock on Saturday. Do *not* send them hungry or sleepy or needing to use the bathroom. Perky and bright and guaranteed to behave. That is my expectation."

"Yes, of course."

"What in heaven's name is that ghastly smell?"

"Rabbits. We've had a problem with them this summer."

I slip away before they can decide to go looking. Mr. Riggs is nowhere around, so it doesn't take me long to get past the fig tree and back to the hill. I don't tell Camellia about the viewing party or that we're supposed to have an extra bath tomorrow. No sense letting her get started on a conniption fit ahead of time.

I've got a bad feeling that I don't need to tell her about the extra bath anyhow.

Camellia hasn't got blond hair.

Turns out, I'm right. After breakfast on Saturday, I find out that Camellia's not on the list. Wherever we're going, she's not going with us.

"I ain't sorry they don't want me if it means another bath." She pushes me away when I try to hug her goodbye.

"Be good while we're gone, Mellia. Don't give anybody trouble, and stay away from the big boys, and don't go past the fig tree, and —"

"I don't need lookin' after." Camellia lifts her chin, but there's a little quiver in her bottom lip. She's afraid.

"May!" one of the workers barks. "In line, now!" They've already got all the kids on the list gathered up.

"We'll be back real quick," I whisper to Camellia. "Don't be scared."

"I ain't."

But then she hugs me after all.

The worker yells at me again, and I hurry into line. The next hour and a half is full of soap, and scrubbing, and hair brushing, and bows, and toothbrushes under our fingernails, and ribbons, and lacy new clothes. We try on shoes from a closetful until we find some that fit.

By the time the workers take us to the cars out front, we don't even look like the same kids. There's the four of us, three other girls, a boy who's five, two babies, and Stevie, who's been told that, if he wets his pants again, he'll get a whipping right then and there.

We're not allowed to talk in the car. On the way over, the worker does the talking. "Girls, you will sit politely with your legs together like young ladies. Do not speak unless you are spoken to. You will be mannerly toward the attendees at Miss Tann's party. You will say only good things about your time at Mrs. Murphy's house. There will be toys and colors, cakes and cookies at the party today. You will . . ."

I lose track of her voice as the car goes over a hill and comes within sight of the river. May fades like a speck of sun on the water, and Rill comes out. She stretches toward the crack at the top of the window, and pulls in air and catches all the familiar scents.

For just a minute, she's home.

Then the car turns a corner, and the river's gone again. Something heavy and sad settles over me. I lean my head against the seat, and the worker tells me to stop; I'm smashing my hair bow.

In my lap, Gabion falls asleep, and I cuddle him close and let his hair tickle my chin, and I'm back home again anyway. These people can control everything about me, but they can't control where I go in my mind.

But my visit to the *Arcadia* is too short. Pretty soon, we pull up to a tall white house that's even bigger than Mrs. Murphy's.

"Anyone who does not behave will be *very* sorry," the worker says, and points a finger in our faces before letting us out of the car. "Be friendly with the guests at the party. Sit in their laps if they ask you to. Smile. Show them that you are good children."

We go inside, and the house is filled with people. Other kids are there too, and babies. Everyone is dressed in pretty clothes, and we have cakes and cookies to eat. There are toys for the little kids, and before I know it, Fern and Gabion and even Lark wander away from me.

A man takes Gabion outside to play with a blue ball. A dark-haired woman sits with Lark, and they color in a picture book together. Fern laughs and plays peekaboo with a pretty blond-headed lady who sits off in a chair by herself looking tired and sad. Fern makes her laugh, and pretty soon, the lady is carrying my sister from toy to toy, like Fern can't walk for herself.

They finally cuddle into a chair to read a book, and my heart squeezes. I think about Queenie and how she used to read to us. I want the woman to let go of Fern, to give her back.

A man comes into the room and tickles Fern on the belly, and the woman smiles and says, "Oh, Darren, she's perfect! Amelia would have been this age." She pats the chair arm. "Sit and read the book with us."

"You go ahead." He kisses her on the cheek. "I have some people to talk to." Then he leaves the room.

Fern and the woman are on their second book when the man comes back. They're so busy, they don't even notice that he sits down next to me on the sofa. "Are you sisters?" he asks.

"Yes, sir," I answer just like I've been told to. *Ma'am* and *sir* to everything.

Leaning away, he takes a good look at me. "You do favor one another."

"Yes, sir." I stare down at my hands. My heart speeds up, bumping around my chest like a wren caught in the shanty house. *What does he want?*

The man lays a hand on my back. My shoulder blades fold around it. Little hairs tug at the bottom of my neck. Sweat drips under my scratchy dress.

"And how old," the man asks, "are *you*?"

Chapter 13

Avery

The cottage is quiet and filled with moonlight as I swing open the door. I fumble for the light switch and brace my cellphone against my shoulder as I wait for my Uncle Clifford to answer the question I've just asked. He's put me on hold while he orders food at a drive-through window.

I'm consumed by the strongest memory of arriving here after dark for a visit, just my grandmother and me. The cottage was exactly like this, moon spears fanning over the floor in the shape of palmetto fronds, the air smelling of salt water, and sandy carpets, and lemon oil, and furniture that has lived long by the sea.

I wiggle my fingers. I can almost feel her hand wrapped around mine. I must've been about eleven or twelve — that awkward age when I'd quit holding her hand in public, but here in our magic place, it was okay.

Standing in the entry now, I reach for that sense of comfort, but this visit is pungent with opposing tastes. Bitter and sweet. Familiar and strange. The tastes of life.

Uncle Clifford comes back on the line. After a long walk along the beach and supper at the Waterfront Restaurant, I've decided that my uncle might be the only means of making progress in my quest, for now. Trent Turner ditched me by taking off in a jeep with the guy in the uniform. I waited around in my car, but the Turner Real Estate office remained closed all afternoon.

So far, this trip is looking like a bust.

"What was it that you needed, Avery? What about the Edisto house?" Uncle Clifford wants to know.

"So, I'm just wondering if you and Dad came here much with Grandma Judy? When you were little, I mean." I'm keeping it casual. Trying not to tip him off to anything. Uncle Clifford was a federal agent in his younger years. "Did Grandma Judy have friends she met here or people she came to see?"

"Well . . . let me think. . . ." He ruminates for a while, then simply says, "I don't guess we went there all that much, now that you mention it. We visited more when I was young. Once we were older, we liked Granny Stafford's place on Pawleys Island better. The house was bigger, and the sailboat was there, and more often than not, we had cousins around to play with. Usually, Mama went to the Edisto cottage by herself. She liked to write there. You know, she dabbled in poetry a bit, and she did the society column for a while."

I'm momentarily dumbfounded. "Grandma Judy wrote a *society column*?" Otherwise known as the weekly gossip.

"Well, not under her own name, of course."

"Under *what* name?"

"If I told you that, I'd have to kill you."

"Uncle Clifford!" While my dad is strait-laced, Uncle Clifford has always been wild and a bit of a tease. He's given Aunt Diana a full head of gray hair, which, as any good Southern lady would, she colors regularly.

"Oh, let your grandmother's secrets stay secret." For a minute, I think there's a hidden message in that, but then I can tell he's just toying with me. "So you're down at the Myers cottage, huh?"

"Yes. I just decided to get away for a few days."

"Well, drop a line in the water for me."

"You know I don't fish. Yuck." Being

saddled with girls, my poor father worked hard to form an avid angler from at least one of us.

Even Uncle Clifford knows it was a lost cause. "Well, now see, that's one way you don't take after your grandmother. She loved to fish, especially down on Edisto. When your dad and I were little, she'd take us there to meet up with somebody who had a little jon boat. We'd go up the river and spend half the day fishing. Don't remember who it was we went with. A friend, I guess. He had a little blond-headed boy I liked to play with. Name started with a *T* . . . Tommy, Timmie . . . no . . . Tr . . . Trey or Travis maybe."

"Trent? Trent Turner?" The current Trent Turner being Trent the Third, his father was a Trent too, and he's around my uncle's age.

"Could've been. There some reason you're asking? Anything wrong?"

Suddenly, I realize I've gone one question too far and inadvertently unlocked the detective's office. "No. No reason. Being on Edisto just started me thinking about things. I wish I'd come down here more with Grandma Judy. I wish I'd asked questions while she could still remember things, you know?"

"Well, that's one of the paradoxes of life.

You can't have it all. You can have some of this and some of that or all of this and none of that. We make the trade-offs we think are best at the time. You've accomplished a lot for a girl — I mean, a *woman* just thirty years old."

Sometimes I wonder if my family doesn't see more in me than is really there. "Thanks, Uncle Clifford."

"That'll be five bucks for the session."

"The check's in the mail."

After we hang up, I think through the conversation as I unpack the single sack of groceries I've picked up at the BI-LO, which I remember as the Piggly Wiggly.

Were there any clues in what Uncle Clifford said?

Nothing jumps out at me. Nothing that leads anywhere. If the little boy in the jon boat *was* named Trent, that tells me that my grandmother had some sort of personal connection to the elder Trent Turner, which I'd already guessed. But if they spent time out fishing together *with* the children, that also pokes holes in my blackmail theory. You don't go fishing with a blackmailer, and you certainly don't take your little boys. You also don't bring children with you if you're having an illicit affair. Especially not children who are old enough to remember the outing.

Maybe the elder Trent Turner was nothing more than a longtime friend. Maybe the envelope merely contains photos . . . something totally innocent. But then, why the deathbed pledge between grandfather and grandson that the packets wouldn't be passed along to anyone other than their owners?

I form theories as I carry my things to the bedroom, open my suitcase, and settle in. I throw darts at the theories, just the way I would if we were gathered in the war room at my old office.

The darts hit their marks, and there's really nothing left. The day is catching up with me anyway. I'm ready for a shower and a good night's sleep. Maybe tomorrow I'll have a stroke of genius . . . or maybe I'll catch up with Trent Turner III and wrestle the truth out of him.

One possibility seems about as likely as the other.

It's not until I'm letting the shower run and realizing that there seems to be no hot water in the cottage that I zero in on something Uncle Clifford said. My grandmother came here *to write.*

Could any of her writings still be here?

Could there be a clue in them?

I'm back into my clothes in a flash. The cold shower really didn't sound so good anyway.

Outside the cottage windows, the sea oats sway over the dunes, and the moon rises above the palmetto thicket. Waves thrum the shore as I rifle through drawers and search closets and blanket chests and wardrobe cabinets. I've almost surrendered to the obvious conclusion that there's nothing here to find when I come up from checking beneath my grandmother's bed and realize the small piece of furniture beside it isn't a desk or a vanity table but a typewriter stand. There's an old black typewriter hanging upside down underneath the center panel. Having grown up in family homes filled with vintage furniture, I more or less know how this thing works. It doesn't take me long to release the right combination of latches and swivel the hinges. The typewriter flips upright with an impressive wallop.

I run a finger over the keys. I can almost hear my grandmother pecking away at them. Leaning close, I study the black rubber roller that pulls the page through. The keys have left tiny indentations behind. If this were a computer, perhaps I could pull something off the hard drive, but no words remain legible here. It's impossible to tell what's been written or when.

"What do you know that I don't know?" I whisper to the machine as I rifle through the drawers. There's nothing in the stand but assorted pens and pencils, yellowed typing paper, a box of carbon sheets, and strips of correction film, chalky white on one side and slick on the other. The top sheet bears the impression of letters. Holding it to the light, I can easily make out the mistyped-then-corrected words, *Plmetto Blvd, Edisto Island . . .*

My grandmother wrote letters here apparently, but either accidentally or on purpose, she cleaned up her tracks. There are no partially used pieces of paper, and the carbon sheets are pristine, no ghosts of words left behind. Strange, because in her desk back home, there was always a folder filled with paper that could be reused for small projects, crafts, or children's drawings.

I push a typewriter key, watch the hammer swing up and strike the roller, leaving behind only the faint, shimmery impression of a *K.* The ink on the ribbon is dry.

The ribbon . . .

The next thing I know, I'm bent over the black metal housing, wrestling it loose so I can get to the spools. It's surprisingly easy. Unfortunately, the ribbon is mostly unused. Only a few inches of it might contain the stamped-out impression of whatever was typed last. Unrolling it and holding it against the light, I squint to make out,

> yduJ,ylerecnissruoY.tihsiwthgimewsayle
> tarepsedsa,tnerT,wonkrevenlliwewspa
> hreP.yteicoSemoHs'nerdlihCeessenneTeh
> tfosdrocerehtnineebevahthgimesletahwg
> nirednowdnadetartsurf

It's gibberish at first, but I've been around Grandma Judy long enough to know how a typewriter ribbon works. It rolls as the keys strike. The letters *have* to be in some sort of order.

The first letters on the top line suddenly take on meaning. *Judy.* My grandmother's name spelled backward, right to left, the way it would have ended up after being typed. Another word rises from the muddle, *Society* just after — or before — the period. Three more capitalized words precede it: *Tennessee Children's Home.*

Grabbing a pencil and paper, I sort out the rest.

. . . frustrated and wondering what else

might have been in the records of the Tennessee Children's Home Society. Perhaps we will never know, Trent, as desperately as we might wish it.

Yours sincerely,
Judy

I stare at my own handwriting, trying to piece together the rest of the story. Children's homes are for orphans and babies given up for adoption. The young woman in May Crandall's photo was pregnant. Was she a relative of my grandmother's — one who found herself in trouble?

Events come to life in my mind — a starry-eyed girl from a good family, a man of dubious reputation, a scandalous elopement — or worse yet, no marriage at all. An out-of-wedlock pregnancy. Perhaps her beau abandoned her, and she was forced to return to her family?

Back in those days, girls were sent away to have their babies and quietly sign them over for adoption. Even now, women in my mother's social circles occasionally whisper about someone who *went to stay with an aunt* for a time. Perhaps that's what Trent Turner is keeping hidden.

One thing is for certain — the last note written on this typewriter was to a Trent

Turner, and though I can't tell how recent it is, there's little doubt that whatever's in the mysterious envelope will answer a lot of questions.

Or create more.

Without rethinking it, I hurry across the house, grab my phone, and dial Trent Turner's number, which I now know by heart.

The phone rings three times before I glance at the clock and realize it's almost midnight. Not at all a proper hour to be calling a near stranger. My mother would be aghast.

If you want to win the man's cooperation, this isn't the way to do it, Avery has just gone through my head when a thick, drowsy " 'Ello, Nrent Nnurner" confirms that I have, indeed, rousted him from bed. That's probably why he answered the phone without checking to see who it was.

"Tennessee Children's Home Society," I blurt out, because I calculate that I have about 2.5 seconds before he comes to his senses and hangs up.

"What?"

"The Tennessee Children's Home Society. What does it have to do with your grandfather and my grandmother?"

"Miss Stafford?" Despite the formal form of address, his thick, sleep-laden tone makes the greeting sound intimate, like pillow talk. A heavy sigh follows, and I hear bedsprings creaking.

"Avery. It's Avery. Please, you have to tell me. I found something. I need to know what it means."

Another long exhale. He clears his throat, but the voice is still deep and drowsy. "Do you have any idea what time it is?"

I glance sheepishly at the clock, as if that somehow excuses my bad behavior. "I apologize. I didn't notice until after I'd dialed."

"You could hang up."

"I'm afraid if I did, you'd never answer again."

A little chuckle-cough tells me I'm right. "True enough."

"Please listen to me. *Please.* I've been digging around the cottage all evening, and I found something, and you're the only one who can tell me what it means. I just . . . I need to know what's going on and what I should do about it." If there's a scandal somewhere in our family's past, it's quite possible that it no longer matters, except perhaps to a few well-preserved members of the Old Guard Gossip Brigade, but there's no way to judge that until I know what I'm dealing with.

"I really can't tell you that."

"I understand your promise to your grandfather, but . . ."

"No." He suddenly sounds wide-awake — wide-awake and in control. "I mean, I *can't* tell you. I've never looked in any of the envelopes. I helped Granddad get them to the people whose names were on them. That's all."

Is he telling the truth? It's hard for me to imagine. I'm the type who carefully peels the tape off the wrapping paper and peeks at the Christmas presents the minute they show up under the tree. I don't like surprises. "But what were they *about*? What did it have to do with the Tennessee Children's Home Society? Children's homes are for orphans. Could my grandmother have been looking for someone who was given up for adoption?"

As soon as I suggest it, I'm afraid I've said too much. "That's just a theory on my part," I add. "I don't have any reason to think it's true." I'm better off not opening the door to a potential scandal. I don't know that I can trust Trent Turner, though it takes a man of integrity to live with sealed envelopes for months on end. The elder Mr. Turner must have known that his grandson was made of solid stuff.

The phone goes silent and stays that way so long that I wonder if Trent has abandoned the call. I'm afraid to speak, afraid anything I say might tip the balance one way or the other.

I'm not terribly accustomed to begging, but finally I whisper, "Please. I'm sorry we got off on the wrong foot this afternoon, but I don't know where else to go from here."

He takes in air. I can almost see his chest filling. "Come over."

"What?"

"Come over to the house before I change my mind."

Stunned silence is all I can manage in response. I'm not sure whether I'm excited or scared to death . . . or if I'm crazy for even thinking about visiting a stranger's house in the middle of the night.

On the other hand, he *is* a reputable and well-known businessman on the island.

A businessman who now knows that I've unearthed at least some part of a secret.

His grandfather's deathbed secret.

What if there's a sinister intention behind this midnight invitation? No one will even know where I am. Who can I tell?

I can't think of anybody I'd want to let in on this right now.

I'll leave a note . . . here in the cottage. . . . No . . . wait. I'll send myself an email. If I go missing, that's the first place they'll check.

The thought feels melodramatic and silly, and then again, it doesn't. "I'll grab my keys and —"

"You won't need your car. I'm four cottages down."

"You're right in the neighborhood?" Parting the kitchen curtains, I try to see through the wall of yaupon and live oak. *All this time, he was practically next door?*

"It's quicker by the beach. I'll turn the back-porch light on."

"I'll be right there."

I rattle around the cottage looking for a flashlight and batteries. Fortunately, whatever relatives have been using the place did leave the basics. My phone rings as I'm thumb-typing an email to myself, documenting my whereabouts and my time of departure. I jump at least three feet, then land hard in a pit of dread. *Trent changed his mind already. . . .*

But the phone number is Elliot's. I'm too wound up to calculate what time it is in Milan right now, but no doubt he's working. "I was tied up when you called yesterday. Sorry," he says.

"I figured. Busy day?"

"Rather," he says vaguely, as usual. In his family, the women aren't interested in business. "How are things on Edisto?"

Honestly, the grapevine in our family is better than microchip tracking. "How did you know I was here?"

"Mother told me," he sighs. "She'd been over to Drayden Hill to get a baby fix, since your sister and Courtney and the boys are visiting. Now she's on the grandkid kick again." Elliot is understandably frustrated. "She reminded me that I'm thirty-one already, and she's fifty-seven, and she doesn't want to be an old grandmother."

"Uh-oh." I wonder sometimes what it'll be like to have Bitsy as a mother-in-law. I love her, and she means well, but she makes Honeybee look subtle.

"Can we book your sister and the triplets to go stay at Mother's for a few days?" Elliot suggests ruefully. "Maybe that'll cure her."

Even though I get the joke, it stings. I adore the triplets, even if they are little wild men. "You could ask." Despite the fact Elliot and I have only talked about kids as an eventual part of our life plan, he's already concerned that multiple births run in my family. He doesn't think he could handle more than one at a time. Every once in a while, I worry that having kids *someday* might be *never* for Elliot. I know we'll work these things out as we go. Don't most couples have to?

"So how long are you at the beach?" he says, changing the subject.

"Just a couple days. If I stay any longer, Leslie will send someone to hunt me down."

"Well, Leslie is looking out for your best interests. You need to be seen. That's the reason you moved home."

I moved home to look after my dad, I want to say, but with Elliot, everything is a step toward something. He's the most achievement-oriented person I've ever met.

"I know. But it's nice to have a little breather. You sound like you could use one too. Get some rest while you're over there, okay? And don't worry about your mother and the grandkid thing. She'll be focused on something else tomorrow."

We say goodbye, and I finish the precautionary email to myself. If I'm never heard from again, someone will eventually check there. *Midnight Tuesday evening. I'm going four doors down from the Edisto cottage to talk to Trent Turner about something involving Grandma Judy. Should be back in an hour or so. Leaving this message just in case.*

It feels dorky, but I send it anyway before

slipping out the door.

Outside, the night is quiet and deep as I walk the path through the dunes, shining my flashlight to keep a lookout for snakes. Along the shore, most of the cottages have gone dark, leaving only the glow of a full moon and a smattering of lights that seem to float over the watery horizon. Leaves and sea grass whisper, and on the beach ghost crabs scuttle sideways through the sand. I sweep the light over them, taking care not to ruin the feeding frenzy by stepping on someone.

The breeze slides along my neck and through my hair, and I want to walk and relax and enjoy the soothing song of the sea. I own meditation music that sounds like this, but I seldom take time for the real thing. Right now, that seems like a shame. I'd forgotten how heavenly this place is, a perfect meeting of land and sea, undisturbed by giant high-rises, or bonfires and ATVs.

I come to Trent Turner's cottage before I want to. My pulse quickens as I slip along a well-worn trail through shrubbery and cross a short boardwalk to a leaning gate. His cottage is of about the same vintage as Grandma Judy's. It sits on short stilts on a large lot, with a small outbuilding in the side yard. A stone path leads to the porch steps. Overhead, moths flutter in circles around a single bulb.

Trent answers the door before I can knock. He's wearing a faded T-shirt with a tear along the neck and sweats that sag around his hips. His suntanned feet are bare, and he's sporting an impressive case of bedhead.

Crossing his arms, he leans against the doorframe, studying me.

I'm suddenly all hands and feet, like an adolescent on a first date to the middle-school dance. I don't know what to do with myself.

"I was starting to wonder," he says.

"Whether I was coming, you mean?"

"Whether the phone call was just a bad dream." But his lips curve upward, and I gather that he's joking.

Even so, I blush a little. This is such an imposition. "I'm sorry. I just really . . . I need to know. What was your grandfather's association with my grandmother?"

"Most likely, he was doing a job for her."

"What kind of job?"

He looks past me toward the tiny cabin tucked beneath the trees in the side yard. I sense the struggle in him. He's wrestling with whether or not he's betraying the deathbed promise. "My grandfather was a finder."

"A finder of *what*?"

"People."

CHAPTER 14

Rill

It's getting on toward dark by the time the viewing party slows down, and the workers start gathering kids to put them into cars and take them back home. By then, I almost don't want to go. All afternoon long, there've been cookies and ice cream and licorice whips and cake and milk and sandwiches and coloring books and new boxes of Crayola colors and dolls for the girls and tin toy cars for the boys.

I'm so stuffed, I can hardly move. After three weeks of not enough food, this place tastes better than anything.

I feel bad that Camellia is missing it all, but then I don't know if she would put up with it either. She doesn't like to be cuddled . . . or touched. I steal a cookie for her and slip it in the front pocket of my pinafore dress and hope nobody checks us over before we leave.

The people all call us *dearie* and *sweetie pie* and *Oh, precious!* So does Miss Tann while we're here. Just like at the bookmobile, she tells tales that aren't true. Her eyes twinkle, and she smiles, like she's enjoying getting away with it.

Just like at the bookmobile, I keep my mouth shut about what *is* true.

"They're perfect in every way," she says to the guests over and over. "Wonderful physical specimens and mentally advanced for their ages as well. Many come from parents with talents in music and art. Blank slates just waiting to be filled. They can become anything you want them to be."

"He's a fine little thing, isn't he?" she asks a man and a wife who've been holding on to Gabion all day. They've played ball and cars, and the man tossed Gabby in the air while he giggled.

Now that it's time to leave, the lady doesn't want to give Gabby back. She walks all the way to the front door, and my baby brother holds on around her neck just like Fern is holding on around mine.

"I 'anna 'tay," Gabby whines.

"We gotta go." I shift Fern to my other hip as Mrs. Pulnik tries to shoo us forward onto the porch. I don't blame Gabby for fussing. I hate that we have to go back to

Mrs. Murphy's house too. I'd rather watch Fern read some more books with the nice lady, but the lady left just a little while ago with her mister. She kissed Fern on the head and said, "We'll see you soon, *dearest,*" before she handed Fern to me.

"Gab . . ." I stop myself just before saying the name that'll get me popped in the head at Mrs. Murphy's house if Mrs. Pulnik hears me. "*Robby,* you can't stay here. Come on, now. We need to find out what happened to Huckleberry Finn and Jim once they got downriver to Arkansas, remember?" I stretch out one arm to him because the other's holding Fern. Gabby won't come, and the woman won't let go either. "We'll read the book when we get back to Mrs. Murphy's. Tell the nice lady goodbye."

"Silence!" Miss Tann looks my way with fire in her eyes, and I pull back, letting my arm drop so quick it makes a loud slap against my leg.

Miss Tann smiles at the woman, then swirls a finger in Gabby's hair. "Isn't our little Robby adorable? So charming." Just as quick as she got mean, she's friendly again. "I think you've hit it off with him."

"Yes, very much so."

The lady's husband steps closer. He gives the collar of his suit jacket a quick tug so that it's good and straight. "Perhaps we should chat a bit. Certainly arrangements can be made so that . . ."

"Quite possibly." Miss Tann doesn't wait for him to finish. "But I must warn you, this little darling is definitely a popular one. I've had *several* ask after him already. Those lovely blue eyes with the dark lashes and the golden curls. Such a rarity. Like a little angel. He could charm most any mother's heart."

They all look at my brother. The man reaches across and pinches Gabby's cheek, and he baby-laughs real cute. He hasn't giggled like that since the police took us off the *Arcadia.* I'm glad he's happy, even if it's just for today.

"Take the other children outside." Miss Tann's voice goes low and flat. She leans close to Mrs. Pulnik and whispers through her teeth, "Put them in the cars. Wait five minutes there before you let the driver pull away." Even a little lower, she adds, "But I don't think we'll be needing you."

Mrs. Pulnik clears her throat and uses a friendly, happy voice we never hear at Mrs. Murphy's house. "To the cars with all of you. Come alongk."

Lark, Stevie, and the other kids scurry to the porch. Fern kicks her feet against my leg and rocks on my hip like she's trying to make a stubborn pony walk out of the barn.

"But Ga . . . Robby." Roots grow under my feet, and I'm not even sure why at first. The people just want to hug and kiss on Gabby a little more. They like to play with little boys. I've been keeping an eye on Gabby, Lark, and Fern all day, whenever I could get away from the couple of men who wanted to know who I was and why I was here, since I'm older than everybody else. I've scampered from room to room and window to window, making sure I knew where the babies were and that nobody was being mean to them.

But in the back of my mind, I've been thinking about Stevie's sister, who left Mrs. Murphy's house and never came back. I know what happens to orphans, which Sherry and Stevie are but we're not. We've got a daddy and a mama who're coming back for us.

Does the woman who's been playing with Gabion know that? Did anybody tell her? She doesn't think he's an orphan, does she?

I take another step toward my brother. "Here. I can get him."

The woman turns her shoulder to me. "He's fine."

"Outside!" Mrs. Pulnik's fingers close

hard around my arm, and I know what'll happen if I don't do what she asks.

I touch Gabby's little knee and say, "It's all right. The lady just wants to tell you bye-bye."

He lifts a fat little hand and waves at me. "Bye-bye," he repeats. His smile fills with baby teeth. I remember when he cut every single one of those.

"To the *car."* Mrs. Pulnik's jagged fingernails dig into my skin. She tugs me, and I trip over the threshold on the way out, staggering onto the porch and almost dropping Fern.

"Oh, goodness. Is she his sister?" the woman with Gabion worries.

"No, certainly *not,"* Miss Tann says, lying again. "The little ones become attached to the older ones in the home. That is all. It can't be helped. They forget just as quickly, of course. The only sibling to this little fellow is an infant girl. Newborn. Adopted by a *very* prominent family, no less. So, you can see that he is no *ordinary* little boy. You've picked out our finest. The mother was a college graduate, an extremely intelligent girl. Died during the birthing process, unfortunately, and the children were abandoned by their father. But they're no worse for the wear. And wouldn't this one be adorable on your California beaches? Of course, our out-of-state adoptions do involve special fees. . . ."

Those are the last words I hear before Mrs. Pulnik drags me down the porch steps, telling me under her breath what Mrs. Murphy will do to me if I don't step it up. Her grip wrenches my arm until I'm sure it's gonna break.

I don't even care. I can't feel anything — not the summer-dry grass crunching under my feet, not the stiff shoes the workers gave me this morning. Not the hot, sticky evening air or the too-tight dress tugging when Fern kicks and wiggles and reaches over my shoulder, whimpering, "Gabby . . . Gabby . . ."

I'm cold on the outside, like I just fell off in the winter river and all the blood's gone deep down inside to try to keep me from freezing to death. My arms and legs seem like they're somebody else's. They move, but only because they know what they're supposed to do, not because I tell them.

Mrs. Pulnik throws Fern and me in the car with the rest of the kids and gets in beside me. I sit stiff and stare toward the big house and wait for the door to open and someone to bring Gabion across the yard. I wish for it so hard, the wishing hurts.

"Where's Gabby?" Fern whispers into my ear, and Lark watches me with her sad, quiet eyes. She hasn't said much since we came to Mrs. Murphy's, and she won't now either, but still I hear her. *You gotta get Gabion,* she's telling me.

I picture him coming across the yard.

I hope.

I watch.

I try to think.

What should I do?

Mrs. Pulnik's wristwatch ticks. *Tick, tick, tick, tick.*

Miss Tann's words flit through my mind, zipping off the way water striders do when someone throws a rock in the river. They go all directions at once.

Died during the birthing process . . .

My mama's dead?

. . . the children were abandoned. . . .

Briny's not coming back for us?

The only sibling to this little fellow is an infant girl. Newborn.

One of the babies didn't die at the hospital? I have a new little sister? Miss Tann gave her to somebody? Is that a lie? Is all of it a lie? Miss Tann can tell a fib so smooth and easy, it seems like even she believes it. Gabby doesn't have a mama who's a college student. Queenie's smart, but she only got through the eighth grade before she met Briny and took off for the river.

It's lies, I tell myself. *Everything she says is a lie. It's gotta be.*

She's trying to make the party people happy, but they'll have to give Gabion back because Miss Tann knows our daddy's coming to get us soon's he can. Briny would never give us up. He'd never let a lady like Miss Tann take my new baby sister, if I had one. Never. Ever. He'd die first.

Is Briny dead? Is that why he hasn't come for us?

The car starts, and I jerk toward the window, pushing Fern off my lap. She slides into the seat as I grab hold of the door handle. I'll run back to the house, and I'll tell those people the truth. I'll tell them Miss Tann is a liar. I don't care what they do to me after.

Before anything else can happen, Mrs. Pulnik has me by the big, fancy hair bow one of the workers prettied me up with this morning. Fern squirms out from between us and lands on the floor with Stevie and Lark.

"You will behave." Mrs. Pulnik's lips touch my ear, her breath hot and sour. It smells of Mrs. Murphy's whiskey. "Shouldt you not, Mrs. Murphy will gif you the *closet.*

And not *only* will this be for you. We will be tying all of you and leavingk you there, hangingk like shoes by the laces. The closet is *cold.* And it is *dark.* Will the little ones enjoy the dark, do you think?"

My heart beats wild as she yanks my head back. My neck crackles and snaps. Hair pops loose from the roots. A white flash of pain shoots over my eyes.

"Is that understoodt?"

I do my best to nod.

She throws me against the door, and my head bounces off the glass. "I did not imagine any troubles would be comingk from you."

Tears storm into my eyes, and I blink hard against them. *I won't cry. I won't.*

The seat bends, sucking me closer to Mrs. Pulnik's bulky body. She lets out a purring sigh, like a cat in a sunny chair. "Driver, take us to home now. It is time."

I worm away and watch out the window as long as I can until the white house with its big columns is gone.

Nobody in the car says a word. Fern crawls back into my lap and we all sit still as stones.

On the way back to Mrs. Murphy's, I look for the river. A little dream finds its way into my mind while Fern hangs on around my neck, and Lark rests against my knee, and Stevie huddles between my feet, his fingers squeezed over the buckles on my shoes. I pretend that when we pass by the river the *Arcadia* will be there, and Briny will see the car.

In my daydream, he runs up the banks and makes the driver stop. Briny opens the door and pulls us out, all of us, even Stevie. When Mrs. Pulnik tries to get in his way, he slugs her in the nose, just like he would if someone tried to steal from him in a pool hall. Briny kidnaps us the way Huck Finn's daddy does in the story, but Huck's daddy was a bad man, and Briny is good.

He goes back to the house and gets Gabion away from Miss Tann and carries us to a far-off place.

But my dream isn't true. The river comes and goes. There's no sign of the *Arcadia,* and soon enough, the shadow of Mrs. Murphy's house covers the car. Inside my skin, I'm empty and cold, like the Indian caves where Briny took us camping one time when we hiked up over the bluffs. There were bones in the caves. Dead bones of people who are gone. There are dead bones in me.

Rill Foss can't breathe in this place. She doesn't live here. Only May Weathers does.

Rill Foss lives down on the river. She's the princess of Kingdom Arcadia.

It's when we're marching up Mrs. Murphy's sidewalk that I think about Camellia. I feel guilty for imagining that Briny rescued us from the car, that he took us away without Camellia.

I'm scared of what she'll say when I tell her we haven't got Gabion with us — that I hope he's coming later on. Camellia will say I should've fought harder, that I should've bit and scratched and screamed the way she would have. Maybe that's right. Maybe I deserve to hear it. Could be I'm just too chicken, but I don't want to get the closet. I don't want them to put my little sisters in there either.

Dread steals over me when we get inside. It's the kind of dread that comes on a swolled-up river when the spring melt happens and you see an ice floe headed straight for the boat. Sometimes, the ice is so big that you know there's no chance of pushing it away with a boathook. It's about to hit and hit hard, and if the edge slices the hull, you're sunk.

It's all I can do not to shake off the babies and turn around and run out Mrs. Murphy's door before it closes behind us. The house stinks of mold, and bathroom smells, and Mrs. Murphy's perfume and whiskey. The smells grab me by the throat, and I can't breathe, and I'm glad when we're told to go outside because the kids haven't come in for supper yet.

"And the clothes are not to be soiledt!" Mrs. Pulnik hollers after us.

I look for Camellia in the places where I told her to stay, the safe places. She's not at any of them. The big boys don't answer when I ask where she is. They just shrug and go on playing a game of conkers with the buckeyes they pick by the back fence.

Camellia's not digging in the dirt, or swinging on the swings, or playing house in the shade under the trees. All the other kids are here, but not Camellia.

For the second time in one day, my heart feels like it'll bust out of my chest. What if they've taken her away? What if she threw a fit after we left, and she got herself in trouble?

"Camellia!" I holler, and then listen, but there are only the voices of the other kids. My sister doesn't answer. "Camellia!"

I'm headed for the side of the house, for the azalea bushes, when I see her. She's sitting on the corner of the porch with her legs pulled tight to her chest and her face buried. Her black hair and her skin are gray with dirt. It looks like she's been in a scrape with somebody while I was gone. There're scratches on her arm, and she's got a skinned knee.

Maybe that's why the big boys wouldn't tell me where she was. Probably they're the ones she tangled with.

I leave the little kids by the persimmons and tell them to stay right there and not to wander, and I go up the stairs and walk down the long porch to Camellia. My stiff shoes echo against the wood, *clack, clack, clack,* but my sister never moves.

"Camellia?" Sitting would get my dress dirty, so I squat down beside her. Maybe she's sleeping. "Camellia? I brought you something. It's in my pocket. Let's go out on the hill where nobody can see, and I'll give it to you."

She doesn't answer. I touch her hair, and she jerks away. A little gray cloud puffs out as my hand slides toward her shoulder. It smells like ashes but not like a fireplace exactly. I know the smell, except I can't place it. "What'd you get yourself into while we were gone?"

I touch her again, and she ducks her shoulder in but lifts her head. She's got a bump on her lip, and there are four round bruises on her chin. Her eyes are puffy and red, like she's been crying, but it's the look inside them that bothers me most. It's like I'm staring through a window into an empty room. There's nothing inside but the dark.

The smell comes off her again, and all of a sudden, I know it. Coal ash. Whenever we tied up the *Arcadia* near railroad tracks, we'd gather up coal that'd fallen off the trains. *Heating and cooking. Free for the taking,* Briny always said.

Has Briny been here?

As soon as I think it, I know how wrong I am. I know how wrong *this* is. Something terrible happened while I was gone. "What's the matter?" I drop down to the porch, too scared to care about my dress. Little splinters poke my legs. "Camellia, what happened?"

Her lips hang open but don't make a sound. A tear squeezes from her eye and cuts a pink river through the coal dust.

"*Tell* me." I lean down to see her better, but she turns and stares the other way. Her hand is knotted in a fist between us. I take it in mine, pry open her fingers to see what she's holding, and the minute I do, all the cookies and ice cream from the party come up in my throat. Dirty, round peppermints are stuck so tight to my sister's palm, they're melted into her skin.

I close my eyes and shake my head and try not to know, but I do. My mind drags me kicking and screaming to Mrs. Murphy's cellar, into the dark corner behind the stairs where ash coats the coal bin and the boiler furnace. I see thin, strong arms fighting, legs thrashing around. I see a big hand closing over a screaming mouth, the dirty, oily fingers squeezing so hard they leave four round bruises.

I want to run in the house, yell, and scream. I want to smack Camellia for being stubborn and going over by the azaleas when I told her not to. I want to grab her and hold her close and make everything better. I don't know exactly what Riggs did to her, but I know it's bad. I also know that, if we tell, he'll make my sister fall out of a tree and hit her head. Maybe he'll even do the same to me. Then who'll take care of the babies? Who'll wait for Gabion to come back?

I grab my sister's hand, slap away the peppermints, and let them bounce onto the porch and fall into the flower bed, where they disappear under a trumpet vine.

She doesn't fight when I pull her to her feet. "Come on. If they see you looking like this when the dinner bell rings, they'll think you been fighting, and you'll get the closet."

I drag her down the porch like a tow sack of wheat and haul her to the rain barrel and, little by little, pour the water over her skin and wash her off, best I can.

"You tell them you fell off the swing." Even though I'm holding her face in my hands, she won't look at me. "You hear? Anybody asks about the skinned places, you say you fell off the swing and that's all."

Over on the steps, Fern and Lark and Stevie wait for us, quiet as mice. "Y'all stay put . . . and leave Camellia be," I tell them. "She ain't feelin' good."

"Yer tummy hurt?" Fern sidles closer, and so does Lark, and Camellia pushes them away hard. Lark looks at me, confused. She's usually the only one Camellia *does* like.

"Let her alone, I said."

"I see London. I see France!" one of the big boys hollers from halfway across the yard. They always start wandering in about now, so they can be first in the supper line. I don't know why. We all get the same thing, every single meal.

"You hush up, Danny Boy," I hiss, and pull Camellia's dress down over her knees. The workers call him Danny Boy on account of he's Irish. Red hair and a thousand freckles, just like James had. He marshals their pack now that James is gone. But Danny Boy is mean to the core.

He wanders closer, props his hands on the rope that's holding up his too-big britches. "Well, ain't you fine and fancy? Guess even them purdy clothes couldn't getcha no new mama and daddy."

"We don't *need* a mama and daddy. We got one."

"Who'd want ya, anyhow?" He catches sight of Camellia's scratched-up arm and leg, pushes in closer to see. "What happened to her? Looks like she's been fightin'."

I step up to Danny Boy. If I have to get the closet to protect my sister, I will. "She fell down and bunged herself around a little. That's all. You got anything to say about it?"

The dinner bell rings, and we line up before anything else can happen.

Turns out that evening it's not me getting the closet I need to worry about; it's Camellia. She's quiet through supper and doesn't eat her food, but when it's time for the bath, she comes alive and throws a wild-eyed fit. She screams like an animal and scratches and kicks and leaves long, red fingernail marks on Mrs. Pulnik's arm.

It takes three workers to hold Camellia down and drag her to the bathroom. By then, Mrs. Pulnik has me by the hair too. "You are *not* to speak. Not *one* wordt, or you will see the consequence." Fern, Lark, and Stevie cling to each other against the wall.

In the bathroom, Camellia roars and squeals. Water splashes. A bottle shatters. Scrub brushes clatter. The door shakes in its frame.

"Riggs!" Mrs. Pulnik yells down the stairs. "Come with my rope. Bring my rope for the closet!"

And just like that, Camellia's gone. The last thing I see of her is a worker hauling her off down the hall, caterpillar-wrapped in a bedsheet so she can't kick or hit.

That night, we're just three. I don't take out our book to read it, and my baby sisters don't beg for more of the story. Lark and Fern and me curl up in one cot together, and I hum one of Queenie's old songs until my sisters fall asleep. Finally, I drift away too.

Sometime before sunup, Fern wets the bed for the first time since she was two and a half. I don't even holler at her for it. I just clean it up the best I can and open the basement window the little crack it'll go. I roll up the wet blanket and Fern's drawers and stick them under the bushes where hopefully nobody will find them. I'll sneak through the azaleas later and spread them out so they'll dry before tonight.

It's when I'm working to spread the blanket over the branches that the wind catches the leaves and they shudder apart long enough for me to see something. Underneath the gaslight by the street, there are people standing and watching the house. In the dawn dark, I can't make out faces or clothes, just the outline of a crooked old man and a tall, thin boy.

They look like Zede and Silas.

Just as quick as they were there, the leaves fall back, and they're gone.

Chapter 15

Avery

The envelope is surprisingly ordinary. Just the plain manila kind that would be used in an office. The contents feel thin — maybe a few sheets of paper, folded in triplicate. It's sealed shut, and my grandmother's name is written on the back in a shaky scrawl that bleeds across to the margin and drops over the edge.

"Granddad's Parkinson's gave him quite a bit of trouble toward the end," Trent explains. He rubs his forehead, frowning at the envelope as if he's wondering again whether he should have broken the oath by giving it to me.

I know I'd be wise to open it before he changes his mind, but guilt stings. Trent looks as if he's failed at something. I'm the cause of that.

I understand loyalty to family all too well. It's the very thing that has driven me here in the middle of the night.

"Thank you," I say, as if that will help.

He kneads an eyebrow with his fingertips and nods reluctantly. "Just so you know, it may make things worse, not better. There was a reason my granddad spent so much of his time helping to find people. After he and my gran married and took over the family business in Charleston, he went to law school so he could handle his own real estate contracts . . . but he also did it for another reason. When he was eighteen, he'd found out he was adopted. Nobody had ever told him. His adoptive father was a sergeant in the Memphis Police Department, and I don't know that they were ever very close, but when Granddad learned he'd been lied to all his life, that was the last straw. He joined the army the next day and never talked to his adoptive parents again. He looked for his birth family for years but never found them. My gran always felt like it might've been better if he hadn't run across his records in the first place. To tell you the truth, she wished his adoptive parents had destroyed them."

"Secrets have a way of coming out." That's a bit of wisdom my father has shared with me many times. *Secrets also make you vulnerable to your enemies, political or otherwise.*

Whatever's inside this envelope, I'm better off knowing it.

Still, my fingers tremble as I slip them beneath the flap. "I can see why your grandfather would've been passionate about helping other people find information and lost family members." *But how is my grandmother involved?*

The adhesive loosens bit by bit as I pull. I work it slowly, like my mother opening a birthday present, taking care not to tear the paper. "Guess there's no time like the present to find out," I say. Gingerly, I remove a smaller envelope that has been opened at some time in the past. The papers inside are folded together like a brochure or an electric bill, but I can tell they're official documents of some kind.

Across the table, Trent looks down at his hands as I lay out the contents.

"I really . . ." There's no point in thanking him again. It won't save him from wrestling with his conscience. "I want you to know you can count on me to do whatever's best with this. I won't let it cause some kind of family issue. I respect your grandfather's concern, given the kind of research he was doing for people."

"He knew firsthand what could happen."

A noise in the house causes both of us to turn as I'm flattening the documents on the table. I recognize the sound of little bedtime feet on a sandy floor. I halfway expect to see one of my nieces or nephews standing in the corridor, but instead there's a three- or four-year-old towheaded boy with sleepy blue eyes and the most adorable cleft in his chin. I know where he got that.

Trent Turner has a son. Is there a Mrs. Turner sleeping back there? The strangest hint of disappointment tinges the thought a faint shade of green. I catch myself checking for a wedding ring before looking back at the little boy and thinking, *Stop that. Avery Stafford, what is wrong with you?*

It's times like this that I wonder what really *is* wrong with me. Why don't I feel like a woman who has bonded with her soulmate, forever and ever, end of story? Both of my sisters fell head over heels for their husbands and seemingly never had any second thoughts. So did my mother. So did my grandmother.

The little boy eyeballs me as he circles the table, yawning and scratching his forehead with the back of one arm. He's dramatic about it. He looks like a silent movie actress practicing an exaggerated swoon.

"Are you supposed to be in bed, Jonah?" his dad asks.

"Ya-huh."

"And you're up because . . ." Trent may be trying to sound tough, but his face has *pushover* written on it. Jonah braces both hands on his daddy's knee, lifts a leg, and begins to climb him like a jungle gym.

Trent hoists the boy up, and Jonah stretches closer to whisper, "Is a peterdactyl in my clod-et."

"A pterodactyl?"

"Ya-huh."

"Jonah, there's nothing in your closet. That's just the movie the big kids let you watch over at Aunt Lou's, remember? You've had another bad dream about it. A dinosaur wouldn't even fit in your closet. There're no dinosaurs in there."

"Ya-huh," Jonah sniffs. Clinging to handfuls of his dad's T-shirt, he swivels enough to study me over a wide-open yawn.

I shouldn't get involved. I might be just making things worse. I have, however, been through this dinosaur thing during holiday sleepovers at Drayden Hill and vacations with my sisters' kids. "My nieces and nephews had the same problem. They were scared of dinosaurs too, but do you know what we did?"

Jonah shakes his head, and Trent gives me a quizzical look, sandy-blond brows twisting together. He has a very flexible forehead.

Two identical sets of blue eyes invite my solution to the closet-dinosaur dilemma.

Fortunately, I have one. "We went to the store the next day and picked out flashlights — really awesome flashlights. If you've got a really awesome flashlight by your bed, then when you wake up at night, and you think you see something, you can turn on the light and shine it over there and check. And do you know what happens every single time when you turn on the flashlight?"

Jonah waits breathless, his little Cupid's bow mouth hanging open, but Dad clearly knows the answer. He looks like he wants to palm-thump himself in the forehead, as if to say, *Why didn't I think of this before?*

"Every single time, when you shine the flashlight, nothing's there."

"Ebry time?" Jonah's not sure.

"Always. Honest."

Jonah turns to his father for confirmation, and a sweet look of trust passes between them. This is obviously an involved dad. He slays monsters and does tuck-in time. "We'll go pick out a flashlight tomorrow at the BI-LO. Sound good?"

I notice he doesn't say, *Mom can take you*

to get a flashlight tomorrow. I also notice that he doesn't tell his son to be a big boy or insist on hustling the poor kid back to bed. He just shifts Jonah to one shoulder and lays a palm on the table, the fingers pointing toward the documents pressed beneath my hand.

Jonah pops a thumb into his mouth and snuggles against his dad's chest.

I look down at the papers, surprised that they temporarily left my mind. Jonah is irresistibly cute.

The top page is a grainy photocopy of some sort of official form. *HISTORY SHEET,* the heading reads in bold, black letters. Below, the subject has been given a number of record: *7501. AGE: inf. SEX: male.* The baby's name is listed as *Shad Arthur Foss, church relationships unknown.* The corner of the form is stamped with a date in October 1939 and was apparently filled out at a hospital in Memphis, Tennessee. *MOTHER'S NAME: Mary Anne Anthony. FATHER'S NAME: B. A. Foss.* The address for both parents is listed as *indigent, river camp.* Both the father and mother were in their late twenties when the baby was born.

The official responsible for the form, Miss Eugenia Carter, has explained the infant's situation in a few short words under clinical-sounding headings. *CAUSE FOR RELEASE TO T.C.H. SOCIETY: Born out of wedlock — unable to provide. HOW RELEASED: Surrender signed by mother and father at birth.*

"I don't recognize these names," I mutter, separating the sheet from the others and setting it quietly on the table. Granted, we have a lot of relatives, but I've never seen a Foss or an Anthony on a wedding invitation or met one at a funeral. "I can't imagine how any of this could be connected to my grandmother. This might've been around the year she was born, I guess." Grandma Judy's age changes every time you ask her. She admits to nothing and considers it gauche for anyone to inquire in the first place. "Maybe Shad Arthur Foss was someone she knew in school later? Could she have been trying to help a friend track down birth information?"

The next page is a copy of a case history sheet on Baby Boy Foss.

BIRTH DATE: September 1, 1939
BIRTH WEIGHT: premature – 4 lbs.
PRESENT WEIGHT: 6 lbs. 9 oz.
BABY: Baby arrived prematurely, weighing only four pounds at birth. He has developed normally in every way. Kahn was

negative, Wasserman and smear on mother were negative. Has had no childhood illnesses or immunizations.

MOTHER: 28 years of age, American born, of Polish-Dutch extraction. High school education, blue eyes, blond hair, about 5 ft. 6 in. tall. Weight 115 lbs. Protestant in religion. Considered very attractive and intelligent.

FATHER: 29 years of age, American born, of Scotch-Irish and Cajun-French extraction. High school education, brown eyes, black hair, about 6 ft. 1 in. tall. Weight about 175 lbs. No church affiliation.

No inheritable diseases exist on either side among the families, and despite extramarital errors of these young individuals, both maternal and paternal families are hardworking and well respected in their own communities. None have interest in custody of the children.

I pass the second document across the

table to Trent, who's looking at the first one. The third page reads:

Parent's or Guardian's
SURRENDER
To
Tennessee
Children's Home
Society

HELP A CHILD FIND A HOME IS OUR MOTTO

Baby Shad's sad story is told again in uneven type on dashed lines beside questions like *Healthy? Robust? Deformed? Crippled? Diseased? Is child ruptured? Is child feebleminded?*

Fit to be placed in a home?

Baby Shad is signed, sealed, witnessed, and delivered. He's transferred to the Memphis Receiving Home for observation and placement.

"I really haven't a clue what any of this means." But I do know there's no way my grandmother would have come here to Edisto repeatedly to meet with Trent Turner, Sr., if it weren't important. I also find it hard to believe that she would have gone this far to help a friend. She had some personal investment here. "Are there more of these packets? Did your grandfather leave anything else?"

Trent looks away as if he's trying to decide what to tell me, struggling with his conscience again. Finally, he offers, "Just a few other sealed envelopes with names on them like that one. Most of the papers Granddad was able to give to the owners before he passed on. The packets that were left he pretty much figured were for people who'd died without his knowing it."

Trent pauses to shift Jonah, who's falling asleep on his shoulder. "Some cases he kept up with for fifty and sixty years, ever since he started doing the research. How he decided which ones to take on, I don't know. I never asked him. I vaguely remember clients coming to him with pictures and sitting at the table in the little cottage outside, crying and talking, but it didn't happen all that often. He did most of his business at the office in Charleston. The only reason I ever saw any of it was that I came here to Edisto with him every chance I got. Once in a while, he'd meet with people here — for privacy, I think. I have a feeling he dealt with some pretty high-profile clients on occasion." He gives me a meaningful look, and I know he's lumping me into that category. My skin suddenly itches, and I squirm under my T-shirt.

"I'm still at a loss as to what this has to do with my grandmother. Is there anything in your grandfather's papers having to do with a woman named May Crandall . . . or maybe even someone named Fern . . . or Queenie? I think they might've been friends of my grandmother."

He rests his chin on Jonah's downy head. "The names don't sound familiar, but like I told you earlier, I didn't go back and read any of the documents after Granddad died. I locked his workshop, and I haven't been in there since." A shrug indicates the tiny cabin slumbering beneath the glow of a yard lamp. "I just took charge of the envelopes, like he asked me to. Whatever else was left out there, I assumed he didn't think was important anymore. He had a lot of respect for people's privacy, given what he went through when he found out the truth about his parents. He never wanted to take the responsibility of altering someone else's history that way. Not unless they asked for the information."

"So that means my grandmother definitely came to him?"

"Based on what I know about my grandfather's work, yes." He worries his bottom lip contemplatively. I catch myself focusing in on it, almost losing track of what he's saying. "If someone else had been looking for your grandmother — a lost relative, say — Granddad would've given them the paperwork and closed out the file once he'd found your grandmother. He always let his clients make the final decisions about getting in touch. The fact that he hadn't closed this file and that he'd left it marked *Judy Stafford* means that your grandmother was looking for someone . . . a person he wasn't ever able to find."

My mind is in hyperdrive now, despite the late hour. "Is there any way I could see the rest of it?" I know how bold it is to request this now, but I'm afraid Trent may change his mind once he's had time to think about things. A lesson from trial law. If you need your witness to switch tracks, ask for a recess. If not, keep driving hard toward whatever you're after.

"Believe me, you don't want to go out there at night. That building is an old slave cabin that was moved onto the property, so it's not exactly sealed up tight. There's no telling what might be living in there at this point."

"I grew up in horse barns. I'm not afraid of much."

His mouth quirks, bringing out a dimple. "Why does that not surprise me?" He shifts Jonah on his shoulder again. "Let me tuck him back in bed."

Our gazes tangle, and for a moment, we're just . . . looking at each other. Maybe it's the dim lighting from the vintage fixtures or the quiet intimacy of the cottage, but I feel something I don't want to feel. It winds through me, languid and warm, noticeable like a tide pool on a summer evening after the air has cooled.

I swirl a toe in the waters, laugh softly, feel myself blush and look down, then steal another glance at Trent. The other side of his mouth curves upward into a smile, and a strange sensation travels all the way to my toes. It's like lightning crackling far off over the water — something unpredictable and dangerous.

It stuns me for an instant, and I forget where I am and why I came here.

Jonah's head rolls off his dad's shoulder, and the spell is broken. I awaken from it like an early-day medical patient coming out of an ether sleep. My mind dawdles. My wits take a moment to line up properly and force me to look away. Somewhere in the process, I glance past my ring finger where, right now, my engagement ring is missing because, before my evening took such a wild track, I removed it so I wouldn't get lotion on it after my shower.

What is going *on*? I've never had something like this happen to me. Ever. I don't do mental lapses. I'm not easily taken in by people. I don't behave improperly with strangers. The paramount importance of *not* doing those things has been impressed upon me since birth, and law school was a good reinforcement.

"I should go." As if on cue, the cellphone in my pocket vibrates, the real world breaking in. My chair squeals as I push back. The sound seems to stop Trent unexpectedly. Was he really thinking of letting me into the workshop tonight? Or was he thinking of something . . . more intimate?

I ignore the phone and thank him for giving me the envelope, then add, "Maybe we could meet tomorrow?" *In the bright, clear light of day.* "Look at whatever else is left?" I'm taking a risk either way I play this. By tomorrow, Trent may have rethought everything. But here, tonight, there are risks of a different kind. "I've imposed on you way too long. It was incredibly rude of me to call this late. I'm sorry . . . I've just been so . . . desperate to figure things out."

He stifles a yawn, blinks, and forces his

eyelids upward. "It's not a problem. I'm a night owl."

"I can tell," I joke, and a laugh escapes him.

"Tomorrow." He speaks the word like a promise. "It'll have to be after work. I've got a full day. I'll see if Aunt Lou can keep Jonah a couple extra hours."

The commitment is a relief. I just hope he feels the same way after he thinks about this. "I'll see you in the evening then. Just let me know what time. Oh, and don't leave Jonah at his aunt's on my account. I have triplet two-year-old nephews. I love little boys." Gathering Grandma Judy's papers and my flashlight, I take a step toward the door, then stop, looking for a pencil and something to write on. "I should give you my phone number."

"I have it." He pulls a face. "On my cellphone about . . . two hundred times."

That should be embarrassing, but instead we laugh together. He turns toward the hallway. "Let me put Jonah down, and I'll walk you out to the beach and watch you till you get home."

My head says *no,* but I have to force myself to form the words. "It's okay. I know the way." Outside the window, the night is alive with moonglow, the water glistening through the palms around the cottage's backyard. Confederate rose and jasmine stir in the sea breeze. It's a perfect combination. The kind only the Lowcountry can create.

He casts a look my way. "It is the middle of the night. Let me be a gentleman about it at least."

I wait while he puts Jonah to bed; then we cross the back porch together and descend the steps. The breeze off the water catches my hair, swirling it into the air, skimming my skin and slipping down my T-shirt. At the bottom of the stairs, I glance at the small slave cabin, study the old wood-paned windows, six of them, that run all the way across the front porch. Are answers hiding behind the salt-hazed glass?

"It dates from around 1850." Trent seems to be fishing for conversation. Maybe we both feel the awkward pressure of a setting that begs for something more than casual chatter. "Granddad moved it here himself when he purchased the property. He originally used it as an office. This tract was his first real estate deal. He bought the acreage adjacent to the Myers cottage and divided it for this house and the two between."

Another connection between Trent Turner, Sr., and my grandmother. Obviously, they knew each other a long time. Did she enlist him to help her look for someone because she knew he dabbled in such things? Or did his dabbling lead him to my grandmother? Did she suggest that he buy the property next to the cottage? Is the current Trent Turner really as much in the dark about these family connections as I am? Has one generation lived intricately intertwined lives that were, for whatever reason, hidden from the next?

The questions tie my brain in knots as we stop at the beach path, where sea oats glisten like strings of spun glass in the moonlight. "Nice night," he says.

"Yes, it is."

"Watch out. Tide's coming up. You'll get your feet wet." He nods toward the sea, and I can't help but look. A trail of glistening waves leads to the moon, and a starry carpet glows impossibly bright overhead. How long since I've just sat in the dark and enjoyed a night like this? Suddenly, I'm so very hungry for it. I'm hungry for water and sky and days that aren't divided by the tiny squares in an appointment book.

Did my grandmother feel this way? Was that the reason she came here so often?

"Thanks again . . . for letting me interrupt your evening." I take a backward step from grass to sand. Something scuttles past my foot, and I squeal.

"Better turn on the flashlight."

The last thing I see before surrounding myself with a sphere of artificial illumination is Trent grinning at me.

I turn and walk away, knowing he is watching.

My phone buzzes again, and when I pull it from my pocket, it's like a gateway to another world. I'm quick to step through. I need something familiar and safe to focus on after that strange moment on the beach with Trent.

But Abby? From the office in Baltimore? Why would she be calling me in the wee hours of the morning?

When I answer, she's breathless. "Avery, there you are. Is everything all right? I got this crazy email from you a while ago."

I laugh. "Oh, Abby, I'm sorry. I meant to send that to myself."

"You have to tell *yourself* where you're going now? *That's* what the posh life in South Carolina has done to you?" Abby is a no-nonsense D.C. girl, an achiever who pulled herself up from public housing to a law degree. She's also a fabulous federal prosecutor. I miss having lunch with her and putting our heads together about ongoing cases.

If there's anyone I could trust with the information about Grandma Judy, it would be Abby, but it's safer to catch up on things at the office, so I do that instead. "Long story. So why are you awake at this hour?"

"Working. Discovery tomorrow. Laundering and mail fraud. Major case. They've hired Bracken and Thompson."

"Ohhh . . . big guns." The legal chatter brings me squarely back home to Baltimore. Whatever nonsense came over me at Trent's house is quickly eclipsed, and I'm glad because I need it to be. "Tell me what's happening." My senses heighten in a way that has nothing to do with the night or a glance over my shoulder that finds Trent still watching me.

Abby launches into the details of the investigation, and my mind homes in. I'm struck by one undeniable fact.

I miss my old life.

Chapter 16

Rill

"Rise and shine. Looks like finally some sun today!" Miss Dodd says as she unlocks the door to the basement room. Miss Dodd is new here, since two days ago. She's younger than the others, and nicer too. If I can get her alone, I plan to ask after Camellia. Nobody will tell me where my sister is. Mrs. Pulnik said to shut my yap about it and stop bothering the workers.

Danny Boy says Camellia's dead. He says he woke up and heard Mrs. Murphy telling Riggs that Camellia died after they put her in the closet and what to do about it. Danny Boy says Riggs carried her body out to the truck to go dump it in the swamp. He saw the whole thing with his own two eyes. He says my sister's gone, and good riddance.

I don't believe a word that comes out of Danny Boy. He's hateful clean through to the bone.

Miss Dodd will tell me the truth.

Right now, she's more worried about the stink in the room. It's moldy and drippy down here when it rains, and on top of that, Fern's been wetting the bed every night since they took away Camellia and Gabion. I tell Fern not to, but it doesn't help.

"Mercy, that smell!" Miss Dodd gives us a worried look. "This ain't a fit place for children."

I move between her and the wet cot. I've piled it with covers because that's all I can figure out to do to hide it. "I . . . I spilled the slop pot."

She looks at the corner. The cement is dry under the pot. "Did somebody have an accident in the bed?"

Tears pop into my eyes, and Lark backs away toward the corner, taking Fern with her. I grab Miss Dodd's apron and duck my head away at the same time because I'm expecting a smack. Even so, I've got to keep her from going upstairs to get Mrs. Pulnik. "Don't tell."

Miss Dodd's brown eyelashes flutter over soft gray-green eyes. "Why in the name a' Saint Francis not? We'll just wipe up the mess, and it'll be all right."

"Fern will get in trouble." I guess Miss Dodd doesn't know yet what happens to kids who wet the bed around here.

"Oh, heaven's sake. No she won't."

"Please . . ." Panic runs inside me like a flood tide. "Please don't tell." I can't lose Fern and Lark. I don't know for sure what's happened to Camellia, and after four days, I figure those people won't be giving Gabby back either. I've lost my brother. Camellia's gone. Lark and Fern are all I've got left.

Miss Dodd puts her hands on either side of my face and holds me real gentle. "Ssshhh. Hush up, now. I'll see it's took care of. Don't you fret, little pea. We'll keep it just 'tween us."

My tears just come harder. Nobody's held me this way since Queenie.

"Quieten down, now." Miss Dodd looks over her shoulder nervous-like. "We best get upstairs before they come lookin' for us."

I nod and choke out "Yes'm." It'd be the worst thing if I got Miss Dodd in trouble. I heard her tell one of the kitchen women that her daddy died last year and her mama's sick with the dropsy and she's got four little brothers and sisters living on a farm up in north Shelby County. Miss Dodd walked and hitched rides to Memphis to find work so's she could send the money home.

Miss Dodd needs this job.

We need Miss Dodd.

I get Fern and Lark together, and we march through the door ahead of Miss Dodd. Riggs is hanging around by the boiler, nosy as a kitchen-door dog. Like always, I keep my head down and watch him from the corner of my eye.

"Mr. Riggs," Miss Dodd says just before we get to the stairs, "I'm wonderin' if you could do me a favor? Ain't no need in tell-in' nobody about it."

"Why, yes'm."

Before I can stop her, she asks, "You think you might could mix up some Clorox and water and rub it over the cot that's settin' there by the door? Just leave me the bucket when you're done. I'll wash up the rest af-terwhile."

"Yes'm. I'll d-do it for ya. I sure will." His crooked teeth poke out of his smile, long and yellow like a beaver's. "Reckon these kids'll b-be movin' up-upstairs soon." He waves at us with the handle of his shovel.

"The sooner the better." Miss Dodd doesn't know how wrong she is. Once we get upstairs, there won't *be* a locked door between us and Riggs. "A room in the base-ment ain't right for young'uns."

"No'm."

"And if the house caught fire, they could wind up trapped."

"If there's a f-fire, I'd b-b-bust down that door. I w-would."

"You're a good man, Mr. Riggs."

Miss Dodd don't know the truth about Mr. Riggs. She just don't.

"Th-thanks, ma'am."

"And no need in tellin' nobody about the cleanin'," she reminds him. "It'll be our secret."

Riggs just smiles and watches us, his eyes white around the edges and winter-bear crazy. You see a bear moving in the winter, you better look out. He's hungry and he aims to find something to fill that hunger. He won't care much what it is.

Riggs's look stays with me through breakfast and even later in the day when the yard's finally dry enough for us to go outside. Crossing the porch, I look down at the corner and think about Camellia and wonder, *Could Danny Boy be telling it true? Could my sister be dead?*

It'd be my fault. I'm the oldest. I was supposed to look after everybody. That was the last thing Briny told me before he hurried off across the river. *You watch over the babies, Rill. Keep care of everybody, till we get back.*

Even the name sounds strange in my mind now. People keep calling me May. Maybe

Rill's still on the river someplace with Camellia, and Lark, and Fern, and Gabion. Maybe they're drifting down in the lazy low-water summer currents, watching boats pass and barges go by and Cooper's hawks circle wide and slow, hunting for fish to dive after.

Maybe Rill is only a story I read, like Huck Finn and Jim. Maybe I'm not even Rill and never was.

I turn and run down the steps and across the yard, my dress sweeping up around my legs. I stretch out my arms and throw back my head and make my own breeze, and for a minute, I find Rill again. I'm her. I'm on the *Arcadia,* our little piece of heaven.

I don't stop when I get to the gate where the big boys have their tunnel. They're busy pestering two new kids who came in during the rain yesterday. Brothers, I think. I don't care anyway. If Danny Boy tried to stop me, I'd make a fist and knock him flat, same as Camellia would. I'd knock him on his back right next to the fence and use him to climb up over it and get free.

I wouldn't stop running until I got all the way to the riverbank.

I circle the old outhouse still going as hard as I can and take a running leap against the iron bars, trying to get high enough to shinny on over, but I can't. I only make it a few feet before I slide down and hit hard. I grab the bars and pull and scream and howl like a wild thing fighting a cage.

I keep on until the bars are slick with sweat and tears and tinted with blood. The bars don't give in to it. They don't move at all. They just hold as I sink to the ground and let the tears take over.

Somewhere outside my own noise, I hear Danny Boy say, "Pretty girl done gone round the bend, she did."

I hear Fern and Stevie wailing and Fern calling my name and the big boys teasing them and pushing them down every time they try to get through the gate. I need to go. I need to help them, but more than anything, I just want to disappear. I want to be alone in a place where nobody can find me. Where nobody I love can be stolen away.

Danny Boy twists Stevie's arm around behind his back and makes him say "uncle," then keeps on until Stevie's scream stabs me deep down in the belly. It hits the place I want to make hard as stone. Like Arthur's sword, Stevie's scream pierces in.

Before I can even think what I'm doing, I'm back across the churchyard, and I've got Danny Boy by the hair. "You let him go!" I yank hard, and Danny Boy's head pops back. "You let him go, and don't you *ever* touch him again. I'll snap your neck like a chicken's. I *will.*" Without Camellia here to do our fighting, all of a sudden, I'm her. "I'll snap your neck and dump *you* in the swamp."

One of the other boys turns Fern loose and backs away. He stares at me, white eyed. From the looks of my shadow, I can see why. There's hair flying all directions. I look like Medusa from the Greek stories.

"It's a fight! It's a fight!" kids yell, and come running to watch.

Danny Boy lets go of Stevie. He doesn't want to get whipped in front of everybody. Stevie tumbles face-first into the dirt and comes up with a mouthful. He spits and cries, and I shove Danny Boy away and grab Stevie's hand and Fern's. We've gotten over to the hill before I even notice who's missing.

My heart hitches. "Where's Lark?"

Fern puts a fist in her mouth like she's afraid she'll be in trouble. Maybe she's scared of me after what she just saw.

"Where's *Lark*?"

"Waydee." Stevie babbles out the first word I've heard him say since the day we came here. "Waydee."

I kneel down in the wet grass, look them both square in the face. "What lady? *What* lady, Fern?"

"The lady got 'er on the porch," Fern whispers through her fingers. Her eyes rim with tears. "Like this." She grabs Stevie by the arm and lifts up, dragging him along a few steps. Stevie nods to tell me that's what he saw too.

"A lady? Not Riggs? Riggs didn't get her?"

Both of them shake their heads. "Waydee," Stevie says.

My head is still cloudy with dried-up tears and leftover hate. Did Lark get in trouble? Was she sick? She couldn't be. When we came to breakfast, she was just like always. They don't take kids to the sickroom unless they're burning with fever or throwing up.

I point Fern and Stevie to the playground. "You two, go. You go over there on the teeter-totter, and you don't get off no matter what, unless I come get you or you hear the bell. You understand?"

Both of them look scared to death, but they nod and link hands. I watch them walk over to the teeter-totter, then I head for the house. On the way past the gate, I let Danny Boy know that if he bothers them, he'll have me to reckon with.

My courage comes and goes on the way across the yard. I keep looking at the house hoping I'll spot Miss Dodd. A hammer pounds in my ears when I tiptoe over the porch and head into the washroom. Depending who sees me here, I could get in bad trouble. Somebody might think I'm trying to steal food.

The colored women are at the washer and the ringer when I go by. Do they know what happened to Lark? Would they tell me if they did? Usually we pass like people who're better off not seeing each other.

They don't look up, and I don't ask. Nobody's in the kitchen, and I hurry through so I won't get caught in there.

The swinging door groans low when I poke my head into Mrs. Murphy's front hall. It's almost too late that I hear her voice and see that her office door is open.

"I think you'll find her delightful." Miss Tann is in the room too. Her voice is sticky sweet, so I know she's talking to someone besides Mrs. Murphy. "Perfect in every way. The mother had a start on a college education before the Depression. Very intelligent young woman and considered quite beautiful. Clearly, it's an inherited trait. This little one is a regular Shirley Temple, and she won't even need a permanent wave. She is a bit quiet but very well behaved and mild mannered. She won't be any trouble to you in public situations, which I know is so important in your line of work. I do wish you'd allowed us to bring her to you there. It isn't our normal procedure to have new parents come to our boarding homes."

"I appreciate your making accommodations." The man's voice is deep. He sounds like an army commander. "It's difficult for us to go anywhere without being recognized."

"We completely understand." I've never heard Mrs. Murphy sound so friendly. "What an honor to have you visiting. Right here in my own home!"

"You've chosen one of our best." Miss Tann comes closer to the door. "And you will be the best, won't you, Bonnie? You'll do everything your new mommy and daddy ask of you. You're a lucky little girl. And you're very grateful for that, aren't you?"

Bonnie is Lark's new name.

I try to hear if Lark answers, but I can't tell.

"Then I suppose we must let you go, though we will miss you dearly," Miss Tann says.

A man and a woman step into the hall, bringing Lark with them. The man is handsome, like a prince in a book of fairy stories. The woman is beautiful, with fancy hair and pretty lipstick. Lark is wearing a frilly white dress. She looks like a tiny ballerina.

Air goes solid in my throat. I push the kitchen door open wide. *You have to stop them,* I tell myself. *You have to make them see that Lark is yours and they can't have her.*

A hand grabs my arm and pulls me back, and the door swings shut with a slap. I stumble and stagger as someone drags me across the kitchen and through the washroom to the porch. I don't even know who's got me until Miss Dodd spins me around and stands me up, holding both of my shoulders.

"You ain't supposed to be in there, May!" Her eyes are wide, her skin washed white. She looks almost as afraid as I feel. "You *know* what the rules are. You bother Mrs. Murphy and Miss Tann, there'll be the devil to pay."

The ball in my throat breaks like a fresh hen egg. It drips down, sticky and hot and thick. "M-my sister . . ."

Miss Dodd holds my face. "I know, darlin', but you've gotta think what's best for her. She's gettin' a mama and daddy that're movie stars." She pulls in a breath like she's just won a prize at the carnival fair. "I know you'll be sad awhile, but it's the best anybody could hope for. Brand-new parents and a brand-new home. A whole new life."

"We've got a mama and daddy!"

"Hush! Hush, now." Miss Dodd starts to drag me down the porch, away from the door. I try to pull free, but she won't let me. "Hush. You can't start carryin' on. I know you wish your mama and daddy could come back after you, but they ain't able. They signed you over to the Tennessee Children's Home Society. Y'all are orphans now."

"We're not!" I wail. I can't help myself. I babble out the truth — all about the *Arcadia,* and Queenie, and Briny, and my brother and sisters. I tell about Camellia and the closet, and the workers saying different stories of what happened to her, and Danny Boy telling me she got dumped in the swamp.

Miss Dodd's chin drops and just hangs there. She holds me by the shoulders so tight my skin twists and burns. "Is all that the God's honest truth?" she asks when I run out of words.

I squeeze my eyes shut, nod, and swallow tears and snot.

"Ssshhh," she whispers, and hugs me close. "Don't say nothin' more now. Not to nobody. You go on out with the other kids. Be good and keep quiet. I'll see what I can learn about it all."

When she lets me go, I grab her hand. "Don't tell Mrs. Murphy. She'll take Fern away from me. Fern's all I got."

"I won't tell. I won't leave you either. I'll find out what happened to your sister. God be my witness, we'll make this right, but you gotta stay real strong." She stares into my eyes, and there's fire in her. The fire's a comfort, but I know what I've just asked her to do. If Mrs. Murphy can make Camellia disappear, she can get to Miss Dodd too.

"D-don't let them c-catch you, Miss Dodd."

"I'm a sharper knife than folks think I am." She shoos me toward the yard, and just like that, we've got a friend here. Finally somebody's listening to our story.

That night, Fern cries and carries on forever, asking for Lark. I even try reading her some of the book, but she won't hush, and I finally can't stand it. I grab her and squeeze her arms hard and pick her up and stick my face in hers.

"Stop it!" My voice echoes around the tiny room. "Stop it, you *stupid*! She's *gone*! It's *not* my *fault*! Stop it, or you're gonna get a *spanking.*" I lift up my hand, and it's only after my sister's eyes blink, blink, blink that

I see what I'm doing.

I drop her on the cot and turn away and grab my hair and pull until it hurts. I want to pull all of it out. Every single piece. I want a pain I understand instead of the one I don't. I want a pain that has a beginning and an end, not one that goes on forever and cuts all the way to the bone.

This pain is changing me into a girl I don't even know.

It's changing me into *them.* I see it in my sister's face. That hurts worst of all.

I fall on the cot that Miss Dodd got all washed and cleaned for us. It smells like Clorox now. Three peppermints roll out from under the dirty pillow, and I throw them at the slop pot.

Fern comes and sits beside me and pats me on the back the way a mama would do to quiet a baby. The day, and this place, and everything that's happened here goes through my mind. I see it like a motion-picture show, the kind we watch for five cents when the carnivals come through the river towns and shine their projectors on the side of a building or a barn. But the show in my mind is wavy, and blurry, and running too fast.

Finally I sink farther, and everything goes dark and quiet.

In the middle of the night, I wake up, and Fern's snuggled in beside me. There's a blanket over both of us. It's twisted and wadded funny, so I know that Fern must've put it there.

I clutch her and dream about the *Arcadia* then, and it's a good dream. We're all together again, and the day is so sweet, it's like the drops of syrup from a honeysuckle vine. I stick out my tongue and taste and taste.

I lose myself in the smell of woodsmoke and morning fog so thick it cloaks the opposite bank and turns the river into a sea. I run along the sandbars with my sisters, and hide in the grass, and wait for them to come find me. Their voices weave soft through the mist, so that I can't tell how close or far they are.

On the *Arcadia,* Queenie sings a song. I sit stone still in the grass and listen to my mama's voice.

When the blackbird in the spring,
On the willow tree,
Sat and rocked, I heard him sing,
Singing, Aura Lee,
Aura Lee, Aura Lee,
Maid with golden hair,
Sunshine came along with thee. . . .

I'm so lost in her song, I don't even hear the basement door unlocking until the knob's turning. I jump up and see it's morning already. Little strings of sun squeeze through the azaleas and slant across the room.

In the corner, Fern's getting off the slop pot and pulling up her drawers. After last night, maybe she's too scared to wet the bed again.

"Good girl," I whisper, and hurry to straighten the cot.

"No need in *that. You're* not going *anywhere* today." The voice from the doorway isn't Miss Dodd's. It's Mrs. Murphy's. It hits me like a whip, crackling all through my body. She's never come down here before.

"How *dare* you!" Her mouth tightens so that her cheekbones poke out. Air hisses through her crooked front teeth. In three quick steps, she's got me by the hair. "How *dare* you use my hospitality, my *kindness,* to tell tales against me! Did you think that little hillbilly, that little know-nothing, would really be of help to you? Oh, of course she was foolish enough to believe your *lies.* But all you've done is cost her a job, and Miss Tann will be picking up the little Dodd brothers and sisters soon enough. They've been reported to the Shelby County Welfare, and their paperwork is being processed even now. Is *that* what you *wanted*? Is *that* what you had in *mind* when you filled her ear with lurid tales about poor Mr. Riggs? My own *cousin,* no less! *My cousin,* who cleans the mess you bloodsucking nits leave in the yard, and fixes your toys, and sees to the boiler so the *little precious ones* won't catch *sniffles* on cold nights!" She turns a hateful smirk toward Fern, who's pushed herself as far as she can into the corner.

"I . . . I . . . I didn't . . ." What can I do? Where can I go? I could try to get away and run out the door, but she's got Fern trapped.

"Don't bother denying it. *Shame.* Shame on *you.* Shame on you for your lies. I've provided you with so much more than *river lice* like you deserve. Well, let's see how you feel after you have some time alone to consider the error of your ways." She pushes me down hard, and I fall backward over the cot. Before I can get up, she's grabbed Fern.

My sister screeches and tries to reach for me.

"Don't!" I shout, scrambling to my feet. "You're hurting her!"

"You're lucky I don't do worse. Perhaps

we should make her pay for your crimes?" Mrs. Murphy shoves me out of the way as she passes by. "Give me any more trouble, and we *will.*"

I want to fight, but I don't let myself. I know that if I do, I'll only be hurting Fern. "Be good," I tell my little sister. "Be a good girl."

The last thing I see is her feet sliding across a spill of coal dust as Mrs. Murphy drags her out the door. The lock turns, and I listen to Fern's cries getting farther and farther away. Finally, they're gone altogether.

I fall on the cot and grab the blanket that still holds the warm spots from Fern and me and cry until there's not a tear left and all I can do is stare at the ceiling.

I wait all day, but nobody comes back for me. I open the cellar window and hear the kids playing outside. The sun goes high, then works its way west. Eventually, there's the dinner bell.

After a while, the ceiling timbers rattle as everyone marches upstairs for bed.

I'm hungry and thirsty, but mostly I just want Fern. They won't make her sleep someplace else, will they? Because of what *I* said?

But they do.

After the house goes quiet, I lay down again. My stomach growls and hurts like a rat's been chewing at it from the inside. My throat feels like someone's scratched it raw.

I sleep, and wake, and sleep, and wake.

In the morning, Mrs. Pulnik comes and brings me a pail of water and a ladle. "Drink only small portions. You will be seeingk no one for some time. You will be on restrictions."

It's three more days before she brings food. I'm so hungry, I've started eating the peppermints Riggs slips under the door, even though I hate myself for it.

One day runs into the next, and the next, and the next. I read all the way through to the end of *Huckleberry Finn,* where Huck decides he'd rather run off to Indian Territory than be adopted.

I close my eyes and pretend I'm running off to Indian Territory too. I have a big, pretty red horse, with white socks and a blaze, like Tony the Wonder Horse and Tom Mix. My horse is faster than anything, and we just run, and run, and run.

I start the book over again, and I'm back in Missouri on the shores of the big river. I travel along on Huckleberry Finn's raft to pass the days.

At night, when the branches blow around,

I watch out the window, looking for Zede, or Silas, or Briny under the streetlamp. Once when it's windy, I see them standing there. A woman is with them. She's too stout to be Queenie. I think it's Miss Dodd.

Just as quick as they're there, they're gone again. I wonder if maybe I'm going soft in the head.

Mrs. Pulnik comes and takes my book away and tells me I got Mrs. Murphy in trouble with the bookmobile ladies. She calls me a thief and smacks me hard across the face for not reminding her that I still had the library's property.

I'm not sure how I'll get by without *Huckleberry Finn.*

I worry about Fern and how she's making out upstairs all on her own.

Days and days and days pass by. I lose count of how many, but it's a long time before Mrs. Pulnik finally takes me out of the room and brings me up to Mrs. Murphy's office. I stink almost as bad as the slop pot, and my hair's knotted in a big, dirty wad. The light upstairs is so bright, I stumble around and bump into things and have to feel my way.

Mrs. Murphy is just a blurry shadow behind the desk. I squint to see her better, and then I realize it's not Mrs. Murphy. It's

Miss Tann. Mrs. Murphy is standing behind her by the window.

Mrs. Pulnik shoves me forward. My legs buckle, and I fall hard on my knees. Mrs. Pulnik grabs a handful of dress and hair and holds me there.

Miss Tann stands up and leans over the desk. "I think that is *exactly* where you belong. On your knees, begging forgiveness for all the trouble you've caused. For all the *lies* you've told about poor Mrs. Murphy. You are a wretched, ungrateful little thing, aren't you?"

"Y-yes'm," I squeak out in a whisper. I'd say almost anything to get out of that room.

Mrs. Murphy rams her fists into her hips. "Telling lies about my cousin. Lurid, horrible little . . ."

"Tssst!" Miss Tann lifts a hand, and Mrs. Murphy clamps her mouth shut. "Oh, I think May *knows* what she's done. I think she was just looking for attention. Is that the problem with you, May? Are you looking for attention?"

I don't know what to say, so I kneel there with my guts trembling and my chin quivering. Mrs. Pulnik shoves me harder into the floor. Pain shoots down from the roots of my hair and up from my knees. Tears build inside me, but I can't let them show.

"Answer me!" Miss Tann's voice fills the room like a thunderclap. She limps around the desk and stands over me with her finger wagging in my face. Her eyes are the cold gray of a winter storm.

"Y-yes'm . . . n-n-no'm."

"Well, which *is* it?"

I open my mouth, but nothing comes out.

Her fingers close around my chin. She stretches my neck and leans close. I smell talcum powder and sour breath. "Not so talkative now, are we? Perhaps you've seen the error of your ways?"

I manage a tiny nod.

A smile pinches her mouth, and her eyes take on a hungry shine, like she can feel the fear in me and she likes it. "Perhaps you should have thought of *that* before you invented some ridiculous story about your fictitious sister and poor Mr. Riggs."

Blood pounds in my head. I try to make sense of what she's saying, but I can't.

"There never was any . . . *Camellia.* You and I both know that, don't we, May? There were *four* of you when you came here. Two little sisters and one little brother. *Only* four. And we've done a marvelous job in finding homes, thus far. Good homes. And for that, you are *most* grateful, aren't you?" She motions to Mrs. Pulnik. The weight lifts off my shoulders. Miss Tann pulls me up by my chin until I'm standing there in front of her. "There will be no more of this nonsense out of you. Do you understand?"

I nod and hate myself at the same time. It's wrong. Everything I told Miss Dodd was true. But I can't go back in the basement. I have to find Fern and make sure they haven't hurt her. Fern's all I've got left.

"Good." Miss Tann lets me go and folds her hands one over the other and rocks back on her heels, her dress swaying around her knees.

Mrs. Murphy laughs under her breath. "Well, the little guttersnipes *do* have brains in their empty heads after all."

Miss Tann's lips curve upward, but it's the kind of smile that makes you cold when you look at it. "Even the most unwilling can be taught. It's only a matter of what means are needed to properly impart the lesson." She squints, looking me over from head to toe before the clock on the fireplace mantel chimes and grabs her attention. "I really must be on about my business." She brushes past, leaving her powdery scent in the room. I try not to breathe it in, but it sticks in my nose.

Mrs. Murphy sits down at her desk and picks up some papers like she's forgotten

I'm there. "From now on, you will be *grateful* for my hospitality."

"Y-yes'm. C-could I see Fern now?" It's all I can do to make myself ask, but I have to. "M-Mrs. Murphy?"

She doesn't look up. "Your sister is gone. She's been adopted. You'll never see her again. You may go outside for playtime with the other children now." Sorting through the papers, she picks up a pen. "Mrs. Pulnik, please be certain that May has a bath before you move her upstairs to her new bed tonight. I can't bear the smell of her."

"I will see that this is accomplishedt."

Mrs. Pulnik wraps a hand around my arm, but I hardly even feel it. When she leaves me outside, I just sit for a long time on the porch steps. The other kids wander by and look at me like I'm an animal from the zoo.

I don't pay them any mind.

Stevie comes and tries to crawl into my lap, and I can't even stand to have him close. It makes me think of Fern.

"Go on and play with the trucks," I tell him, then walk off across the yard, all the way to the fence behind the church house, and crawl up under a nest of wild grapevines to hide.

I look through the leaves at the bedroom windows where the girls sleep and I wonder,

If I jump from one tonight, will I die?

I can't live without Fern. We've been joined at the heart since she was born.

Now my heart's gone.

I lay my head down and feel the pinpoints of sun on my neck, and let sleep come over me, and hope I won't wake up.

When I do, someone's touching my arm. I jerk away and wobble into a squat, thinking it's Riggs. But the face that looks back at me makes me believe I'm still in a dream.

I must be.

"Silas?"

He puts a finger to his lips. "Sssshhhh," he whispers.

I reach through the bars, my hands shaking and stretching. I have to see if he's real.

His fingers close over mine. He holds tight. "We found where you was, finally," he says. "A lady at the hospital got your mama and daddy to sign some papers right after the babies came. They told your daddy if he'd sign it all, he could get Queenie's doctor bill paid for and the babies would be buried proper. But that ain't what the papers was for at all. It let them come and take you off the *Arcadia.* When Briny and Zede went to the police, they said Briny had signed y'all over to the Tennessee Children's Home Society — there was nothin' to be done about it, and that's that. We been hunting y'all for weeks. That lady, Miss Dodd, she finally found us and told us where y'all was. I been comin' here and watchin' this place every chance I get, hopin' to see that you's still here."

"They've been keeping me inside. I got in trouble." I look around in the vines. I still can't believe what's happening. I must be making it up in my head. "Where's Queenie and Briny?"

"Takin' care of the *Arcadia.* Getting her ready to set off on the river again. She's been tied up a long time."

I sag against the bars. My skin goes hot and red. Sweat runs under the ragged nighty I've been wearing for weeks now. What'll Briny think of me when he knows the truth? "They took everybody. They took everybody but me. I couldn't do what Briny said. I couldn't keep us together."

"It's all right," Silas whispers. He strokes my hair while I cry, his fingers tangling in the mess. "I'm gonna get you out. I'm gonna come tonight and cut through one of the bars . . . over there under the holly berries where the brush is good and thick. Can you come out here tonight? Can you sneak off?"

I hiccup and sniff and nod. If James could

get down to the kitchen to steal food, I can get to the kitchen too. If I can get to the kitchen, I can get to the churchyard.

Silas studies the fence. "You gimme a little while. A couple hours after it's full dark to slip in here and cut that bar. Then you come. The less time they've got to miss you, the better."

We make the plan, and then he tells me he better go before anybody sees him. It's all I can do to let loose of him and crawl out from under the vines and walk away.

It's only a few more hours, I tell myself. *Just the rest of the day, then supper and one more bath, and I'll be home. Back home on the* Arcadia.

But when I start across the yard, I see Stevie looking for me, and I think, *What about him?*

Danny Boy comes out to rough Stevie up at the churchyard gate.

"You leave him be." I close the space between us and stand over Danny Boy. I think I got taller while I was in the basement. Thinner for sure. The fist I wave in Danny Boy's face looks so bony it could be sticking up out of a grave.

"I ain't gonna fight ya. Ya stink too much." Danny Boy swallows hard. Maybe he figures, if I made it for weeks downstairs, I'm too tough to tangle with. Maybe he's afraid, if he gets in a wrangle, they'll do the same thing to him.

He doesn't give me or Stevie any trouble all the rest of the day.

When we line up to go in for the evening, I take the front spot for Stevie and me. Danny Boy doesn't like it, but he hasn't got the guts to stop me. He settles for making fun of my hair and how I smell. "Heard they're bringin' your stupid little sister back tomorrow," he says behind my back when we go in. "Heard them people don't want her after all, 'cause she's too dumb not to wet the bed."

It's probably just more of his lies, but a little hope sparks fires anyway. I don't stamp it out. Instead, I give it tinder and breathe on it real soft. After supper, I get up my guts to ask one of the workers if it's true that Fern's coming back. She tells me it is. In the whole time she's been gone, Fern hasn't stopped carrying on and asking for me and wetting herself.

"It looks like bullheadedness runs in the family," the worker says. "Shame. She may never find a home now."

I try not to look happy about it, but I am. Once Fern's back, we can both get away, but I'll need to make Silas wait another day.

Tonight, I'll sneak outside and tell him.

I just have to figure out how to do it without the workers catching me. They might be watching me close since it's my first time to stay upstairs. But it's not the workers I'm most worried about; it's Riggs. He must know where I'll be sleeping tonight too.

And he knows there's no lock on the door.

Chapter 17

Avery

If you have to kill time, Edisto Island isn't a bad place to do it.

The breeze off the water sifts through the screens and teases the hem of the simple wrap dress I've slipped on after whiling away the day. I forgot to grab my cellphone charger before leaving home. Now the battery is at half-mast, and there's not a compatible charger available anywhere on the island. Rather than answering email or scouring the Internet for anything pertaining to last night's revelations, I've been forced to entertain myself the old-fashioned way.

Kayaking the ACE Basin was worth a second barely lukewarm shower and getting a pair of shorts permanently stained by the blackish mix of mildew and pluff mud from the seat of the rental kayak. I feel as if I've rediscovered my childhood self.

The paddle trip brought back long-lost memories of a sixth-grade excursion to Edisto with my dad. I'd been working on a science-fair project about the black-water ecosystems in the Lowcountry. Being the driven little perfectionist that I was, I'd wanted to collect my own samples and take my own photographs rather than just pulling things from books. My dad had obliged. Our overnight visit here yielded one of our few exclusive father-daughter moments that wasn't tied to a horse show or a press op. The memory is still golden, even all these years later.

I also remember that it was Elliot who helped me put together the massive backdrop for my exhibit. We'd salvaged the parts from a closet full of old campaign materials, then painted over the signs and argued at length over how to make the huge pieces of cardboard stand up on their own. Neither of us was very handy with tools.

I don't know why you didn't just buy something, he'd complained after our second epic failure. By then, it was late at night and we were still in my father's horse barn, up to our elbows in paint smears and poorly nailed lumber.

Because I want to put it in my paper that the exhibit was built from recycled materials. I want to be able to say I made it myself.

I don't see what the difference is. . . .

The rest of the argument has been, quite fortunately, lost to the sands of time. I do remember that it got loud enough for Dad's stable manager to venture in with a set of heavy wooden standards used for horse jumps. He added a big box of zip ties and some duct tape. Elliot and I took it from there.

The science-fair memory makes me laugh. I glance at my watch thinking I'll call Elliot and share, but I don't want to be tied up on the phone when the call from Trent Turner comes in. Worry creeps up as I think about the time. It's after five, and I haven't heard from him. Maybe he's working late this evening?

Maybe he's changed his mind about letting me see the rest of his grandfather's records.

Another half hour ticks by. I'm as anxious as a hamster in a very small cage. I sit. I stand. I move around the cottage checking my cell to make sure it has reception.

I finally surrender to the urge to slip down to the beach and covertly scan for signs of life at Trent's cottage. When the phone rings, I've inched at least halfway there, peeking around dunes and sea oats.

I'm so startled by the ringtone that I jump, lose my footing in the sand, and end up juggling the cell.

"I was about to give up on you," Trent says when I finally pick up. "I knocked three times, and nobody answered. Thought maybe you'd changed your mind."

I try to keep my eagerness from showing, but it's hopeless. "No. I'm here. I was just out back." *Did he say knocked? He's at my door?*

"I'll come around."

I look toward the Myers cottage and realize how far away I am. He'll know what I've been doing. "I think the gate has poison ivy growing over it."

"Nope. Doesn't look like it."

I spin around and bolt for the backyard, but I'm running in sand, the long wrap dress clinging around my legs, my flip-flops slapping. I catch the flash of a blue shirt near my grandmother's palmetto hedge just in time to put on the brakes and act casual coming up the boardwalk.

Even so, Trent reacts with a quizzical look. "You look a little fancy . . . for digging around in my granddad's shed. I told you it's a mess in there, right? And it's hot."

"Oh . . . this?" I glance down at the wrap dress. "It's the last thing I had in my suitcase. I took a kayak out this morning and trashed a set of clothes. I'm a wreck."

"You don't look like a wreck." I try to decipher whether he's just being nice or flirting, and I can't quite tell. I can see why he's successful in the real estate business. He oozes charm. "Ready?" he adds.

"I am."

I close the back gate, and we stroll down the beach together. He apologizes for getting home late. "A little excitement at Aunt Lou's today. Somehow — none of the cousins really want to confess the details — Jonah poked a Cocoa Puff up his nose. I had to stick around and help with the extraction."

"Did you get it out? Is he okay?"

Trent grins. "Black pepper. The obstruction was cleared via compressed air from inside the nasal passages. In other words, he sneezed. Whether Aunt Lou gets a confession out of the cousins as to who's responsible remains to be determined. There are seven of them. All boys, and Jonah is the youngest by three years, so he learns life lessons the hard way."

"Poor little guy. I can sympathize. Being the baby isn't easy. Our family is all girls, though, and that was bad enough. If you need to go get him . . ."

"Are you kidding? I'd have a mutiny on my hands if I did. He loves it there. Two of my mother's sisters and a cousin live on the same street, and my mom and dad are usually here part of the year, so the food and the action are constant, and there's always someone to play with. That was the biggest reason I moved here and bought the real estate office after Jonah's mother died. I needed to cut my working hours back to something reasonable, but I also wanted Jonah to have family around. I didn't want him to grow up in an apartment with just me."

Questions rush through my mind. Most of them seem far too personal. "Where did you live before?" I already know the answer. I researched him back when I was following the blackmail theory.

"New York." Given the khakis, polo shirt, casual boat shoes, and slight Texas accent, it's hard to picture him in the buttoned-up basic black of a New York professional. "Commercial real estate."

I feel an unexpected sort of kinship with Trent Turner. We're both adjusting to new surroundings, new lives. I envy his. "Big change, huh? Do you like it here?"

There's a hint of something, a little regret. "It's a lot slower pace . . . but yes. It's good."

"I'm sorry about your wife." I wonder at the details, but I'm not going to ask. What I thought might be flirtation on his part is probably just the kind of loneliness that would be natural only a few months after such a loss. I don't want to lead him on in any way. I'm wearing my engagement ring, but it's a princess-cut emerald, so people don't always realize it's not just decorative jewelry.

"We weren't married."

I blush instantly, feeling like a ninny for making assumptions. These days, you never know. "Oh . . . sorry. I mean . . ."

His smile puts me at ease. "It's okay. It's complicated, that's all. We were co-workers . . . and friends. She and I crossed some lines we shouldn't have after her divorce. I suspected Jonah was mine, but Laura said he wasn't. She was moving upstate to give it a try with her ex-husband again. I left it alone. I didn't know the truth about Jonah until after her car wreck. Jonah had internal injuries, and he needed a liver donor. Her sister got in touch with me because they hoped I'd be a match. I was, and that was that."

"Oh . . ." is all I can come up with.

He catches my gaze. We stop walking before turning onto the path toward his house, and I know the rest of the story is coming. "Jonah has two half brothers he almost doesn't remember anymore. It doesn't look like he'll get the chance to know them unless they decide to reconnect as adults. After the custody hearing, their father wouldn't let them have anything to do with Jonah, or me. That's not the way I want it, but that's the way it is. I understand the people my granddad helped better than you might think."

"I can see why you would." I'm surprised by his openness. The depth of his pain and disappointment are obvious. He doesn't even try to conceal the fact that he's conflicted about his decisions or that a past error in judgment resulted in a situation filled with difficult choices. Those realities will affect Jonah for the rest of his life.

I come from a world where we would never openly admit to such things, certainly not to someone who's practically a stranger. In the world I know, a polished exterior and an unblemished reputation are paramount. Trent makes me wonder if I've become too accustomed to the constraints that go with upholding public appearances.

What would I do if I faced a situation like his?

"Jonah seems like a really great kid," I say.

"He is that. I can't imagine any other kind of life now. I guess every parent feels that way."

"I'm sure."

He waits for me to start along the path, then follows. A spiderweb catches me in the face when we enter the yard, and then a second one. Now I remember why my cousins and I always fought about who'd be first on the trails when we rode horses in Hitchcock Woods back home. I pick off the silk and grab a dried-up palm frond to swish the air ahead.

Trent chuckles. "You're not as urban as you look."

"I told you I grew up in horse barns."

"I didn't really believe you. I thought Granddaddy's workshop might scare you away when you saw it."

"Not a chance." When I glance over my shoulder, he's grinning. "Were you hoping it would?"

The path opens into the yard, and he sobers as we cross to the small, low-roofed cabin and climb the steps. "I'm not sure. I wish my granddad were here to make these decisions for himself." Concern draws deep lines over his tanned forehead as he fishes the keys from his pocket and bends to look at them.

"I understand. I really do. I've wondered more than once if I should be digging around in my grandmother's past, but I can't help myself. I feel like the truth matters more."

He slips the key into the dead bolt and opens the lock. "Spoken more like a reporter than a politician. You'd better watch out, Avery Stafford. That kind of idealism will come back to bite you in the political world."

I bristle at that. "Spoken like someone who's dealt with the wrong kind of politicians." He's not saying anything that Leslie hasn't said to me already. She's afraid I'm too highbrow and not realistic about what a Senate run could mean. She forgets that all my life I've had to listen to random strangers offering their opinions about everything from our clothes to the tuition costs of the private schools we attended. Actually, not just strangers but friends. "In my family, public service is still *public* service."

His face is impassive, so I can't tell whether he agrees with me or not. "Then you won't like what you're about to find out in relation to the Tennessee Children's Home Society. It's not a pretty story any way you look at it."

"Why?"

"The place was incredibly well respected, and the woman who ran it, Georgia Tann, operated in powerful circles, socially and politically. She was well thought of publicly. People admired what she was doing. She changed the general perception that orphans were damaged goods. But the *reality* is that the Tennessee Children's Home Society in Memphis was rotten to the core. It's no wonder Granddad never wanted to talk about what he did in this little building. The stories are sad, and they're gruesome, and there are literally thousands of them. Kids were *brokered.* Georgia Tann made money by charging huge fees for adoptions, transportation, delivery out of state. She took children from poor families and sold them to celebrities and people with political influence. She had law enforcement agencies and family court judges in her pocket. She duped women in hospital maternity wards into signing surrender papers while they were still under sedation. She told people their babies had died when they hadn't." He pulls a folded piece of paper from his back pocket and hands it to me. "There's quite a bit more than that. I printed this off today between appointments."

The paper is a printed scan of an old newspaper story. The title pulls no punches.

It reads, "Adoption Matron May Have Been Most Prolific Serial Killer."

Trent stops with his hand on the door-knob. He's waiting for me to look over the article. "Nobody ever came out here but my grandfather and, occasionally, clients — not even my grandmother. But she didn't share his interest in the topic either. I told you that she felt that the past should have been left in the past. Maybe she was right. My grandfather must have felt that way in the end too. He told me to clean this place out and destroy whatever was still here. Just be warned before we go in. I have no idea what's on the other side of this door."

"I understand. But I am . . . was a federal prosecutor in Maryland. Not much shocks me."

Yet just the title of the article *is* shocking. I can tell that Trent's not letting me through the door until I've read the story — until I've been warned. He wants me to understand that what lies inside won't be warm and fuzzy stories about lonely orphans finally finding homes.

I turn back to the article, and begin scanning the text:

> Once heralded as the "Mother of Modern Adoption" and consulted by the likes of

Eleanor Roosevelt in efforts to reform adoption policies in the United States, Georgia Tann did, indeed, facilitate the adoptions of thousands of children from the 1920s through 1950. She also guided a network that, under her watch, allowed or intentionally caused the deaths of as many as five hundred children and infants.

"Many of the children weren't orphans," said Mary Sykes, who, along with an infant sister, was stolen from the porch of her unmarried mother's home at only four years old and placed in the care of the Tennessee Children's Home Society. "Many had loving parents who wanted to raise them. The children were often literally kidnapped in broad daylight, and no matter how birth parents tried to fight in court, they were not allowed to win." Mrs. Sykes would live for three years in a large white house operated by Georgia Tann and her network of helpers.

Mary's infant sister, just six months old when a woman claiming to be a social services nurse took them from the family's porch, would live in the TCHS facility for only two months.

"The babies weren't given proper food or medical care," said Mrs. Sykes. "I remember sitting on the floor in a room full of cribs, reaching through the bars and just patting my sister's arm. She was too weak and dehydrated to even cry. No one would help her. Once it was clear that she was too far gone to recover, a worker put her in a cardboard box and carried her away. I never saw her again. I heard later that, if babies got too sick or cried too much, they'd set them in the sun in a carriage and leave them. I have children, and grandchildren, and great-grandchildren now. I can't imagine how anyone could do those things to kids, but it happened. We were tied to beds and chairs; we were beaten, held under the bathwater; we were molested. It was a house of horrors."

Over the course of three decades, children under the care of TCHS are reported to have disappeared en masse, their paperwork often vanishing along with them, leaving no record of their lives. If biological family members came looking for information or petitioned the courts, they were simply told that the children had been adopted and the records were sealed.

Operating under the protection of Boss Crump, Memphis's notorious political kingpin, Georgia Tann's network was seemingly untouchable.

The remainder of the article gives details about the brokering of children to wealthy parents and Hollywood celebrities, the grieving birth families left behind, the allegations of physical and sexual abuse. The last lines are a quote from a man who runs a website called The Lost Lambs.

> "The Memphis branch of the Tennessee Children's Home Society had scouts everywhere — at social services offices, at rural medical clinics, in poor neighborhoods and shacktowns. Babies were often given to social workers and officials who might stand in Tann's way. Adoptive parents were sometimes blackmailed for more money, threatened with having their adopted children taken from them. Georgia Tann cultivated the protection of Boss Crump and the family court system. Ultimately, she enjoyed the freedom to alter lives at her discretion. She played God and seemingly had no regrets. In the end, Georgia Tann died of cancer before she could be forced to answer charges. Powerful people wanted to see the case closed, and so it was."

"This is . . ." I pause to search for a word. I'm about to say *incredible,* but it isn't the right term. "Appalling. It's hard to imagine that something like this could happen, and on such a large scale . . . for years."

"TCHS wasn't forced to close until 1950." Clearly, Trent shares my mix of horror, astonishment, and rage. Mary Sykes's story of touching her dying sister makes me think of my nieces and nephews and the bonds they have with their siblings. Courtney used to climb into the triplets' cribs and fall asleep with them if she heard them crying at night.

"I just can't . . . I can't imagine." I've prosecuted abuse cases and corruption cases, but this is so large-scale. Dozens and dozens of people must have known what was happening. "How could everyone have just ignored this?"

It dawns on me then. I have family from Tennessee. They were political, influential. They held various state, judicial, and federal offices. Were they aware of this? Did they turn a blind eye to it? Was that the reason Grandma Judy involved herself with Trent Turner, Sr.? Was she trying to right the family wrongs?

Maybe she didn't want it to come out that her family had cooperated with these monstrous acts, perhaps even supported them?

The blood drains from my head, and I

reach out to steady myself on the wall. My cheeks feel cold despite the warmth of the summer day.

Trent's face offers concern as he stands poised to open the door. "You're sure?"

He doesn't look any more certain than I am. We're like two kids trying to dare ourselves into forbidden territory. Is he hoping I'll change my mind and spare both of us whatever details await?

"The truth always comes out sooner or later. I'm of the belief that you're better off knowing about it first." But even as I say it, I wonder. My entire life, I've been so certain that we were above reproach. That our family was an open book. Maybe that was naïve of me. What if, all these years, I've been wrong?

Trent looks down at his shoes, kicks a loose shell off the porch decking. It bounces against a red toy tractor that looks particularly poignant at this moment. "I'm afraid what I'm going to find out in here is that my grandfather's adoption was something like the ones in that article where it mentions giving kids to government officials to keep them quiet. My granddad's adoptive father was a Memphis police sergeant. They weren't the kind of people who would've had a bunch of money to fund an expensive adoption. . . ." He trails off as if he doesn't want to put any more words to the story, but in his eyes there's a mirror of my own fear. Do we carry the guilt from the sins of past generations? If so, can we bear the weight of that burden?

Trent opens the door and, perhaps, the mystery.

Inside, the cottage is low-roofed and shadow-filled. The white plank walls are crackled and faded, and window glass hangs crooked in the wooden frames. The air smells of dust and mildew and something else that takes a moment to register. Pipe tobacco. The odor instantly reminds me of my Grandpa Stafford. His office at the Lagniappe house always held this scent and still does.

Trent flips on the light, and the bulb flickers stubbornly in a Deco-era fixture that is out of step with the rest of the place.

We move into the tiny one-room structure. It contains a large desk that looks as if it could have been bought at a library sale, two file cabinets, a small wooden table, and a couple odd chairs. An old, black rotary phone still sits on the desktop. There's a canister of wooden pencils, a stapler, a three-hole punch, an ashtray that hasn't been cleaned, a gooseneck desk lamp, an electric typewriter in faded olive green. Shelves along the back wall sag under their load of stacked file folders, aging binders, loose papers, magazines, and books.

Trent sighs, running a hand through his hair. He seems too big for this small space. His head is only about six inches from the rafters, which I see now are hand-hewn with notches in them, most likely salvaged shipwreck timbers.

"Are you okay?" I ask.

He shakes his head, then shrugs, indicating a hat, a vintage umbrella with a dragon carved into the handle, and a pair of blue boat shoes. All three wait by the coat hooks, seemingly in hopes of their owner returning. "It feels like he's *here,* you know? He smelled like this place most of the time."

Trent opens the blinds, illuminating the bulletin boards that line the walls.

"Look," I whisper, dust catching in my throat.

There are literally dozens of photos, some bearing the bold colors of modern photography, some in the washed-out hues of old Polaroids, some in shades of black and gray with white frames around the edges bearing dates: *July 1941, December 1936, April 1952 . . .*

Trent and I stand side by side, staring at

the wall, each lost in our own thoughts, awed and horrified at once. I take in images — children's faces juxtaposed with adult faces. The resemblances are evident. These are mothers and fathers and kids, presumably birth families who were separated from one another. The children's pictures now hang next to more recent photos of the adults they became.

I look into the eyes of a beautiful woman, her smile vibrant, her hip jutting out as she rests a baby on it. An oversized dress and an apron hang loose on her frame, making her seem like a child playing dress-up. She couldn't be more than fifteen or sixteen.

What could you tell me? I wonder. *What happened to you?*

Beside me, Trent thumbs a few of the photos. There are even more underneath them, images layered over images. Trent Senior was thorough in his work.

"There's nothing on the backs," Trent observes. "I guess that's why he didn't worry about asking me to take care of these. You wouldn't be able to tell who they were unless you knew already."

Sadness tinges my thoughts, but it's a vague feeling. My attention is focused on a photo of four women, standing arm in arm on a beach. Even though the picture is black-and-white, I imagine the bright colors of their sixties-era sundresses and broad-brimmed hats. I can see the golden glint of sunlight on their long blond curls.

One of the women is my grandmother. She's holding her hat in place. The dragonfly bracelet dangles from her wrist.

The other three women bear a resemblance to my grandmother. Same blond curls, same pale eyes, probably blue. They could easily be relatives, yet I don't recognize any of them.

Each wears a dragonfly bracelet that matches my grandmother's.

In the background, just out of focus, little boys squat by the tide line, their knees poking upward as they labor over buckets and sand towers.

Is one of them my father?

I reach for the photo, and Trent stretches up to take it down for me. When he pulls the thumbtack, something small and white falls, drifting like a kite losing the wind. It's familiar even before I bend to pick it up.

A larger version of it rests in a pearlescent frame in May Crandall's nursing home room.

A voice disturbs the air, but I'm so focused I almost don't realize I'm the one who's speaking. "I've seen this photo before."

Chapter 18

Rill

The house is black as pitch inside. There's no lights left burning, and the curtains block the moon outside the bedroom windows. Around me, kids rustle in their beds and whimper and grind their teeth in their sleep. After all that time trapped in the basement by myself, it's a comfort to be with anybody, but, truth is, this is no safe place. These girls tell tales. They say Riggs comes at night sometimes and gets whoever he wants — mostly the little kids he can carry easy.

I'm too big to carry. I hope. But I don't want to find out.

Quiet as a shadow, I slide from under my blanket and tiptoe across the floor. I already walked it real careful before getting into my new bed tonight. I know where the squeaky boards are. I know how many steps it is to the door, how many to the stairs, the safest way past the parlor room off the kitchen where the workers will be dozing off in their chairs. James told me all about going downstairs to the kitchen at night to steal Mrs. Murphy's tea cakes. I know just how he got away with it.

But all the things James had figured out didn't save him in the end, so I need to be careful about sneaking out to tell Silas I'm waiting here for Fern to get back. Soon's she does, I'll grab her up, and we'll slip off in the dark, and Silas will take us home to the river, and all the terrible times will finally be over.

What if Briny and Queenie don't want me back after what I've done? Maybe they'll hate me as much as I hate myself. Maybe they'll look at the skinny, sad girl I am now and see someone nobody wants.

I shush my mind, because your mind can ruin you if you let it. I have to pay attention, to do everything right so I don't get caught.

It's not as hard as I thought it would be. I'm down the back stairs in no time. A small circle of light seeps from the room off the kitchen. Someone's snoring loud inside. Near the door, a pair of feet in heavy white shoes is flopped outward like moth wings. I don't even look to see whose they are. I just slip around the wall by the stove, staying in the shadow like James talked about. My toes test each new floorboard, real careful. The ragged hem of my nightgown catches on the oven's rough iron surface. I imagine it making noise, but really it doesn't.

The screen door in the washroom squeaks a little when I tug it open. I stop, hold my breath, stretch my ears toward the house, listen.

There's nothing.

Soft as a whisper, I go on out. The porch boards are wet with dew, just like the deck of the *Arcadia.* Overhead, katydids and crickets give the sky a heartbeat, and a million stars shine like far-off campfires. The half-moon hangs heavy, rocking on its back. Its twin rides the ripples in the rain barrel as I pass.

All of a sudden, I'm home again. I'm wrapped in the blanket of night and stars. The blanket is part of me, and I am part of it. No one can touch me. No one can tell one of us from the other.

Bullfrogs croak, and dark birds call as I run across the yard, the thin white gown skimming my legs, light as milkweed silk. Near the back fence, I cling close to the holly bushes, give a whippoorwill's call.

An echo answers. I smile and breathe in

the sweet, heavy smell of jasmine and hurry toward the sound, pushing my way along the big boys' tunnel until I'm there at the fence. Silas is on the other side. In the moon shadows, I can't see his face, only the outline of his applejack hat and his knobby legs bent up like a frog's. He reaches through the bars for me.

"Let's go," he whispers, then locks on to one of the bars like he means to pull it loose with his bare hands. "I cut this one most of the way through. It oughta . . ."

Grabbing his hand, I stop him. If he opens the hole, the big boys will see it in the morning when they come to their hideout. "I can't." Everything inside me screams, *Go! Run!* "I can't leave yet. Fern's coming back. The people who took her don't want her anymore. I have to wait till tomorrow night, so I can bring her with me."

"You gotta get away now. I'll come back here for Fern."

Doubts dart through my mind, skittering this way and that. "No. Once they know I'm gone, once they see the hole in the fence, we'll never get her out of here. I can sneak away again tomorrow night. And there's another little boy, Stevie. He's from the river too. I can't just leave him here." How am I gonna manage it? I know where Stevie sleeps, but getting him from the toddler room and bringing Fern and not letting anyone see us . . .

It doesn't seem possible.

Even so, Silas being here makes me sure of myself. It makes me brave. I feel like I can do anything. I'll find a way. I can't leave Fern or Stevie here. They belong to the river. They belong to us. Mrs. Murphy and Miss Tann stole enough from me already. I want it back. I want to be Rill Foss again.

Before this is over, I'll find all my sisters and my baby brother and bring them home to the *Arcadia.* That's what I'll do.

Silas reaches out, and his long, thin arms circle me. I lean toward him, and his cap tumbles off. His forehead rests against my cheek, his raven's-wing hair tickling my face.

"I don't want you to go back in there." He slides a hand over my hair, soft and careful. My heart speeds up.

It's all I can do not to bust through the fence right now. "It's only one more day."

"I'll be here tomorrow night," Silas promises.

He kisses me on the cheek. Something new shivers through me, and I close my eyes hard against the feeling.

Leaving him there is as hard as anything I ever did in my life. As I crawl off, he packs mud on the bars so nobody'll see the fresh cuts in the metal. If one of the big boys happens to lean against the fence while they're in their tunnel, I hope it doesn't break.

I'm back to the house and up the stairs without even breathing again, it feels like. At the top, I check the hall and listen for sounds before starting around the railing where we line up for our baths. There's nothing but moon shadows from the stairway window and sleep noises. One of the little kids talks in his dreams. I freeze, but then he goes quiet just as quick.

Only fifteen more steps and I'll be back in my room again. I've made it. Nobody will know where I went. Tomorrow, it'll be even easier now that I've done it once. James was right. It's not that tough to get away with things here, if you're smart.

I can fool all of them. The idea swells inside me. It makes me feel like I took something from them, something they stole that was *mine.* Power. I've got power now. When we're safe on the *Arcadia,* the river carrying us far away from here, I'll forget all about this place. I'll never tell anybody what happened here. It'll be like it never happened at all.

A bad dream with bad people in it.

I'm so caught in the idea, I step wrong. A

floorboard creaks under my foot. I hold back a gasp, look down, then decide the best thing I can do is hurry on in case one of the workers shows up. If I'm in the bed, they won't have any way to know who was —

I almost don't see Mr. Riggs till I'm right on top of him. He's coming out of the toddler room. He stumbles back, and so do I. His shoulder hits the wall, and he whispers, "Ooof."

I turn to rush off, but he grabs me by a fistful of nightgown and hair. His big hand clamps over my mouth and nose. I smell sweat and whiskey, tobacco and coal ash. He bends my head back so far, I think, *He'll snap my neck right here. He'll snap my neck and drop me down the stairs and say I fell. That's how it ends. . . .*

I strain my eyes to see him. He looks around, tries to decide where he can take me. I can't let him get me to the basement. If he does, I'm dead. I know it. Fern will come back tomorrow, and I won't be here.

Checking the stairs, he wobbles on his feet. His boot comes down hard over my toe, and stars shoot across my eyes, and I moan. He clamps his hand harder, cutting off my air. I hear my backbone crack. I twist and push and try to get free, but he only crushes me tighter against him, lifting me off my feet and dragging me down the hall into the shadows by the bathroom door. His fingers fumble for the handle to open it. I whimper and struggle and pull until finally he growls low in his throat and pins me to the wall so he can get at the door. His belly crushes my chest, and blackness circles around my eyes, and my lungs choke for air.

His face comes close to my ear. "Y-you and me can b-b-be friends. I can git ya p-peppermints and c-c-cookies. Anythin' y-you want. We can b-b-be best friends." He rubs his cheek along my chin and my shoulder, his whiskers scrubbing hard as he smells my hair, then sticks his face in around the neck of my nighty. "Y-you smell like out-outside. Y-you b-been meetin' one of the b-big boys down there? Y-you got a b-boyfriend again?"

His voice seems like it's coming from far off, echoing the way foghorns do on the river's cold mornings. My knees buckle. My feet go prickly and numb. I can't feel the wall or him. My ribs jerk like a fish's gills when it's hanging on the stringer.

I see sparkle fairies. They dance wild in the dark.

No! I tell myself. *No!* But there's nothing left to fight with. My body's gone. Maybe

I'll suffocate and die. I hope so.

Just as quick, he lets loose of me, and cool rushes in where his body was, and a breath pours into my belly. I slide down the wall and land in a pile, dizzy, blinking and trying to push off the floor.

"Mr. *Riggs*?" The sharp voice of a worker comes from the stairway. "*What* are you doing up here at this hour?"

My eyes clear, and I see him standing in front of me, so she won't see. I pull back into the shadows, squeeze tight against the wall. If they catch me here, I'll be the one who's in trouble, not him. I'll get locked away again . . . or worse.

"H-heard thunder while ago. G-gotta close up the w-windows."

The worker comes around the railing. The moonlight catches her, and I see she's the new one that came since Miss Dodd left. I don't know much about her or if she's mean or not. She *sounds* mean. She doesn't like Riggs being up here, that's clear enough. If she gives him trouble, she won't last long at Mrs. Murphy's.

"I didn't hear anything." She twists back and forth, looking toward the bedroom doors.

"I'z out-outside when I h-heard it. Was s-some s-s-stray cats yowlin'. T-took my rifle out to k-kill ’em.”

“Good heavens. You’d have woken the whole place. Surely the cats aren’t hurting anything.”

“C-cousin Ida don’t like nothin’ prowling round where it don’t b-b-belong.” By Cousin Ida, he means Mrs. Murphy. He also means to let the new worker know her place.

“I’ll check the windows myself.” She’s not backing down, and I don’t know whether I’m glad or not. If she keeps coming closer, she’ll see me. If she leaves, Riggs will drag me off into the bathroom. “No need in disturbing your sleep, Mr. Riggs, when I’m being paid to watch the children at night.”

He moves away from me and closer to her, his steps uneven and wobbly. At the corner of the railing, he blocks her path. The two shadows melt into one. He whispers something.

“Mr. Riggs!” Her hand swings out of the shadow and back in. Skin slaps on skin. “Have you been drinking?”

“I s-s-seen how you b-been watchin’ me.”

“I have done *no* such *thing.*”

“Y-you b-b-be nice, or I’ll tell Cousin Ida. She d-don’t like nobody to g-gimme trouble.”

She sidles to the wall and slides past him,

and he lets her by. "You . . . you will keep away from me, or . . . or I . . . I'll tell her myself. I'll tell her you got liquored up and were fresh with me."

He lumbers on toward the stairs. "Y-you oughta look — see the li'l boys first. S-s-somebody tumped outta bed in there." His feet fall heavy as he walks on down. The boards squeak and sing.

Hugging her arms around herself, the worker watches him before going to see about the toddlers. I stand up on shaky legs and hurry to my bed, and pull the covers all the way to my neck and wrap up. It's a good thing, because the worker comes in our room next, maybe thinking Riggs was closest to it.

She walks along and lifts covers and looks at every one of us like she's checking for something. When she comes to my bed, I breathe long and deep and fight hard not to shiver as she pulls the covers off me and feels my skin. Maybe she wonders why I'm wrapped up so tight when it's sticky hot. Maybe she can smell the night on me like Riggs did.

She stays over my bed awhile.

Finally, she's gone, and I lay there looking up at the dark. *One more day,* I tell myself. *You only gotta get by one more day.*

I think it over and over again, like a promise. I have to. Otherwise, I'd find a way to get that screen off the window, and I'd jump out and hope it's high enough to kill me.

I can't live like this.

I fall asleep knowing it's true.

Morning comes in fits and jerks. I wake and sleep, waiting on the voices of the workers to tell us to get out of our beds and put on our clothes. I know better than to move before that. Mrs. Pulnik made sure to tell me the upstairs rules before she showed me my bed and the little crate underneath where I keep my clothes.

But I won't be needing that crate for long. I'll get us out tonight, all three of us — me, and Fern, and Stevie — no matter what it takes. *If I've gotta grab a kitchen knife and stab it into somebody to get us past, I'll do it,* I tell myself. *I won't let anyone stop me.*

It's not till we're downstairs for breakfast that I know I've been making promises that'll be hard to keep. First rattle out the box this morning, Mrs. Pulnik spotted sandy footprints in the kitchen. They're dried, so she knows they were put there last night. They fade out before the stairs, which means she can't tell where the trail would end up, but the prints are big enough that she's sure it was one of the older boys. She's got them lined up, and she's trying them one by one against the tracks to see who fits.

She hasn't noticed yet that I've got big feet. Standing by my place at the table with the rest of the girls, I squeeze my toes in and hope she won't look my way.

Maybe one of the boys is the size of the prints, I think, and I know that's wrong, because I'd be getting somebody in trouble. Bad trouble. Mrs. Murphy's in the room too, and she's hotter than a jar fresh out of the canning pot. She's got an umbrella with all the cloth torn off. She means to whip somebody with it. After that, it'll probably be the closet.

I *can't* get the closet.

But can I stand by and let it happen to somebody else when it's my fault? It'd be the same as if I was swinging the umbrella myself.

Through the washroom, I see Riggs by the back screen door. He's watching the show. He nods and smiles at me, and my skin goes cold.

The new worker looks on from the corner, her dark eyes skittering. She's never seen anything like this. "It . . . it could've been me," she babbles out. "Mr. Riggs mentioned stray cats outside, and I went to shoo them away."

Mrs. Murphy barely even hears her. "You will *not* interfere!" she screeches. "And *your* feet are too small. *Who* are you covering up for? *Who?*"

"No one." Her eyes dart off toward me.

Mrs. Murphy and Mrs. Pulnik try to follow them. Time slows down.

Be still. Be still, I think. *Don't move.* I stay frozen.

"C-could be those w-was there last evenin'. Th-th-there's mud round the rain b-barrel," Riggs tosses in, now that everyone's looking at my side of the table. At first, I think Riggs wants to help, and then I understand he just doesn't want me locked up tonight where he can't get at me.

Mrs. Murphy bats a hand at him. "You *hush.* Honestly, you're far too kind to these little *ingrates.* Give them an inch and they'll take a mile." She slaps the umbrella against her palm, studying my side of the table. "Now . . . if it wasn't one of the boys . . . then who could it be?"

The girl who was in the bed across from me last night, Dora, tips her head back and wobbles around and faints dead away on the floor.

Nobody moves.

"Not *her,* I guess," Mrs. Murphy says. "And if not *her,* then *who*?" The umbrella swings in a circle like a magic wand. "Step away from the table, girls." Her eyes sparkle. "Let's see who our little Cinderella might be."

The phone rings, and everybody jumps. Then we stand still as statues, even the workers, while Mrs. Murphy decides whether or not to answer. When she does, she half yanks the phone off the wall, but her voice goes honey sweet soon's she knows who it is.

"Why, *yes.* Good morning, Georgia. How delightful to hear from you so early." She pauses and then says, "Yes, *yes.* Oh, why *certainly.* I've been up for *hours.* Let me walk back to my office and pick up your call in private."

The words echoing through the phone come fast like the *rat-a-tat-tat* of the Gatling guns in cowboy western movies.

"Oh, I *see.* Of course." Mrs. Murphy sets down the umbrella and lays a palm on her forehead, her lips pulling back from her teeth in a way that makes me think of Queenie the last night I saw her. "Well, yes, we can accomplish it by ten, but I don't think it's advisable. You see . . ."

More talk comes through the phone, loud

and fast.

"Yes, I understand. We won't be late," Mrs. Murphy says past her teeth, and when she slams the earpiece back into its holder, she points my way with her eyes narrow and her mouth squeezed into a tight ball. "Take *her* and clean her up and put her in a Sunday dress. Something blue to match her eyes . . . and with a pinafore. Miss Tann wants her downtown at the hotel by ten."

Mrs. Pulnik's face looks like Mrs. Murphy's. The last thing they want to do with me right now is wash me up, brush my hair, and get me in a dress. "But . . . she . . ."

"Do *not* question me!" Mrs. Murphy howls, then swats Danny Boy in the head hard, because he's the one closest. Everybody shrinks away as she sweeps a finger around the room. "What are all of *you* looking at?"

The kids don't know whether to sit down or stay where they are. They wait until Mrs. Murphy pounds through the swinging door. Then they slink into their chairs while the hinges are still creaking.

"I will be takingk care with *you* myself." Mrs. Pulnik grabs me by the arm, squeezing hard. I know she's about to get revenge on me one way or the other.

But I also know that, whatever Miss Tann

has planned, it could be even worse. There are stories about what happens to kids when the workers take them to hotels.

"And don't leave any bruises on her!" Mrs. Murphy's order echoes in from the hall.

Just like that, I'm saved, but then again, I'm not. Mrs. Pulnik yanks my hair and wrenches me around. She tries hard to make the next hour hurt as much as possible, and it does. By the time I'm finally walked out to the car to join Mrs. Murphy, my head is pounding, and my eyes are red from the tears I've been told I better not cry.

Mrs. Murphy doesn't say a word in the car, and I'm glad. I just press myself close to the door and look out the glass, scared and worried and sore. I don't know what's about to happen to me, but I know it won't be good. Nothing here is good.

On the way downtown, we pass by the river. I see tugs and barges and a big showboat. Its calliope music pushes into the car, and I remember how Gabion used to dance on the deck of the *Arcadia* when the showboats went by. He'd make us laugh and laugh. My heart strains toward the water, hoping to see the *Arcadia,* or Old Zede's boat, or any shantyboat at all, but there's nothing. Across the way, a river camp sits empty. There's only dead fire pits, trampled circles of grass, and a stack of drift somebody gathered up but never burned. The shantyboats are all gone.

It hits me for the first time that it must be about October by now. Pretty soon, the maples and the gum trees will change, bits of red and yellow edging along their leaves. The river gypsies have already started the long, slow drift south, down to where the winters are warm and the water's chock full of fat catfish.

Briny's still here, I tell myself, but all of a sudden, I feel like I'll never see him, or Fern, or anybody I love ever again. The feeling swallows me whole, and all I can do is let my mind leave my body. I'm not there when the driver parks the car in front of a tall building. I barely hear Mrs. Murphy threatening what'll happen to me if I don't behave. It hardly even hurts when she pinches through my dress and twists the skin over my ribs and tells me I better do whatever I'm asked to do in here, and I'm not to tell anyone no, or cry, or carry on about it.

"You'll be as sweet as a little kitten." She squeezes my skin harder and holds her face close to mine. "Or you'll be sorry . . . and so will your little friend, Stevie. You wouldn't want anything to happen to *him,* would you?"

She gets out on the curb and drags me with her. Around us, men pass by in business suits. Women stroll along with bright packages. A mama in a red coat pushes a baby carriage out of the hotel and glances at us as she goes by. She has the kindest face, and I want to run to her. I want to grab on to her coat and tell her everything.

Help me! I'll say.

But I can't let myself. I know they'll take it out on Stevie if I do. And probably Fern too, once they get her back to Mrs. Murphy's house. No matter what, I have to be good today. I have to do everything they say, so they won't lock me up when we get home tonight.

I straighten my back and tell myself this is the last time. *This is the last time they'll ever be able to make me do anything.*

Whatever it is, I'll go along.

But my heart flutters, and my stomach tightens like a fist. A man in a uniform holds open the door. He looks like a soldier or a prince. I want him to rescue me the way the princes do in fairy books.

"Good day." Mrs. Murphy smiles and raises her nose and marches on.

Inside the hotel, people are laughing, and talking, and having lunch at a restaurant. It's a pretty place, like a castle, but it doesn't seem pretty today. It seems like a trap.

The elevator man stands like a statue by the buttons. It doesn't even seem like he breathes while the little box takes us up, and up, and up. When we get off, the man sends a sad look my way. Does he know where they're taking me — what's about to happen?

Mrs. Murphy walks me down the hallway and knocks on a door.

"Come in," a woman calls, and when we do, Miss Tann is sprawled out on a sofa like a cat resting in the sun. Behind her, the curtains are open and a big window shows the whole city of Memphis. We're so far up, we look down on the roofs. I've never been this high in the air in my life.

I squeeze my hands into fists and hide them in the ruffled pinafore and try not to move.

Miss Tann's got a half-full glass in her hand. She looks like she's been here a while. Maybe she lives in the hotel?

She swirls the brown drink, lifts it toward a door across from the sofa. "Put her in the bedroom, and then that will be all, Mrs. Murphy. Close the door as you leave her . . .

and instruct her to sit quietly until she's told otherwise. I'll speak with him out here first, to make certain our . . . arrangement is in order."

"I don't mind staying, Georgia."

"If you'd rather." She watches me as we cross to the door, Mrs. Murphy holding me up under the armpit, so I can't help but walk uneven. "Honestly, there would be better choices, but I can see why he wants her," Miss Tann says.

"I don't know why *anyone* would want her."

Inside the bedroom, Mrs. Murphy sits me on the bed and fluffs the frilly dress around me, so I look like a pillow doll. She yanks my hair forward over my shoulders, letting it hang in long curls, and then tells me not to move an inch. "Not *one,*" she finishes when she's heading out the door. She closes it behind her.

I hear her and Miss Tann talking in the other room. They chat about the view and share a drink. Then, there's nothing but quiet and the faraway sounds of the city. Horns honk. A streetcar rings its bell. A newspaperboy yells.

I don't know how much time goes by before there's a knock at the front door. Miss Tann answers, sticky sweet, and I hear a man's voice, but I can't make out the words until they come closer.

"Of course, she's *all* yours . . . *if* you're certain you still want her, that is," Miss Tann says.

"Yes, and I appreciate your altering our arrangements on such short notice. My wife has struggled terribly these last few years, often to the point of taking to her bed for weeks on end, locking herself away from me. What else can I do?"

"Indeed. I can see where the girl might serve your needs, but I do have other children who are more . . . tractable," Miss Tann suggests. "We have many older girls. Yours for the asking."

Please, I think. *Pick somebody else.* And then I know that's wrong. I shouldn't wish bad things on the other kids.

"No, I wanted her specifically."

I squeeze the bedcovers. Sweat coats my palms and seeps into the fabric. I dig in my fingernails.

Be good. Whatever it is, be good.

Silas is coming tonight. . . .

"What else can I do?" the man asks again. "My wife is so very fragile. The child will not stop carrying on. I cannot have the constant upheaval and noise around the house. I am a composer, you know, and it interferes with my work. I've several scores for films due by the holiday season, and time is running short."

"Oh, sir, I can practically assure you that this girl will bring you *more* trouble, not *less,*" Mrs. Murphy pipes up. "I thought . . . I assumed you only wanted her for . . . I had no *idea* you planned to take her with you *permanently,* or I would have spoken up sooner."

"It is of no matter, Mrs. Murphy," Miss Tann snaps. "The girl is certainly old enough to be compliant with *whatever* Mr. Sevier should desire."

"Yes . . . yes, of course, Georgia. Pardon my interruption."

"The girl is perfect in every way, I can assure you, sir. Unblemished."

The man says something I can't make out, and then Miss Tann talks again. "Very well then. I have her documents for you, and of course, as with your other adoption, it will be one year before the process is decreed final, but I would anticipate no trouble with that, especially for a client of your . . . stature."

The conversation goes quiet. Papers rustle. "I only want Victoria to be happy again," the man says. "I love my wife dearly, and these past years have been a torment. The doctors say that the only hope of overcoming her blue moods is to give her a compelling reason to look forward rather than back."

"Such situations are, of course, our very reason for existing, Mr. Sevier." Miss Tann's voice trembles like she's halfway to crying. "These poor lost children and the families who need them are my impetus and inspiration for the tireless work I do. Day in and day out, I endure my arduous labor and the sad beginnings of these little waifs so that I might rescue them and give them life and add life to countless empty homes. Certainly, coming from a fine family myself, I could have chosen an easier path, but someone must make the sacrifice to protect those who cannot protect themselves. It is a calling. It is *my* calling and one I willingly accept with no expectation of accolades or personal gain."

The man sighs, sounding impatient. "I am most grateful, of course. Is anything else needed to conclude our business?"

"Not a thing." Footsteps echo, but they're going away from the bedroom door, not toward it. "All the paperwork is in order. You've provided the payment for her fees. She is yours, Mr. Sevier. She is waiting there in the bedroom, and we will leave you two to get acquainted . . . in whatever way you see fit."

"I would urge you to use a firm hand with her. She . . ."

"Come along, Mrs. Murphy."

Then they're gone, and I sit very still on the bed, listening for the man. He comes to the door, and stops on the other side of it. I hear him take in a breath, then blow it out.

I clutch the dress hard over my knees, my body shaking.

The door opens, and he stands in it, just a few feet away.

I know his face. He sat beside me on the sofa at the viewing party and asked me how old I was.

His wife was the one who read books to Fern.

CHAPTER 19

Avery

The driver in front of me slows down, but I'm so lost in watching two teenage girls trot their horses alongside the road that I don't hit the brakes until it's almost too late. The car turns off on a road that leads toward the equestrian events center. I wonder if that's where the girls might be going with their horses. It's the right time of year for the derby series. When I was younger, I would've been there either watching or competing, but these days I barely have time to lament that grown-up life leaves no time for activities I was once so passionate about, like riding.

Right now, my mind is already several miles down the road, entering May Crandall's room at the nursing home. I've had Ian, the friendly intern, make a few low-key calls to determine her current location and condition. She's back at the care facility and feeling well enough to give the attendants trouble again.

Behind me, Trent taps his horn and lifts a hand in the air, as if to say, *Pay attention up there,* but he's smiling beneath his sunglasses.

If he weren't in a separate car, I'd say, *You insisted on coming along. I warned you that things could be unpredictable.*

He'd probably laugh and tell me there's no way he's missing this.

We're like a couple of sixth graders playing hooky from school for the first time. Neither of us is where we're supposed to be this morning, but after discovering that photo last night in his grandfather's workshop, neither of us can say no to this journey. Even an early-morning missed call from Leslie and a half-dozen new customer inquiries at Trent's real estate office couldn't change the plan we impulsively formed last night. One way or another, we're going to find out what our grandparents were hiding and how my history and his are tied together . . . and what May Crandall has to do with it.

I've intentionally failed to answer Leslie's summons, and Trent has slapped a note on the door of the real estate office, and we're on the lam, after having taken off at first light.

A little over two hours later, we're in Aiken. We plan to see May Crandall after her breakfast. Depending on what we find out from May, we may go to my grandmother's house on Lagniappe next.

I try to focus on the driving as we wind through graceful, tree-lined streets, the sleepy magnolias and towering pines slipping their calming shade over the SUV, seeming to say, *Why the rush? Slow down. Enjoy the day.*

For a moment, I relax into it, persuade myself that this is just any other late-summer morning. But the instant the nursing home appears around the corner, the illusion vanishes. As if to punctuate this, my cellphone rings again, and Leslie's name is on the screen for the fourth time. I'm inconveniently reminded that, as soon as this visit with May Crandall is over — whatever it yields — I'll have to check in. The world of present-day issues has come calling. Literally.

At least I know that, if the summons had anything to do with my father's health, one of my sisters would be phoning me, not Leslie. So it's definitely business related. Something that has cropped up since I talked to

Ian yesterday evening, or else he would have mentioned it then. Leslie probably has a can't-miss press op lined up, and she wants me to come home early from my minivacation on Edisto. Little does she know, I'm already here.

The idea of diving back into the political stewpot pinches a little. I really don't want to think about it. Putting my phone on vibrate, I tuck it into my purse without checking the stack-up of texts. There are probably emails too. Leslie does *not* like to be ignored.

All thoughts of Leslie vanish as I park, grab the folder that holds the antique photos from the bulletin board and the papers from Grandma Judy's envelope, and get out of the car.

Trent meets me on the curb. "If we're ever traveling cross-country, I'll drive."

"What, you don't trust me?" A strange little tingle slides down my back, and just as quickly, I shrug it away. Being in Aiken again is a stark reminder that, as much as I find Trent likeable, this will never be anything more than a friendship.

I made sure to slip a mention of my fiancé into the conversation before we left Edisto, just to be fair to all concerned.

"You I trust. Your driving . . . maybe not."

"It wasn't even a near miss." We banter back and forth on the way up the sidewalk, and by the time we reach the door, I'm laughing without meaning to. The scent of air freshener and the oppressive quiet sobers things up.

Trent's expression morphs almost instantly. His smile vanishes. "This brings back memories."

"You've been here?"

"No, but it looks a lot like the place we moved my gran into after her stroke. There wasn't any choice, but it was tough on Granddad. They'd never been separated more than a night or two in over sixty years."

"It's so hard when you reach the point where there aren't any good options." He knows about Grandma Judy's situation. It came up last night while we were sitting on the porch of the little cabin talking about the photos and what they might mean.

An attendant in colorful scrubs passes by. She greets us, appearing to wonder if she recognizes me. Then she moves on. I'm glad. The last thing I need is anyone picking up on the fact that I'm here. If this gets back to Leslie and my father, there will be an intense round of questions, and I haven't a clue what I'd say.

At the doorway to May Crandall's room, I

suddenly realize I'm not sure what I plan to say to her either. Should I just burst in there with the photos and ask, *Who were you and my grandmother to one another? How was Trent Turner, Sr., involved?*

Should I try to lead into it more subtly? From my short association with May, I have no idea how she'll react to our coming here. I'm hoping that Trent's presence may work a bit of extra magic. May did, after all, most likely know his grandfather.

What if it's all too much for her, the two of us showing up? She *has* been sick. I don't want to cause her any more problems. In fact, being back here nudges me toward the realization that I should do something to help her. Maybe I could talk to Andrew Moore at the seniors' rights PAC. Perhaps he could give me some suggestions about organizations that serve seniors like May whose families live far away.

Trent stops at the door and motions to the nameplate. "Looks like we're here."

"I'm nervous," I admit. "I know she's been sick. I'm not sure how strong she'll —"

"Who's hovering around out there?" May puts my uncertainty to rest before I can finish voicing it. "Go away! I don't need anything. I won't have you whispering about me!" A slipper flies through the small opening between the door and the frame, and then a hairbrush sails past and clatters across the hall.

Trent recovers the discards. "She's got a good arm."

"You leave me be!" May insists.

Trent and I share uncertain looks, and I lean close to the door, avoiding the line of fire just in case May has more ammo at hand. "May? Just listen a minute, okay? It's Avery Stafford. Remember me? We met a few weeks ago? You liked my dragonfly bracelet. Do you remember?"

Silence.

"You said my grandmother was a friend of yours. Judy. Judy Myers Stafford? You and I talked about the photo you had beside your bed." It seems as though my whole world has changed since that day.

"Well?" May snaps after a moment. "Are you coming in or *not*?" Beyond the door, there's the sound of a body shuffling and bedcovers moving. I don't know if she's preparing to greet us or loading up to take another shot.

"Are you finished throwing things?"

"I don't suppose you'd leave if I weren't." But there's a note of anticipation in her voice this time. She's inviting me in, so I enter, leaving Trent safely in the hall.

She lies propped up in bed, wearing a blue housecoat that matches her eyes. Even with a stack of pillows behind her, there's something regal about the way she watches me, as if she was accustomed to service in bed long before her nursing home years.

"I was hoping you'd feel well enough to talk with me today," I venture. "I asked my grandmother about you. She mentioned Queen . . . or Queenie, but that was about all she could remember."

May seems stricken. "She's *that* bad?"

"I'm afraid so." I feel terrible for being the messenger. "Grandma Judy isn't unhappy. She just can't remember things. It's hard for her."

"And hard for you too, I would imagine?"

May's sudden insight leaves me floundering emotionally. "Yes, it is. My grandmother and I were always very close."

"Yet she never told you about the people in my photograph?" Beneath the question, there is the insinuation that this woman knows my grandmother intimately. I'm not sure I'll be able to resign myself to it if I never find out the truth — if May won't tell me.

"I have a feeling Grandma Judy would now, if she could. But I'm hoping that, since she can't, you will."

"It has nothing to do with you." May turns her shoulder away from me, as if she's afraid to have me look directly at her.

"I have a feeling it does. And maybe . . ."

Her attention shifts toward the door. "Who is that out there? Who *else* is listening?"

"I brought someone with me. He's been helping me try to figure out what my grandmother hasn't been able to tell me. He's just a friend."

Trent steps inside and crosses the room with his hand outstretched, flashing the sort of smile that could probably sell snow cones to Eskimos. "Trent," he says, introducing himself. "Nice to meet you, Mrs. Crandall."

She accepts the greeting and imprisons his hand in both of hers, holding him slightly bent over the bed while she turns back to me. "Just a *friend,* you say? I doubt that."

I draw back a little. "Trent and I only met a few days ago, when I went down to Edisto."

"Lovely place, Edisto." She focuses on Trent, her eyes narrowing.

"Yes, it is," I agree. *Why is she studying him that way?* "My grandmother spent quite a bit of time there over the years. Uncle

Clifford told me that she liked to write at the cottage. It seems that she and Trent's grandfather may have done some . . . business there." Just as if I were working a witness on the stand, I watch for changes in her demeanor. She tries to hide them, but they *are* there, and they're obvious — more so with each sentence.

She's wondering how much I know.

"I don't believe I caught your last name." She blinks at Trent.

The air in the room seems to tighten as she awaits the answer, but when he offers a more formal introduction, she nods and smiles. "Mmmm," she says. "Yes, you do have his eyes."

I get the little tingle I always have when I know a witness is about to crack. Often, it's this very thing that does it — the surprise appearance of the face that's familiar, a tie to something hidden in the past, the fringes of a secret that's been kept too long.

May's trembling fingers lift away from Trent's hand. She touches his jawline. Moisture mats her lashes. "You favor him. He was a looker too." She offers a closed-lipped smile that tells me she was probably quite the flirt in her day, a woman who had no difficulty operating in a man's world.

Trent even blushes a little. It's cute. I can't

help enjoying the exchange.

May wags a finger my way. "This one's a keeper. Mark my words."

It's my turn to blush. "Sadly, I'm already committed."

"I don't see a wedding band, yet." May grabs my hand and makes a show of examining my engagement ring. "And I know a spark when I see it. I *should* know. I've outlived three husbands at this point."

A puff of laughter spills past Trent's lips, and he ducks his head, sandy-blond hair falling forward.

"And I had nothing to do with any of their deaths, in case you're wondering," May informs us. "I loved each of them dearly. One was a teacher, one was a preacher, and the last was an artist who found his calling later in life. One taught me to *think,* one taught me to *know,* and one taught me to *see.* Each inspired me. I was a musician, you understand. I worked in Hollywood and also traveled with big bands. That was back in the glory days, long before all this digital foolishness."

My phone buzzes in my purse, and she frowns toward it. "Those infernal things. The world would be better off if *they* had never been invented."

I silence the phone completely. If May is

finally ready to tell me the story of that photo on her nightstand, I want nothing to distract us from it. In fact, it's time to redirect the witness right now.

I open the envelope and slide out the pictures from the cabin at Trent's. "Actually, it's these we were wondering about. These, and the Tennessee Children's Home Society."

Her face instantly hardens. She flings a fiery look my way. "I could do without ever hearing those words again."

Trent cups her hand in both of his, looks down at their intertwined fingers. "I'm sorry, Mrs. Crandall . . . if we're dredging up painful memories. But my grandfather never told me. I mean, I knew he was adopted when he was fairly young, and I knew he broke ties with his adoptive parents after he found out. But I didn't know much about the Tennessee Children's Home Society — not until recently. Maybe in passing I'd overheard people mention it to my grandfather over the years, when visitors would stop by. I was aware that my grandfather helped those people in some way, and that he felt the need to conduct those meetings in private — in his workshop or out on the boat. My grandmother never liked any kind of business talk in the house, real estate or otherwise. I didn't know anything about my grandfather's hobby, or side business, or whatever it was, until I helped him take care of the remaining files before he died. He asked me not to read the papers, and I didn't. Not until Avery came to Edisto a few days ago."

May's mouth falls open. Tears rim her eyes. "He's passed, then? I knew he was very ill."

Trent confirms that he lost his grandfather months ago, and May pulls him close for a kiss on the cheek. "He was a good man and a dear friend."

"Was he adopted from the Tennessee Children's Home Society?" Trent asks. "Was that why he was interested in it?"

A somber nod answers. "Yes, indeed he was. And I was as well. That was where we met. Of course, he was just three years old then. He was such a cute little thing, and sweet. His name wasn't Trent at the time. He didn't change it to that until years later, when he found out who he really was. He had a sister who was separated from him during our stay at the home. She was two or three years older, and I think he always hoped that using his real name might help her to find him. But that's the irony of it. The man who aided so many of us in recon-

necting with one another again never was able to locate his sister. Perhaps she was one of those who didn't survive. There were many. . . ."

Her voice cracks and trails away. She pushes upright in the bed, clears her throat. "I was born on the Mississippi River in a shantyboat my father built. Queenie was my mother and Briny was my father. I had three little sisters, Camellia, Lark, and Fern, and a brother, Gabion. He was the youngest. . . ."

She closes her eyes, but I can see them moving under thin, blue-veined lids as she continues her story. It is as if she's dreaming, watching the images float by. She talks about being taken off the boat by the police, ending up in the children's home. She describes weeks of uncertainty and fear, workers who were cruel, separation from her siblings, horrors like the ones Trent and I have read about.

The story she tells is heartbreaking yet mesmerizing. We stand on either side of the bed, barely breathing as we listen. "I lost track of my other three siblings at the home," she says at the end. "But Fern and I were fortunate. We were kept together. Adopted."

She stares out the window, and for a mo-

ment, I wonder if she's told us all she intends to. Finally, she returns her attention to Trent. "The last time I saw your grandfather as a child, I was afraid he would be one of those who wouldn't survive the home. He was such a timid little thing. Always in trouble with the workers without meaning to be. He was practically like a little brother by the time I left. I never thought I'd see him again. When a man named Trent Turner contacted me years later, I assumed he was a fraud. I didn't recognize the name, of course. Georgia Tann habitually gave new names to the children — to help prevent their birth families from finding them, no doubt. I can tell you that I remember her as a horrible, cruel woman and that I believe the extent of her crimes may never be fully told. Few of her victims were able to do what your grandfather did — reclaim a birth name and a heritage. He even found his biological mother before she died, and he reunited with other relatives. He became Trent again, but when he was little, I knew him as Stevie."

Her attention wanders again, her mind seeming to travel with it. I shift the photo of the four women just a bit, make a few inferences. In court, this would be leading the

witness, but here it's just helping to uncover the story. "Are these your sisters in the photo with you and my grandmother?"

I know the three women on the left must be sisters or cousins. It's obvious enough, even with the hats shading their faces. I'm still troubled by their similarities to my grandmother. The hair color. The pale eyes that seem to reach beyond the photo. But the facial structures, at least as much as I can see of them, are different. The features of the three sisters are substantial, perfectly chiseled. They have wide, square chins, and ski-slope noses, and almond-shaped eyes that slant upward slightly at the edges. They are beautiful. My grandmother is lovely as well, but her features are thin and birdlike, her blue eyes almost too large for her face. They are luminous, even in black-and-white.

May takes the photo and holds it in her shaky hands. Her study seems endless. I have to force myself not to prod. *What's going on in her mind? What is she thinking of? What is she remembering?*

"Yes. The three of us — Lark, Fern, and me. Bathing beauties." She gives a quick, wicked giggle and taps Trent's hand. "I think your grandmother worried a bit whenever we came around. But she needn't have. Trent loved her dearly. We were so grateful to him for helping us to find one another. Edisto was a special place for us. It was where we were first reunited."

"Was that where you met my grandmother?" I crave a simple answer to all of this. One I can live with. I don't want to find out that my grandmother was somehow paying penance for our family's involvement with the Tennessee Children's Home Society — that my grandfathers were among the many politicians who protected Georgia Tann and her network, who turned a blind eye to atrocities because powerful families did not want her crimes revealed or their own adoptions nullified. "Was that where the two of you became friends?"

Her finger traces the white frame on the photo. She's looking at my grandmother. If only I could climb inside her mind or, better yet, inside the picture. "Yes, yes it was. We'd crossed paths at society events before I ever knew her, though I will say, I had a completely wrong impression of her prior to making her acquaintance. She grew to be a dear friend. And she was so very generous to loan my sisters and me the cottage on Edisto from time to time, so we could get away together. That photo was taken during one of our trips. Your grandmother joined us there. It was a lovely late-summer day on the beach."

The explanation soothes me, and I'd like to stop there, but it doesn't explain why the words *Tennessee Children's Home Society* were on the typewriter ribbon in my grandmother's cottage . . . or why Trent Turner, Sr., was in communication with my grandmother.

"Trent's grandfather left an envelope for my Grandma Judy," I say. "Judging by her daybook, I think she was making plans to pick it up before she got so sick. Inside the envelope, there were documents from the Tennessee Children's Home Society. Health assessments and surrender papers for a baby boy named Shad Arthur Foss. Why would she have wanted those?"

I've caught May off guard now. There *is* more to this story, but she's biting down hard on it.

Her eyelids flutter and descend. "I'm so very . . . so very . . . tired all of a sudden. All this . . . this talking. It's more than I usually . . . do . . . in a week."

"Was my grandmother involved with the Tennessee Children's Home Society? Was my family involved?" If I don't find out today, I have a feeling I never will.

"You'd have to ask her about that." May

presses into the pillows, draws an exaggerated breath.

"I can't. I told you that. She isn't able to remember things. Please, whatever it is, just give me the truth. Arcadia. Does it have anything to do with this?" My grip tightens around the bed rails.

Trent reaches across and lays a hand over mine. "Maybe it's better if we quit here for today."

But I can see May withdrawing into herself, the story vanishing like chalk art on a rainy day.

I scramble after the running colors. "I just want to know if my family was . . . responsible in some way. Why did my grandmother have such an intense interest in this?"

May pats along the railing until she finds my fingers. She squeezes them reassuringly. "No, of course not, dear. Don't fret. At one time, Judy was helping me to write my story. That's all. But I thought better of it. I've found in life that bygones are a bit like collard greens. They tend to taste bitter. It's best not to chew on them overly long. Your grandmother was a fine writer, but it was so difficult for her to hear about our time in the home. Her talent was meant for happier tales, I believe."

"She was helping you write your story?

That's all?" Could this really be the sum total of it? No big family secret, just Grandma Judy using her abilities to help a friend, to shed light on an old injustice, the effects of which still lingered? A sense of relief washes through me.

It all makes perfect sense.

"That's everything there is," May confirms. "I wish I could tell you more."

That last part tickles my senses like a stray puff of smoke from a fire that's supposedly been put out. Witnesses who aren't telling the truth have a hard time stopping on an absolute yes or no.

What does she wish she could tell me? Is *there more*?

May finds Trent's hand, squeezes it, then lets go. "I'm so sorry about your grandfather. He was a godsend to many of us. Before the state's adoption records were opened in '96, we had little means of discovering where our relatives might be — who we really were. But your grandfather had his ways. Without him, Fern and I would never have found our sister. They're both gone now, of course — Lark and Fern. I would appreciate it if you'd refrain from disturbing their families, even so . . . or mine, for that matter. We were young women with lives and husbands and children by the time we were brought together again. We chose not to interfere with one another. It was enough for each of us to know that the others were well. Your grandfather understood that. I hope you will respect our wishes." She opens her eyes and turns my way. "Both of you." Suddenly, all signs of exhaustion have faded. The look she gives me is intense, demanding.

"Of course," Trent says. But I can tell it's not Trent's answer she's after.

"I didn't set out to bother anyone." Now I'm the one tap-dancing around the issue . . . which is that I shouldn't make promises I can't keep. "I just wanted to know how my grandmother was involved."

"And now you do, so all's well." She punctuates this with a resolute nod. I'm not sure which one of us she's trying to sell on this — me or herself. "I have made peace with my past. It is a story I hope never to tell again. As I said earlier, I thought better of sharing the whole thing with your grandmother even. Why release such ugliness into the present? We all have difficulties. Mine may be different than some, but I have come through them, as did Lark and Fern and, I would assume, though we were never able to find him, my brother as well. I prefer to hope it was so. He was my one true reason for wanting to have the story written, years ago when I coaxed your grandmother into helping me with the project. I suppose I thought a book or a newspaper article might somehow reach him if he was still out there, and if he was one of the many who'd simply vanished under the care of the Tennessee Children's Home Society, it would provide a memorial for him. Perhaps for my birth parents as well. There are no stones to lay flowers upon. None that I would know how to find, in any case."

"I'm so . . . I'm so sorry for what you've been through."

Nodding, she closes her eyes again, shutting me out. "I should rest now. Soon enough, they'll come around to poke me, or prod me, or haul me off to that infernal physical therapy room. Honestly, I'm almost ninety years old. What do I need with muscle tone?"

Trent chuckles. "Now you sound like my grandfather. If he'd had his way, we would've put him in a jon boat and let him drift off down the Edisto River."

"That seems perfectly lovely. Would you be so kind as to arrange the boat? And then I'll find my way home to Augusta and float away down the Savannah." She closes her eyes, smiling a bit. Within moments, her breaths lengthen, and her eyelids flutter in their pleated frames. The smile remains. I wonder if she is once again that little girl drifting on the muddy waters of the Mississippi aboard the shantyboat her father built.

I try to imagine having a history like hers, having lived two lives, having been, effectively, two different people. I can't. I've never known anything but the stalwart stronghold of the Stafford name and a family who supported me, nurtured me, loved me. What was May's life really like with her adoptive parents? I realize now, she never really told that part of the story. She only said that, after a heartbreaking stay in the children's home, she and her sister had been given to a family.

Why did she stop the story there? Was the rest too private?

Even though she's answered the question I came here to ask, and she's requested that we not pry any further, I can't help wanting to know more.

Trent seems to be feeling the same way. Of course he would. His family history is tied to May's.

We hover on either side of the bed a few minutes, both of us watching her, lost in our own thoughts. Finally, we take our photographs and reluctantly withdraw from the room. Neither of us speaks until we're out of earshot.

"I never knew any of that about my grandfather," he says.

"It must be hard, finding out."

Trent's brows fold together. "It's strange to think that Granddad came through that kind of thing growing up. It makes me admire him all the more — what he did with his life, what kind of person he was. But it also makes me mad. I can't help wondering what his life would've been like if he hadn't been in the wrong place at the wrong time, if his parents hadn't been poor, if someone had stopped the Tennessee Children's Home Society before they ever got to him. If he'd grown up with the family he was born into, would he have been the same person? Did he love the river because he came from it or because the father who raised him fished on the weekends? May said he met some of his biological relatives. How did he feel about that? Why didn't he ever introduce us to any of them? There are so many questions I'd like to ask him now."

We wander to a stop just outside the front door, both of us reluctant to part ways and move toward our own cars. Our reason for being together has been swept away by May's story. This should be goodbye, but I feel as if ties now exist and they're not meant to be severed. "Do you think you'll try to find any of them — your grandfather's family?"

Tucking his hands in his jean pockets, he shrugs, looking down at the sidewalk. "It's so far back, I can't see the point. They'd be distant relatives of ours by now. Maybe that's why my grandfather never bothered. I might do some more research, though. I'd like to know details . . . for Jonah and my nieces and nephews, if nothing else. Maybe they'll ask someday. I don't want any more secrets."

The conversation wanes. Trent lightly runs his tongue along his lip, as if he wants to say something but can't quite decide whether he should.

When we start up again, we tumble over each other.

"Thank you —"

"Avery, I know we —"

For some reason, we both find it funny. Laughter diffuses the tension a little.

"Ladies first." He gestures my way, as if he's ushering the words I'm about to say. I really don't have the right ones. After what we've journeyed through these past few days, it seems almost inconceivable that this is the end. We're bonded, or at least it feels that way.

Maybe I'm being silly. "I was just going to say thank you for all of this. For not sending me away empty-handed. I know that breaking the promise to your grandfather was hard. I don't . . ." Our gazes meet. The rest of the sentence vanishes. My cheeks blaze. I'm once again aware of an unexpected chemistry between us. I thought it was the pull of the mystery, but now the mystery has been solved and the tickle of fascination is still there.

A random thought comes, completely unbidden, entirely unwanted: *Maybe I'm making a mistake . . . with Elliot.* And then I realize it's not as random as it seems. I've only been sidestepping the question until now. Are Elliot and I in love, or are we just . . . in our thirties and feeling like it's time? Do we have a deep, long-standing friendship, or do we have passion? Even though we've been telling ourselves we won't be ramrodded by our families, have we allowed it to happen anyway? A bit of Leslie's savvy political coaching comes back to me. Suddenly, it seems like evidence. *If we do need to raise your public profile, Avery, a well-timed wedding announcement could fill the bill. Aside from that, it's not advantageous for a pretty young thing to be single in Wash-*

ington, no matter how well she minds her body language in social situations. The wolves need to know there's officially no availability there.

I try to shake off the thought, but it's like a sandbur in a horse's forelock. Strands are twisted all around it. I can't imagine changing course now. Everyone, *everyone* is expecting an announcement soon. The fallout would be . . . unthinkable. Honeybee and Bitsy would be heartbroken. Socially and politically, I'd look like a flake, a person who can't make up her mind, who doesn't know her own heart.

Am I?

"Avery?" Trent's eyes narrow, and his head cocks to one side. He's wondering what I'm thinking.

I can't possibly tell him. "Your turn." I don't trust myself to say anything more, considering the wild track my mind has taken.

"Doesn't matter now."

"Not fair. What were you about to say, really?"

He surrenders without too much of a fight. "I'm sorry we got off on the wrong foot that first day. Usually I wouldn't talk to a customer that way."

"Well, I wasn't really a customer, so you're

excused." He was actually pretty decent about it all, considering how pushy I was. In the end, I'm a Stafford through and through. I tend to assume that I'll get what I want.

Which, I realize with a shiver, makes me eerily like the adoptive parents who inadvertently funded Georgia Tann's business. No doubt some were well-meaning people and some of the children really did need homes, but others, especially those who knew that exorbitant fees were being forked over for made-to-order sons and daughters, must have had some idea of what was happening. They just assumed that money, power, and social position gave them the right.

Guilt stains this realization of mine. I think of all the privileges I've been given, including a Senate seat practically prepackaged for me.

Do I have a right to any of this, just because of the family I come from?

Trent's hands tuck awkwardly back into his pockets. He glances at his car, then turns my way again. "Don't be a stranger. Look me up next time you're on Edisto."

The idea strikes me like the sound of the bugle going off at the beginning of a cross-country hunt, when the horse's muscles tense and I know that if I just loosen the reins, all that potential energy will be unleashed in one direction. "I'd really love to know what else you discover about your grandfather's family . . . if you find anything, I mean. No pressure, though. I don't want to be nosy."

"Why stop now?"

I cough, pretending to be offended, but we both know it's the truth. "It's the lawyer in me. Sorry."

"You must be a good lawyer."

"I try to be." I swell with the sense of pride that comes from having someone else affirm an accomplishment I care about. One I worked for myself. "I like to see things set right."

"It shows."

A car pulls up into a nearby parking space. The intrusion reminds both of us that we can't stand here forever.

Trent takes a last look at the nursing home. "It sounds as if she's lived quite a life."

"Yes, it does." It stings to imagine May, my grandmother's friend, languishing in this place day after day. No visitors. No one to talk to. Grandkids living far away in a complex blended-family situation. It's not anyone's fault. It's just a reality. I'll definitely get in touch with Andrew Moore at the PAC and see if he can suggest any organizations that could help her.

A horn sounds on the street, and nearby a car door closes. The world is still moving, and Trent and I should too.

His chest heaves outward and then relaxes. His breath grazes my ear as he leans in to kiss me on the cheek. "Thanks, Avery. I'm glad I know the truth."

His face lingers against mine. I smell salt air, and baby shampoo, and a hint of pluff mud. Or maybe I'm only imagining it.

"Me too."

"Don't be a stranger," he says again.

"I won't."

From the corner of my eye, I catch a glimpse of a woman coming up the sidewalk. White blouse, pumps, black skirt. Her rapid-fire steps feel unwelcome, out of keeping with the day. Heat boils into my cheeks, and I jerk away from Trent so quickly, he gives me a confused look.

Leslie has tracked me down. I should've known better than to ask Ian to check on May's condition for me. Leslie's chin recedes into her neck as she regards Trent and me. I can only imagine what she's thinking. Actually, I don't have to imagine it. I can *see* what she's thinking. The exchange she just witnessed looked intimate.

"Thanks again, Trent." I try to diffuse the impression she must have. "Take care on the drive home." I step back, clasp my hands one over the other.

His eyes search mine. "Yeah," he mutters, cocking his head to one side and squinting at me. He has no idea someone is standing behind him or that the real world has come rushing in with gale force.

"We've been looking for you." Leslie makes her presence known without taking time for pleasantries. "Cellphone not working this morning, or are you in hiding?"

Trent moves aside, glances from my father's press secretary to me.

"I was on vacation," I say. "Everyone knew where I was."

"On Edisto?" Leslie retorts with a nip of sarcasm. Clearly, I'm not on Edisto now. She directs another suspicious glare in Trent's direction.

"Yes . . . well . . . I . . ." My mind scrambles. Sweat beads under the cotton floral tourist dress I bought so I'd have something clean to wear today. "It's a long story."

"Well, I'm afraid we don't have time for it. You're needed at home." She means to let Trent know we have business to tend to and he's not welcome here any longer. It works. He gives me one last quizzical look, then excuses himself, saying he has someone he wants to visit while he's in Aiken.

"Take care, Avery," he says, and starts toward his car.

"Trent . . . thanks," I call after him. He lifts a hand and waves over his shoulder in a way that says, whatever is going on here, he wants no part of it.

I wish I could run after him and at least apologize for Leslie's abrupt dismissal, but I know I shouldn't. It'll only raise more questions.

"My phone was off, I think." I preempt Leslie before she can start an inquisition. "Sorry about that. What's going on?"

She blinks slowly, lifts her chin. "Let's not talk about that for a minute. Let's talk about what I just saw when I came up this sidewalk." She waves a hand toward Trent, and I hope he's far enough away not to hear her. "Because *that* was disturbing."

"Leslie, he's a friend. He was helping me track down some family history. That's all."

"Family history? Really? Here?" Jerking her chin up, she snorts in frustration. "Of what sort?"

"I'd rather not say."

Leslie's eyes flash. Her lips squeeze into a thin line. She takes a breath, blinks again, levels a heated gaze at me. "Well, let me tell you something. *Whatever* I just witnessed there is exactly the kind of scene you cannot afford. *Nothing* that could possibly be spun, used, or misinterpreted, Avery. *Nothing.* You have to be pure as the driven snow, and that did *not* look pure from a distance. Can you imagine how it would have played in a photograph? All of us, the entire team, are putting *everything* we have into you. In case you're needed."

"I know that. I understand."

"The last thing this family can withstand is one more battle to fight."

"Point taken." I paint a layer of confidence over the words, but inside I'm confused; I'm embarrassed; I'm aggravated that I have to deal with Leslie right now. I'm torn between appeasing Leslie and running after Trent. I'm afraid to even look up to see whether he's made it to his car yet.

The engine starts, and answers my question. I hear him back out and drive away. *It's probably for the best,* I tell myself. *Of course it is.* I had my whole life planned before I went to Edisto. Why would I want to jeopardize that over . . . ancient family history, things that don't matter anymore, a man with whom I have no connection other than a story that even those who lived it want to forget?

"There's been a development." Leslie's words take a moment to register even though I'm looking right at her. "*The Sentinel* just rolled out a massive exposé about corporate-owned nursing care and the responsibility dodge. It's only a matter of time before the major media pick it up. The article highlighted the South Carolina cases. They have cost comparisons between Magnolia Manor and the kind of care facilities that have been named in some of the injury lawsuits. They have photos of victims and their families. They titled it 'Aging Unevenly,' and they headed it up with a long-range picture of your dad and your grandmother walking in the gardens at Magnolia."

I stare at her, openmouthed, a feverish anger igniting deep within me. "How dare they! How dare . . . anyone! They have no right to harass my grandmother."

"This is politics, Avery. Politics and sensationalism. There *is* no safe ground."

CHAPTER 20

Rill

The man's name is Darren, and the woman's name is Victoria, but we've been told that we're to call them Papa and Mommy, not Darren and Victoria or Mr. Sevier and Mrs. Sevier. It doesn't bother me much. I've never called anyone Papa or Mommy, so the words don't have a place in me one way or the other. They're just words. That's all.

Queenie and Briny are still our folks, and we're still going back to them, soon as I can find a way. It won't be hard as I thought it might be. The Sevier house is big and filled with rooms no one uses, and out back there's a wide porch that looks over fields of tall trees and green grass, and all of it slopes on down to the best thing ever — the water. It's not the river; it's a long, skinny oxbow lake that drains off into a place called Dedmen's Slough . . . and Dedmen's Slough goes all the way down to the Mississippi. I found that out because I asked Zuma, who cleans this place and fixes the meals and lives over the old carriage house, where Mr. Sevier parks his cars. He has three cars. I've never even met anybody that has three cars.

Zuma's husband, Hoy, and their girl, Hootsie, live out there with her. Hoy keeps the yard and takes care of a pen of chickens, Mr. Sevier's hunting dogs that bark and howl all night, and a pony Mrs. Sevier has been telling us for two weeks now we can go riding on if we want to. I said that we don't like ponies, even though it's not true. I let Fern know she better not say any different.

Zuma's husband is big and scary and black as the dickens, and after being at Mrs. Murphy's, I don't want some yardman getting me or Fern off by ourselves anyplace. I don't want us alone with Mr. Sevier. He's tried to take us out to the pony too, but only because Mrs. Sevier made him. He'll do just about anything to keep her from wandering off down the path to the garden where two babies born dead and three that were never born at all have graves with little stone lambs on top. When Mrs. Sevier goes out there, she lays on the ground and cries. Then she comes home and gets in her bed and stays. There's old scars across her wrists. I know why they're there, but I don't tell Fern, of course.

"Just sit in her lap, and let her fix your hair and play dolls with you. Make sure she's happy," I tell Fern. "No crying and don't wet the bed. You hear me?" That's the only reason the Seviers brought me here in the first place — because Fern wouldn't stop crying and bed-wetting and carrying on.

Mostly, Fern's been doing pretty good now. Some days, though, there's not a thing that'll help Mrs. Sevier. Some days, she don't want to be touched by another living soul. She only wants the dead.

When she lays up in her bed and cries over the babies she lost, Mr. Sevier hides in his music room, and we're stuck with Zuma, who thinks having us around makes too much work for her. Mrs. Sevier used to buy things for Zuma's little girl, Hootsie, who's ten, two years younger than me. Now Mrs. Sevier buys things for us instead. Zuma ain't one bit happy about that either. She's weaseled enough information out of Fern to know where we're from, and she can't see why somebody fine as Mr. and Mrs. Sevier would want river trash like us anyhow. She lets us know it, but she can't say it where Mrs. Sevier might hear, of course.

Zuma doesn't dare hit us, but she'd like to. When Hootsie acts up, Zuma wears out Hootsie's skinny behind. Sometimes, Zuma shakes that long wood spoon our way when nobody's looking and says, "Oughta be grateful. Oughta be kissin' the missus feet, her even lettin' you in this fine house. I know what you is, and don' you be fo'gettin' it neither. You's only here till the missus gits a baby a' her own. Mister thinks, if she quit worrin' about it so hard, it gonna happen. When it do, you li'l river rats be gone like smoke. Out wit' the trash. Y'all only here fo' now. Don' be makin' yo'self to home. I seen it all befo', jus' so you know. You ain't here fo' long."

She's right, so I got no reason to argue. There's food here, at least, and plenty of it. There's frilly dresses, even if they are scratchy and stiff, and hair ribbons, and Crayolas, and books, and shiny new Mary Jane shoes. There's a little tea set for tea parties with cookies in the afternoons. We've never even had a tea party before, so Mrs. Sevier has to show us how to play the game.

There's no lining up for bath time. We don't have to get naked while other people look on. Nobody hits us in the head. Nobody threatens to tie us up and hang us in the closet. Nobody gets locked in the basement. At least not so far, and like Zuma says, we won't be here long enough to find out whether it'd happen after the new wears off.

One thing I know for sure is that, whenever the Seviers get tired of us, we're not going back to Mrs. Murphy's. At night, after I'm safe in the room next to Fern's, I look way down across the pasture and see the water through the trees. I watch for lanterns drifting along the oxbow lake, and I spot a few. Sometimes, I see lights, even far off in the slough, floating like fallen stars. All I have to do is find us a way onto one of the boats, and we can go through Dedmen's Slough to the big river. Once we're there, it'll be an easy trip downwater to where the Wolf meets the Mississippi at Mud Island, and that's where Queenie and Briny will be waiting for us.

I just need to find us a boat, and I will. After we're gone, the Seviers won't have the first idea what happened to us. Miss Tann didn't tell them we're from river folk, and I bet Zuma won't either. Our new mommy and papa think our real mama was a college girl and our daddy was a professor. They think she took sick with pneumonia and died and he lost his job and couldn't keep us. They also think Fern's just three years old, but she's four.

I don't tell the Seviers any different. Mostly, I just try to be good so nothing will happen before Fern and me can get away.

"*There* you are," Mrs. Sevier says when she finds us down at the dining table waiting on breakfast. She frowns, seeing that we're already dressed in the clothes that were set out for us last night. Fern's wearing a pair of blue check pants with a little top that buttons up the back. It has puffy ruffles around her arms and shows her tummy under the lace at the bottom of the shirt. I've got on a purple dress that's ruffly and fluffy and a little too small at the top. I had to suck in to get it buttoned, and I shouldn't need to, but I'm growing, I guess. Queenie says we Foss kids always get bigger in spurts.

Either I'm in a growing spurt, or it's because we eat a lot more than just corn mush here. Every morning, we all sit down to a big meal, and at lunch Zuma makes us sandwiches on a tray. In the evening, we have a big supper too, unless Mr. Sevier is busy in his music room at supper. When that happens, we have sandwiches on a tray again, and Mrs. Sevier plays parlor games with us, which Fern likes to do a lot.

"May, I *told* you there's no reason for you

to be up so early and making little Beth get dressed too." She crosses her arms over the silky bathrobe that looks like it oughta be on Queen Cleopatra. Fern and me have robes that match. Our new mommy had Zuma make them just for us, special. We haven't put them on since. I figure it's best we don't get used to fancy things, since we're not staying long.

Besides that, there's two little bumps poking out on my chest, and the gowns are shiny and thin, and it makes the bumps show, and I don't want anybody to see.

"We waited . . . awhile." I look down at my lap. She doesn't understand that all our lives we've been up at first light. There's no other way to live on a shantyboat. When the river comes awake, you do too. The birds speak, and the boats whistle, and the waves wash up one after another if you're tied anyplace near a main channel. The lines have to be watched, and the fish are biting, and the stove needs kindling. There's things to do.

"It's time you learned to sleep until a decent hour." Mrs. Sevier shakes her head at me, and I don't know whether she's playing or if she doesn't like me very much. "You're not in an orphanage anymore, May. This is your home."

"Yes, ma'am."

"Yes, *Mommy.*" She lays a hand on my head and leans over to kiss Fern's cheek, then pretends to gobble up her ear. Fern giggles and squeals.

"Yes, Mommy," I repeat. It ain't natural, but I'm getting better at it. Next time, I'll remember.

She sits at the end of the table and looks down the long hall, resting her chin on her hand, frowning. "I guess you haven't seen Papa this morning?"

"No . . . Mommy."

Fern shrinks in her seat and gives our new mommy's frown a worried look. We all know where Mr. Sevier is. We can hear the music drifting up the hall. He's not supposed to go in his music room before breakfast. We've heard them fighting about it.

"Dar-ren!" she hollers, clicking her fingernails on the table.

Fern slaps her hands over her ears, and Zuma rushes in with a covered china bowl rattling in her hands. The lid almost slides off before she catches it. The white shows all around her eyes, and then she sees that Mrs. Sevier isn't mad at *her.* "I'll go for 'im, Missus." She sets the bowl on the table and hollers over her shoulder toward the kitchen, "Hootsie, you bring them platters in befo' they go cold!"

She sweeps past the table, stiff as a whisk broom, and shoots a mad look my way when our new mommy isn't looking. Back before we came, Zuma didn't have to dirty up all these dishes for breakfast. She only had to make a tray and take it to Mrs. Sevier's bedroom. Hootsie told me. Before we came, sometimes Hootsie'd stay upstairs all morning with the missus, just looking at *Life* magazines and picture books and trying to keep her happy so the mister could work.

Now Hootsie's gotta help in the kitchen, and that's *our* fault.

She sticks a foot under the table and stomps on my toes when she sets down the eggs.

In a minute, Zuma comes up the hall with Mr. Sevier. She's the only one who can get him out of his music room when the door's closed. She raised Mr. Sevier since he was a little boy, and she still takes care of him like he is one. He listens to her when he won't even listen to his missus.

"You gotsa eat!" she says as she follows him up the hall, her hands waving in and out of the morning shadows. "Here I been, cookin' up all this food, and it done gone half-cold a'ready."

"Woke with a melody in mind earlier. Had

to work it out before it left me." He stops at the end of the hall, puts one hand to his stomach, and holds the other one in the air. He dances a little jig like he's an actor onstage. Then he takes a bow for us. "Good morning, ladies."

Mrs. Sevier's frown tugs upward. "You *know* what we agreed, Darren. *Not* before breakfast, *and* meals at the table *together.* How will the girls ever learn to be a family if you're locked away by yourself all hours?"

He doesn't stop at his chair but rounds the table and kisses her square on the lips. "How's my muse this morning?"

"Oh, *stop* that," she complains. "You're only trying to shake me off."

"Am I succeeding at it?" He winks at Fern and me. Fern giggles, and I just pretend I didn't notice.

Something tugs in my chest, and I stare down at my plate, and I see Briny kissing Queenie just that same way when he passed through the shanty heading to the afterdeck.

The food doesn't smell good all of a sudden, even though my stomach growls for it. I don't want to eat these people's breakfast or laugh at their jokes or call them Mommy and Papa. I have a mama and a daddy, and I want to go home to them.

Fern shouldn't giggle and carry on with

these people either. It ain't right.

I reach under the table and pinch her leg, and she yelps a little.

Our new mommy and papa bend their foreheads at us, trying to figure out what happened. Fern doesn't tell.

Zuma and Hootsie bring out the rest of the dishes, and we eat breakfast while Mr. Sevier talks about his new music and how just the right tune came to him in the middle of the night. He talks about scores and rests and notes and all kinds of things. Mrs. Sevier sighs and looks out the window, but I can't help listening. I've never heard anything about how people write music down on paper. All the tunes I know come from listening when Briny plays his guitar or harmonica or maybe even the piano in a pool hall. The music always goes deep down inside me and makes me feel a certain way.

Now I wonder if Briny ever knew that people write tunes on paper like a storybook and it gets put in the movies, the way Mr. Sevier talks about. His new music is for a movie. At the end of the table, he moves his hands around in the air and talks wild and excited about a scene where Quantrill's Raiders ride through Kansas and burn a whole town.

He hums the tune and uses the table for a

drum, and the dishes rattle, and I can feel the horses running and hear the guns blasting.

"What do you think, dear?" he says to Mrs. Sevier when he finishes.

She claps and Fern claps too. "A masterpiece," Mrs. Sevier says. "Of course it's a masterpiece. Don't you think so, Bethie?"

I can't get used to them calling Fern Beth, which they think is her real name, of course.

"Madderpees." Fern tries to say the word *masterpiece* with her mouth full of grits.

The three of them laugh, and I just look down at my plate.

"It's so good to see her happy." Our new mommy leans around the table to tuck Fern's hair out of the way so she won't get grits in it.

"Yes, it is." Mr. Sevier is looking at his wife, but she doesn't know it. She's busy petting Fern.

Mrs. Sevier twirls Fern's hair around her finger, blending tiny spirals into bigger curls, like Shirley Temple's. Mrs. Sevier likes it that way best. Most days, I put mine in a braid behind my back, so she won't get any ideas about doing that to me. "I was worried we'd never get to this point," she tells her mister.

"These things take time."

"I was so afraid I'd never be a mother."

His eyes round upward, like he's happy. He looks across the table. "She's ours now."

No she's not! I want to scream. *You're not her mother. You're not our mother. Those dead babies in the graveyard, those are yours.* I hate Mrs. Sevier for wanting Fern. I hate those babies for dying. I hate Mr. Sevier for bringing us here. If he'd left us alone, we'd be back on the *Arcadia* by now, Fern and me. Nobody would be twirling my sister's hair into Shirley Temple curls or calling her Beth.

I clench my teeth so hard the pain travels all the way to the top of my head. I'm glad for it. It's just a little ache, and I know where it comes from. I can stop it any time I want. The one in my heart is way bigger. I can't fix it no matter how hard I try. It scares me so much that I can't even breathe.

What if Fern decides she likes these people better than she likes me? What if she forgets about Briny and Queenie and the Arcadia? We didn't have fancy dresses and scooter toys on the porch and stuffed teddy bears and Crayolas and little china tea sets there. All we had was the river, but the river fed us and carried us and set us free.

I have to make sure Fern doesn't forget. She can't turn into Beth on the inside.

"May?" Mrs. Sevier is talking, and I haven't even heard her. I put on a sunshine face and look her way.

"Yes . . . Mommy?"

"I said, I'm going to take Beth into Memphis for a fitting of special shoes today. It's important that we correct the leg that turns inward before she's any older. Once a child is grown, it's too late, they tell me. That would be a shame, when it's something that can be cured." Her head crooks sideways a bit. She looks like an eagle when it's watching for fish. Pretty, but the fish better be careful. I'm glad my feet are under the table so she can't see my right leg. We all have the foot that toes in a little. We get it from Queenie. Briny says it marks us as part of the royal line of the Kingdom Arcadia.

Now I feel myself straightening it just in case she takes a notion to look.

"She'll have to sleep in a brace at night," Mrs. Sevier tells me. Beside her, Mr. Sevier opens the newspaper, eyeballing it as he eats his bacon.

"Oh," I mutter. *I'll slip the brace off Fern's leg at night. That's what I'll do.*

"I thought I'd take her by myself." Mrs. Sevier's words come real careful, her deep blue eyes fastening to me underneath blond curls that remind me of Queenie even if I don't want them to. Queenie is *much* prettier, though. She *is.* "Beth must get accustomed to spending time with her new mommy, just the two of us . . . without carrying on about it." She smiles at my sister, who's busy chasing one of Zuma's canned strawberries around her plate with a little silver baby fork. The Seviers don't like anybody eating with their fingers.

Mrs. Sevier claps her hands to get Mr. Sevier's attention, and he lets the paper down a bit, poking his nose over it. "Darren, Darren, look at her. How cute!"

"Keep at it, trooper," he says. "After you capture that one, you can have another."

Fern spears the strawberry, pops it into her mouth whole, and smiles with juice dripping out the sides.

Our new mommy and daddy laugh. Mrs. Sevier dabs Fern's cheek with a napkin, so she won't spoil her blouse.

I try to decide whether I should beg to go along to the shoe doctor or not. I'm afraid to let her take Fern away from me. She'll buy things for Fern, and Fern will like her. But I don't want to go to Memphis. The last thing I remember about that place is being taken downtown by Mrs. Murphy and given to my new papa in a hotel room.

If I stay home while Mrs. Sevier is gone, I

can probably get outside and look around some. She doesn't like us wandering out there mostly. She's afraid we'll catch poison ivy or be bit by a snake. She's got no way of knowing that we river kids understand all about those things from the time we're old enough to walk.

"You'll be starting school soon." Our new mommy isn't happy that I didn't answer right away about Fern going to the doctor. "Beth is still too young for that, of course. She'll have two years at home yet before it's time for kindergarten . . . if we send her to kindergarten at all. I might keep her here an extra year. It'll depend . . ." A slim-fingered hand travels to her stomach, spreading gently over it. She doesn't say the words, but she's hoping there's a baby.

I try not to think about that. And I try not to think about school either. Once they send me, Mrs. Sevier will have all day with Fern. Fern will like her better than me for sure. I have to get us away from here before that happens.

Mrs. Sevier clears her throat, and her mister lets the paper down again. "What's on your schedule for today, darling?" she asks.

"Music, of course. I want to finish the new score while it's fresh in my mind. Then I'll call Stanley and play a bit of it for him over the phone . . . see if he thinks it's right for the film."

She sighs, and the wrinkles squeeze around her eyes. "I thought perhaps you'd have Hoy hitch up the pony cart, and the two of you could take a ride." She looks from Mr. Sevier to me. "Would you like that, May? With Papa along, you wouldn't have to be afraid of the pony. She's really very sweet. I had one like her when I was little, back home in Augusta. She was my favorite thing in the whole wide world."

My muscles tighten up, and my face goes cold. I'm not scared of the pony. I'm scared of Mr. Sevier. Not because he's done anything to me but because, after Mrs. Murphy's house, I know what can happen. "I don't wanna be any trouble."

My palms sweat, and I rub them on my dress.

"Mmmm . . ." Mr. Sevier's brows lower. He doesn't like the idea any better than I do, and I'm glad. "We'll have to see how the day transpires, darling. They've run so far behind in production on this film, my timeline is shorter than usual, and with the house so chaotic these past weeks because . . ." His wife lifts her chin, shaking it slightly, and he stops, then says, "We'll see how the day goes."

I stare at my lap, and nothing more gets said about riding in the pony cart. We finish breakfast and Mr. Sevier disappears to his music room fast as he can. Pretty soon, Fern and Mrs. Sevier are gone too. I take my Crayolas and a book and sit out back on the wide porch that looks down toward the trees and then the lake. Piano music spills from Mr. Sevier's studio. It mixes with the birdsongs, and I close my eyes and listen and wait for Zuma and Hootsie to wander off to the carriage house, so I can slip away and look around a little. . . .

I drift off to sleep and dream that Fern and me are down on Mr. Sevier's fishing dock. We're sitting on one of those big suitcases they store in the pantry room, near Zuma's mops and brooms, and we've got it packed full of toys to share with Camellia, Lark, and Gabion. We're waiting for Briny and Queenie to pick us up.

The *Arcadia* comes into view at the far end of the oxbow lake. She's fighting her way upwater real slow. Then, all of a sudden, the wind kicks her, pushing her away. I look over my shoulder and there's a big black car bouncing across the field behind us. Miss Tann's face is pressed against the window glass. Her eyes are boiling mad. I grab Fern and try to get to the water so we can swim away.

We start running, but the harder we run, the longer the dock gets.

The car grinds right up the dock behind us. A hand snatches me up by my dress and hair.

"You're an ungrateful little wretch, aren't you?" Miss Tann says.

I jerk awake, and Hootsie's standing there with a glass of tea and a lunch plate for me. She smacks them down on the wicker table. The drink splashes all over the tray and the plate. "Be like river food now, won't it? Nice 'n' soft." She gives me a squinty smile.

I pick up the soggy sandwich and take a big old bite and smile back at her. Hootsie hasn't got any idea how things were for us before we came here. I can eat corn mush with weevils in it and not think twice. Tea spilled on a sandwich isn't gonna set me off. Neither is Hootsie, no matter how hard she tries. She's not tough. I've seen kids who are tough.

She huffs and sticks her nose in the air, and then she's gone. After I finish the plate, I set the napkin over it to keep the flies from gathering. Then I wander down the long porch toward the music room. Everything's quiet now, but I'm careful when I get to the end of the house and round the corner. There's no sign of Mr. Sevier. I check first before I sidle closer.

When I slip through the screen door, his music room is shadowy, the drapes pulled tight. In the corner, a projector shines a blank square of light on the wall. It makes me think of the traveling picture shows in the river towns. I walk closer and see my shadow, long and thin, little curly pieces of light shining through the hair. I think how Briny made shadow puppets in the window light on the *Arcadia* sometimes. I try to do one, but I can't remember how.

Beside the projector, a needle bobs back and forth on a spinning phonograph record. A soft, scratchy sound comes out the side of the cabinet it's in. I walk over to it, look down into the box, and watch the black circle spin. For a little while, we had one of these on the back porch of our shantyboat, but it was a hand crank. Briny found it in an old house along the river where nobody lived anymore.

He traded it off for firewood a while later.

I tell myself I hadn't oughta touch this one, but I can't help it. It's the prettiest thing I've ever seen. It must be brand new.

I pick up the silver ball that holds the needle, move it back just a hair so the last tiny bit of music plays. Then I do a little more and a little more. It's turned down soft enough I figure nobody else will hear it.

After a minute, I go over to the piano and think of how Briny and me used to sit together in the pool halls or on the showboats when they were empty. He'd teach me how to play tunes. Of all of us kids, I was the one who was best at picking it up; that's what Briny said.

The last of the music ends on the phonograph, and the needle scratches.

I find the notes on the piano, just real quiet. I only push the keys a little. It's not too much work to figure out the music. I like it, so I set the needle back and do a bit more. That part's tougher, so I have to try harder, but I get it finally.

"Well, bravo!"

I jump up and see Mr. Sevier standing there with one hand on the screen door. He lets go and claps. I scoot off the piano bench and look around for a place to run.

"I'm sorry. I shouldn'ta . . ." Tears ball up in my throat. What if this makes him mad, and he tells Mrs. Sevier, and they get rid of me before Fern and me can take to the river and go home?

He comes in and lets the screen close.

"Don't worry. You're not going to hurt the piano. But Victoria was determined we should take the pony cart out while she's gone. I asked Hoy to hitch it up. I have some people coming to build a little cottage along by the lake — a quiet place for my work when the house is too chaotic. We'll drive the pony cart down and take a look and then rattle around the property a bit. When we come back, I'll show you how to . . ."

He moves a few more steps into the room. "Well, you know what? On second thought, the pony won't mind waiting. She's a patient old sort." Mr. Sevier whirls a hand toward the piano. "Do that again."

The tears drain down my throat. I swallow what's left of them as he walks across to the phonograph.

"Here. I'll reset the needle. How much can you do?"

I shrug. "I dunno. Not much. I gotta listen at it real hard first."

He lets the record go a little farther than I've already tried, but I think real quick and get it mostly right.

"Have you ever played before?" he asks.

"No, sir." He puts the needle back even farther, and we do it all again. I only get a little bit wrong, just on the new part.

"Impressive," he says.

It ain't really, but it feels good to have him say it. At the same time, I wonder, *What's he want? He don't need me to play the piano. He's real good at it on his own. He's better than the phonograph record even.*

"Again." He wheels a hand one more time. "Just from memory."

I do it, but something's off.

"Ooops," he says. "Hear that?"

"Yessir."

"It's a sharp; that's why." He points to the piano. "I can show you, if you like."

I nod and turn back to the piano and put my fingers on the keys.

"No, like this." He bends over from behind me and shows me how to stretch out my hand. "Middle C for the thumb. You've got good, slim fingers too. Those are the hands of a piano player."

They're Briny's hands, but Mr. Sevier doesn't know that.

He touches my fingers, one by one. The keys play the tune. He shows me how to do the sharp I've been getting wrong.

"That's the way," he says. "Hear the difference?"

I nod. "I do! I hear it!"

"You know where the note goes now?" he asks. "In the melody, I mean."

"Yessir."

"All right then." Before I have time to think about it, he's sitting down beside me. "You play the melody, and I'll play the chords. You'll see the way they come together. That's how a piece is created, like the one you heard on the record."

I do what he says, and he plays the keys on his end, and we sound just like the record! I feel the music coming from the piano and slipping through my body. Now I know what it's like for the birds when they sing.

"Can we play it again?" I ask when we get to the end. "More of it?" I want to do more, and more, and more.

He spins the record and helps me find the right keys, and then we play the music together. He's laughing when we finish, and I am too.

"We should see about arranging some lessons for you," he says. "You have a talent."

I look at him real hard to see if he's teasing. *A talent? Me?*

I push a hand over my smile and turn back to the keys, and my cheeks go hot. *Does he mean it?*

"I wouldn't say that if it weren't true, May. I might not know much about raising little girls, but I do know about music." He leans close, trying to see my face. "I understand that it's hard for you, coming here to a new home, at your age . . . but I think you and I can be friends."

All of a sudden, I'm back in the hallway at Mrs. Murphy's house, in the pitch dark, and Riggs has me pinned between his belly and the wall, and he's pressing hard into me, blocking out the air, making my body go numb. The smell of whiskey and coal dust slides up my nose, and he whispers, *Y-you and me can b-b-be friends. I can git ya p-peppermints and c-c-cookies. Anythin' y-you want. We c-can b-b-be best friends. . . .*

I jump up from the piano bench, smashing the keys so that a handful play all at once. The noise mixes with the sound of my shoes clattering against the floor.

I don't stop running until I'm upstairs curled in the bottom of my closet with my feet braced on the door so nobody else can get in.

CHAPTER 21

Avery

When the Stafford camp circles the wagons, we're a formidable force. For almost three weeks now, we've been hunkered down behind the barricades fighting off the press, whose main goal is to paint us as criminally elitist because we've engaged premium nursing home care for my grandmother, who can *afford* it, by the way. It's not as if we're asking the public to pay her fees . . . which is what I really want to say to every reporter who accosts us with a microphone as we make our way to and from public events, meetings, social commitments . . . even church.

Driving into Drayden Hill after accompanying my parents to church and a Sunday brunch, I spot my sisters in one of the broodmare paddocks with Allison's triplets. In the riding arena, Courtney has a sweet old gray gelding out for a canter. She's riding bareback, and as I park, I imagine the rhythm of Doughboy's strides, his muscles tightening and releasing, the rise and fall of his broad back.

"Hey, Aunt Aves! Want to go out on the trails with me?" Courtney calls hopefully as I walk to the fence. "You can take me home after."

I'm about to say, *Let me go grab a pair of jeans,* but Courtney's mom beats me to the punch. "Court, you have to get ready for camp!"

"Awww, *man,*" my niece whines, then canters off on Doughboy.

I slip through the paddock gate and totter across the broodmare pasture in my high heels. Along the far fence, the boys are delighting themselves by poking flowers and spears of grass between the slats for this year's foals to nuzzle. Allison and Missy snap rapid-fire photos with their iPhones. The boys' little seersucker shorts and bow ties don't look quite as pristine as they did in church.

Missy squats down and snuggles one of the boys while helping him pull a wildflower. "Awww . . . I miss these days," she says wistfully. Her teenagers are away at the Asheville summer camp we attended throughout our childhood. Court leaves tomorrow for a shorter stay.

"These three hooligans are up for rent anytime you want." Allison's eyes widen hopefully as she tucks her thick auburn hair behind her ear. "I mean *anytime.* You don't even have to take all three. Just one or two."

We laugh together. It's a nice moment of stress relief. The last few weeks have tied everyone in knots.

"How was Daddy at the brunch?" As usual, Missy steers back to practical matters.

"Okay, I think. They stayed after, chatting with some friends. Hopefully Mama will make him go kick up his feet once they're home. We have a dinner to go to later." My father is determined to keep up the pace, yet the controversy over Grandma Judy is wearing him down. The fact that his mother has become a target in this latest political scuffle is hard for him to bear. Senator Stafford can handle the shots across his own bow, but when his family is caught in the cross fire, his blood pressure skyrockets.

On days when he has to wear the chemo pump strapped to his leg, he looks as though he might collapse under the additional weight.

"We'll go ahead and scoot out of here before they show up then." Allison glances toward the driveway. "I just wanted to get a few pictures of the foals and the boys while we still had the church clothes on. Leslie thought some baby-animal-baby-Stafford pics would be a good distraction on the social media pages. Something innocuous and cute."

"Well, they'd distract *me.*" I kiss one of my nephews on the head, and he reaches up and sweetly pats my face with his grassy little palms.

"Hey, Aunt Aves, check this out!" Courtney takes Doughboy over a tiny jump.

"Courtney! Not without a saddle and a helmet!" Allison yells.

"She's a girl after my own heart," I say.

"She's *way* too much like you." Missy shoulder nudges me.

"I can't imagine what you're talking about."

Allison's ski-slope nose scrunches. "Oh, yes you can."

"Come on, Al. Let her stay and ride." I can't help intervening on Court's behalf. Besides, I have some free time, and a ride sounds nice. "I'll bring her home in an hour . . . or two. She can pack for camp then."

Court takes Doughboy over another jump. "Courtney Lynne!" Allison scolds.

I'm about to protest that they're just little jumps and, besides, Courtney sits a horse like a Mongolian nomad, but I'm distracted by a car pulling up to the barn. I recognize the silver BMW convertible immediately. A ten-pound barbell lands on my chest.

"Bitsy's here?" Missy asks.

"This can't be good." I shouldn't say it, especially of my future mother-in-law, but the last thing I need today is more wedding-planning harassment from Bitsy. She means well, but she's been after me every chance she gets.

The weight lifts when someone else steps from the car — someone tall, dark, and decidedly handsome.

"Well, look who's here to see his ladylove. I didn't know your fella was in town." Missy grins at me, then waves toward the barn. "Hi, Elliot!"

I'm dumbstruck. "He didn't . . . He never told me he was going to be in Aiken. When we talked yesterday, he was in D.C. for a meeting and he had to fly out to California today."

"I guess he changed his mind. How romantic is that?" Allison pushes me toward the gate. "You'd better go give that man a hug."

"And a kiss," Missy chimes in. "And

whatever else comes to mind."

"Y'all *stop.*" Maybe it's all the childhood years Elliot and I spent deflecting my sisters' taunts about us being boyfriend and girlfriend when we *weren't,* but my neck and cheeks heat up as Elliot waves and starts toward the paddock gate. He looks good in his smooth-fitting gray suit. He's definitely dressed for business. Why is he here?

Suddenly, I can't wait to find out. I kick off my shoes and run across the grass and throw myself into his arms. He lifts me off my feet, then sets me down and gives me a quick kiss. Everything about it is wonderful. It feels familiar, and sweet, and safe, and I realize that's exactly what I need right now.

"What are you doing in Aiken?" I'm still shocked by his sudden appearance — thrilled, but shocked.

His deep brown eyes glitter. He's pleased with himself for having pulled off a surprise. "I changed my flight so I could lay over here for a few hours before I fly out to L.A."

"You're flying on to L.A. yet today?" I hate to sound disappointed, but I'd already started making plans in my head.

"This evening," he answers. "Sorry I couldn't fit in a longer visit. But hey, it's better than nothing, right?"

I hear a car coming up the drive, and I

pull him toward the barn. That could be Dad and Honeybee returning from the luncheon. If they see us, we'll never get any alone time. "Let's go for a walk. I want to have you all to myself." Hopefully, the folks won't notice the extra car parked next to Allison's SUV.

Elliot frowns at my bare feet. "Don't you need your shoes?"

"I'll grab some muck boots from the tack room. If I go up to the house, everyone will know you're here, and Mama will want you to stay and chat." The words have barely cleared my lips when a dose of reality hits. "Does your mother know you're in town?" Bitsy will kill us both if Elliot comes and goes and doesn't spend time with her.

"Relax. I've already been by to see her. We had a late breakfast together."

That explains why Bitsy wasn't at the brunch earlier. "Your *mother* knew you were coming, but you didn't tell me?" I hate to be jealous, but I am. Elliot shows up in town, and the first person he spends time with is Bitsy?

He pulls me to his side and kisses me in a way that lets me know who he really likes best. "I wanted to surprise you." We amble along the stable aisle together. "And besides, I wanted to get Mother out of the way. You know how that can be."

"I see your point." As always, he's handled the situation with Bitsy in the best possible way. And he's spared us from having to visit her together, which would have turned into an intense wedding discussion. "Did she harass you about nailing down our plans?"

"Some," he admits. "I told her you and I would talk about it."

I refrain from pointing out that *We'll talk about it* means *Yes, we'll do whatever you want* in Bitsy's vernacular. Really, the last thing either one of us wants to focus on is his mother.

He opens the tack room door for me and hangs his jacket on a hook. "How's your dad doing now?"

I give him the latest rundown on Daddy's health while I find a pair of muck boots about the right size, slip them over my feet, and tuck my slacks inside.

"Nice," he teases, studying my outfit when I'm done. Elliot isn't a muck-boots-with-slacks kind of guy.

"I could go up to the house and find something better while Honeybee talks to you about spring weddings. . . ."

He chuckles, rubbing his eyes, and I can tell he's tired. That makes it even sweeter that he detoured to come here. "Tempting but . . . no. Let's walk awhile, and then maybe we can sneak out for a little drive."

"Sounds perfect. I'll text Allison and Missy and ask them not to tell the folks you're here." I send a quick message while we start toward the riding trails. As always, Elliot and I fall into easy conversation. His hand slips over mine, and we talk about business, family issues, his trip to Milan, politics. We catch up on everything we haven't had time to discuss on the phone. It feels good, like coming home after a long journey.

The rhythms of conversation and movement are ones we've learned over time. We both know where we're headed — down to a little spring-fed lake, where we'll sit in the pine-shrouded gazebo that's been there as long as I can remember. We've almost reached it when I find myself spilling the story of May Crandall, the Tennessee Children's Home Society, and Grandma Judy's strange warning to me about *Arcadia.*

Elliot stops at the base of the gazebo stairs. He leans against a post, crosses his arms over his chest, looks at me like I've just sprouted horns. "Avery, where is all this coming from?"

"All . . . what?"

"All this . . . I don't know . . . digging

into things that are ancient history? Things that have nothing to do with you? Don't you have enough on your plate with your dad, and the hubbub over the nursing home cases, and Leslie always trying to whip you into shape?"

I'm not sure whether to be offended or to take Elliot's protest as the voice of reason speaking. "That's just the point. What if it *did* have something to do with us? What if Grandma Judy was so interested in the Tennessee Children's Home Society because our family had some connection to it? What if they were involved in the legislation that legalized all of those adoptions and sealed the records?"

"If they did, why would you want to know about it? What does it matter, decades after the fact?" He frowns, his brows drawing together in a dark knot.

"Because . . . well . . . because it mattered to Grandma Judy, for one thing."

"That's exactly why you need to be careful of it."

I'm dumbfounded for a minute. Heat rises under the silky sleeveless blouse I wore to church. Suddenly, my fiancé sounds way too much like his mother. Even the intonation of the sentence reminds me of Bitsy. Over the years, she and my grandmother have found themselves on opposite sides of various issues around town, often with Honeybee as a wishbone in the middle. "What is *that* supposed to mean?"

Maybe Elliot is just tired, and or maybe Bitsy got under his skin about something at breakfast, but I'm shocked when he flips a hand into the air. It falls and hits his leg with a dull slap. "Avery, you *know* that Judy Stafford has always been too outspoken for her own good. It isn't any big secret. Don't act like no one's ever said it before." He looks me in the eye with an annoyingly calm countenance. "She came close to ruining your grandfather's career a few times . . . and your father's."

I'm instantly offended. "She believed in speaking up when something was wrong."

"Your grandmother relished controversy."

"She did *not.*" A pulse pounds in my neck, but underlying it, there's a teary sensation. I feel slightly betrayed by his hidden opinion of my family, but mostly I'm thinking, *Elliot's finally here, and we're arguing?*

He reaches out, rubs a palm gently down my arm, and takes my hand. "Hey . . . Aves." His voice is conciliatory, soothing. "I don't want to fight. I'm just giving you my honest opinion. And that's because I love you and want what's best for you."

His gaze meets mine, and it's as if I can see all the way through to his heart. He's completely earnest. He does love me. And he is entitled to his opinion. It just bothers me that it's so different from mine. "I don't want to fight either."

The argument ends where all of our arguments do — on the altar of compromise.

He brings my hand to his lips and kisses it. "I love you."

I look into his eyes and see all the years, and miles, and experiences we've shared. I see the boy who was my friend, who's now a man. "I know. I love you too."

"I guess we should talk about the wedding." One eye winces shut, and I get the sense that the drill at breakfast was not an easy one. He pulls out his cellphone and checks the time. "I promised Mother we would."

We migrate to our same old spots in the gazebo and sit awhile, but it's too hot to stay there very long, certainly not long enough to settle on any details. Finally, we go to our favorite little restaurant downtown to do what we did in childhood, in our teenage years, during college — hash out what *we* want and try to separate it from what everyone else wants for us.

We really haven't come to any conclusions

by the time Elliot needs to drive back to the airport, but we're caught up on life, and we're simpatico with each other, and that's what matters most.

Honeybee meets me at the door when I return to the house. She strains toward the driveway. Somehow, she's found out about Elliot's visit, and she's disappointed that he didn't come inside with me.

"He's busy, Mama," I say, making an excuse for him. "He had a flight to catch."

"I would've had one of the guest rooms made up for him. He's always welcome."

"He knows that, Mama."

She pauses, tapping a finger while she holds the door open and wistfully watches the driveway. She has probably air-conditioned half the estate before she finally pushes the door shut and gives up on Elliot. "Bitsy called. She said she'd discussed your wedding plans — or your lack of them — with Elliot this morning and he promised that the two of you would talk things over. I just assumed, once you were finished having some time alone, you'd come to the house together."

"We did chat through some possibilities. We just haven't come to any decisions yet."

She chews her lip, her brows knotting. "I don't want everything that's going on to be a . . . distraction for you two. I don't want you to feel that you have to put off your future."

"Mama, we don't feel that way."

"Are you *sure*?" The disappointment and desperation on her face hurt. An upcoming wedding would be happy news, something to create forward focus. It would also mean the type of public announcement that could subtly indicate the Stafford camp is confident enough to do business as usual.

Maybe Elliot and I are just being self-serving by holding everyone in suspense. Would it kill us to plan a time and a venue, maybe even the azalea garden in spring? That would make everyone in the family so incredibly happy. And if you're sure you're marrying the right person, what does it matter where or when it happens?

"We'll decide something soon. I promise." But in the darkest corner of my mind, there are those words, *Avery, you* know *that Judy Stafford has always been too outspoken for her own good. It isn't any big secret.* What Elliot doesn't realize — or maybe doesn't want to face — is that my grandmother and I are so very much alike.

"Good." The worry wrinkles soften around Honeybee's eyes. "But I'm not pushing you."

"I know."

She lays cool hands on either side of my face, looks at me adoringly. "I love you, Peapod."

The childhood nickname makes me blush. "I love you too, Mama."

"Elliot is a lucky man. I'm sure he realizes that every time you two are together." She tears up a little, which makes me tear up too. It feels good to see her so . . . happy. "Go on. You'd better go change or we'll be late to the choral fundraiser tonight. The concert portion starts at seven with a children's choir from Africa. I hear they're fabulous."

"Yes, Mama." I promise myself that I'll talk to Elliot about the wedding again as soon as he's back home from L.A. The fact that tomorrow is my day to go visit Grandma Judy at Magnolia Manor only reinforces my determination. I want my grandmother to share the wedding celebration with us. Since childhood, I've imagined the day with her in it. There's no telling how much more time we have.

I mull over various ideas while the evening passes. I try to form mental pictures of a garden wedding. Elliot and me, several hundred friends and acquaintances, a perfect spring day. It could be truly lovely, a modern version of an old tradition. Grandma Judy and my grandfather were married in the gardens at Drayden Hill.

Elliot will agree, no matter how much he instinctively resists the idea of his mother or mine running our lives. If a garden wedding is really what I want, he'll want it too.

In the morning, I drive to Magnolia Manor with a new agenda in mind. I'll ask Grandma Judy for details about her special day. Maybe there are some favorite moments we can re-create.

As if she senses that I've come with important business this time, she greets me with a bright smile and a look of recognition.

"Oh, there you are! Sit right here next to me. I have something to tell you." She tries to pull the other wing chair close but can't. I drag it forward a bit, then perch on the edge, so our knees are touching.

Grabbing my hand, she looks at me so intensely I'm pinned to the spot. "I want you to destroy the contents of my office closet. The one at the Lagniappe house." Her gaze strains into mine. "I don't suppose I'm ever getting out of here to take care of it myself. I wouldn't want people reading my daybooks after I'm gone."

I steel myself against the inevitable sting

of grief. "Don't say that, Grandma Judy. I saw you in exercise class the other day. The instructor said you were doing great." I play dumb about the daybooks. I can't stand the idea. It'll be like saying goodbye to the busy crusader she once was.

"There are names and phone numbers there. I can't have them falling into the wrong hands. Start a fire in the backyard and burn them."

Now I wonder if she has slipped away again, yet she *seems* lucid. Start a fire in the backyard . . . on a city street filled with meticulously preserved old homes? The neighbors would call the police in 2.5 seconds.

I can picture how that would look in the papers.

"They'll only think you're burning leaves." She smiles and gives me a conspiratorial wink. "Don't worry, Beth."

It's suddenly very clear that we're not in the same place. I have no idea who Beth is. I'm almost relieved that Grandma Judy doesn't know who she's talking to. It gives me an excuse not to abide by her closet-clearing request.

"I'll look into it, Grandma," I say.

"Wonderful. You've always been so good to me."

"That's because I love you."

"I know. Don't open the boxes. Just burn them."

"The boxes?"

"The ones with my old society columns. It won't do for me to be remembered as Miss Chief, you know." She covers her mouth and pretends to be embarrassed about her days as a gossip columnist, but really she's not. That's evident in her face.

"You never told me you wrote a society column." I wag a finger, scolding.

She pretends to be innocent of keeping secrets. "Oh? Well, it was a long time ago."

"You didn't say anything in those columns that wasn't true, did you?" I tease.

"Why, of course not. But people don't always take well to the truth, do they?"

Just as quickly as we got *on* the track of Miss Chief, we're off it again. She talks about people who have been dead for years, but in her mind, she's just lunched with them yesterday.

I ask her about her wedding. In answer, she offers up a mishmash of memories from her wedding and others she has attended over the years, including those of my sisters. Grandma Judy loves weddings.

She won't even remember mine.

The conversation leaves me sad and hollow. There are always just enough sparks of lucidity to get my hopes up, but the waves of dementia quickly sweep them out to sea.

We're floating far from shore by the time I kiss her and tell her goodbye and that my father will be by today, hopefully.

"Oh, and who is your father?" she asks.

"Your son Wells."

"I think you must be mistaken. I don't have a son."

As I walk out of the building, I desperately want to talk to someone and unload all of this. I pull up my favorites list, then stop with my finger over Elliot's number. After what he said about Grandma Judy yesterday, it seems almost disloyal to tell him how much she's slipping.

I don't realize until my phone rings and I see the name on the screen that there *is* someone I can talk to. I think of the expression on his face when he spoke of those difficult last promises to his grandfather, the promises that kept May Crandall's secrets and my grandmother's, and instinctively I know he'll understand.

Something in me rushes headlong across the distance, even though we haven't spoken since that day at the nursing home several weeks ago. I told myself I wouldn't get in touch with him again, that it was better to leave things be and move on.

As soon as I answer, he seems unsure of why he's called. I wonder if he's been thinking the same thing I have — there's no place for a friendship between the two of us. Our parking lot encounter with Leslie proved that point. "I just . . ." he says finally. "I've seen some of the press about the nursing home exposé. You've been on my mind."

A warm, pleasant sensation rushes through me. I'm completely unprepared for it. I will it not to show in my voice. "Ohhhh, don't remind me. If this keeps up much longer, I'm liable to go all Ninja Turtle on someone."

"No you aren't."

"You're right, I guess. But I'd like to. It's so incredibly . . . frustrating. I understand that my father is in public office, but we're still human, you know? You'd think some topics would be off the table . . . like cancer for one. And watching your grandmother struggle to remember anything about who she is, for another. It feels like people will poke a spear in anyplace they can draw blood these days. It wasn't that way when I was growing up. Even in politics, people had some . . ." I search for the word, and the best thing I can come up with is "decency."

"We live in an entertainment-driven

world," Trent says soberly. "Everything's fair game."

I open my mouth to further vent about the attacks on my family and then think better of it. "Sorry. I didn't mean to unload on you. Maybe I need another trip to the beach." It's not until the words are out that I realize how flirty they sound.

"How about lunch instead?"

"What?"

"I just thought I'd see if you were free, since I'm in Aiken. I've been doing a little digging around in my granddad's papers and talking to people who helped him with his searches. One of them is a man who was a courthouse worker in Shelby County, Tennessee, back when all the adoption records were still sealed. From what I can tell, he funneled quite a bit of information to Granddad."

Instantly, I'm back in the thick of it. The scents of that tiny Edisto cabin tease my senses. I smell pipe tobacco, old newspaper clippings, dried-out bulletin boards, peeling paint, faded photos. "You mean so that your grandfather could help adoptees find their relatives, right? So . . . you're taking up where he left off then?"

"Not really. I was nosing around for May Crandall. Thinking maybe I'd uncover something about the little brother she never found, Gabion."

I'm momentarily stunned. This guy is genuine to the core. He's also a better person than I am. I've been so obsessed with family problems, I've been delaying calling the seniors' rights PAC about May's situation. Now I realize that I've been brushing this task aside on purpose. I'm afraid to have anything to do with her, given all the controversy after the "Aging Unevenly" article. If word got out that I was helping her, our political enemies would accuse me of using her to prop up our bruised public image.

I can't be seen having lunch with Trent either. I can't possibly go, but I can't quite make myself say no, so I continue the sidetrack. "That's really nice of you. What did you find?"

"Nothing significant so far. There was an address in California in the court paperwork. I wrote to it just to see if they might know anything about a two-year-old boy adopted from the Tennessee Children's Home Society in 1939 . . . or possibly even just who lived at that address in the late thirties. It's a long shot, though."

"So you drove here to tell May that?"

"Nah . . . I don't want to get her hopes

up unless something comes of it. I actually came here for jelly. When I left you last time, I went by to visit my aunt outside Aiken. She was putting up blackberry preserves. They're ready now."

A little laugh puffs out of me. "Two and a half hours is a long way to drive for jelly."

"You've never tasted my aunt's blackberry preserves. Besides, Jonah loves to go there. Uncle Bobby still has a mule."

"So Jonah's with you?" Lunch suddenly seems a possibility if it'll be the three of us. Even if we *were* seen, no one would think twice about it with Jonah there. I rush through my mental queue of the afternoon's plans, trying to calculate whether I can re-arrange a few things and sneak away long enough. "You know what? I'd love to have lunch with you two."

"I think I can tear Jonah away from Uncle Bobby and the mule. Tell me when and where. Any particular place you'd like to go? We're pretty flexible . . . as long as it's not during naptime. That can get ugly."

Again, his comment makes me chuckle. "When's naptime?"

"Around two."

"All right, then. How does an early lunch sound? Maybe about eleven? Is that too soon?" I don't have any idea how far out of town his aunt's house is, but if there's a mule involved, it isn't close to where I am right now. No one has farmed around Magnolia Manor for years. The estates here are pristine. "You pick the place, and I'll meet you there. Nothing too upscale, though, all right? Something kind of out of the way would be good."

Trent laughs. "We don't do upscale. We're actually into eateries with playscapes. Know one of those, by chance?"

My mind skips back in time and lands on a nice memory. "Actually, I do. There's an old drive-in with a little playground not far from my grandmother's house. She used to take us there when we were kids." I give him directions, and we're set. Best of all, if we meet at eleven, no one will even miss me at home.

I am an adult, I rationalize, navigating a U-turn and starting toward Grandma Judy's neighborhood. *I shouldn't have to feel like a teenager sneaking out just because I make lunch plans with a . . . a friend.*

I do have a right to some sort of life of my own, don't I?

I lose myself in my mental debate for a while, my thoughts turning corners along with the car. Maybe I've gotten spoiled up in Maryland, living in my own little anonymous world, working a job that was mine and only mine, not tied to a support staff, to offices in D.C. and the home state, to constituents, contributors, and an entire political network.

Maybe I never realized how much being a Stafford is an all-consuming thing, especially here in our native territory. The collective identity is so overwhelming, there's no room for an individual one.

Once upon a time, I liked that . . . didn't I? I enjoyed the perks that came with it. Every path I stepped on was instantly smoothed down before me.

But now I've had a taste of climbing my own mountains my own way.

Have I grown beyond this life?

The idea splits me down the middle, leaving half of my identity on each side of the divide. Am I my father's daughter, or am I just me? Do I have to sacrifice one to be the other?

Surely this is only a . . . a reaction to all of the stress lately.

Pausing at a stop sign, I look down Grandma Judy's street, past the dip in the road where we kids splashed in puddles when it rained, past the neatly trimmed hedge and the mailbox with the iron horse head atop.

There's a taxi sitting in my grandmother's driveway. In a town the size of Aiken, it's not a typical sight.

I hesitate at the intersection and watch the cab a moment. It doesn't back away and leave. Maybe the driver is unaware that nobody lives there anymore? He must be waiting in front of the wrong house.

Turning down her street, I fully expect him to be leaving when I pull in, but he's not. In fact, he seems to be . . . dozing in the driver's seat? He doesn't move when I drive past him and get out of my car.

He looks young, almost like a teenager, but he must be old enough to have a commercial driver's license. There's no passenger in the backseat and no one around the house as far as I can see. I'd suspect that this was related to some sort of hideous news exposé, a reporter skulking around snapping photos to show how the other half lives, but why would someone like that travel by cab?

The driver jumps about a foot when I knock on the half-open window. His mouth hangs open as he tries to blink me into focus.

"Ummph . . . guess I fell asleep," he apologizes. "Sorry, ma'am."

"I think you're in the wrong place," I tell him.

He glances around, stifles a yawn, flutters his thick, dark lashes against the bright late-morning sunlight. "No . . . no, ma'am. The reservation's for ten-thirty."

I check my watch. "You've been here for almost a half hour . . . sitting in the drive-way?" *Who would've directed a cab to my grandmother's house?* "You must have the wrong address." Some poor customer is probably pacing the floors about now.

The driver doesn't seem worried in the least. Straightening in his seat, he glances at the console. "No, ma'am. It's a standing reservation. Every Thursday at ten-thirty. Prepaid, so my dad . . . I mean my *boss* says come here and sit, since it's already paid for."

"Every Thursday?" I cycle through the schedule — what I can remember of it — from the time when Grandma Judy was still living here with a full-time caretaker. The day she ended up lost and confused at a shopping mall, she was in a cab. "How long have you been doing this — coming here every Thursday?"

"Ummm . . . maybe I should . . . call the office, so you can talk . . ."

"No. It's okay." I'm afraid the office won't

answer my questions. The kid behind the wheel doesn't seem to know any better. "When you picked my grandmother up on Thursdays, where did you take her?"

"Over by Augusta, a place on the water there. I only drove her a few times, but my dad and my grandpa did for . . . maybe a couple years. We're a family company. Four generations." The last part sounds sweetly as if he plucked it straight from the billboard.

"Years?" I'm so confused, the word doesn't even begin to describe me right now. There was nothing in my grandmother's daybooks about a standing Thursday appointment. She *had* no standing appointments, other than bridge circles and beauty shop visits. And Augusta? That's thirty minutes or so each way. Who in the world would she have been visiting regularly in the Augusta area? And in a cab? And for *years*?

"And she went to the same place every time?" I ask.

"Yes, ma'am. As far as I know." He looks extremely uncomfortable now. On the one hand, he realizes I'm grilling him. On the other hand, he doesn't want to lose what has obviously been a long-standing fare. I can't imagine what the price for the trip to

Augusta might be.

My hand settles over the top of his window. It might be silly, but I want to make sure he doesn't try to flee the scene while I sort out the barrage of information. *A place on the water there . . .*

Something completely unexpected pops into my mind. "A place on the water. You mean on the river?" The Savannah River runs through Augusta. When Trent and I talked to May, she mentioned Augusta. Something about going home and drifting down the Savannah River.

"Well, yeah, the place could be on the river. The gate's all . . . kinda overgrown like? I just drop her off there and wait. I don't know what happens after she goes in."

"How long did she usually stay?"

"A few hours. Pop used to walk down to the bridge and fish while he waited. She didn't care. She'd come out and honk on the cab horn when she was ready to go."

I just stand there gaping at him. I can't even begin to reconcile all of this with the grandmother I knew. The grandmother I *thought* I knew.

Was she writing May Crandall's story after all? Or is there more?

"Can you take me there?" I blurt out.

The cabby shrugs. He moves to exit the

car so he can open the back door for me. "Sure. Yeah. The fare's paid for."

My pulse inches upward. Goosebumps dot my arms. *If I get in this car, where will I end up?*

My phone buzzes, reminding me that I was headed someplace before this detour. It's a text from Trent telling me he and Jonah are holding down a table for us. The hamburger stand is already crowded this morning.

Instead of texting back, I slip away from the cabby and call Trent. I apologize for not being there and ask, "Can you . . . could you . . . come with me to do something?" The explanation of where I am and what's happening sounds even more bizarre when I voice it out loud.

Fortunately, Trent doesn't decide that I've lost it. Actually, he's intrigued. We make plans for the cab to swing by the restaurant so Trent and Jonah can follow in their car.

"Meantime, I'll grab a burger to go for you," Trent offers. "World-famous shakes here. Jonah's giving it the thumbs-up already. Want one?"

"Thanks. That sounds good." But I'm not sure I could eat a thing at the moment.

On the short ride to the restaurant, I can hardly stay focused, I'm so on edge. Trent is waiting in the parking lot with Jonah already buckled in. He hands me a sack and a shake and tells me he'll be right behind me.

"You okay?" he asks. Our gazes catch for a moment, and I'm lost in the deep blue of his eyes. I find myself relaxing into them, thinking, *Trent's here. It'll be all right.*

The thought almost lifts the mass of dread that's growing inside me. Almost.

Unfortunately, I understand the feeling well enough to know I shouldn't ignore it. It's the sixth sense that always comes alive when I'm about to learn something practically unthinkable about the players in a case I'm working on — the trusted neighbor was responsible for the child's disappearance; the innocent-looking eighth grader was stocking up on pipe bombs; the clean-cut father of four had a computer full of disgusting pictures. That sense is preparing me for something; I just don't know what.

"I'm fine," I say. "I'm just afraid of where this cab is going to end up . . . and what we might find."

Trent lays a hand on my arm, and my skin seems to heat up under his fingers. "You want to ride with us? We can just follow the cab." He glances toward his car, where Jonah is waving madly from his booster seat, trying to get my attention. He'd like to share his fries with me.

"No. But thanks. I need to talk to the driver some more on the way." Really, I think he's told me all he knows, but I want to keep the young man busy so he doesn't check in with the office. His father may have a different opinion of my using Grandma Judy's fare to transport me to a mystery location. He may be savvy enough to realize this could bring up a privacy issue. "And I don't want to take any chances on his getting away from us."

Trent's fingers trail down my arm as he lets go . . . or maybe that's just my imagination. "We'll be right behind you, okay?"

I nod and wave at Jonah, who gives me a fries-and-teeth grin, and then we're off. The midday traffic is light on the thirty-five-minute trip, so it's easy for the driver to chat. He tells me his name is Oz and that when he drove my grandmother she always gave him cookies, or chocolates, or sweets left over from parties and gatherings. Because of that, he remembers her well. He's sorry to hear she's in a care facility now. Clearly, he's oblivious to all the newspaper coverage and controversy. He's been busy working after having taken over much of the driving for his father, who's having some health problems.

"I was worried about her the last time I brought her here," he admits as we leave the highway and wind through rural roads, presumably drawing near our destination. Walls of lowland shrubs, climbing vines, and tall pine trees tighten around us, pressing inward as we turn, then turn again. "She was getting around okay, but she seemed kinda confused. I asked her if I could walk her in the gate, but she wouldn't let me. She said there'd be a golf cart waiting for her on the other side, like always, and not to worry. So I let her off. That was the last time I drove her."

I sit silently in the backseat, attempting to conjure the images as Oz talks. I try, but I just can't fathom the things he's describing.

"The week after that was my dad's heart surgery. We had a substitute driver filling in for a month or so. Next time I drove on a Thursday, I came to the house, and there was nobody there. Been that way ever since. The substitute driver didn't have any idea what happened. Last he saw of her, he let her off at a shopping mall, and she said she'd see him again the next Thursday. We've tried calling the number on her bill, but nobody answers, and nobody's there when I show up. We wondered if something might've happened to her. Sorry if we caused a problem."

"It's not your fault. Her caretakers shouldn't have been letting her leave alone in the first place." Good help is hard to find these days, but my grandmother was also surprisingly adept at convincing her helpers that *she* was perfectly competent and *we* were being overly controlling. Obviously, they were allowing her to take off in a cab on Thursdays. Then again, she was the one writing their paychecks, and they weren't unaware of that fact. She wasn't above dismissing household help that gave her trouble.

The car bumps over an old WPA bridge with crumbling cement railings and moss-covered arches. The driver slows, but I don't see any sign of houses or mailboxes. From all appearances, we're out in the middle of nowhere.

Good thing Oz knows exactly where he's going. Anyone who didn't would've missed the turn completely. The barely visible remnant of a gravel driveway sketches two scraggly paths through the roadside grass and across a drainage culvert. Just beyond, a massive stone entranceway lies hidden among trumpet vines and blackberry brambles. Heavy iron gates, each perhaps eight feet in height, hang askew, their weight supported by leaves and runners, the hinges long since rusted away. A decaying chain and padlock seem almost like somebody's idea of a joke. No one has driven through these gates in decades. Just beyond them, there's a sycamore tree six inches across, its muscular arms reaching through the bars and slowly lifting one gate higher than the other.

"There's the way in." Oz points out a narrow path leading to a walk-through entrance beside the main one. It's obviously functional, the trail beneath it patted down enough that the summer grass hasn't completely taken over. "That's where she always went."

Behind us, a car door slams. I jump and glance back before remembering it's Trent.

When I turn around again, I'm struck by a strong feeling that the gateway should be gone. *Poof.* I'll wake up in my bed at Drayden Hill thinking, *Now that was a strange dream. . . .*

But the gate hasn't vanished, and the path is still waiting.

CHAPTER 22

Rill

Fern freezes halfway across the sitting room. Her body goes stiff so that I can see every little string of muscle. A second later, she's wetting herself for the first time in weeks.

"Fern!" I snap under my breath because I don't want Mrs. Sevier to hear me and come see what Fern's just done. Our new mommy's so proud of Fern that she takes us to the movies and talks about trips we'll go on together and how we'll see Santa at Christmas and what he'll bring for us. She's even got it in her head that we should all drive to Augusta to visit her mama. I don't want to go to Augusta, but I also don't want any trouble now that Mrs. Sevier has started letting us out of her sight a little more.

I hurry across the room and strip off Fern's dress and shoes and socks, use them to sop up the puddle. "Go on upstairs before she sees."

I can hear Mrs. Sevier talking to someone in the front parlor.

Fern's mouth quivers, and her eyes fill up with tears. She just stands there while I roll up the wet clothes and stuff them behind the ash bin where I can take care of them later.

All of a sudden, I know why Fern's not moving. There's another voice in the parlor. The closer I get, the more it sends ice slivers through me, right down to the bone.

"Go hide under your bed," I whisper against Fern's ear, and push her toward the stairs.

Fern runs up to the second floor and disappears. Breath comes in and out my nose in short gasps as I flatten myself against the stairway wall and creep closer to the open parlor door. In the kitchen, Zuma turns on the electric mixer. I can't hear the voices for a minute, but then I do.

". . . a very unfortunate situation, but it does happen," Miss Tann is saying. "It's never my wish to take the children away once we've found good homes for them."

"But my husband . . . the papers . . . We were promised that the girls would be ours to keep." Mrs. Sevier's voice wavers and cracks.

A teacup rattles against a saucer. It seems

like forever before Miss Tann answers. "As well they should be." She sounds like she feels sorry for our troubles. "But adoptions are not final for one year. Birth families can be *so* difficult. The grandmother of these children has petitioned to gain custody of them."

I gasp, then hear the soft sound of it and slap a hand over my mouth. We don't even have a grandmother. Not that I know of, anyhow. Briny's folks are dead, and Queenie hasn't seen her people since she ran off with Briny.

"This can't . . ." Mrs. Sevier lets out a sob that sounds like it'll break her in two. She sniffles and coughs and finally forces out some words. "We . . . we can't let this . . . D-Darren will be home for . . . for lunch. Please . . . please wait. He'll know what . . . what to do."

"Oh my, I'm afraid I've upset you more than is necessary." Miss Tann sounds sticky sweet, but I can picture her face. She's smiling the same mean smile she had when Mrs. Pulnik was holding me down on my knees. Miss Tann likes the way people look when they're afraid. "I wasn't planning to take the children with me *today.* You can fight this foolishness, of course. You *should,* in fact. The grandmother has no real means of providing for the girls. They would have a terrible life. May and little Beth are depending on *you* to protect them. But you must realize that . . . legal work can be . . . costly."

"C-costly?"

"For people of your obvious means, that shouldn't be a difficulty, now, should it? Not when the fate of two innocent children is at stake. Two children whom you've come to dearly love."

"Yes, but . . ."

"Three thousand dollars, perhaps a bit more. That should go quite a distance toward resolving these legal issues."

"Three . . . three thousand?"

"Perhaps four."

"What are you *saying*?"

Another pause and then, "Nothing matters more than your family, don't you agree?" I can hear that horrible smile in Miss Tann's voice. I want to run in there and tell the truth. I want to point at her and yell, *Liar! We don't even have a grandma! And I had three sisters, not two. And a baby brother, and his name was Gabion, not Robby. And you took him away, just like you took my sisters.*

I want to tell all of it. I can taste the words on my tongue, but I can't say them. If I do, I know what'll happen. Miss Tann will take us back to the children's home. She'll give Fern to someone else, and we won't be together anymore.

Mrs. Sevier sniffles and coughs again. "Of . . . of course, I agree, but . . ." She breaks down in sobs again, apologizing for it all the while.

A chair creaks and groans, and heavy, uneven footsteps cross the floor. "Talk with your husband. Express your sincere feelings on the matter. Tell him how much you need the children and how much they need you. I won't bother with seeing the girls today. I'm sure they're doing quite well under your care. Thriving, even."

Her footsteps move closer to the doors at the other end of the room. I push off the wall and run up the stairs. The last thing I hear is Miss Tann's voice echoing through the house: "No need getting up. I can show myself out. I'll expect to be hearing from you by tomorrow. Time is of the essence."

Upstairs, I hurry to Fern's room. I don't even get her out from under the bed. I just slip under there with her. We lay face-to-face the way we always did on the *Arcadia.* "It's all right," I whisper. "I won't let her take us back. I promise. No matter what."

I hear Mrs. Sevier pass by in the hallway. Her sobbing echoes off the wood walls and the high ceiling with the gold edges. The door closes at the end of the hall, and I hear her take to her bed and cry and cry and cry, just like she used to when I first came here. Zuma comes up and knocks on the door, but it's locked, and Mrs. Sevier won't let anyone in. She's still in the bed when Mr. Sevier comes home for lunch. By then, I've got Fern cleaned up, and I've read her a book, and she's sound asleep with her thumb in her mouth and the teddy bear she calls Gabby, like it's our baby brother.

I listen while Mr. Sevier unlocks their bedroom. After he goes inside, I tiptoe out where I can listen better. I don't even need to be very close to hear how mad Mr. Sevier is after his missus tells him what happened. "This is blackmail!" he shouts. "It's nothing but outright blackmail!"

"We can't let her take the girls, Darren," Mrs. Sevier pleads. "We can't."

"I will *not* be blackmailed by this woman. We paid the adoption fees, which, by the way, were exorbitant, particularly the second time around."

"Darren, *please.*"

"Victoria, if we let this get started, there will be no stopping it." Something metal topples over and clatters across the floor. "Where does it end then? Tell me that."

"I don't know. I don't know. But we have to *do* something."

"Oh, I'll do something, all right. That woman doesn't know who she's dealing with." The door handle rattles, and I hurry to my room.

"Darren, please. Please. Listen to me," Mrs. Sevier begs. "We'll go to Mama's home in Augusta. Bellegrove has more than enough space, and the place is too much for her now that Daddy is gone. The girls will have aunts and uncles and all of my friends there. We'll take Hoy and Zuma and Hootsie. We can stay as long as need be. Permanently, even. Mama is lonely, and Bellegrove House needs a family. It's a wonderful place to grow up."

"Now, Victoria, *this* is our home. I've finally gotten my little studio building under way down by the lake. The McCameys aren't the fastest workers, but they have the piers and the flooring in place, and they're making progress on framing up the walls. We can't let Georgia Tann put us out of our home, my *family* home, for heaven's sake."

"Bellegrove has acres and acres along the Savannah River. You can build another studio. A bigger one. Any kind you want." Mrs. Sevier talks so fast I can hardly make out the words. "Please, Darren, I can't live here knowing that woman could come knocking on our door at any moment to take our children!"

Mr. Sevier doesn't answer. I close my eyes and dig my fingernails into my fuzzy pink wallpaper, waiting, hoping.

"Let's not do anything rash," Mr. Sevier says finally. "I have a meeting to go to in the city tonight. I'll pay a visit to Miss Tann and settle this matter face-to-face, once and for all. We'll see how bold she is in her demands then."

Mrs. Sevier doesn't argue any more. I hear her crying softly and the bed creaking and him comforting her. "Come now, darling. No more tears. It'll be taken care of, and if you'd like to take the girls to visit in Augusta, we can arrange that as well."

I stand there with my mind rushing through a hundred thoughts, and then it stops and settles on one. I know what I have to do. There's no more time to waste. I hurry to my dresser to get what I need and then run downstairs.

In the kitchen, Zuma has lunch ready, but she's over in the corner with her head in the laundry chute, so she can listen to what's happening with the Seviers. Hootsie's probably halfway up the chute telling everything she hears. On the chopping block, there's a little picnic basket ready to go down to the McCameys' construction camp. Normally, Zuma would make Hootsie take it down there. Hootsie hates that, and so does Zuma. Zuma says the McCameys are nothing but white trash and they'll steal Mr. Sevier blind if he turns his back. The only good thing is Zuma and Hootsie hate us less now, because they're busy hating the McCamey boys and their daddy.

I grab the basket and run out the door, yelling, "I'll take this to the camp. I've got a movie handbill to give to the boy down there anyhow." I'm gone before Zuma can argue that I'll be late for lunch.

I bolt out the back, jump off the veranda, and cross the yard as fast as my legs will take me, all the while looking over my shoulder to see if Hootsie's following me. It's a relief that she doesn't.

Down by the lake, Mr. McCamey is more than ready to settle under a shade tree when I show up with the basket. Near as I can figure, he's always willing to stop working. The only reason he's got a sweat worked up today is because his two biggest boys went to the neighbor's place to help cut a lightning-felled tree off their barn and fix the roof. They won't be back for a day or two, until that job's done. The only help

Mr. McCamey's got right now is the youngest boy — Arney is his name, but Mr. McCamey just calls him boy.

I nod at Arney, and he follows me up the path to a willow tree where we've sat and talked before. I slip under the branches and give Arney a sandwich, an apple, and two sugar cookies I squirreled away in my pocket. Arney's a scrawny little thing, so usually when I come down here I bring him food he doesn't have to share with the rest of the McCameys. I figure he needs it. He's a year older than me but not even as tall as I am yet.

"Brought you something else today." I give him the handbill from the movie theater.

He holds the picture of a cowboy on a tall yellow horse and whistles long and low. "It sure is purdy. Tell me how the tale went. Was there lotsa shootin'?"

He sits down, and I sit down with him. I want to share all about the movie Mrs. Sevier took us to and the theater with its big red velvet seats and tall towers that looked like they should've been on a king's castle. But there isn't time to talk about those things. Not today. Not with what's happened. I have to get Arney to say yes to what I asked him yesterday.

The moon will be full tonight, and on the

water it'll be almost bright as high noon. With Arney's brothers gone, there won't be a better time. I can't let Mrs. Sevier drag us off to Augusta. I can't let Miss Tann make us go back to the home. And besides that, Fern's starting to think of Mrs. Sevier as her mama. Little by little, her mind's letting loose of our *real* mama. At bedtime, I sneak over to Fern's room and tell her about Queenie and Briny, but it's not working anymore. Fern's forgetting the river and Kingdom Arcadia. She's forgetting who we are.

It's time for us to go.

"So, what we talked about yesterday. You're gonna take us, right?" I ask Arney. "Tonight. The moon'll be up early and long." You don't live all your life on the river without knowing how the moon travels. The river and its critters choose their moods according to the moon.

Arney jerks away like I've slapped him. He pinches his brown eyes closed. A shock of thin, reddish-brown hair falls across his forehead and parts over his long, bony nose. He shakes his head in a nervous way. Maybe he never meant to help us at all. Maybe it was just big talk when he said he could run his daddy's boat and he knows how to get through the oxbow lake and Dedmen's

Slough all the way to the big river.

But I told him the truth about Fern and me. The whole story. I even gave him our real names. I thought he understood why we needed his help.

He rests his elbows on his dirty overalls where his knees poke through. "I'd sure enough miss ya if 'n you'z gone. Y'all been the only thang good 'bout this place so far."

"You can come with us. Old Zede's fetched up lots of boys. He'd take you on, I bet. I'm sure he would. You'd never have to see this place again. You could be free. Just like we're gonna be." Arney's daddy drinks every night, and works his boys like sawmill mules, and beats on them all the time, especially Arney. Hootsie saw Arney get whopped upside the head with a hammer handle just for bringing his daddy the wrong peck of nails. "And either way, the pearls are yours, just like I promised."

I dig in my pocket and pull them out and hold them in my hand where Arney can see. I feel bad about the pearls. Mrs. Sevier gave them to me the night after she took Fern to get fitted for the special shoes. She thought it was my birthday on account of that's what the papers from the Tennessee Children's Home Society said. The Seviers figured I'd forgot all about it being my special day, and they surprised me with a party at supper. I was surprised all right. My birthday was five and a half months ago, and I'm already a whole year older than they think I am. But my name isn't May Weathers either, so a birthday in the fall didn't matter too much to me.

The pearls are the prettiest things that have ever been mine, but I'd give them up for Queenie and Briny and the river. I'd hand them over quick as a wink.

Besides, Arney needs the price they'll fetch more than I do. Half the time, they've got whiskey but no food in their camp.

Arney touches the pearls, then pulls his hand away and picks at a scab on his knuckle. "Awww . . . I couldn't leave my fam'ly. My brothers 'n' such."

"Think on it real hard. About staying on the river with us, I mean." Truth is that Arney's brothers are practically grown, and they're just about as bad as Arney's daddy. Once they get tired of working like dogs and finally decide to light off, Arney's likely to starve to death or get beaten till he breaks right in two. "Briny and Queenie can find you a place, I promise. They'll be so happy you brought Fern and me back, they'll find you a really good place. If Zede's not there at Mud Island anymore, you can stay with us on the *Arcadia* till we come across Zede again."

A little worry sliver pokes under my skin. Really, I haven't got any way of being sure Briny and Queenie are still tied up in our same spot . . . except that I just *know.* They'd wait there forever if they had to, even though the nights are getting cooler, and the leaves are falling, and it's time to be headed south down the river to warmer country.

What I'm afraid won't go easy is getting Briny and Queenie to cast off once Fern and me are back on the *Arcadia.*

Has Silas told them that only me and Fern are left, that Camellia's gone and Lark and Gabion are far away? Do they know?

I can't think about it too hard, because it hurts. *Don't borrow trouble from round the bend,* Briny always said. Right now, I just have to concentrate on getting down the slough to the big river. From there, we'll stay close to the shore and watch out for the wakes off the boats and the barges . . . and keep an eye on the drift piles and strainer trees and such. Many's the night here at the Seviers' house, I've climbed way up in the cupola and looked out. I can't see the river from there, but I can feel it. I'm sure I hear the foghorns and the whistles, far off distant. At the edge of the sky, I can see the Memphis lights. From what Arney's told me, I figure the slough that drains off this lake must hit the Old Man River someplace between the Chickasaw Bluffs and the bars up-water from Mud Island. Arney's not exactly sure, but I can't be wrong by much.

Arney nods, and it's a relief. "All right. I'll take ya. But it's gotta be tonight. No way of knowin' when my brothers'll git back."

"Good. Fern and me will sneak down here soon's the moon comes up over the treetops. We'll meet you at the boat. You be sure your daddy gets into his whiskey early this evenin'. Let him eat real good too. That'll make him sleepy. I'll check that Hootsie brings down plenty of food for supper." That won't be hard. All I have to do is tell our new mommy the boy here in the camp is hungry and didn't have enough to eat. She'll make Zuma rustle up extra.

Mrs. Sevier has a heart that's soft as a dandelion puff. It's just as fragile too. I don't want to think about how she'll get by once we're gone. I *can't* think about it. Queenie and Briny need us too, and they're our folks. It's simple as that. There's no other way to look at it.

It's time for us to go.

Arney nods again. "All right. I'll be there

at the boat, but if'n we're to trek downriver together, they's somethin' you oughta know first. Might be it'd change some thangs."

"What's that?" My breath hiccups a little.

Arney's bone-thin shoulders lift and fall, and he cuts a narrow look at me before coming out with it. "I ain't no boy." He unbuttons his shirt neck, which isn't much more than rags anyhow. There's a strip of dirty old sack muslin wrapped around under there like a doctor's bandage, and Arney ain't a boy. "Arney's for Arnelle, but Daddy don't want nobody knowin' it. People won't cotton to me workin' if'n they find out."

Now I'm sure more than ever that Arney needs to stay down the river with us. On top of the fact that he's a *she,* and this is no kind of life for a girl, there're bruises all over her skinny body.

But what'll Zede say about a girl on his boat?

Maybe Briny and Queenie will let us keep Arney on the *Arcadia.* Somehow, I'll make a way. "It don't matter if you're a girl, Arney. We'll find you a place. You just be ready tonight once the moon's over the trees."

We pinky-promise on it, and then Arney's daddy hollers for her from the other side of the trees. Lunch is over.

All afternoon, I wonder if Arney will be at the boat tonight when Fern and me get there. But I figure she will, because when she thinks about it, she'll see there's not much to hold her here. She needs to get away down the river as much as we do.

The Seviers talk in their bedroom again before Mr. Sevier heads into Memphis for his meeting. When they come down, he's carrying a little overnight bag.

"If the meeting runs late, I may stay in the city," he says, and then he kisses Fern on the head and me too, which he's never done before. I grit my teeth and try really hard to be still while he leans over me. All I can think about is Mr. Riggs. "You three take care of each other." He looks at Mrs. Sevier. "Don't worry. Everything will be fine."

Zuma hands him his hat as he walks out the door, and then it's just us womenfolk. Mrs. Sevier tells Zuma and Hootsie they can go on out to the carriage house and kick their feet up. There's no need to fuss over a meal. We girls will just have ourselves a tray of finger sandwiches.

Zuma fixes the tray real cute before she leaves.

"A little pajama party just for us. *Captain Midnight* is on the radio tonight," Mrs.

Sevier says. "And hot cocoa too. Maybe it'll settle my stomach." She licks her lips and presses a hand over her tummy.

"I don't think my stomach feels too good either." I'm itching to get upstairs and gather some things together. I won't take any more than I have to of what the Seviers bought for us. It's not right. Anyhow, we have things on the *Arcadia.* Not fancy things like these, but we've got what we need. What would a river gypsy want with ruffled dresses and shiny leather shoes? The clackety soles would scare all the fish away.

"You girls go on and wash up, and put your gowns on. May, you'll feel better once we're all settled in with some cocoa and treats." Mrs. Sevier wipes her forehead with the back of her hand, then pushes her lips into a smile. "Come on, now. We'll make a lovely evening of it. Just us girls."

I take Fern's hand and head upstairs.

Fern's so excited about our party with Mrs. Sevier, she washes herself and gets her pajamas on lickety-split, even if her nighty is backward.

I fix it and put her robe on over the top and get mine on too, but I keep my clothes underneath. If Mrs. Sevier notices, I'll just tell her I was chilly. Lately, it's been cool in the house at night. One more reminder that it's time to get back to the river before winter sets in.

I try to act like I'm happy about our radio party, but I'm nervous as a cat while we're eating our finger sandwiches. I drop one on my robe and stain it, and Mrs. Sevier wipes the mess up for me.

She checks my forehead for a temperature. "How are you feeling now that you've had a little something to eat?"

All I can think is that I wish she was Queenie. I wish Queenie and Briny owned this big house, and I wish Mrs. Sevier could have babies one right after the other like Queenie does so she wouldn't be lonesome after we're gone.

I shake my head and whisper, "I might oughta just go on up to bed. I can take Fern with me and get her settled."

"No need for you to bother." She runs a hand along my hair, gathering it in her fingers and lifting it off my neck the way Queenie used to. "I'll bring her up when she's ready. I'm her mommy, after all."

Everything in me goes cold and hard again. I barely even feel it when she kisses me on the cheek and asks if I need her to come tuck me in.

"No . . . Mommy." I hurry out of the room quick as I can, and I don't look back even once.

Upstairs, it seems like forever before Mrs. Sevier brings Fern to bed. Through the wall, I hear her sing a lullaby. I push my hands tight over my ears.

Queenie and me sang that song to the babies a lot.

Hush-a-bye, don't you cry,
Go to sleep, little baby.
When you wake,
You shall have
All the pretty little horses.

All of it tangles in my head: The *Arcadia* and this place. My real parents and Mrs. Sevier and Mr. Sevier. Queenie and Mommy and Briny and Papa. The big river. The oxbow lake. The slough. Long white porches and little ones that drift, and drift, and drift over the water, not painted at all.

I play like I'm asleep when Mrs. Sevier comes into my room and feels my forehead again. I'm afraid she'll try to wake me up and ask how I am, but then she leaves. The door closes at the end of the hall, and I can finally breathe easy.

The moon's just coming up when I put on my coat and shoes, strap a little poke onto my back, and slip into Fern's room and lift her out of bed. "Sssshhh . . . be real quiet. We're gonna walk to the river and see if we can spot some fireflies. If anybody hears us, they won't let us go."

I wrap my little sister in a blanket, and she's asleep on my shoulder before we're down the stairs and out the door to the porch. It's dark and shadowy there, and I hear something scratching in the gardens near the house, a coon or a skunk maybe. Mr. Sevier's hunting dogs bark when I step off into the grass, but they quiet after they see it's just me. Nobody lights a lamp in the carriage house. Dew flicks up and sprinkles my legs as I hold Fern tight and hurry toward the trees. Over branches, the moon shines high and full, as bright as the lantern Briny always hangs on the *Arcadia* at night. There's plenty of light to see by, and that's all we need. We're down to the lakeshore quick. Arney is waiting, just like she promised.

We whisper, even though she tells me her daddy's dead-dog out cold from whiskey, like usual. "If he wakes some and wants me, he ain't gonna git hisself upright to come lookin'." But Arney hurries us into the boat anyhow. Her eyes are wide white circles in her thin face when she checks over her shoulder toward the camp.

At the last, she stands there with one hand on the little jon boat and two feet on the shore. It seems like forever that she's turned toward the camp, just watching.

"Get in," I whisper. Fern's waking up a little in the bottom of the boat, yawning and stretching and blinking around. If she figures out what's going on, I'm afraid she might raise a fuss.

Arney's fingers drift off the boat until only the tips are touching.

"Arney." *Is she thinking of sending us on alone?* I've got no idea how to run the motorboat by myself, and I don't know the way through the slough. We'll get lost in there and never come out. "Arney, we gotta go."

Past the treetops, the shadows shift on the lawn, and I think I see streams of light moving over the grass. They're gone by the time I stand up for a better view. Maybe they were only in my mind . . . or maybe Mr. Sevier decided to come home tonight instead of staying in the city. Could be he's parking his car and walking into the house right now. He'll look in our bedrooms and know we're gone.

I wobble across the hull and grab Arney's arm, and she jumps like she's forgot all about me. Her eyes grab on to mine through the moonlight. "I don't know if I oughta," she says. "I won't never see my people again."

"They treat you bad, Arney. You have to leave. You have to come with us. *We'll* be your people now. Me and Fern and Briny and Queenie and Old Zede."

We stare at each other for a long time. Finally, she nods and casts off the boat so fast I fall over the top of Fern. We take the paddles and row out a ways, letting wind and the current pull us along toward the slough until we're well out from shore.

"Where's . . . a fi . . . fireflies?" Fern mumbles when I crawl over her.

"Sssshhh. We gotta get all the way to the river first. You might oughta sleep awhile yet." I pull her blanket up tight and put her shoes on her bare feet to keep them warm and let her use the poke for a pillow. "I'll wake you up when it's time to look." There won't be any gators, but when Fern finally sees the *Arcadia,* she won't care a bit.

Arney starts the motor and sits down in the stern to run it. I take my paddle and move to a place up front to watch for drift logs. "Light the lamp," Arney says. "There's matches in the box there."

I do what she asks, and just a few minutes later, we're slipping down the middle of the wide, clear lake, stirring the night critters as they skitter away from the circle of lantern glow. I feel free as the Canada geese that pass by overhead, honking their call notes and dotting out the stars. They're headed the same way we are. South to the river. I watch them pass and wish I could catch on to one and let it fly me home.

"Best keep a lookout up there." Arney slows the boat when the lake narrows and the trees squeeze in closer. "Push off the drift if ya spy any. Don't let us run up on it."

"I know."

The night air cools and thickens and smells of the slough. I button my coat tighter. Trees shut out the sky, their bottoms wide and twisted and rooty. Their branches reach at us like fingers. Something scrapes along the hull and lifts us on one side.

"Keep us offa them," Arney barks. "One splits the boat, we're goners."

I watch for logs and cypress knobs and any sort of driftwood. I push it away with the paddle, and the miles go by slow. Here and there, skiffs sit tied ashore and swamp houses float on skids, their lanterns flickering, but mostly we're alone. There's nothing except us and miles of low, boggy country where the otters and the bobcats live and moss hangs heavy from the branches overhead. The trees make shapes that look like monsters in the dark.

A screech owl sounds off, and both Arney and me duck low. We hear it pass right over our heads.

Fern roots around in her sleep, bothered by the noise.

I think of Briny's tales about ol' rougarou and how he carries little children off to the swamp. A shiver runs through me, but I don't let Arney see it. There's no monsters here worse than the ones that're waiting for us at Mrs. Murphy's house if we're sent back.

No matter what else happens, Fern and me can't get caught.

I watch the water and try not to think about what might be out there in the swamp. Arney turns us this way and that, finding the channel time after time just like she said she could.

Finally, we run out of moonlight, and the kerosene in the lamp goes dry. The flame sputters until it's just the wick burning. The breeze snuffs it out as we draw to shore and tie the bowline to a tree branch. My arms and legs are heavy like the water-soaked logs I've been shoving away with the paddle.

They ache and crackle when I crawl to the center of the boat to get under the blanket beside Fern, who's been asleep almost this whole time.

Arney comes too. "Ain't far to the end of the slough from here," she says, and the three of us curl up together, cold and wet and wanting sleep. From someplace, I think I hear music, and I tell myself it's a showboat and that means the river's nearby, but it could just be my mind playing tricks. As I drift away, I'm sure there's the sound of the boats and barges far off. Their foghorns and whistles travel on the night. I listen close, try to decide if I know which ones they are. The *Benny Slade,* the *General P,* and a paddle-wheeler with its telltale *puff, slap, slap, slap, puff.*

I'm home. I'm wrapped in the lullaby I know by heart. I let the dark and the night sounds come inside me, and there's not a dream or a worry anywhere. The mother water rocks me soft and gentle until nothing else is around me at all.

I sleep the deep sleep of a river gypsy.

In the morning, voices pull me from the quiet. Voices . . . and wood pounding on wood. I throw off the blanket, and Arney snaps upright on the other side of Fern. We look at each other for a minute, remembering where we are and what we've done. Between us, Fern turns over and blinks up at the sky.

"I tolt ya they's somebody in that boat, Remley." Three little colored boys stand watching us from the cypress knees, their overalls rolled up above skinny, muddy legs.

"That one's a *girl*!" the biggest boy says, stretching out his chin to get a better look at me and tapping the boat with the end of his frog gig. "And they's a little girl too. White girls!"

The others step back, but the biggest boy — he can't be much more than nine or ten — stands his ground and leans on his gig. "What're you doin' here? You lost?"

Arney stands up and swats a hand at them. "Scamper off! Y'all better git gone if'n ya know what's good for ya." Her voice is deeper, like the one she used before I knew she was a girl. "We been out fishin'. Just waitin' on mornin' to start up again is all. One a' y'all clamber up there 'n' unhitch that line, so's we can git on our way."

The boys stay where they are, still watching us, wide-eyed.

"Hurry on now, ya hear me?" Arney shakes the paddle toward the branch where we're tied. The water pulled us around while we slept, and the rope's tangled in the limbs. It'll be hard to get at it ourselves.

I scrabble in the poke and hold up a cookie. In the Sevier house, it's never hard to make off with Zuma's baked goods. I've squirreled some away the last few days to have them ready for our trip. Now they'll come in handy. "I'll throw you a cookie if you do."

Fern rubs her eyes and whispers, "Where's Mommy?"

"Hush," I tell her. "You be real still, now. No more questions."

I hold the cookie up for the colored boys. The littlest one grins, then drops his gig pole and climbs the branch as good as any lizard could. He works at the knot a bit, but he gets it loose. Before we drift off, I toss three cookies up on the bank.

"No need in givin' them any," Arney complains.

Fern stretches toward me and licks her lips.

I hand Fern and Arney the last two cookies. "We'll have lots of food once we get to the *Arcadia.* Queenie and Briny are gonna be so happy to see us, they'll cook up a mess so big you won't be able to believe your natural-born eyes." Ever since we started this trip, I've been promising Arney things to keep her going. I can tell she still wants to be back with her people. It's funny how what you're used to seems like it's right even if it's bad.

"You'll see," I tell her. "Once we're on the *Arcadia,* we'll cast off down the river where nobody can give us trouble. We'll go south, and Old Zede, he'll be right behind us."

I tell myself that over and over and over while we start the little motor and work our way to the mouth of the slough, but it's like there's a line inside me and it's still tied to something back yonder. It gets tighter and tighter, even after we turn a corner, and the trees open up, and I see the river, ready to carry us home. There's a worry growing in me, and it's got nothing to do with the wakes from the big boats jostling and rocking us around as we putter along toward Memphis.

When Mud Island finally does come into sight, the worry gets my breath altogether, and I half wish a runaway barge would plow us under as we cross toward the backwater. What'll Briny and Queenie say when they see that Fern's the only one left besides me?

The question gets heavier and heavier as we pass the old shantyboat camp, which is almost empty now, and I guide Arney into the backwater I've traveled a hundred times in my mind already. I've come here from

Miss Tann's car, and Mrs. Murphy's cellar, and the sofa at the viewing party, and the lacy pink bedroom at the Seviers' big house.

It's hard to believe, even when we clear the bend and the *Arcadia* is waiting there, that she's real. She's not just another dream.

Zede's shantyboat is tied up just down the way, but the closer I get, the more things look wrong about the *Arcadia.* The porch rail is broken out. Leaves and downed branches litter the roof. A shattered window shines its sharp fangs in the sunlight near the stovepipe. The *Arcadia* lists in the water, her hull mired up on the bank so high, I wonder how we'll ever break her loose.

"Arcadia! Arcadia!" Fern cheers, and claps, and points, her sun-gold curls bouncing up and down. She stands in the center of the boat the way only a river girl can. "*Arcadia*! Queenie! Queenie!" she yells again and again as we come closer.

There's no sign of anybody around. *Maybe they got up this morning and went off to fish or hunt? Or maybe they're down at Zede's?*

But Queenie doesn't leave the boat much. She likes staying home unless she's got womenfolk nearby to visit with. There's nobody else around here.

"This it?" Arney sounds doubtful.

"Must be they're not home just now." I

try to seem sure of myself, but I'm not. A thick black feeling comes over me. Queenie and Briny wouldn't ever let the boat look like this. Briny was always prideful about the *Arcadia.* He kept things up real nice. Even with five kids around, Queenie made our little home spotless. *Shipshape,* she called it.

The *Arcadia* is a long way from shipshape now. It looks even worse as Arney steers us close to the gangplank, then cuts the motor so we can float in. When I grab the porch rail to pull us to, a piece of it comes off in my hand, and I almost topple into the water.

We've no sooner gotten tied up than I see Silas running down the bank, his long legs pumping through the sand. He jumps over a brush pile, nimble as a fox, and for a minute, I think of Camellia scampering away when the police came.

That seems like years ago, not just months.

Silas meets me when I climb off the boat. He grabs me in a bear hug and swings me and holds me up over the sand while his feet sink down into it. Then he sets me on the end of the plank.

"You're a sight for sore eyes," he says. "I never thought I'd see you again."

"I wondered too." Behind me, I hear Arney helping Fern, but all I can do is look at

Silas. *He's* a sight for sore eyes, that's what he is. "We're home. We made it home."

"You did. And you got Fern here too. Wait'll Zede sees!"

He hugs me again, and this time my arms aren't pinned down by his. I hug him back.

It's not till Fern talks that I remember there's anybody else watching. "Where's Queenie?" she asks.

The minute I let go of Silas and step back to look at him, I know something's wrong. Nobody's come out of the shanty, even with all the racket we've made. "Silas, where's Queenie? Where's Briny?"

Silas holds me by the shoulders. His dark eyes stare hard into mine. The corner of his mouth quivers a little. "Your mama died three weeks ago, Rill. The doctor said it was blood poisonin', but Zede told me she just had a broke heart. She missed y'all too much."

The news guts me out like a fish. I'm empty inside. *My mama's gone from this world? She's gone from this world, and I'll never get to see her again?*

"Where . . . where's Briny?" I ask.

Silas holds me tighter. I can tell he's afraid that if he lets go, I'll crumple like a ragdoll. For a second, I think I will. "He ain't been well, Rill. He took to the bottle after he lost y'all. He's worse since Queenie died. Worse by twice."

Chapter 23

Avery

Trent and I stand side by side gazing up at the ancient columns that line the perimeter of a decaying stone and concrete foundation. They stand like sentinels, military in stature, their feet lost in ivy and lush grass, their hats crowned with carved scrollwork and moss-hued cherubs.

A few moments pass before either of us realizes that Jonah has climbed the steps to investigate what must have once been a multilevel veranda. Rusted second-story railings loop along the columns high above our heads, binding them like faded strings of gold braid.

"Hey, come on back over here, buddy," Trent calls to Jonah. The stones look solid, but there's no way of knowing how stable this place is.

A plantation house once stood here, tucked on a gentle hill along the Savannah

River not far from Augusta. Whose was it? Nearby, an icehouse and other outbuildings stand derelict, their burgundy-shingled roofs slowly decaying, broken timbers poking forth like severed bones.

"What in the world was my grandmother *doing* here?" It is impossible to imagine Grandma Judy — the woman who fussed if I came in from the barn with horsehair on my breeches and made the mistake of sitting on the furniture — in a place like this.

And *every* Thursday for *years*? Why?

"One thing's for certain. Nobody would bother you here. I doubt if anyone still realizes this place exists." Trent moves to the steps and reaches for Jonah's hand as the little boy gleefully hops down. "Stay here by Dad, buddy. I know it looks awesome, but there might be a snake."

Jonah stretches upward to see over the foundation. "Where a 'nake?"

"I said there might be."

"Ohhh . . ."

I'm momentarily distracted by the two of them. They look like a magazine photo, the bright midday sunlight cascading through the old-growth trees and settling over them, highlighting their sandy-blond hair and look-alike stances.

I finally turn back to the remains of the

house. It must have been grand in its day. "Well, judging by the fact that she used a cab rather than having her own driver bring her, she didn't want anyone to know where she was."

I want the truth to be that innocent, but I know better. It's too much of a coincidence that May Crandall mentioned Augusta and my grandmother has returned here time and time again. This involves the two of them somehow. This is May's place, I know it. Her association with Grandma Judy reaches far beyond working together on some tragic adoption story once upon a time.

"Looks like the road continues on down that way." Trent motions toward the path we've walked from the gate. With grass grown up in the middle and seed heads bowing over the worn tire tracks, it barely qualifies as a road, but it has obviously been both driven on and mowed since last season's growth. Someone was keeping this place up until fairly recently.

"I guess we should see where it goes." But part of me — most of me — is afraid to know.

We start down the road, crossing what was once the lawn. Jonah lifts his legs high with each step, wading through the unmown grass like he's testing waves along the seashore. Trent swings him up and cups him in one arm as the grass deepens and the path leads us into the trees.

Jonah points out birds and squirrels and flowers, making our trek seem innocent — a little nature walk with friends. He wants both his dad and me to comment on his finds. I do my best, but my mind is running a million miles a minute down the hill. Through the trees, I can see water. It's sunlit, slightly ruffled by a breeze. The river, no doubt.

Jonah calls me Ay-ber-wee. His dad corrects him, saying, "That's Miss Stafford." Trent smiles sideways at me. "My family's old school. No first names for adults."

"That's nice." I was raised that way too. Honeybee would've grounded me to my room if I'd failed to properly use *Mr.* and *Mrs.* for grown-ups. The rule stood until I was out of college, officially fully grown.

Ahead, the path skirts what looks like the remains of a rusted wire garden fence. It's so overgrown with trumpet vines that I don't realize it's actually delineating a yard until we're almost on top of it. There's a tidy little house tucked among red climbing roses and snowy-white crepe myrtles. Situated on a gentle hill above the river, it's like an enchanted cottage in a children's fairy tale — the sort of hideaway that would shelter a princess in disguise or a wise old hermit who was once a king. From the yard's front gate, a boardwalk leads downhill to a dock that leans into the water.

Even though the gardens around the house are overgrown right now, they were obviously an elaborate labor of love. Arbors and benches and birdbaths wait beside carefully laid stone paths. The little house sits on short piers, prepared to withstand high water. Judging by the weathered wooden window frames and the tin-paneled roof, I'd say it's been here for decades.

So this was my grandmother's destination. It's easy to imagine that she enjoyed coming here. This would've been a place where she could leave behind her obligations, her cares, her duties, the family reputation, the public eye — everything that filled those carefully managed appointment books.

"You wouldn't know this was here." Trent admires the little hide-away as we walk around to the front, where a wide screened porch peeks through the trees. Lace curtains hang inside the front windows. A wind chime sings the sweet, soft music of midday. Twigs and leaves on the steps confirm that no one has swept since before the last set of storms.

"No, you wouldn't." *Is* this May Crandall's home, the place where she was discovered keeping company with her sister's dead body?

Trent lets us through the crooked gate. It scrapes the stone path, protesting the intrusion. "Looks pretty quiet. Let's see if anyone's home."

We climb the steps together, and he sets Jonah down on the porch as the screen door creaks its way closed behind us.

We knock on the door and wait, and finally peer through the lace curtains. Inside, a flowered settee framed with Queen Anne tables and Tiffany lamps seems out of step with the humble river cottage. Paintings and photos line the walls of the small living room, but I can't see them clearly from here. At the far end, there's a kitchen. Doors off the main room appear to lead to bedrooms and a back porch that's been closed in.

I've moved to the other window to get a better view when I hear Trent trying the doorknob.

"What are you *doing*?" Glancing over my shoulder, I half expect sirens or, worse yet, a shotgun aimed our way.

Trent winks at me, a mischievous twinkle in his eye as the knob clicks. "Checking on a potential listing. I think somebody called me to do an appraisal of the place."

He's inside before I have the chance to argue. I'm not sure I would anyway. I can't leave without knowing more, without finding out what's been going on here. It's hard to picture how someone in May's condition could have lived this far off the beaten path.

"Jonah, you stay right there on the porch. No going out the screen door." Trent casts a commanding look over his shoulder.

" 'Kay." Jonah is busy picking up acorns that some squirrel must have spirited through the torn corner of the screen door. He's counting them when I follow Trent inside. "One, two, fwee . . . seven . . . eight . . . fowty-fow."

The count drifts away as I stand on the small rag rug inside the doorway and look around the room. It's not what I expected. There's no layer of dust, no gathering of dead insects along the windowsills. Everything is neat as a pin. There's a definite sense of occupation, but the only sounds come from the wind chime, the birds, the leaves, Jonah's whispery voice, and the call of a river bird.

Trent fingers an envelope that's lying on the kitchen counter, twists to look at it. "May Crandall." He presents the evidence, but I only half see it.

I'm focused on a painting over the fireplace. The bright sun hats, the crisply ironed sixties sundresses, the smiles, the golden curls lifted by the salt breeze, the laughter you can see but not hear . . .

I recognize the scene, if not the exact pose. In this one, the four women are looking at one another and laughing. The boys playing in the sand are gone from the background. The photo I found in Trent Senior's workshop was black-and-white, and the women were smiling for the camera. The snapshot that inspired this painting must have been taken an instant before or after the other one. The portrait artist added the vibrant colors. There is no hue for painting laughter, yet the captured moment radiates joy. The women stand with their arms linked at the elbows as they throw back their heads. One of them kicks a spray of seawater at the photographer.

I move closer to the painting to study the signature in the bottom corner. *Fern,* it reads.

A brass plate on the frame titles the work: SISTERS' DAY.

My grandmother is on the left. The other three, based on the story told to us at the nursing home, are May, Lark, and Fern.

With their heads tipped back and sun rather than shadow over the faces, the women really *look* like sisters.

Even my grandmother.

"That's not the only one." Trent pivots, surveying the room. Everywhere, there are photographs. Different decades, different locations, an assortment of frames and sizes, but always these same four women. On the dock by the river, their jeans rolled up and fishing poles in their hands; enjoying tea by the climbing roses behind this little house; in red canoes, paddles at the ready.

Trent leans over a table, opens a frayed black photo album, and leafs through. "They spent a lot of time here."

I take a step toward him.

Suddenly a dog barks outside. Both of us freeze as the sound rushes closer. Toenails clatter up the porch steps. In four hurried strides, Trent is across the room and out the front door, but he's not fast enough. A big black dog is growling from the other side of the screen, and Jonah stands frozen.

"Easy, buddy . . ." Trent moves forward, grabs Jonah's arm, and shifts him back to me.

The dog raises its head and bays, then scratches at the bottom of the door, trying to cram its nose through the torn corner.

Not far off, some sort of engine rumbles. A lawnmower maybe. It's coming our way. Trent and I have no choice but to wait. I don't even dare to close the front door to the house behind us. If the dog breaks through, we'll need an escape.

We're like felons caught in the act. Actually, we *are* felons caught in the act.

Only Jonah, who's innocent of any crime, is excited. I keep a hand on his shoulder while he bobs up and down, trying to see what's making the engine noise.

"Oh . . . tractor! Tractor!" He cheers when a man in overalls and a straw hat comes chugging into view on a red-and-gray tractor of inestimable age. A faded two-wheeled cart rattles in tow with a Weed Eater and a few twigs inside. The sun slides over, dappling the man's burnished brown skin as he pulls up near the gate and kills the engine.

On closer inspection, I see that he's younger than his garb makes him look. Maybe about my parents' age . . . in his sixties, perhaps?

"Sammy!" His voice is deep and demanding as he steps off the tractor and calls the hound. "You cut that out, now! Hush up! Come outa there!"

Sammy has his own mind. He waits until the man is almost within reach before obeying the command.

The stranger stops halfway up the steps, but he's so tall we're almost eye-to-eye.

"I help you folks?" he asks.

Trent and I look at each other. Clearly, neither one of us has planned for this moment.

"We were talking to May in the nursing home." Trent is salesman smooth. He makes that seem like an explanation, even though it really isn't.

"I — Is this is hers . . . her . . . her house?" I babble, making us look even more guilty.

"You got a tractor!" Of the three of us, Jonah has the most intelligent comment.

"Yes, sir, I do there, li'l fella." The man braces his hands on his knees to talk to Jonah. "That there was my daddy's tractor. He bought her when she was brand-new in 1958. I just come start her up when I get time, knock down the weeds around the farm, pick up the branches, and look in on Mama. The grandbabies love comin' with me. I've got one over there right now who's just about your size."

"Oh . . ." Jonah is properly impressed. "I'm fwee." He works hard to hold up the three middle fingers on one hand and fold down the pinky and thumb.

"Yep, Bart's just about your age then."

The man agrees. "Three and a half. Named after his papaw. That's me."

Big Bart straightens back up, studying Trent and me. "You relatives of May's? How's she doin'? Mama told me her sister died and they had to take Mrs. Crandall off to the rest home. Said the grandkids put her in a facility all the way over in Aiken, thinking it'd be better if she wasn't so close to home. Sad thing. She loved this place."

"She's doing as well as can be expected, I guess," I tell him. "I don't think she likes it very much there. After visiting her house here, I can see why."

"You a niece or granddaughter?" He zeroes in on me. I can see him searching his mental catalog, trying to decide who I might be.

I'm afraid to lie to the man. No telling whether May even *has* a granddaughter. Bart might be testing me.

A lie won't really solve my problem anyway. "I'm not . . . exactly sure, to tell you the truth. You said your mother lives nearby? I wonder if she might know anything about the" — *the secret my grandmother was keeping* — "pictures in the house and the painting above the fireplace? My grandmother is one of the women in it."

Bart gives the cottage a clueless look.

"Couldn't say. Haven't been inside in years, myself. Mama's been the one to take care of the place here for a long time. Since before the big house got burned down by lightning in '82, even."

"Could we possibly . . . talk to her? Would it be too much of an imposition?"

He tips back his hat, smiling. "My mercy! Not a bit. She loves it when anybody comes to visit. Just be sure you've got time to kill. Mama can *talk.*" He leans back and looks around the edge of the cabin. "Did y'all walk down here on foot from the old house? There's an easier route out right through there. Little driveway up to the farm lane. May kept her car parked in the garage by Mama's place."

"Oh, I didn't know." But that explains a few things, like the overgrown condition of the front entrance and the rough trail that led us here. "We walked in from the old iron gate."

"Oh slap, you'll have chiggers by tomorrow. Remind me to give you some of Mama's chigger soap. She makes it herself."

I immediately start itching.

"Y'all hop in my li'l box trailer there. I'll give you a ride over to Mama's house. Unless you'd just as soon walk?"

I look across the way, and all I see are billions of chiggers waiting to attach themselves to me and make me itch for all eternity.

Jonah is already vibrating in place and tugging his daddy's pant leg and pointing at the tractor.

"I think we'll ride," Trent decides.

Jonah claps and cheers, seconding the motion.

"You come on then, young fella." Bart opens the screen door, and Jonah reaches for him as if he's an old friend. He swings Jonah into the air and down the steps, and it's clear that Bart is experienced at this kind of thing. Obviously he's a top-notch grandpa.

Jonah is in heaven when we climb into the little two-wheeled wooden trailer, which reminds me of the manure wagon the stable hands use at Drayden Hill. I even suspect this cart may have been employed the same way. Suspicious-looking substances bounce around underneath the pile of twigs. Jonah doesn't mind a bit. He looks happy as a duck in a puddle as we motor through some underbrush at the edge of the yard and follow what is clearly a well-used trail, perhaps for a four-wheeler or a golf cart.

Our route runs away from the river, taking us to a rural road, where we turn in to the first driveway. The freshly painted blue house looks like the sort of place where an old farmwife would live. Chickens peck in the yard. A spotted milk cow lounges under a shade tree. Laundry flaps lazily on a multistrand clothesline. Sammy bounds ahead, barking and baying to announce our arrival.

Bart's mother shuffles onto the porch dressed in a colorful muumuu, house shoes, and a bright yellow scarf. A matching silk flower adorns the fluffy gray bun atop her head. When she sees us in the tractor cart, she draws back and shades her eyes. "Who ya got there, Barthol'mew?"

I let her son offer an explanation, since I don't have one. "They were over at Mrs. Crandall's place. Said they been to visit her in the nursing home."

The old woman's chin disappears into the leathery, cinnamon-colored folds of her neck. "Who you say you is?"

I climb off the wagon before she can decide to have her son take us back where he found us. "Avery." It's only two steps onto her porch, and I hurriedly offer my hand to shake hers. "I was asking your son about the pictures and the paintings over at May's house. My grandmother is in them."

The old woman glances from me to Trent, who's waiting at the bottom of the steps while Jonah investigates the tractor with Bart. A boy about Jonah's size emerges from a nearby barn and runs across the yard to join them. Introductions aren't needed, but they're quickly offered. This is little Bart.

The old woman turns her attention to me again. She cranes upward and looks long and hard, as if she's mapping the contours of my face, comparing them to something. Is it my imagination, or is there a spark of recognition? "Now, who you say you is?"

"Avery," I repeat more loudly this time.

"Av'ry who?"

"Stafford." I purposely haven't offered that information until now. But I don't want to leave here without answers, and if this is what it takes, this is what it takes.

"You Miss Judy's daughter?"

My heart starts pumping so hard I can feel my eardrums pulsating. "Granddaughter."

Time seems to slow down. I lose all consciousness of little-boy chatter, and tractor talk, and big Bart, and chickens clucking, and the cow swatting flies, and the endless song of a mockingbird.

"You wanna know 'bout that place next door. 'Bout why she go there." It's not a question but a statement, as if this woman has been waiting for years, knowing that sooner or later someone would come asking.

"Yes, ma'am, I do. I'd ask my grandmother, but to tell you the truth, she's not doing all that well mentally. She can't remember things."

She shakes her head slowly, her tongue making a soft *tsk, tsk, tsk.* When she focuses on me again, she says, "What the mind don't 'member, the heart still know. Love, the strongest thang of all. Stronger than all the rest. You wanna know 'bout the sisters."

"Please," I whisper. "Yes. Please tell me."

"It ain't my secret to tell." She turns and shuffles toward the house, and for a moment I think I've been dismissed, but a quick glance over her shoulder tells me otherwise. I'm being asked to follow her inside.

Told to.

I stop just past the threshold, waiting while she opens the slant top on an oak secretary desk and draws out a dented tin crucifix. From beneath it, she takes three rumpled sheets of paper originally torn off a yellow legal pad. Even though they've been wrinkled and then straightened, they don't look particularly old, and they're certainly not of the same vintage as the pressed tin piece.

"I only took it fo' safekeepin'," the woman says. She hands me the tin piece and the papers separately. "That cross been Queenie's, long time ago. Miss Judy write the other. It's *her* story, but she never write the rest. They decide they all gon' carry it to they graves, I guess. But I figure somebody might come askin' one day. Secrets ain't a healthy thang. Secrets ain't a healthy thang, no matter how old they is. Sometimes the oldest secrets is the worst of all. You take yo' grandmother to see Miss May. The heart still know. It still know who it loves."

I look down at the crucifix, turn it over in my hand, then unfold the yellow sheets. I recognize the handwriting. It's my grandmother's. I've looked at enough of her daybooks to be certain.

"Sit down, child." Bart's mother guides me to a wing chair. I half sit and half collapse. The top of the page reads:

PRELUDE

Baltimore, Maryland
August 3rd, 1939

The date of my grandmother's birthday and the place she was born.

My story begins on a sweltering August night, in a place I will never set eyes upon. The room takes life only in my imaginings. It is large most days when I conjure it. The walls are white and clean, the bed linens crisp as a fallen leaf. The private suite has the very finest of everything. . . .

I float through time, tumbling back years and decades, moving through space to a hospital room in August 1939, to a tiny life that enters the world and leaves it in the same moment, to blood and grief and an exhausted young mother who sinks into merciful sleep.

There are the whispered conversations of powerful men. A grandfather who, for all his wealth and position, cannot save his tiny grandchild.

He is an important man . . . a congressman, perhaps?

He cannot rescue his daughter. Or can he?

I know of a woman in Memphis. . . .

A desperate choice is made.

This is where the written story ends.

And where another story begins. The saga of a fair-haired infant girl who, if Georgia Tann's sordid history is any indication, is taken from her mother immediately after birth. Falsified papers are signed, or perhaps the exhausted new mother is simply told that her child was stillborn. The baby is spirited away in Georgia's arms, secretly delivered to a waiting family that will claim her as their own and bury their desperate secret.

The tiny girl becomes Judy Myers Stafford.

This is the truth my heart has been reaching for since the day I saw the faded photograph on May's nightstand and was struck by the resemblance.

The photo in the nursing home is of Queenie and Briny. They aren't just people from May Crandall's remembrances. They are my great-grandparents. River gypsies.

I might've been one myself had fate not taken an unthinkable twist.

Bart's mother moves to the space beside me. She sits on the arm of the wing chair, and rubs my back, and hands me a handkerchief as my tears flow. "Oh, honey. Oh, child. The best thing is to *know.* I always tell 'em, best to be who you *is.* What you *is* deep down inside. Ain't no other good way of livin'. But it ain't my decision to make."

I'm not sure how long I sit there, the old woman patting and soothing while I contemplate all the things that kept the children of the *Arcadia* from one another. I think of the way May explained their choices: *We were young women with lives and husbands and children by the time we were brought together again. We chose not to interfere with one another. It was enough for each of us to know that the others were well. . . .*

But the truth is, it wasn't enough. Even the ramparts of reputation, and ambition, and social position couldn't erase the love of sisters, their bond with one another. Suddenly, the barriers that created their need for hidden lives and secret meeting places seem almost as cruel as those of brokered adoptions, altered paperwork, and forced separations.

"You take your grandmother to see her sister." A trembling hand squeezes mine. "They the only two left. The only two sisters. You tell them Hootsie say it's time to be who they is."

Chapter 24

Rill

The whippoorwill call tries to take me from my dream, but I push it away and hold on. In the dream, we're all on board the *Arcadia . . .* Briny, and Lark, and Fern, and Gabion. We're drifting down the wide Mississippi full out in the middle, just like we own the deed on the whole big river. The day is clear and fine, and there's not a tugboat or a barge or a stern-wheeler in sight.

We're *free.* We're free, and we're letting the river take us south. Far, far away from Mud Island and everything that happened there.

Silas and Zede are with us too. And Camellia and Queenie.

That's how I know the whole thing isn't true.

I open my eyes and toss off the blanket, and for a minute I'm sunblind and lost. It's the middle of the day, not nighttime. Then I realize I'm curled in the skiff with Fern, and we were squirreled up under the ragged canvas, not a blanket. The skiff is tied to the back of the *Arcadia,* heading nowhere. It's the only place we can go to rest during the day and be sure Briny won't sneak up on us.

The whippoorwill call comes again. It's Silas, I know. I look for him in the brush, but he's got himself hidden.

I wiggle from under the canvas, and Fern wakes up and grabs my ankle. Since we've come back to the *Arcadia,* she's scared to be by herself even for a minute. She's never sure whether Briny will push her away so hard she falls down or grab her up and hold her so tight she can't breathe.

I answer the whippoorwill call, and Fern scrambles up trying to see into the woods.

"Ssshhhh," I whisper. When we snuck out to the skiff this morning, Briny was rambling around with a bottle of whiskey. He's probably asleep on the porch by now. I just can't be sure. "We better not let Briny find out Silas is here."

Fern nods and licks her lips. Her tummy rumbles. She probably knows that Silas'll bring us something to eat. If it weren't for Silas and Old Zede and Arney, we would've starved to death in the three weeks we've been back on the *Arcadia.* Briny hasn't got much need for food. He mostly lives on whiskey now.

I lift the canvas up for Fern. "You go back under there a minute." If Briny sees that Silas came over and starts into a fit about it, I don't want Fern in the way.

I have to peel her off to put her back under the canvas, but she stays.

Silas is waiting in the brush. He hugs me hard, and I bite my lip to keep from crying. We move off a little farther together, but not so far that I can't hear Fern if she needs me.

"You all right?" Silas asks when we sit down in the clear spot under a tree.

I nod. "Fishing wasn't any good this morning, though." I don't want to ask for food, but I'm hoping that's what's in the little poke he's carrying.

He hands over a bundle no bigger than two fists, but it means a lot. Zede's supplies are running low, and he's got Arney to feed too. She's moved onto his boat, where she'll be safe. Zede wanted Fern and me to go too, but I know Briny won't hurt us.

"Some flapjacks and a little salt fish. An apple you can split up." Silas leans back on his hands, pulls a breath, and looks through the brambles toward the river. “Briny any better today? He comin’ around at all?”

“A little.” I’m not sure if it’s true or if I just want it to be. Briny mostly wanders around the boat and drinks and yells at night. Then he sleeps it off during the day.

“Zede says we’ll have rain this evenin’.”

I’ve seen the rain signs too. It worries me. “Don’t come back and try to untie the lines again, all right? Not yet. Maybe in a few more days. A few more days, and I think Briny’ll be ready.”

For two weeks, we’ve stayed in at the bank across from Mud Island while the weather’s turned colder. Even though Silas and Zede warned Briny it’d be easy for the police to find us here if they come looking, Briny won’t let anybody unhitch the shore lines. He almost shot Silas’s hand off for trying. He nearly shot poor Arney too. I gave her some of Queenie’s clothes to use, and Briny decided she was Queenie, and he was mad at her for dying.

“Just a little longer,” I plead with Silas.

Silas rubs his ear like that’s not what he wants to hear. “You oughta bring Fern and come onto Zede’s boat with me. We’ll move her down into the main channel and see if Briny don’t come along.”

“Just a few more days. Briny’ll get better.

He's gone out of his head for a while, that's all. It'll pass."

I hope I'm right, but the truth is that Briny doesn't want to leave Queenie, and Queenie's buried in the thick Mississippi soil not far from here. A Catholic priest said final words over her, Zede told me. I never even knew my mama was a Catholic. Until I lived with the Seviers, I didn't even know what that meant. Zuma wore a little cross like the one on our shanty wall. She'd hold it and talk to it sometimes, just the way Queenie did, but not in Polish. The Seviers didn't care for that too much, because they're Baptists.

I figure, either way, it's a comfort to know my mama was buried proper and a preacher was there to say prayers at her grave.

"Zede wants you to tell Briny that, in four days at the outside, he's moving our boat, and if Briny don't want to come along, he's taking you and Fern off the *Arcadia.* You're goin' downwater with us."

"Who'ssss out'ere?" Briny's voice booms from somewhere near shore. The words are thick with leftover liquor. He must've heard Silas talking. "Who'ssss out'ere round?" Briny comes crashing through the brush and dead grass.

I grab the poke, tuck it under my dress,

and shoo Silas away. Briny staggers around while I slip away to the skiff, gather up Fern, and take her to the shanty.

Briny finds us there when he finally comes back. I pretend like I've just fried the flapjacks up in the skillet. He doesn't even notice there's no fire in the stove.

"I got supper almost ready." I make a show of dishing up plates. "You hungry?"

He blinks and scoops up Fern and sits down at the table and holds her tight. She watches me, her face pale and scared.

A fist grabs my throat. How am I going to tell Briny that Zede's only waiting four more days? I can't, so I say, "Flapjacks and salt fish and apple slices."

I put the food on the table, and Briny sets Fern in her place. It feels just like we've been having a proper meal together every single day. For a while, everything's like it should be. Briny smiles at me through dark, tired eyes that remind me of Camellia.

I miss my sister, even if we did fight all the time. I miss how tough and stubborn she was. How she never gave in.

"Zede says, four days yander, the currents'll be good, and it's time to take to the river. Go downwater where the fishin's fine and the weather's warm. He says it's time."

Briny braces an elbow on the table and rubs his eyes, shaking his head slowly back and forth. His words are muddled, but I hear the last few anyway. ". . . not without Queenie."

He gets up and heads for the door, grabbing his empty whiskey bottle on the way. A minute later, I hear him rowing off in the skiff.

I listen until he's gone, and in the quiet that's left after, I feel like the world is coming down around me. When I was at Mrs. Murphy's and then the Seviers' house, I thought if I could just get back to the *Arcadia,* that'd fix everything. I thought it'd fix *me,* but now I see I was fooling myself, just to keep on going, one day to the next.

Truth is, instead of fixing everything, the *Arcadia* made everything real. Camellia's gone. Lark and Gabion are far away. Queenie's buried in a pauper's grave, and Briny's heart went there with her. He's lost his mind to whiskey, and he doesn't want to come back.

Not even for me. Not even for Fern. We're not enough.

Fern crawls into my lap, and I hold tight to her. We wait out the evening listening for signs of Briny, but nobody comes. He's probably gone into town to hustle pool halls until he can get some more to drink.

Finally, I tuck Fern into her bunk and slip into mine and lay there trying to find sleep. There's not even a book to keep me company. Everything that can buy whiskey has already been traded off.

Rain starts before I fall asleep, but there's still no sign of Briny.

I find him in my dream. We're whole, and everything's the way it should be. Briny plays his harmonica as we picnic in the sand along the shore. We pick daisies and taste honeysuckle. Gabion and Lark chase after little frogs until they've caught a whole jarful.

"Ain't your mama pretty as a queen?" Briny asks. "And what's that make you? Why, Princess Rill of Kingdom Arcadia, of course."

When I wake up, I hear Briny outside, but there's no music. He's hollering into the deepening storm. Sweat sticks the bedsheet to my skin, so I have to peel it off as I sit up. My mouth is pasty and dry, and my eyes don't want to clear. The air around is black as pitch. Rain rattles the roof. The woodstove has been filled and the damper must've been turned wide open, because it's crackling and whistling and the room is boiling hot.

Outside the shanty, Briny cusses a blue streak. A lantern flashes by the window. I swing my feet around to get up, but the boat sways crazy wild, knocking me back onto the ticking. The *Arcadia* bobs side to side.

Fern rolls clean over the rail on her bunk and tumbles onto the floor in a heap.

All of a sudden, I know . . . we're not tied up onshore anymore. We're on the water.

Silas and Zede came and cut us loose after Briny got back. That's the first thing I think. *He's out there hollering because he's mad they did it.*

But just as quick, I'm sure they wouldn't set us adrift at night. It's too dangerous, with the logs and sandbars and the wakes from the big boats and barges. Silas and Zede know that.

Briny does too, but he's half out of his mind out there. He's not trying to get us to shore. He's daring the river to take us. "C'mon, you blaggard!" he hollers, like Captain Ahab in *Moby-Dick.* "Try 'n' win! Take me! C'mon!"

Thunder booms. Lightning crackles. Briny cusses at the river. He laughs.

The lantern disappears from the window, then bobs up the side ladder as Briny climbs onto the roof.

I stumble across the room to check on

Fern and put her back in her bunk. "You stay there. Stay until I tell you different."

She grabs my nightgown, croaks out, "Noooo." Since we've been back on the *Arcadia,* she's been scared to death at night.

"It'll be all right. I think the lines came loose, that's all. Briny's probably trying to get us back ashore."

I hurry on, leaving her there in the bed. The *Arcadia* wobbles as I stagger across the floor, and a tug blows its horn, and I hear the creaks and pings of barge hulls, and I know that bigger wakes are coming. I reach out for the door and grab on just in time. The *Arcadia* rises up a wake, then tips hard coming down. Wood slides through my fingernails, driving splinters underneath. I fall forward, land on the porch in the cold. The boat nods the other direction, spinning sideways to the current.

No, no! Please no!

The *Arcadia* rights herself like she's heard me. She rides the next swell clean and slick.

"You think you can take me? You think you can take me?" Briny yells from up top. A bottle shatters, and glass tumbles down from the porch roof, glistening in the night rain and the tug's searchlight. It seems to fall slow. Then it plinks into the black water.

"Briny, we've gotta get her ashore!" I yell.

"Briny, we gotta tie up!"

But the tug's horn and the storm whip my voice from my mouth.

A man someplace yells curses and warnings. An emergency whistle sounds. The *Arcadia* rises up a huge wake, balances like a dancer on tiptoes.

She lists as she falls. Cold water rushes over the porch.

We spin sideways to the river.

The tug's light sweeps and catches us.

A piece of drift aims itself for our bow — a giant strainer tree with all the roots and dirt still attached. I see it just before the light moves on. I scramble for the boathook to push it away, but the pole isn't where it should be. There's nothing I can do but hug the porch post and yell to Fern to hang on and watch the tree hit, its roots spreading around the *Arcadia* like fingers, catching my ankle, turning, and pulling hard.

Inside the cabin, Fern screams my name.

"Hold on! Hold on tight!" I yell. The tree pulls and rips, twirling the *Arcadia* like a spinning top, whirling her around, then breaking free and leaving us listing in the current. The wakes come over us hard, rushing through the shanty.

My feet slide out from under me.

The *Arcadia* moans. Nails bust loose.

Timbers splinter.

The hull hits something hard, the porch post jerks out of my hands, and next thing I know, I'm flying through the rain. Breath kicks out of my chest. Everything goes black.

I lose the noise of splintering wood and yelling voices and far-off thunder.

The water's cold, yet I'm warm. There's a light, and inside it I see my mama. Queenie reaches for my hand, and I stretch for hers, and just before I can get to her, the river tugs me away, yanking me back by the waist.

I kick, and fight, and come to the surface. I see the *Arcadia* in the tug's lights. I see a skiff coming our way. I hear whistles and yelling. My legs go stiff, and my skin's icy cold.

The *Arcadia* hangs wedged against a huge drift pile. The Mississippi goes after her like the mouth of a giant dragon, slowly eating up her stern.

"Fern!" My voice gets lost in water and noise. I swim for all I'm worth, feel the swirl and the downward pull as I ram into the drift pile. The eddy tries to yank me back, but I fight against it, climb on top, and balance my way to the deck and scramble uphill to the door.

It falls inward with a crash when I open it.

"Fern! Fern!" I yell. "Fern! Answer me!" Smoke chokes my voice. The woodstove lays tipped over. Hot red coals roll across the floor. They sizzle on the wet deck and hiss under my feet.

Everything is turned around, and I can't see. I go the wrong way first, end up at the table, not Fern's bunk. The flour-sack quilt from Briny and Queenie's bed swims by like a colorful whale, carrying a lick of flame. Nearby, fire flicks up the curtains.

"Fern!" *Is she gone? Did she fall off into the river? Did Briny get her out already?*

A wave rushes in, grabs the red coals, and sweeps them out the door. They pop and squeal as they die.

"Riiiiill! Get me! Get me!"

The searchlight sweeps over us, pressing through the window in a long, slow circle. I see my sister's face, wide-eyed and terrified under her bunk. She reaches for me, and then the next second I've grabbed her hand, and I'm trying to pull her, but the water's got us both. A chair skitters by and hits me hard in the back, knocking me onto the floor. Water flows over my face and ears. I cling to Fern for all I'm worth.

The chair tumbles on. I grab my sister, stumble and crawl across the cabin to the side door.

The searchlight goes through again. I see the picture of Briny and Queenie hanging on the wall with Queenie's cross below it.

I shouldn't, but I pin Fern there with my leg and grab the picture and my mama's cross and shove them down the front of my nighty and into the top of my drawers. They bump against my skin and dig in as we climb out and shinny over the rail and make our way onto the drift pile, scrambling over the tangle of branches, plank wood, and trees. We're quick as mice. We've done this all our lives.

But we both know enough to understand that a drift pile isn't a safe place to be. Even when we get to the other end, I can feel the heat from the fire. I hold Fern's hand, turn and look toward the *Arcadia,* and lift an arm to shield my eyes. Flames curl and stretch upward from the shanty, burning through the roof and the walls and the deck, skinning the *Arcadia* down to her bones, stripping her of her beauty. Pieces float on the air. Up, and up, and up they whirl until they fly overhead like a million new stars.

Cooled by the rain, they fall and settle over our skin. Fern yelps when one lands, still warm. I wrap a hand around the neck of her nighty, squat down, and push her into the water, tell her to hold real tight to the tangled branches. There's too much current here for us to swim to shore. Her teeth chatter, and her face goes pale.

The drift pile is starting to burn. The fire'll work its way to us soon enough.

"Briny!" The name rips from me. He's here somewhere. Surely he's gotten off the boat. He'll save us.

Won't he?

"Hold on!" somebody yells, but it's not Briny's voice. "Hold on. Don't move!"

A tank explodes on the *Arcadia.* Cinders rocket out and fall everywhere. One lands on my foot, and the pain drives right through me. I scream and kick and stick my leg in the water and hang on to Fern.

The drift pile shifts. It's smoldering in a dozen places now.

"Almost there!" the man's voice calls out.

A small boat sifts out of the darkness, two rivermen with hoods pulled over their heads straining hard at the oars. "Don't let go, now. Don't let go!"

The branches crackle. Logs whine and whistle. The entire drift pile shifts downriver a foot or two. One of the men in the lifeboat warns the other that they'll get swamped if the drift breaks loose.

They come on anyway, snatch us into the

boat, and throw blankets over us and row hard.

"Was there anyone else on the boat? Anybody else?" they want to know.

"My daddy," I cough out. "Briny. Briny Foss."

Nothing feels quite so good as the shore when they drop us there and go back to look for Briny. I cuddle Fern close inside my blanket, the picture and Queenie's cross between us. We shiver and shake and watch the *Arcadia* burn until finally the drift pile breaks loose and takes what's left of her with it.

Fern and me stand up and move to the edge of the water and watch as Kingdom Arcadia disappears into the river bit by bit. Finally, it's gone altogether. There's not a trace. It's like it never was.

Against the dawn gray to the east, I watch the men and boats. They search on, and on, and on. They call out, and their lights sweep, and they row.

I think I see somebody standing down shore. A slicker flaps around his knees. He doesn't move, or call out, or wave at the lights. He just watches the river, where the life we knew has been swallowed away.

Is it Briny?

Cupping my hands around my mouth, I

call to him. My voice carries through the morning mist, echoing over and over.

A searcher in one of the boats looks my way.

When I squint down shore again, I can hardly make out the man in the slicker. He turns and walks toward the trees until the dawn shadows cover him over.

Maybe he was never there at all.

I move a few steps closer and yell again and listen.

My voice echoes away, then dies.

"Rill!" When there's finally an answer, it doesn't come from downriver. It's not Briny's voice.

A jon boat motors up to the sandy bank, and Silas hops out before the *Jenny* even makes it to a stop. He tugs the line at a run, hurrying toward me until he grabs me in his arms. I cling to him and cry.

"You're all right! You're all right!" He breathes into my hair, squeezing me so tight the picture frame and Queenie's cross push deep into my skin. "Zede and me and Arney was scared half out of our minds when we seen the *Arcadia* gone."

"Briny cut us loose last night. I woke up, and she was on the river." I sob out the rest of the story — Briny on the roof talking out of his head, the near miss with the barge, hitting the drift pile, the fire, ending up in the water, seeing Queenie, then coming back up and climbing onto the *Arcadia* as the river was eating her whole. "Some men pulled us off the drift before it broke loose," I say, finishing our sad tale, my body shivering in the cold. "They went to look for Briny." I don't tell Silas that I think I've already seen him and that, instead of coming to find us, he walked away.

If I don't tell *anyone,* it'll never be true. It'll never be the way Kingdom Arcadia ended.

Silas then holds me at arm's length to look me over. "But you're all right. Y'all two are in one piece. Thank the saints! Zede and Arney will be bringin' Zede's boat downwater soon's they can. We'll find Briny too. You'll all be with us. We'll go where it's warm and the fishin's good, and . . ."

He chatters on about how Zede and Briny will gather boards and scrap from the riverbanks and build us a new boat. A new *Arcadia.* We'll start all over again and always travel together from now until forever.

My mind wants to color in those pictures, but it can't. Zede's boat is too small for all of us, and Briny's gone. Zede's too old to run the river much longer. He's too old to raise Fern. She's just a baby yet.

Hanging on my leg, she burrows under the blanket and tugs my dress. "I wannnn' Mom-meee," she sniffles. Her fingers almost touch the edge of Queenie's picture, but I know that's not who she means.

I look Silas full in the face as the dawn rays catch him. My heart squeezes so tight it hurts. I wish we were older. I wish we were old enough. I love Silas. I know I do.

But I love Fern too. I loved Fern first. She's all I've got left of my family.

Just down the bank from us, the search for Briny is simmering down as the early sun sheds its glow on the river. Any minute, the men will see that there's no hope of finding another survivor. They'll come back for Fern and me.

"Silas, you've gotta take us out of here. You've gotta take us *now.*" I pull away from him and move toward the jon boat, dragging Fern along.

"But . . . Briny . . ." Silas says.

"We have to *go.* Before the men come over here. They'll take us to the children's home again."

Silas understands then. He knows I'm right. He gets us in the boat, and we move off quiet until we're far enough away that no one notices the motor revving up. We keep to the shore on the other side from the cotton warehouses and docks and Mud Island and all of Memphis. When we get to our little backwater, I tell Silas I don't want him to carry us to Zede's boat except long enough to say goodbye.

I have to bring Fern back upriver and hope the Seviers will take her in again. It's not her fault we left. It wasn't her idea to steal things. It was mine. What happened wasn't Fern's doing.

If we're lucky, they'll let her come back . . . if they haven't already got some other little girl from the children's home. Maybe even if they have, they'll still keep Fern. Maybe they'll promise to love her some and keep her safe from Miss Tann.

What'll happen to me after that, there's no way to know. The Seviers won't want me for sure — a liar and a thief. I can't let Miss Tann find me again. Maybe I can get work someplace nearby, but these are lean times. I won't come back to the river. Old Zede can't feed any more mouths, but that's not the real reason I can't stay.

The real reason is I have to be close to my sister. We've been stitched together at the heart since she was born. I can't breathe in a world where she isn't near.

I tell Silas what I want him to do for us. He shakes his head, and his face gets longer and longer the more I talk about it.

"Take care of Arney," I tell him finally. "She hasn't got anything to go back to. Her people treated her in a bad way. Find her a place, all right? She don't mind workin' hard."

Silas looks down at the water as it passes, not at me. "I will."

Maybe Silas and Arney will marry in a few years, I think.

My heart squeezes again.

Everything I wanted my life to be, it won't be now. The path that brought me here is flooded over. There's no going back. That's the real reason, when we find Zede's boat, I tell him that the Seviers will sure be glad to get Fern and me back. "I just need Silas to take us upriver." I don't want Zede to come along. I'm afraid he won't let us go when it gets right down to it.

He looks through the open door into his shanty like he's trying to decide if he can keep all of us for good.

"Fern's got lots of nice clothes and toys back at the Seviers'. And Crayolas. I'll start up with school pretty soon." My voice quivers, and I swallow hard to steady it.

When Zede's eyes turn my way, it feels like he's looking right through me.

Fern reaches for him, and he picks her

up, tucking his head over hers. "Li'l bit," he chokes out, and then pulls me in and hugs us both hard. He smells of ashes, and fish, and coal oil, and the big river. Familiar things.

"You ever need me, you get word to the river," he says.

I nod, but when he turns loose of us, we both know this is goodbye forever. The river is a big place.

Sadness lines his face. He wipes it away before he nods, then sets his mouth and puts Fern in the *Jenny* so we can leave.

"I oughta go along, seein's you don't know the slough," Arney says. "But I ain't stayin' once we get there. I'll take my pa's jon boat and leave it tied up someplace near. You can let him know where to find it. I don't want nothin' of his." She doesn't wait for an answer but goes after the jon boat. Even with all her family's done to her, she's been worried how they'd get by without it.

I don't cry when we shove off again. The Waterwitch has to fight our way upstream, but eventually we make it to the mouth of the slough. The trees lean close after we turn, and I take one look back. I let the river wash away something inside of me.

It washes away the last of Rill Foss.

Rill Foss is princess of Kingdom Arcadia.

The king is gone, and so is the kingdom.

Rill Foss has to die with it.

I'm May Weathers now.

Chapter 25

Avery

"And *that* is where my story ends." May's blue eyes, clouded and moist, study me across the lamp table in an alcove of the nursing home. "Are you happy that you know? Or is it only a burden? I've always wondered how you young ones would feel. I expected that I'd never find out."

"I think . . . it's a little of both." Even after taking a week to think about it since our visit to the river cottage and Hootsie's farm, I'm still struggling to assimilate this history with *my* family history.

Over and over, I've weighed Elliot's admonitions that I'm playing with fire — that the past should be left in the past. Even the startling revelations from my visit to the Savannah River cottage haven't changed his opinion. *Think about the repercussions, Avery. There are people who wouldn't . . . see your family the same way anymore.*

By *people,* I have a sense that he means *Bitsy.*

The sad thing is, Bitsy's not the only one. If all of this became public, there's no telling what would happen to political futures, reputations, the Stafford name.

Times have changed, but the old doctrines still apply. If the world were to find out that the Staffords aren't really what we've claimed to be, the fallout would be . . .

I can't even imagine.

That scares me in a way I don't want to contemplate, but the truth is that I can't bear the thought of my grandmother and her sister spending the last of their lives separated from each other. Ultimately, I have to know I did what was right for Grandma Judy.

"A time or two, I've considered telling my grandchildren," May offers. "But they are settled in their lives. Their mother remarried to a man with children after my son passed away. They're wonderful young people raising their own broods among gaggles of aunts, and uncles, and cousins. It's much the same with my sisters' families. Lark married a businessman who built a department store empire. Fern married a prominent doctor in Atlanta. Between them, there were eight children and two dozen grandchildren and of course great-grandchildren. They are all successful and happy . . . and busy. What can ancient history give them that they don't already have?"

May looks at me deeply, watches me teeter on the dividing line that has shifted from her generation to mine. "Will you share the story with your family?" she asks.

I swallow hard, at war with myself. "I'll tell my father. It's his decision more than mine. Grandma Judy is his mother." I have no notion of how my father will respond to the information or what he'll do with it. "Part of me thinks Hootsie is right. The truth is still the truth. It has value."

"Hootsie," she grumbles. "This is the thanks I get for selling her that piece of land next to my grandmother's old place so she and Ted could have their farm on it. After all these years, she tells my secrets."

"I really think she felt it was in your best interest. She wanted me to understand the connection between you and my grandmother. She was thinking of the two of you."

May swats at the idea like it's a fly buzzing around her face. "Pppfff! Hootsie just likes to stir the pot. She has always been that way. You know, she was the reason I ended up staying with the Seviers at all. By the time we reached their home, Silas almost had me talked into taking to the river with him. He stood on the shore and grabbed me by the shoulders and kissed me. The first time I'd ever been kissed by a boy." She giggles, her cheeks reddening and her eyes taking on a childlike glitter. For a moment, I see that twelve-year-old girl on the banks of the oxbow lake. " 'I love you, Rill Foss,' he said to me. 'I'll wait here an hour. I'll wait for you to come back. I can take care of you, Rill. I can.'

"I knew he was making promises he couldn't keep. Only a few months before, he'd been hoboing trains, trying to survive. If there was one thing I'd learned from watching Briny and Queenie, it was that love doesn't put food on the table. It doesn't keep a family safe."

She nods at her own conclusion, frowning. "Wanting to and doing are two different things. I guess in a way, I knew it wasn't meant to be for Silas and me. Not while we were so young, anyway. But when I started up the path with Fern, all I wanted to do was run back to that dark-haired boy and back to the river. I might've done it if it hadn't been for Hootsie. She made the choice for me before I could choose for myself. My plan was to sneak to the edge of the trees, hide there, and watch to be certain the Seviers would take Fern in again. I was scared to death that if they caught me, they'd send me back to the children's home or off to some sort of workhouse for bad girls or even to jail. But Hootsie was out digging roots for her mama, and she spotted us there near the yard, and she went to hollering. Next thing I knew, there was Zuma, and Hoy, and Mr. and Mrs. Sevier rushing down the hill, and the dogs bounding ahead. I had no place to run, so I just stood there and waited for the worst to happen."

She pauses, and I feel myself dangling on the precipice where she's left me. "What *did* happen?"

"I learned that you need not be born into a family to be loved by one."

"So they welcomed you back?"

A smile teases the corners of her mouth. "Yes, they did. Papa Sevier, and Hoy, and the other men had been out searching the swamps for us for weeks. They knew we must have left in the jon boat with Arney. By the time we came back, they'd given up hope that we would ever be found." She laughs softly. "Even Zuma and Hootsie hugged us that day, they were so relieved to see us alive."

"You were happy with the Seviers after that?"

"They were understanding of what we had done, after they knew the truth about the *Arcadia,* that is. Or what I could bring myself to reveal of the truth. I'd made up my mind never to tell them that there were other siblings beyond just Fern and me. I suppose in my twelve-year-old heart, I was still ashamed that I'd failed to protect Camellia, and Lark, and Gabion. I feared that the Seviers wouldn't love me if they knew. The Seviers were good people — patient and kind. They taught me to find the music."

"The music?"

She reaches across the table. "Yes, the music, darling. You see, there is one thing I learned from following in Papa Sevier's footsteps as I grew up. Life is not unlike cinema. Each scene has its own music, and the music is created for the scene, woven to it in ways we do not understand. No matter how much we may love the melody of a bygone day or imagine the song of a future one, we must dance within the music of today, or we will always be out of step, stumbling around in something that doesn't suit the moment. I let go of the river's song and found the music of that big house. I found room for a new life, a new mother who cared for me, and a new father who patiently taught me not only how to play music, but how to trust. He was as good a man as ever I've known. Oh, it was never like the *Arcadia,* but it was a good life. We were loved and cherished and protected."

A sigh lifts her shoulders, then releases her. "To look at me now, you would think I'd never understood the secret. This music of old age . . . it isn't made for dancing. It's so . . . lonely. You're a burden to everyone."

I think of my grandmother, of her empty house, of her room in the nursing home, of her inability to recognize me most days. Tears well up in my eyes. The music of old age is difficult to hear when it's playing for someonc you love. I wonder if my grandmother will recognize May when they're finally together again. Will May even consent to coming with me? I haven't asked her yet. Trent is waiting down the hall. He's driven up from Edisto. After discussing the possibilities, we decided it might be better if I talked to May alone at first.

"Did you ever see Silas again?" The question pops out, and at first it seems random. Then I realize I've asked it because I was thinking of Trent . . . and of May's tale of first love. Strangely enough, that's been on my mind lately. Trent's smile, his silly jokes, his nearness, even just his voice on the phone stirs something in me. The fact that it matters not a whit to him what my family history may be or what decisions I make about it touches me in a way I'm not prepared for. I don't know how to categorize it or fit it into my life.

I only know that I can't ignore it.

May's countenance bores through me. It's as if she's digging in and following the veins of ore all the way to my soul. "I wished for it, but some wishes don't come true. Papa Sevier moved us over to Augusta to protect us from Georgia Tann. Our family was quite well known there, so I imagine he felt that she wouldn't dare trifle with him across state lines. Silas and Old Zede wouldn't have known where to find us. I never learned what became of them. My last sight of Silas was through the tangles of my new mother's hair as she hugged me close. He stood at the edge of the trees where I had been only moments before, and then he turned and went back to the water. I never saw him again."

She shakes her head slowly. "I always wondered what he might've become. Perhaps it was for the best that I never knew. I was growing into a different life, a different world, a different name. I did hear from Arney again years later. A letter came just out of the blue. My mother had it waiting for me when I arrived home from the college term. I'd always imagined that perhaps Arney and Silas had married, but they hadn't. Zede had found a place for Arney on a dairy farm soon after I left them. Arney was made to work hard, but the people were fair with her. She eventually took a job in a bomber plant and married a soldier. They were living overseas when she wrote to me, and she was quite happy to be seeing the world. She never thought she'd have that sort of opportunity." Even now, the story brings a smile.

"I'm glad things turned out well for her after such a rough start in life." Given that May is ninety and Arney was older than her, it's unlikely that Arney would still be alive now, but I feel a warm sense of relief. May's story has made Arney and Silas and all the people of the river real to me.

"Yes." May nods in agreement. "She gave me a fire in my belly for all those young, dewy-eyed women who found themselves taken advantage of by the playboys in Hollywood. I met so many during my years there, and I made it my business to help them — to provide a place to sleep or a shoulder to lean on. It happened very often, girls ending up in terrible situations. I always thought of Arney's words to me at the end of her letter."

"What did she say?"

"She said that I saved her." May dabs at a sheen of moisture near her eye. "But of course, it wasn't true. We saved each other. If not for Arney taking me back to the river, if not for what happened on the *Arcadia,* I could never have released Briny, and Queenie, and the river. I would've reached for that music all of my life. By taking me back, Arney brought me forward. I told her that in my reply."

"I imagine that meant a lot to her."

"People don't come into our lives by accident."

"No, they don't." Again, I think of Trent. Again, I feel the tug-of-war between my own feelings and the hopes and plans my family has always held for me. The plans I always thought I held for myself.

"Arney and I kept in touch over the years," May continues, and I try to slip into her story again, to leave behind the worry over how the rest of this day will go. "She was a very inspiring woman. She and her husband started their own construction company when they came home. She worked right alongside him, right alongside the men, and she held her own. I imagine those homes were as solidly built as can be. They'll outlast us all."

"No doubt they will."

May turns to me with purpose, stretches intimately close as if she plans to impart a secret. "A woman's past need not predict her future. She can dance to new music if she chooses. Her *own* music. To hear the tune, she must only stop talking. To herself, I mean. We're always trying to persuade ourselves of things."

I'm struck by the profoundness of what she's saying. Can she sense that, since visiting the cottage on the river, since learning about my grandmother, I've questioned everything about my life?

I don't want to hurt anyone, but I want to find my own music. May makes me believe it *is* possible. Which brings me to my real purpose for visiting her today. "I'm wondering if you'll come somewhere with me this afternoon," I say finally.

"Might I inquire where?" But she's already pressing out of her chair, her hands gripping the armrests.

"Are you willing to go if I don't tell you ahead of time?"

"Is it outside these dastardly drab walls?"

"Yes."

She's surprisingly spry getting to her feet. "Then I suppose I don't care *where* we're going. I am all yours. As long as you're not bringing me to some political event, that is. I despise politics."

I laugh. "It's not a political event."

"Excellent." We start down the hall together, May pushing her walker with surprising speed. I half expect her to throw it aside and start sprinting toward the door.

"Trent's waiting outside to drive us."

"The handsome one with the blue eyes?"

"Yes, *that* one."

"Oh, now I really am looking forward to this." She frowns down at her pajama-like cotton shirt and pants. "I'm not dressed very nicely. Perhaps I should change?"

"I think you'll be fine in that."

She doesn't protest when we reach her room. In fact, she stops only long enough to grab her purse.

Trent rises from his chair when we reach the front entrance. He smiles and gives me a thumbs-up behind May's back as she informs the attendant that we'll be taking her *out* for the afternoon. She turns the walker over to me and opts for Trent's arm as we pass through the door. I'm left to fold the apparatus and put it in the trunk while

Trent gets May settled. Fortunately, I've had some experience with this sort of thing.

May tells Trent her story while we drive — all of it, not just the parts she shared with us after our first foray through the workshop behind Trent's house on Edisto. Trent catches my gaze in the rearview mirror repeatedly, shakes his head with a sad sort of awe. It's hard to believe that, not so many years ago, orphaned children were little more than chattel.

May is so lost in the tale or so smitten with Trent that she doesn't notice where we're going. It's not until we're drawing closer to Augusta that she bends toward the window and sighs. "You're taking me home. You should've told me. I would have worn my sneakers."

Trent glances at May's flat slipper shoes. "It'll be all right. Your neighbor mowed the grass."

"Hootsie did raise the sweetest children. Hard to believe. She was such a rotter herself. I tangled with her more than I ever did my sisters."

Trent grins. "After getting to know her a little, I don't find that hard to believe." He's spoken with Hootsie about today's trip. She and Bart have moved heaven and earth to help make it possible.

May notices the difference when we drive past Hootsie's house on the farm lane and the road is cleared all the way through the woods to the cottage. We park on new gravel near the gate.

"Who did all of this?" May looks around at the freshly mown grass, the newly trimmed gardens, the porch with chairs waiting behind the screen.

"I was afraid you wouldn't be able to make the trek down here," I tell her. "This seemed like the best way. I hope you don't mind."

She only wipes her eyes, her lips pressing together hard, trembling.

"I thought you might want to visit more often, after this. My grandmother had a standing appointment with the cab company. They know the way here."

"I'm not sure if they'll . . . let me." A whisper is all she can manage. "The nursing home. I don't want them calling my grandchildren and bothering them either."

"I've been talking about that with a friend, a man who runs a group that advocates for senior citizens. I think we can get some help for you with some of those issues. You're not a prisoner at the care facility, May. They're just trying to make sure you're safe." I'll let that sink in for now. Later we can talk more about the suggestions from Andrew Moore, including his idea that May might gain a sense of purpose by doing some volunteer work for the PAC. Andrew is an amazing person, filled with ideas. I think May would like him.

Right now, she is too mesmerized by the scenery to talk about anything else. She leans close to the front window, tears spilling forth. "Oh . . . oh, I'm home. I never thought I'd see it again."

"Hootsie and her granddaughter have been keeping it clean for you."

"But . . . I haven't been able to pay her . . . since . . ." Tears interrupt the words. "Since they took me away."

"She says she doesn't mind." I reach for my door as Trent walks around the car. "She really does love you, you know."

"She didn't *say* that?"

"Well, no, but it's obvious."

May puffs out a skeptical breath, and once again I see the precociousness of a river gypsy. "You had me worried that Hootsie might be losing her marbles." She smirks at me, allowing Trent to help her from the car. "Hootsie and I have always kept one another sharp. It'd be a shame to ruin it by going sentimental now."

I look through the trees toward the ruins

of the plantation house as I stand up and stretch. It's hard to wrap my mind around the complexities of the relationships between these two women over the years. "You can tell that to Hootsie in person if you want. She'll be over later. I asked her to give us some time to ourselves first."

May casts a suspicious look my way as she moves through the gate, her hand crooked in Trent's elbow. "What was it that you were planning to do here? I've told you everything this time. There is no more to the story."

In the distance, I can already hear another car grinding along the farm lane. May hasn't noticed it yet, which is probably for the best. I'd intended to get her to the cottage and settle her there first. But the timing may not work out as I'd planned. Leave it to my mother to show up early, even though she has no idea where she's going or what she's arriving for.

"I've asked my parents to come." I can't think of a way to make them believe all of this that would be better than just showing them. Otherwise, I'm afraid they might think I've completely lost my mind.

"The senator?" May's face widens with horror, and she immediately starts patting her hair.

Trent tries to move May through the gate,

but she catches the post and holds on like a grade-school kid being hauled to the doctor for a shot.

"Good heavens!" she says. "I asked you if I needed to change clothes. I can't meet them like this."

I sense my best intentions bumping up against the barriers of propriety, and those walls crumble for no one. Getting my parents to cooperate with my mysterious plans for this Sunday afternoon has been nearly impossible. I've told them it has to do with a favor for a friend, but my mother can smell a fib a mile away. She'll be on full alert when she gets here, particularly considering the strangeness of the request and the remote location.

This thing *is* happening, whether any of the parties involved want it to or not, and deep down, I know I've arranged it this way on purpose. I was afraid if I didn't roll it like a downhill snowball, I'd lose my nerve.

"Well, hurry!" May starts toward the house, yanking Trent off balance. "The rest of my clothes are still in the closets. I can find something decent in there."

Through the trees, I can see the cab company's white limo. "There isn't time. They're coming up the road."

May's nostrils flare. "Did *Hootsie* know

about this?"

"Yes and no, but it was my idea. Please. Just trust me. I really do think this is for the best." After today, we'll either be bonded, or May will never speak to me again.

"I believe I'm going to faint." May sags against Trent. I'm not sure whether it's a performance or not.

Trent slips an arm around her, prepared to hold her up. "How about I take you to the house?"

She moves along, too stunned to protest.

I wait at the gate. When the limo pulls up, my mother exits on her side without even waiting for Oz to get out and open the door. Honeybee is hopping mad. "Avery Judith Stafford, what on earth is going on here? I thought for certain the driver was lost or we'd been kidnapped." It's evident in her red, slightly shiny face that she's been working up to a dither for miles, probably complaining to my father and harassing poor Oz, who's only been drafted into this operation because he knows the route. "I've called your cellphone at least fifteen times. Why didn't you answer?"

"I don't think there's any reception down here." I have no idea if that's true. I've had my phone turned off all morning. If Honeybee couldn't get in touch with me to cancel or alter the plans we'd agreed upon, she would have no choice but to come. Honeybee never falters on a commitment.

"Now, girls." My father is in a much more accommodating mood. Unlike Mama, he enjoys the rugged outdoors. Now that the intestinal bleeding has been stopped by the laparoscopic surgery, his blood counts are better, and his strength is returning. Functioning at almost full capacity, he's a match for his attackers on the nursing home issue. He's begun to systematically put it to rest. He's also building support for legislation that will prevent care facility owners from using shell corporations to avoid lawsuit payouts.

He gives the river an interested look. "It was a lovely Sunday drive. We haven't been over toward Augusta in a while. I wish I'd brought along a fishing pole and some tackle." He smiles at me, and instantly our life together flashes through my mind, from little-girl visits to his office, to ill-fated fishing trips, to proms and cotillions and graduations . . . and more recently briefings and strategy sessions and public events. "It's not often that she asks anything of us, Honeybee." He adds an indulgent wink that's just for me. "Not this one."

He means to reassure me that, whatever I

have planned today, he's up for it, but it only reminds me of how much I have to lose here — my father's favor being chief among those things. I'm his favorite. I've always been his golden girl.

How will he handle the fact that, for weeks, I've been sneaking around, digging up information that my grandmother had kept hidden to protect the Stafford legacy?

What will happen later, when I tell him how this journey has changed me? I don't want to live the life my grandmother lived. I want to be who I am at the core. That may or may not mean that the Stafford political dynasty ends with my father. Chances are, he'll be well enough to continue in office for some time. In full health, he'll master this nursing home controversy, and some good will come of it; I'm convinced of that.

I'll be here to help him in whatever way I can, but the truth is that I'm not ready for a political run. I'm not experienced enough. I haven't paid my dues. The office shouldn't be handed to me just because of who I am. I want to earn it the old-fashioned way. I want to gain an understanding of the issues — all of them, not just a limited few — and decide where I stand. If it *is* ever my turn, I will run the race on my own merits, not as my father's little girl. In the meantime,

Andrew Moore mentioned that his seniors' rights PAC needs a good lawyer. The pay is undoubtedly low, but that isn't the point. If I want to dip my toe in the murky world of politics, that is the sort of place an average person wades in, and I *am* a good lawyer.

Will my father understand?

Will he still love me?

Of course. Of course he will. He's always been a dad first. I know it's true. Yes, there will be disappointment when I inform my parents of my plans. Yes, there will be some fallout, but we'll make it through. We always do.

"Avery, I am *not* letting your grandmother out of the car here." Honeybee surveys the little cottage, the river down the hill, the overgrown trees hanging low over the porch roof. She hugs herself and rubs her hands up and down her arms.

"Honeybee," Dad attempts to placate my mother, smiling at me indulgently. "Avery wouldn't have brought us all this way without a good reason." He leans close, slips an arm around Honeybee's waist, and squeezes the ticklish spot only he knows. It's his secret weapon.

She struggles against a smile. "Stop that." The look she turns my way isn't nearly as cheerful. "Avery, for goodness' sake, was all of this really necessary? Why so cloak and dagger? Why are we coming *here* in a *limousine,* of all things? And why in the *world* did we need to drag your grandmother along? Taking her out of Magnolia Manor is so confusing for her. It's hard to settle her into the routines again afterward."

"I wanted to see if she'd remember something," I say.

Honeybee's lips smack apart. "I doubt she'd remember this."

"Some*one,* actually."

"She wouldn't *know* anyone who lives here, Avery. I think it's best that —"

"Just come inside with me, Mama. Grandma Judy *has* been here before. I have a feeling she might realize that."

"Is anyone going to get me out?" My grandmother beckons from the car.

Oz looks to us for approval. My father nods. He's afraid that if he lets go of Honeybee right now, she'll bolt.

I take charge of my grandmother at the gate, and we move along the path together. Despite her mental decline, Grandma Judy is only seventy-eight and still gets around quite well. That makes the dementia all the more unfair.

I watch her as we walk. With each step, she brightens. Her gaze darts about, landing on the climbing roses and azaleas, the bench by the river, the old picket fence, a trellis of wisteria, a trumpet vine, a bronze birdbath featuring statues of two little girls playing in the water.

"Oh," she whispers. "Oh, I do love this place. Has it been a while?"

"I think so," I answer.

"I've missed it," she whispers. "I've missed it so."

My mother and father hesitate at the top of the porch steps, blink at my grandmother and at me, agog. Honeybee is in a situation she can't control, and because of that, she hates it already, no matter what it is. "Avery Judith, you had better start explaining all of this."

"Mama!" I snap, and Honeybee draws back. I've never spoken to my mother that way. Not in thirty years. "Just let Grandma Judy see what she remembers."

Laying a hand on my grandmother's shoulder, I guide her across the threshold into the cottage. She stands for a moment, her eyes adjusting to the change of light.

I watch as she takes in the room, the photographs, the painting over the old stone fireplace.

It's a moment before she notices that the space is occupied. "Oh, oh . . . May!" she says as naturally as if they had just seen one another yesterday.

"Judy." May tries to get off the sofa, but it's saggy, and she can't push to her feet, so she stretches out her arms instead. Trent, who was about to help her up, backs away.

My grandmother crosses the room. I let her make the journey alone. May's eyes fill, and she lifts her arms, her fingers opening and closing, beckoning her sister to her. Grandma Judy, who is so often unsure of people now, shows no hesitation. As if it is the most natural thing in the world, she leans over the sofa and into May's arms. They share the shaky embrace of old age, May's eyes closing as she nestles her chin on her sister's shoulder. They cling to one another until, finally, my grandmother sinks exhausted into the armchair beside the sofa. She and her sister hold hands across the end table. They gaze at one another as if there's no one else in the room.

"I thought I'd never see you again," May admits.

My grandmother's buoyant smile seems innocent of all the obstacles that have kept them apart. "You know I'll always come. On Thursdays. Sisters' Day." She motions to the rocker by the window. "Where is Fern this afternoon?"

May lifts their joined hands, shakes them a bit. "Fern is gone, sweetheart. She passed in her sleep."

"Fern?" My grandmother's shoulders slump, and her eyes grow watery. A tear squeezes out and trickles alongside her nose. "Oh . . . Fern."

"It's just the two of us now."

"We have Lark."

"Lark died five years ago. The cancer, remember?"

Grandma Judy sags a little more, wipes another tear. "Goodness, I'd forgotten. I only have a little of my mind left."

"It doesn't matter." May stretches to cover their joined hands with her other one. "Remember when we spent that first week on Edisto?" She nods toward the painting over the fireplace. "Wasn't that a fine time? All four of us together? Fern loved it there."

"Yes, it was," Grandma Judy agrees. I can't tell if she really remembers or is just trying to be polite, but she smiles at the painting, and suddenly there's a look of clarity. "You gave us the dragonfly bracelets. Three dragonflies to remember the three we never saw again. Camellia, Gabion, and my twin brother. We were celebrating Camellia's birthday the afternoon you gave them to us, weren't we? Camellia was the dragonfly with the onyx." The light of memory shines in my grandmother's eyes. The love of sisters warms her smile. "My, but we were lookers back then, weren't we?"

"Yes, we were. All of us with Mama's lovely hair, but you were always the only one who had her sweet face. If I didn't know that was you in the painting, I'd think it was our mama standing there with us."

Behind me, my mother whispers through her teeth, "What *is* going *on* here?" I feel the heat radiating off her body. She's sweating, and Honeybee never sweats.

"Maybe we should step outside." I try to gather my parents and move them back to the porch. My father seems almost reluctant to leave the room. He's busy staring at the photos, trying to make some sense of all this. Is there a part of him that remembers his mother's unexplained absences? Does he recall being in the background of that photograph taken on Edisto? Has he always suspected that his mother is more than just the woman he knew?

Trent nods across the room at me just before I close the door between the porch and the cottage. His encouragement makes me feel strong, capable, confident. He's a believer in letting the truth be what it is. He and Hootsie have that in common.

"You'd better sit down for this," I say to my parents.

Honeybee reluctantly balances on the edge of a rocker. My father takes the two-seat glider and assumes a posture that lets me know he's expecting something grave and unpleasant. He leans forward with his feet firmly planted, elbows resting on his knees, fingers steepled together. Whatever the situation is, he's ready to analyze it and do damage control.

"Just let me tell you all of it," I plead. "Don't ask me anything until I'm finished, okay?" Without waiting for an answer, I gather a deep breath and begin the story.

My father listens from behind the usual stoic mask. My mother eventually sinks against the rocker with a wrist braced against her forehead.

When I'm done, the air hangs silent. No one knows what to say. It's obvious that even my father had not an inkling of this, although there's also something in his expression that tells me a few details about his mother's behavior have begun to make sense now.

"How . . . how do you know all of this is true? Maybe . . . maybe this woman . . ." My mother trails off, looks toward the cottage window. She's thinking of what she heard in there, of the photos on the walls. "I just don't see how it's possible."

My father breathes over his joined fingertips, graying eyebrows gathering together. He knows it's possible; he just doesn't want it to be. But I've told him what Trent and I have learned about the Tennessee Children's Home Society, and I can see that most of it wasn't new information to him or my mother. No doubt, they've heard of the scandal, perhaps seen the TV shows that have reenacted events at Georgia's notorious children's home.

"I can't . . . My *mother*?" Dad mutters. "Did my father know?"

"I don't think anyone knew. Grandma Judy and her sisters were grown women by the time they were reunited. May told me they didn't want to interfere with each other's lives. Considering that the paper trail was set up to keep birth families from finding one another, it's a miracle that even four of the siblings were brought back together."

"My God." He shakes his head as if he's trying to rearrange the thoughts there, to put them in some workable order. "My mother has a twin?"

"She was born a twin. She did search over the years, but she was never able to find out what happened after that — whether her twin died or survived and was adopted."

My father rests his chin on his hands. He looks upward through the trees. "My dear God in heaven."

I know what he's thinking. I've been turning the same things over in my mind since the day I learned the truth. All week long, I've gone back and forth between taking the secret to the grave with me . . . and setting the truth free, come what may. In the end, it boils down to this: My father deserves to know who he is. My grandmother deserves whatever time she has left to spend with her sister.

The five little river gypsies who suffered at the hands of the Tennessee Children's Home Society deserve to have their stories carried forward into the future. But for a strange twist of fate, my father's mother would have grown up on a riverboat, among common folk, surrounded by the poverty of the Great Depression.

She wouldn't have been of the class to have met my grandfather, much less married him.

We wouldn't be Staffords.

My mother regains herself a bit, lifts her chin, and reaches across to unfasten my father's hands and hold one of them. "It's ancient history. There's no sense in agonizing over it now, Wells. There's no reason to be bringing it up at all." A glance slides my way — a warning.

I resist the urge to wilt. For me, there's no turning back. "Dad, what you decide to do from here is your choice. All I ask is that Grandma Judy be able to have time with her sister . . . for however long they have left. They've spent their whole lives hiding away from the world, for our benefit. They deserve to be at peace now."

My father kisses my mother's fingers, folds them between his, and nods. Silently, he's telling both of us he'll mull this over and make his own decisions.

Honeybee leans closer to me. "What about this . . . the *man* in there? Can he be trusted not to . . . well . . . to *use* this information? With the Senate run coming up next year, there's nothing Cal Fortner would like more than a personal scandal to distract from the issues."

I'm relieved when she automatically looks to my father, not me, in regard to the next Senate race. I feel life shifting toward its old balance, and I'm glad. It'll be easier to tell them there won't be a politically advantageous wedding in our garden during azalea season. I'm not ready to broach the subject yet, but I will.

Being here, seeing May and my grandmother together, makes me all the more certain of it. All the more certain of myself. "You don't have to worry about Trent. He wouldn't do that. He's a friend. If it weren't for his grandfather, Grandma Judy's sisters never would have found her. She wouldn't have learned the truth about her past."

My mother's expression indicates that she's unconvinced it wouldn't have been better that way.

My father's face says otherwise. "I'd like to talk to Mrs. Crandall a bit."

Honeybee's mouth falls open a little. Then she pops it shut, straightens herself, and nods in acquiescence. Whatever path my father chooses, she will walk it right beside him. This is how my parents have always been.

"I think May would welcome that. We can leave the four of you alone so she can tell you her story." Hearing it from May, in her own words, will bring it home to my father, I hope. This is our family history.

"You can stay," my mother says uncertainly.

"I'd rather just let you have a bit of time." Really, I want to be alone with Trent. I know he's dying to ask how my parents took the news about Grandma Judy. He keeps looking at me through the cottage window.

He's obviously relieved when we stand and cross to the door. Inside, my grandmother is talking about a boating trip down the river. She speaks of it as if it happened yesterday. Apparently, May bought a jon boat at one time. Grandma Judy is laughing about the four of them floating off down the Savannah River when the motor wouldn't start.

My father moves tentatively to a chair, looks at his mother as if he's never seen her before. In a way, he hasn't. The woman he remembers was an actress playing a role, at least partially. For all the years since her sisters found her, there have been two people inside the body of Judy Stafford. One of them is a senator's wife. The other carries the blood of river gypsies.

In this little cottage, on yet another Sisters' Day, the two meld into one.

Trent is more than happy to vacate the premises with me.

"Let's walk up the hill," I suggest. "I wanted to grab a few pictures of the plantation house ruins . . . just in case this whole thing falls apart and we never come back here again."

Trent smiles as we pass through the gate and leave the cottage gardens behind. "I don't think it will."

We walk the path to the edge of the trees. I think of Rill Foss becoming May Weathers all those years ago.

Could she ever have imagined the life she would live?

The sunlight warms me as we cross into the open field and start up the hill. It's a beautiful day — one that hints at the up-coming change of the seasons. The shadow of the mansion's ancient remains falls on the grass, making the towering structure seem solid again. My hands shake as I take out my phone and snap photos. This isn't really why I wanted to come here. There was a reason I felt the need to move out of sight of the cottage . . . and out of earshot.

Now I can't find the words . . . or the courage. Instead, I take a ridiculous number of pictures. Eventually, my ruse runs out.

I swallow a sudden onslaught of butterflies, try to muster up the necessary fortitude.

Trent beats me to it. "You're not wearing the ring," he observes, his eyes filling with questions when I turn to him.

I look down at my hand, think about all that I've learned since I accepted Elliot's proposal, then moved back to South Carolina to do what was expected. That feels like a different life, the music of a different woman. "Elliot and I talked. He doesn't agree with my decisions about Grandma Judy and May, and he probably never will, but it's more than that. I think we've both known for a while now that we're better as friends than as a couple. We have years of history between us, a lot of fond memories, but there's just something . . . missing. I think that's why we've avoided setting a date or making firm plans. The wedding was more about our families than it was about us. Maybe in some way, we've known that all along."

I watch Trent as he studies our shadows on the grass, frowning contemplatively.

My heart flutters, then pounds. The seconds seem like taffy, sticky and slow-moving. *Does Trent feel the way I do? What if he doesn't?*

He has a young son to consider, for one thing.

I don't know exactly where I'm going in life, for another. Working with the PAC will give me time to find out who I want to be. I like setting things right that were wrong. I think that's why I've dug so deeply into May's story, why I've brought my grandmother and May here this afternoon.

An old wrong has been set right today,

inasmuch as is possible all these years later.

There's a sense of satisfaction in that, but now the questions about Trent eclipse it. *How does he fit into the future I've only begun to imagine? His family and mine are so different.*

His eyes catch the light when he looks back at me. They're the blue of deep water, and for the first time I realize that perhaps we're not as different as we seem. We share a rich heritage. We're both descended from the river.

"Does this mean I can hold your hand?" He smiles along with the words, raises an eyebrow, and waits.

"Yes. I think it does."

He turns his palm up, and I put my hand in it.

His fingers close over mine, a warm, strong circle, and we walk up the hill away from the ruins of a life that was.

And into a life that can be.

CHAPTER 26

May Crandall
Present Day

Our story begins on a sweltering August night, in a sterile white room where a single fateful decision is made amid the mindless ravages of grief. But our story does not end there. It has not ended yet.

Would I change the course of our lives if I could? Would I have spent my years plucking out tunes on a showboat, or turning the soil as a farmer's wife, or waiting for a riverman to come home from work and settle in beside me at a cozy little fire?

Would I trade the son I bore for a different son, for more children, for a daughter to comfort me in my old age? Would I give up the husbands I loved and buried, the music, the symphonies, the lights of Hollywood, the grandchildren and great-grandchildren who live far distant but have my eyes?

I ponder this as I sit on the wooden bench, Judy's hand in mine, the two of us quietly sharing yet another Sisters' Day. Here in the gardens at Magnolia Manor, we're able to have Sisters' Day anytime we like. It is as easy as leaving my room, and walking to the next hall, and telling the attendant, "I believe I'll take my dear friend Judy out for a little stroll. Oh yes, of course, I'll be certain she's delivered safely back to the Memory Care Unit. You know I always do."

Sometimes, my sister and I laugh over our clever ruse. "We're *really* sisters, not friends," I remind her. "But don't tell them. It's our secret."

"I won't tell." She smiles in her sweet way. "But sisters are friends as well. Sisters are special friends."

We recall our many Sisters' Day adventures from years past, and she begs me to share what I remember of Queenie and Briny and our life on the river. I tell her of days and seasons with Camellia, and Lark, and Fern, and Gabion, and Silas, and Old Zede. I speak of quiet backwaters and rushing currents, the midsummer ballet of dragonflies and winter ice floes that allowed men to walk over water. Together, we travel the living river. We turn our faces to the sunlight and fly time and time again home to Kingdom Arcadia.

Other days, my sister knows me not at all other than as a neighbor here in this old manor house. But the love of sisters needs no words. It does not depend on memories, or mementos, or proof. It runs as deep as a heartbeat. It is as ever present as a pulse.

"Aren't they so very sweet?" Judy points to the young couple strolling the garden paths near Manor Lake, hand in hand. They make a lovely picture together.

I pat Judy's arm gently. "That is your granddaughter. I imagine she's come here to visit with you. And she's brought her beau along. He's a looker, that one. I told her the first time I saw them together, he was a keeper. I recognize a spark when I see it."

"Oh, of course, my granddaughter." Judy pretends to have known it all along. Some days she would have, but not on this particular day. "And her beau." She squints toward the garden path. "I'm having trouble calling up the names just now. My silly mind, you know."

"Avery."

"Oh yes . . . Avery."

"And Trent."

"We knew a Trent Turner once, didn't we? He was a dear man. He sold the cottage lots adjacent to the Edisto place, I think."

"Yes, he did. That is his grandson coming up the walk with Avery."

"Well, do tell." Judy waves enthusiastically, and Avery waves in response. Then she and her beau disappear momentarily behind the arbor. They don't come out as quickly as they might.

Judy presses a hand over her mouth, chuckling. "Oh my."

"Indeed." I remember lost loves and loves that never were. "We Fosses have always been an impassioned lot. I don't suppose that will ever change."

"I don't believe it ever should," Judy agrees, and we fall together in the sweet embrace of sisters, laughing at our own secrets.

A NOTE FROM THE AUTHOR

As you close these pages, perhaps you're wondering, *How much of this story is true?* That question is, in some ways, difficult to answer. If you'd like to dig more deeply into the real-life history of baby farms, orphanages, changes in adoption, Georgia Tann, and the scandal surrounding the Tennessee Children's Home Society in Memphis, you'll find excellent information in *Pricing the Priceless Child: The Changing Social Value of Children* by Viviana A. Zelizer (1985), *Babies for Sale: The Tennessee Children's Home Adoption Scandal* by Linda Tollett Austin (1993), *Alone in the World: Orphans and Orphanages in America* by Catherine Reef (2005), and *The Baby Thief: The Untold Story of Georgia Tann, the Baby Seller Who Corrupted Adoption* by Barbara Bisantz Raymond (2007), which also contains interviews with several of Georgia

Tann's victims. For a view of the scandal as it broke, see the original *Report to Governor Gordon Browning on Shelby County Branch, Tennessee Children's Home Society* (1951), which is available through the public library system. There are also many newspaper and magazine articles available about the scandal as it happened and about the reunions of birth families in later years, as well as coverage in episodes of *60 Minutes, Unsolved Mysteries,* and Investigation Discovery's *Deadly Women.* All of these sources were invaluable to me as research materials.

The Foss children and the *Arcadia* were formed from the dust of imagination and the muddy waters of the Mississippi River. Though Rill and her siblings exist only in these pages, their experiences mirror those reported by children who were taken from their families from the 1920s through 1950.

The true story of Georgia Tann and the Memphis branch of the Tennessee Children's Home Society is a bizarre and sad paradox. There is little doubt that the organization rescued many children from deplorable, dangerous circumstances, or simply accepted children who were unwanted and placed them in loving homes. There is also little doubt that countless children were taken from loving parents without cause or due process and never seen again by their desperately grieving biological families. Survivor accounts bear out that empty-armed birth mothers pined for their missing children for decades and that many of those children were placed in holding facilities where they were neglected, molested, abused, and treated as objects.

Single mothers, indigent parents, women in mental wards, and those seeking help through welfare services and maternity clinics were particular targets. Birth mothers were duped into signing paperwork while under postpartum sedation, were told that turning over temporary custody was necessary to secure medical treatment for their children, or were often simply informed that their babies had died. Children who lived through stints in the home's custody — those who were old enough to have memories of their prior lives — reported having been whisked from front porches, from roadsides while walking to school, and, yes, from houseboats on the river. Essentially, if you were poor and you lived, stayed, or stopped over in the proximity of Memphis, your children were at risk.

Blonds like the Foss siblings were particularly popular in Georgia Tann's system and were often targeted by "spotters" who worked in medical facilities and public aid clinics. Average residents of the city, while unaware of her methods, were not unaware of her work. For years, citizens watched for newspaper advertisements bearing photos of adorable babies and children, underscored by captions like "Yours For the Asking," "Want a Real, Live Christmas Present?" and "George Wants to Play Catch, But He Needs a Daddy." Georgia Tann was heralded as the "Mother of Modern Adoption" and was even consulted by Eleanor Roosevelt on matters of child welfare.

To the general public, Tann was simply a matronly, well-meaning woman who devoted her life to rescuing children in need. Her celebration of children adopted by wealthy, well-known families helped to popularize the idea of adoption in general and dispel the widespread belief that orphaned children were undesirable and inherently damaged. Georgia's high-profile list included political figures such as New York governor Herbert Lehman and Hollywood celebrities such as Joan Crawford and June Allyson and her husband, Dick Powell. Former staff members of Tann's orphanage in Memphis whispered of as many as seven babies at a time being spirited away under cover of darkness for transportation to "foster homes" in California, New York, and other states. In reality, these children were often being shipped off to profitable out-of-state adoptions in which Tann pocketed the lion's share of the exorbitant delivery fees. When interviewed about her methods, Georgia unabashedly extolled the virtues of removing children from lowly parents who could not possibly raise them properly and placing them with people of "high type."

From a modern perspective, it's hard to imagine how Georgia Tann and her network managed to operate largely unchecked for decades or where she found workers willing to turn a blind eye to the inhumane treatment of children in the organization's group homes and in unlicensed boarding facilities, like the one where Rill and her siblings land, yet it happened. At one point, the U.S. Children's Bureau sent an investigator to Memphis to probe the city's soaring infant mortality rate. In a four-month period in 1945, a dysentery epidemic had caused the deaths of forty to fifty children under the care of Georgia's facility, despite the efforts of a doctor who volunteered medical services there. Georgia, however, insisted that only two children had been lost. Under pressure, the state legislature passed a law mandating the licensing of every children's boarding home in Tennessee. The newly passed legislation included a subsection providing an exemption for all boarding homes employed by Georgia Tann's agency.

While Mrs. Murphy and her home in the story are fictional, Rill's experiences there were inspired by those reported by survivors. There were also many who, due to abuse, neglect, illness, or inadequate medical attention, did not live to tell their stories. They are the silent victims of an unregulated system fueled by greed and financial opportunity. Estimates as to the number of children who may have simply vanished under Georgia Tann's management range as high as five hundred. Thousands more disappeared into adoptions for profit in which names, birth dates, and birth records were altered to prevent biological families from finding their children.

One would assume, given these awful statistics, that Georgia Tann's reign would have eventually ended amid a firestorm of public revelations, police inquiries, and legal action. If *Before We Were Yours* were entirely fictional, that's how I would have written its end, with scenes of swift and certain justice. Sadly, this was not the case. Georgia's many years in the adoption business did not draw to a close until 1950. At a press conference that September, Governor Gordon Browning skirted the heartbreaking human tragedy of it all and instead discussed the money — Miss Tann, he reported, had benefited illegally to the tune of $1 million (equivalent to roughly $10 million today) while employed by the Tennessee Children's Home Society. Despite the revelation of her crimes, Tann was, by then, beyond the reach of legal action. Within days of the press conference, she succumbed to uterine cancer and died at home in her own bed. A newspaper exposé ran opposite her obituary on the front page of the local paper. Her children's home was closed and an investigator appointed, but he soon found himself stymied by powerful people with secrets, reputations, and, in some cases, adoptions to preserve.

While the closing of the home gave grieving birth families reason to hope, that hope was quickly snatched from them. Legislators and political power brokers passed laws legalizing even the most questionable of her adoptions and sealing the records. Of the twenty-two wards remaining in Tann's care at the time of her death, only two — who had already been rejected by their adopted families — were returned to their birth parents. Thousands of birth families would never know what became of their children. The general public sentiment was that, having been given over from poverty to privilege, the children were better off where they were, no matter the circumstances of their adoptions.

While some adoptees, separated siblings, and birth families were able to find one another through pieced-together memories, documents spirited from courthouse files, and the assistance of private investigators, Georgia Tann's records would not finally be opened to her victims until 1995. For many birth parents and adoptees, who grieved their losses throughout their lifetimes, that was simply too late. For others, it was the beginning of long-delayed family reunions and the opportunity to finally tell their own stories.

If there is one overarching lesson to be learned from the Foss children and from the true-life story of the Tennessee Children's Home Society, it is that babies and children, no matter what corner of the world they hail from, are not commodities, or objects, or *blank slates,* as Georgia Tann so often represented her wards; they are human beings with histories, and needs, and hopes, and dreams of their own.

ACKNOWLEDGMENTS

Story people are a bit like real people — no matter where their humble beginnings may lie, their journeys are shaped by family, friends, neighbors, co-workers, and all manner of acquaintances. Some encourage them, some guide them, some offer them unconditional love, some teach them, some challenge them to be their best. This story, like most stories, owes its existence to a village of unique and generous individuals.

First and foremost, I am thankful to my family for supporting me through all these writing years, even when it meant late nights, crazy schedules, and foraging for whatever was left in the kitchen. Particular thanks this year goes to my eldest son for falling in love and finally adding a girl to the family. Not only is a wedding a great distraction from editing, writing, rewriting, and editing some more, but now at long last I have someone who doesn't mind riding to book events with me and talking all the way there and back.

Thank you to my mother for being my official assistant, and also a fabulous first reader. Not everyone is lucky enough to have a helper who will tell you when your hair or your last chapter needs a little spiffing up. Thank you to my sweet mother-in-law for helping with address lists and for loving my grown-too-soon boys, and to Paw-paw for making sure that the next generation of Wingates knows how to tell a great tale around the dinner table. Thanks also to relatives and friends far and near for loving me and helping me and hosting me as I travel. You're the best.

I'm grateful to special friends-who-are-like-family, especially Ed Stevens for research help and constant encouragement, and Steve and Rosemary Fitts for hosting us on Edisto Island. If there's a better place to go for a research trip, I haven't been there yet. Thanks also to the fabulous team who help with early readings and tour plans: Duane Davis, Mary Davis, Virginia Rush, and last but not least, my wonderful Aunt Sandy, who has a great sense of plotlines and an equally great sense of humor. To Kathie Bennett and Susan Zurenda of Magic Time Literary, thank you for having planned great book tours in the past, for jumping behind this book from its earliest stages, and for working with gusto to bring it to the world.

On the publishing side, I am forever in debt to my fabulous agent, Elisabeth Weed, for encouraging me to write the book and then working expertly to make sure it found just the right publishing home. Thank you to editor extraordinaire Susanna Porter for pushing me to deepen the experiences of the Foss children and Avery's journey into her family's hidden past. Thank you to the fabulous publishing team behind this book: Kara Welsh, Kim Hovey, Jennifer Hershey, Scott Shannon, Susan Corcoran, Melanie DeNardo, Kristin Fassler, Debbie Aroff, Lynn Andreozzi, Toby Ernst, Beth Pearson, and Emily Hartley. There are no words to express how much I appreciate each of you and your bringing this story to the market with such tender loving care. Loads of gratitude are also due to the teams in art, design, production, marketing, publicity, and sales. Thank you for contributing your incredible talents. Without your work, stories would literally sit on shelves undiscovered and unread. You connect books to readers, and in doing that, you connect people to one another. If books can change the world, those of you who help bring them to the world are the change agents.

Lastly, I'm grateful to the many readers who have shared past journeys with me and are now sharing this one. I treasure you. I treasure the time we spend together through story. Thank you for picking up this book. Thank you for recommending my past books to friends, suggesting them to book clubs, and taking time to send little notes of encouragement my way via email, Facebook, and Twitter. I'm indebted to all of you who read these stories and also to the booksellers who sell them with such devotion. As Mr. Rogers once said, "Look for the helpers. You will always find people who are helping."

You, my friends, are the helpers.

And for that, I am most grateful.

ABOUT THE AUTHOR

Lisa Wingate is a former journalist, an inspirational speaker, and the bestselling author of more than twenty novels. Her work has won or been nominated for many awards, including the Pat Conroy Southern Book Prize, the Oklahoma Book Award, the Carol Award, the Christy Award, and the RT Reviewers' Choice Award. Wingate lives in the Ouachita Mountains of southwest Arkansas.

lisawingate.com
Facebook.com/LisaWingateAuthorPage
@LisaWingate
Pinterest.com/lisawingatebook